10

STAR
QUALITY

JOAN COLLINS

STAR QUALITY

Thorndike Press • **Chivers Press**
Waterville, Maine USA **Bath, England**

This Large Print edition is published by Thorndike Press, USA and by Chivers Press, England.

Published in 2003 in the U.S. by arrangement with Hyperion, an imprint of BuenaVista Books, Inc.

Published in 2003 in the U.K. by arrangement with Robson Books.

U.S. Hardcover 0-7862-4694-4 (Core Series)
U.K. Hardcover 0-7540-1911-X (Windsor Large Print)
U.K. Softcover 0-7540-9274-7 (Paragon Large Print)

Copyright © 2002 Pisces Worldwide Limited

The text of this Large Print edition is unabridged.
Other aspects of the book may vary from the original edition.

Set in 16 pt. Plantin by Minnie B. Raven.

Printed in the United States on permanent paper.

British Library Cataloguing-in-Publication Data available

Library of Congress Cataloging-in-Publication Data

Collins, Joan, 1933–
    Star quality / Joan Collins.
      p. cm.
    ISBN 0-7862-4694-4 (lg. print : hc : alk. paper)
    1. Actresses — Fiction.   2. Motion picture actors and actresses — Fiction.   3. Hollywood (Los Angeles, Calif.) — Fiction.   4. West End (London, England) — Fiction.
5. Mothers and daughters — Fiction.   6. New York (N.Y.) — Fiction.   7. Large type books.   I. Title.
PR6053.O426 S73 2003
    813'.54—dc21   2002073225

To my family

"All the world's a stage,
And all the men and women
merely players."
— *As You Like It*,
William Shakespeare

PROLOGUE

LONDON
MARCH 2002

The ancient woman held the heavy blue envelope, franked with the Royal "E II R" cipher, by the tips of her arthritic fingers. She studied it carefully for several minutes, then slit it open and removed the card with the Queen's coat of arms printed at the head. Her lips moving slowly, she read the message:

> I am pleased to know that you are celebrating your one-hundredth birthday. I send my congratulations and best wishes to you on such a special occasion.

Visions of the past hundred years passed before her eyes, each image more tormenting than the last. Her grip tightened on the card before she tore it into pieces and, with all the force of her frail arm, threw them into the fire, watching as the flames consumed Her Majesty's words. She glanced around the kitchen, where she had spent the best part of the past eighty-five years. It was now a dank, cavernous place, which no longer echoed to the laughter and chatter of the housemaids, menservants, and butlers who had worked and lived in this Eaton Square mansion so long ago.

Now she was the only one of them left, an old woman left to molder beside the fireplace, having relinquished the tending of the household to a young Asian couple who barely spoke English, let alone spoke to her. She sipped at her soothing glass of gin, then picked up the morning tabloid, for the hundredth time, to stare in loathing at the front-page picture of three smiling women. None of them was young, one was only a few years younger than herself, but the joy and excitement on their faces gave them a vibrancy that overcame the barriers of age.

Next to their photograph was another picture of a beautiful, feisty teenage girl. A guitar was strung carelessly across her half-naked body, and flaming red ringlets and braids fanned out against the wind machine as she undulated to the beat of some unheard melody. The girl was gloriously youthful, her joie de vivre almost palpable. The old woman stared at the images of the four women for some time, unaccustomed emotion contorting her withered features. Then she crunched the newspaper up into a ball and cast it onto the flames to join the

10

charred face of the Queen.

"Bitches!" she whispered, watching the fire lap at their images. "Bitches and whores! May they all rot in hell. They deserve everlasting damnation for what they did to me."

PART ONE

Millie

Chapter One
1917

The highly polished brass doorknocker was molded in the shape of a lion's head. Squinting at the pale winter sun reflecting off the beast's forehead, Millie tapped again tentatively, hoping she hadn't made a mistake with the time. Five o'clock, Bridget had said. At five the family would have finished both luncheon and tea, and the staff in the basement would have almost completed the monotonous task of washing and drying the delicate china and fine silverware.

She heard footsteps and the heavy door was opened by a balding man of indeterminate age, who stared at her with ill-disguised impatience. "What can I do for you?" he asked imperiously.

"I — I'm Millie McClancey, Bridget McClancey's cousin. I've come for the job of tweeny maid."

Thin eyebrows rose disdainfully as he pointed down the street. "If you've come for a position, *that's* the servants' entrance; don't *ever* use this door again."

The door slammed in Millie's face, the lion's grim features mocking her as the noise reverberated down the street. She nervously took a step back and, glancing to her left, saw narrow stone stairs a few yards away, encircled by high black iron railings with a discreet plaque that read "Tradesmen and Employees."

Millie climbed down the steep steps apprehensively but, before she reached the sturdy brown door at the bottom, it was flung open and her cousin rushed out to hug her.

"Jesus, Mary and Joseph, *whatever* were you doing at the front door?" Bridget scolded, dragging Millie into a dimly lit hallway that smelled strongly of cooking. "That's only for the nobs."

"Sorry, Bridget, I didn't know."

Bridget took a long look at her cousin. This was her first time in London. Indeed, her first time out of the tiny Irish village where she'd lived the entirety of her seventeen years. Millie smiled back at the big rawboned girl who had the fine red hair of the family but neither the texture nor the brilliance of Millie's own hair. She hadn't seen Bridget for almost two years and was excited to see her, as the two were extremely close; more like sisters.

"Look at you." Bridget pinched her cousin's pale cheek. "Sure, you're nothing but skin and bone, girl."

"There's not much to eat at home these days." The thought of Aunt Mary stooped over in her allotment, trying to find a few potatoes or onions left in the hard earth, briefly crossed Millie's mind.

Millie took off her shabby woolen cloak and bonnet while Bridget examined her tiny bundle of possessions. "Is this all you've brought?"

Millie nodded. Totally exhausted by the two-day boat journey from Ireland in crowded steerage, she would have given anything to sit down and have a cup of tea, but Bridget dragged her into a vast warm kitchen bustling with activity that immediately ceased when they entered.

"Well, well, and who have we here?" Cook glanced up from her pastry table, where she was artfully running a wooden rolling pin up and down the thick yellow dough. Round-faced, ruddy-cheeked, and sweating profusely, she was the benevolent queen of her domain.

"It's my cousin Millie from County Cork, and we've been expecting her, haven't we?" Bridget brooked no nonsense from anyone.

A maid who looked no more than fourteen peered shyly over at the new arrival, her face drenched with sweat as she stirred several steaming pots on the enormous coal-fired range. A wonderful aroma filled the kitchen; of freshly baked bread, sausage rolls, and mutton. Millie's head started to swim. She'd barely eaten in two days, and it was so hot in the cavernous, yet comforting, kitchen. Although the walls were discolored with the residue of bygone cooking, and the furniture looked old and rickety, it was still a cozy place. At least six or seven people were bustling about making the initial preparations for dinner, shooting covert glances at the newcomer.

"Enough of your sauce, girl," said the stout man who'd originally opened the main door to her. "Let's have a good look at what the cat's dragged in." He looked Millie up and down, taking in her shabby serge skirt and threadbare jacket with frayed sleeves. Her fiery auburn curls, which framed a provocatively attractive face and accentuated her wide-apart green eyes, weren't wasted on him either. She felt herself shrivel as his stare burrowed into her.

"Scrawny little thing," he remarked. "Arms like matchsticks — shouldn't think she'd be much good at hauling coals up to the bedrooms."

"But I'm very strong," Millie piped up defensively, although she was feeling light-headed with tiredness and had to grip the back of a nearby chair to steady herself. "At my Auntie Mary's I brought water from the well several times a day, and I chopped all the firewood too."

"She even chopped down trees," Bridget chimed in. "She's hardy, Mr. Kingsley. She may look like a slip of a girl, but she's strong as an ox, I guarantee it."

Kingsley pressed a meaty hand around Millie's upper biceps so hard that she bit her lip.

"Oh, aye — there's a muscle here — the size of a walnut, but it's there all right."

Another maid, Patsy, even younger than Millie, with beautiful bronze hair and an angular but pretty face, stared at Millie coldly while the rest of the staff let out sycophantic giggles at Mr. Kingsley's attempt at wit. Millie felt uncomfortable at Patsy's hostile inspection.

"You wanted a maid of all work and here she is," Bridget said firmly. "She's young, she's tough, and she's cheap. So what do you say, Mr. Kingsley? Will you take her, or shall I go next door to Mrs. Lorrimer — you know she's been looking for a good strong housemaid."

"No, she'll do, I suppose." Kingsley was still regarding her, and Millie thought she could detect an unnerving flash of male desire in his piglike eyes.

"Take her up to your quarters, Bridget. Show her the ropes. And mind you behave yourself, girl. Her Grace may look like her head's in the clouds, but she notices *everything,* and if it's not to her liking it'll be my head on the block — and if that happens, you go."

"Yes, sir," said Bridget airily. "But can I

19

give the girl a cuppa and a bit of bread and dripping first? She looks fairly famished."

"Don't overfeed her — remember, there's a war on."

"Yes, sir," Bridget said again, this time with a mocking bow, and Kingsley returned to his deep armchair next to the huge coal-burning fireplace and buried his head in *The Times.*

"You'll be cleaning that fireplace three times a week with black lead and ammonia," said Bridget. "I'll show you how. It's easy, really."

She clucked around Millie, sitting her down and giving her a plate of potatoes, scraps of stewed trout, and some bread with lard left over from lunch.

"Now mind you eat all that up, girl," said Cook, busily pressing pastry into an iron skillet. "Everything costs an arm and a leg today with this blessed war — so waste not, want not, dearie."

"Don't worry, ma'am." Millie was filling her mouth as fast as she could. "In Ireland we never waste a thing. Can't afford to."

"Everything's so dear today." Cook wiped the sweat from her brow with a floury hand. "Even a glass of gin at the pub costs thruppence ha'penny."

Millie drank several cups of steaming tea while trying to listen carefully to Cook's conversation and learn the strict rules and regulations of the Duke and Duchess of Burghley's residence.

"They're going away tomorrow. They're usually only here for four months in the summer. But the daughters are staying." Bridget made a face. "They're trying to snare husbands even before the Season starts!"

"Season? What season?" Millie was completely ignorant of the ways of London society.

"Oh, you know, all the posh people come up to London from their country estates and dress up and go to each other's fine houses and give big parties and balls."

"Even with the war?" asked Millie.

"Oh yes — and we've got to work three times as hard in those months. I told Mr. Kingsley you'd do the work of two and be twice as fast about it," Bridget said gaily, her blue eyes sparkling. She had been enjoying her service with the Burghleys for the past two years, and it was she who had arranged Millie's passage from Ireland. "You know, the last two scullery maids we had were carried off by all the work, and this nasty influenza's keeping the morgues busy."

"Well, that's happening in Ireland too," said Millie, trying hard not to think about the harrowing weeks that she'd spent nursing her mother through the deadly disease. She'd only been thirteen when her mother had finally succumbed, and her father took to his bed wailing with grief, praying that the Blessed Virgin Mary take him too. The saint hadn't disappointed him. Within a fortnight Liam McClancey had joined his wife, and little Millie was an orphan with only her aunt and cousin Bridget for family.

Bridget looked at Millie sympathetically. "Now now, girl, you mustn't dwell on the past." She grinned suddenly. "Feast your eyes on this." She flicked a switch on the wall and the dim kitchen was suddenly lit by a pure even light.

"Mary, mother of God, what's that?" Millie blinked in the harsh light. "I've never seen anything like it."

"Electric light," said Bridget proudly, "and we've got it in all the rooms."

"Except ours," chimed in Patsy. "Of course it's too good for the likes of us."

"Stop your moaning, Patsy," said Bridget.

"Turn that thing off," barked Kingsley. "You're wasting electricity."

Bridget made a face. "Come on upstairs, Millie. I'll show you your room." She handed her a candlestick and the two girls scampered up the seven flights of stairs at the back of the house to their tiny room.

"You know, I don't know the first thing about scullery maiding," said Millie that night, as she lay on a straw mattress resting on thin metal slats. The walls were paper thin, and she could hear Patsy talking to May, the youngest maid. ". . . well, *she* won't last long that one, stuck up and too skinny she is. Mr. Kingsley'll have her out of here very soon, mark my words . . ."

"Don't take any notice of that cow," said Bridget. "She hates the world, that one does."

"Why?" asked Millie.

"Sure, I don't know — just the way she's made, I suppose. She's had a hard life, but haven't we all?" Bridget wriggled into her cambric nightdress, well patched and darned like the sheets and blankets, which covered her from neck to ankles. It was freezing cold in the dormer room under the eaves, which was no more than a small closet. The wind whistled in through the ill-fitting window-panes, but nevertheless it seemed cozy enough to Millie, who admired the small prints of meadows and flowers on the walls. There was a threadbare carpet on the bare wooden floor and the curtains were flimsy and worn, but Millie, used to sleeping on a couple of blankets on the floor of her Aunt Mary's cottage, thought it little short of a palace. She watched as Bridget unpacked Millie's few possessions and listened as she instructed her on life at Eaton Square.

"Now, it's easy here, really, Millie dear. Much easier than trying to make a living at me mam's farm."

Bridget sat next to Millie and put her arm around her. "You get up at six and clean all the fireplaces. Well, not all, because I'll help you and we don't have to do the big one in the hall — young Tom, the footman, does that. Then you light the fire in the young mistresses' dressing rooms, the breakfast room, and the morning room, and clean the privies and, after that, it's time for a bite yourself before you take the mistresses' trays up to them."

"The mistresses are the daughters?" asked Millie.

"Yes. And ugly beasts they are too. Her Grace's been trying everything to get them hitched to some well-heeled chumps, but they've both got faces that'd frighten the horses on a dark night, so none of the toffs want to know."

"Are they nice?" asked Millie, running her hands down the soft cotton counterpane.

"Nice!" Bridget pealed with laughter. "Cinderella herself couldn't have been cursed with two worse relations. And they're old too."

"How old?" asked Millie.

"Twenty-five and twenty-six — regular old maids. Shouldn't think anybody'd ever want them if it wasn't for the duke being so rich."

"Is he very rich?"

"Ooh, Millie! They say he's one of the richest men in England," Bridget said. "One of the stingiest too. No one gets anything from him for free — except Toby, of course."

"And who's Toby?" Millie yawned. She

could hardly keep her eyes open, even though this was the most exciting day of her life and she wanted to know everything about the family in whose service she now found herself.

"Aah, Toby — you'll meet him soon enough," winked Bridget. "You watch out for him, he's got a bit of a wandering eye that one. Better keep out of his way."

Millie snuggled deeper under the blankets. "I shouldn't think he'd have much interest in me."

"You'd be surprised, dear," said Bridget mysteriously. "When the young master gets drunk there's no telling what he'll get up to. Now, I'll tell you more about the rest of them tomorrow." Bridget blew out the candle. "Get some rest, Millie dear. You've a long day ahead of you."

The following morning, Millie crept down the steep, red-carpeted stairs and marveled as Bridget opened the double doors to the drawing room.

"It really is a palace," she gasped, gazing at the sumptuously decorated room. The walls were covered in eau-de-nil shot silk, which was almost obliterated by the dozens upon dozens of seventeenth- and eighteenth-century pictures, which hung in geometric splendor. Several blond satinwood chairs upholstered in pale Adam-green brocade flanked the profusion of sofas on which Aubusson and needlepoint cushions jostled for attention.

But Millie couldn't marvel for long, for below the impressive portrait of the duke, by the fashionable American painter John Singer Sargent, the ornate marble Adam fireplace held the ashes of last night's fire — Millie's first job for the day.

"We'll be cleaning that grate soon enough," said Bridget. "What do you think of the room? Gorgeous, isn't it?"

"I've never seen anything so beautiful," breathed Millie. "It's like Aladdin's cave."

"The whole house is like this." Bridget sounded proud. "It's the best house in the square. Everyone says so."

Half an hour later Millie caught sight of the duke and duchess as they swept through the main entrance hall and outside to where their new automobile stood, ready to drive to their estate in Gloucestershire.

The duke was a tall, thickset man of fifty, with piercingly fierce eyes and pepper-and-salt hair matched by a beard and bristling mustache. He wore heavy tweed plus fours with a matching jacket, thick argyle socks with sturdy brown brogues, and was carrying a shooting stick with a flourish.

The duchess by contrast was a pale-skinned, sweet-faced woman with an expression of vagueness in her watery blue eyes.

26

She was tightly corseted beneath a nondescript fawn gabardine two-piece suit, and her maid had pinned up her wispy brown hair under a large wide hat, which was tied under her chin by a floating muslin scarf.

Kingsley and Tom followed them outside to the pavement, where the duke's shining conveyance was attracting attention. The new Daimler looked like a large, glossy black beetle, and it shuddered and belched exhaust smoke. The old chauffeur, smart in his bottle-green livery, cranked up the engine of the massive machine, then held open the side door with a respectful, "Ready to go, Your Graces?"

The duke and duchess nodded a dismissive good-bye to their staff, and Millie turned to Bridget with shining eyes. "A motorcar! I've never seen one of them before. Whatever next?"

"There's so much more to see," said Bridget. "Just wait until I show you the new cleaning-up machine. It's called a vacuum cleaner and sucks up dust from the floors ever so well. You'll never believe how clever it is."

"Oh, this is really what everyone back in Ireland said it would be," beamed Millie.

"It's an exciting old world all right, what with all these newfangled inventions. Just wait 'til you see the things they've got in the kitchen," said Bridget. "We've got an icemaker, d'you believe it?"

"It makes ice?" Millie was incredulous.

"Sure it does, and then we've got the absolute latest thing — an electric toaster!"

"A what?"

"It makes toast, girl, out of bread. You pop in a white slice and it comes out brown. Wait until you see it. It's like magic," giggled Bridget. "But you've got to watch it, otherwise it'll set itself on fire!"

"Well, I never," Millie gasped. "Whatever next?"

"Well, well, well. And who have we here?" drawled an alluring voice.

Millie peeped up from beneath her cambric mobcap, pushing some of her escaping russet curls out of the way. A delightful vision lounged in the doorway, elegantly clad in morning coat and gray striped trousers, a cigarette hanging languidly from rosy lips. Pale blue eyes surveyed Millie quizzically as she hastened to get up from the fireplace that she'd been sweeping out with characteristic vigor.

"Speak up, girl, who are you?" the young man asked with a tinge of amusement, for the pretty servant girl had smudges of ash all over her face and her uniform was streaked with soot.

"Millie McClancey, sir, is my name. I'm the new maid." She gave a little bob and lowered her eyes exactly as Bridget had told her. He was so good-looking, this boy with his tumbling blond hair and his languid gaze, that she'd have liked to have had a really good stare.

"Replacing the two dead ones, are you? Poor things, they weren't nearly as pretty as you." His eyes twinkled and Millie felt herself blushing, but she twinkled back at him as she boldly met his eyes.

He was almost too handsome. Tall and twenty-something, he carried himself with the careless grace of the ruling class. They stood summing each other up for several seconds and Millie remembered what Bridget had said — to watch out for him. He was too good-looking for his own good, that was for sure.

Toby broke her reverie by saying softly, "I'd like to see what you look like cleaned up a bit. Try it some time." Then he turned on his heel and was gone. Millie blinked. She'd been working for the Burghleys for over a month now, and this was the first time she'd seen the young master, Tobias Swannell, marquis of Leybourne, heir to the dukedom and all of its properties, apple of his parents' eye and delight of every debutante.

Of the ugly sisters she'd seen more than enough, for after their first glimpse of Millie's pretty face and trim figure they had adopted her as their slave — "Do this, do that, and be quick about it, girl."

"All they ever do is make me their drudge," Millie said to Bridget later that day, as the girls ran down the back stairs and out onto the street, breathless and excited. "I can't believe those two hags are Mr. Toby's sisters."

"You think he's a bit of all right then, do you?" asked Bridget.

Millie smiled shyly. "I've never seen the likes of him in Ireland. He looks like a god. A Greek god at that."

"Well, keep well away from him, dearie," warned Bridget. "He's dangerous, I've heard, so don't get involved."

"Don't worry, I won't," laughed Millie. "But I can look, can't I?"

"Well, you'd better not touch," said Bridget darkly. "He's got a soft spot for servant girls, does Mr. Toby."

"I won't, I promise."

"C'mon, we'll be late!" Bridget shoved her straw hat onto her head at a saucy angle. "I'm about to show you the best time of your life, little cousin. And you'd better take advantage of this half day off, 'cos we're only given it once a fortnight."

"Are you going to tell me where we're off to?" asked Millie.

"To the Alhambra Music Hall and Variety Palace," announced Bridget. "The greatest place of entertainment in the world."

★ ★ ★

The theater, though grandly named, was actually nothing but a "penny gaff," hidden down one of the many narrow back streets of London. It had once been a grocery shop, and was one of the last remaining places of its kind in London.

In spite of its seedy appearance, a large crowd jostled for admission outside its gaudy entrance, where newly installed electric lights flashed and crude photographs of the singers, dancers, and entertainers were displayed. Millie's eyes widened when she saw some of the salacious poses the dancers adopted.

"Their skirts — they're holding them above their knees," she gulped. "I can see their bloomers."

"Girl, this is modern life," laughed Bridget. "Women are getting bolder now that many of them are going out to work. The government is insisting on using women for all sorts of jobs now, 'cos all the young men are at the front. C'mon, c'mon," she urged, pulling Millie away from the photographs. "Give us your penny. This gaff only holds two hundred, and it looks fit to burst already."

The tiny auditorium was lit by smoking gas lamps and the audience, clustered close together on hard wooden benches, was smoking pipes and cigarettes, swilling beer, and munching on meat pies and cod and chips that young girls sold from trays slung around their shoulders as they jostled through the aisles. Although the atmosphere was debauched, it was convivial and the shabby but roistering, good-humored bunch was mainly, like the girls, from the lower classes.

They squeezed onto the end of a bench next to a young costermonger who stank of fish. Millie wrinkled her nose and the lad gave her an insolent stare back. Ignoring him, Millie gazed fascinated at the wooden platform below the stage on which were perched a motley group of pipers, drummers, and violinists who were playing with wild enthusiasm but little aptitude.

When every aisle was filled, with some people even standing on upturned pails at the back, a florid man in a flashy black-and-white striped suit, derby hat, and big fake red nose strode out self-importantly in front of the worn red velvet curtain. Whistles, catcalls, and applause greeted him, and he acknowledged his ovation with a dignified bow before calling for quiet and introducing the first act.

"Ladies and gents, with pleasure I give you the great Harry Hunter — comic genius and singer supreme."

The curtain rose to reveal two jets of flame on each side of the stage, and a painted back flat of bright blue sky, a large yellow sun, and bilious green grass.

A comical-looking old man wearing a battered top hat and a huge red-and-white polka-dotted bow tie tottered on, to tumultuous shouts. Obviously a favorite, he sang three extremely suggestive songs with such salacious glee that Millie blushed. But the audience of petty tradesmen, costermongers, shop girls, soldiers, sailors, and servants whooped with delight, shouting out the lines before they'd even been sung. When Harry Hunter finished to hoots and whistles of approval, Millie's cheeks were flushed and she clutched her cousin's arm with excitement as the red-nosed master of ceremonies introduced the next act.

"A lovely little lady of only fourteen summers, Miss Ada Sproggs."

A charming child in a simple shift sang a plaintive ballad, about being orphaned, with such pathos that several girls in the audience started to sob in sympathy and Millie's own eyes filled with tears. At the end of her turn a few of the patrons flung halfpennies onto the stage and the girl scrabbled about for them, curtsied prettily, and skipped off.

A dozen more turns followed, and Millie became more and more engrossed in the excitement. She was just thinking it couldn't get much better when suddenly there was a tremendous roll of drums before the master of ceremonies introduced the next act.

"Our own Lily of the Valleys, the girl who put the oomph in oom-pah-pah, the one, the only — Miss Lily la Plante."

The curtain rose to reveal a battered birdcage center stage containing a scrawny canary that squeaked plaintively to the appreciative "oohs" and "aahs" from the audience. Then a vision of red ringlets, tightly corseted tartan, pink fishnet tights, and daring black boots laced to the knee bounced onto the stage to screams of delight. The audience erupted as Lily la Plante picked up the birdcage and with tremendous verve sang a song about her "old man" who told her to "follow the van" and not to "dilly-dally on the way."

Millie was enthralled by this fiery whirling dervish of a figure who, after acknowledging a delirium of applause, promptly broke into another bright ditty called "When Father Painted the Parlor." Lily sang three more numbers, each one saucier and more risqué than the last, finishing with the patriotic "Pack up Your Troubles in Your Old Kit Bag," which left many in the audience sobbing with emotion. Millie wanted the show to go on forever, but suddenly it was over. Lily took her bows, picked up her birdcage, and sashayed off, and the master of ceremonies hustled the audience out into the foyer where the next group of patrons was jostling to get in.

"Again," said Millie, breathlessly. "Oh please! Let's stay and see it again."

"Are you mad?" said Bridget. "It costs a penny and besides," she looked around beadily, "this new lot's coughing a lot. I don't like the look or sound of some of them."

She nodded toward a poster on the wall, which proclaimed starkly:

```
INFLUENZA
Is prevalent at this time in England.
If you have a cold and are coughing
or sneezing
PLEASE DO NOT enter this theater.
GO HOME AND GO TO BED UNTIL
YOU ARE WELL.
HELP KEEP LONDON HEALTHY.
The Management.
```

A young man with bad acne, bumping into them in his haste to enter, caught sight of the poster and guffawed, "Flu, pah! It's only the weak and the old that catch that."

"That may be so," Bridget whispered to Millie. "Our last two maids thought they had it, but in the end the doctor said it was consumption . . . there seems to be an awful lot of that around." She glanced behind them at an old woman in a shawl who was bent over and wracked with coughing. "C'mon, let's go. Better be safe than sorry. We'll come back next fortnight, Millie dear, I promise you."

★ ★ ★

But Millie wasn't prepared to wait that long. She was enraptured by Lily la Plante, and when she found out that the Alhambra had continuous performances every day, she took to escaping there while Kingsley and the other servants were too busy to check on her. She sat entranced on the hard benches drinking in all the performances, but most of all worshiping the brazen cheeky charms of Lily.

The following fortnight she cajoled Bridget into waiting with her at the end of the last performance to see her idol leave the theater. They stood out front shivering in the cold night air until Millie spotted the short, stout figure stomping through the auditorium. She ran up to Lily, almost incoherent. "You're the best singer I've ever seen! You're wonderful!" she gushed.

"You haven't seen *that* many," said Bridget, sotto voce. Millie stared at her idol who, up close, Bridget could see was no ingenue. Her red curls didn't even look remotely real, and her complexion was mottled, puffy, and wrinkled. "Thanks, dearies," said Lily graciously enough, but she was in no mood to linger and after a few pleasantries she was gone, in a whiff of cheap cologne and gin. "Sure, she's no spring chicken, is she?" laughed Bridget. "Forty if she's a day."

"Doesn't matter. She's wonderful. She's

brilliant. She's a star. I want to be like her one day."

"Star!" Bridget almost fell over laughing. "What do you know about stars, girl? She's a singer in a penny gaff, that's all. You want to see a star, we'll have to go to a proper palace of varieties."

"When?" asked Millie eagerly. "When can we go?"

"Next fortnight. We'll go and see Marie Lloyd at the Finsbury Park Empire — then you'll see a *real* star."

Chapter Two

Millie could hardly breathe for excitement as they joined the hundreds of people jostling for position outside the Finsbury Park Empire. The British government was encouraging Londoners to visit music halls. The war was still raging, food prices were soaring, rumors were rife about sugar and meat rationing, and the whole country was suffering extreme hardship. The politicians believed that encouraging their citizens to venture out to enjoy themselves occasionally would not only be good for morale but also save on gas and electricity. The gas street lamps flickered in the icy wind, which made the girls hang on to their bonnets and shawls. They had both worn their finest clothes for this special outing. Millie wore a hat that Cook had given her, trimmed with some disintegrating pheasant feathers, while Bridget made an effort at refinement in one of the duchess's cast-off black bombazine jackets, which she had painstakingly altered to fit her tiny frame. The girls clutched their sixpences, desperate not to miss the night's main performer, Marie Lloyd.

Millie stared at the bold black letters on the billboard.

THE LEADING MUSIC HALL ARTISTE OF THE WORLD ENGAGED AT ENORMOUS EXPENSE FOR FIVE NIGHTS ONLY.

THE GREAT, THE ONE, THE ONLY MARIE LLOYD — THE QUEEN OF COMEDY, WHO WILL PERFORM A SELECTION OF ALL HER MOST FAMOUS SONGS AND DANCES.

"So tell me more about this Marie Lloyd," asked Millie excitedly. She'd been pestering Bridget all afternoon for more and more details, but couldn't get enough to satisfy her.

"She's ever so old now, but no one's a greater music hall turn. Well over forty — it's a miracle she can still strut about, just you wait and see. Now c'mon, let's get in the queue."

There was a surge from the crowd and the girls were thrust forward to the front of the unruly queue and pushed up the stairs to the gallery, the cheapest seats in the house. The auditorium, dress, and upper circles were already brimming with an impatient audience eager to see its idol, "Our Marie." The girls managed to squeeze onto the end of a hard wooden bench at the front, giggling at the fat lady next to them who muttered to herself as she swigged from a bottle of ale. All of the patrons seemed to be either eating, drinking, or smoking, and a pall of smoke hung over the packed auditorium.

Millie and Bridget leaned forward, resting their faces in their hands, riveted by every sight and sound.

The front rows of the stalls were filled with a selection of aristocratic and middle-class people in elaborate finery. "I can smell their scent from up here," whispered Millie.

The less prosperous middle classes filled the middle and back rows, while in the boxes military men with fine mustaches, their uniforms resplendent with frogging and encrusted with medals, sat stiffly beside their ladies, who shimmered in satin and lace. Leaning over further, the girls could see some of the upper circle, which was composed of the more shabbily dressed middle class of the audience and the many troops on leave in their assorted army and naval uniforms.

High in the gallery, pale sickly faces leaned down, some of them pitted with smallpox scars or even the ravages of opium, hungry for the entertainment that would let the poorest of the poor forget their miserable lives for a few hours.

On either side of the proscenium arch, illuminated plaques announced the turns. Suddenly, to a burst of applause, the conductor in white tie and tails strode into the orchestra pit and started the overture. When it was over, two pretty girls in daringly short skirts and pink stockings placed a sign on the plaques — *Alfred Hutchings and His Performing Dogs.*

The house lights dimmed and the spotlight hit a tiny man who minced on stage followed by a pack of leaping, yapping terriers.

The canine performers received a lukewarm reception and were followed by a Mr. Ronaldo Frankau, an effete-looking young man billed as *"The Aristocrat of Entertainers."* He sang mournful ballads in an affected falsetto and fared worse than the dogs as several bad eggs and rotten bits of fruit were thrown at him.

A smutty comic told crude jokes, at which the bawdier members of the audience screamed with laughter, and then in quick succession came "Ramona — The Shooting Star," a brilliant trapeze artiste whose contortions made the audience gasp; "The Singing Silvester Sisters — Syncopation in Rhythm and Dance"; "Mr. Jack Blot — Naughty but Nice"; and a troop of performing seals who slithered all over the stage to shrieks of delight from the crowd.

At the intermission, people ate jellied eels and oranges and smoked and drank while the girls sat staring at the colorful audience.

"This is the most thrilling day of my life," Millie breathed. "In Ireland our idea of entertainment was looking into the fire — if we could afford a fire, that is."

"Just wait," said Bridget, "wait 'til you see Our Marie."

"When will she come on?"

"Oh, not until the end, dear — she's the star turn — but this is the Empire, so there'll be lots of good acts to see, mark my words."

After several more entertainers, the master of ceremonies strode center stage and announced the main turn, booming out proudly, "The one, the only — our very own Marie Lloyd!" The audience started whooping and cheering. Some of the men threw flowers onto the stage — one or two even threw their hats — and to the patriotic strains of "Now You've Got Your Khaki On" a plump, toothy woman wearing a flamboyant black ruffled dress and an enormous hat covered in red flowers and satin bows pranced onto the stage. Once she had finished that number, she launched into "A Little of What You Fancy Does You Good" in a throaty yet plaintive contralto voice. Millie was captivated, leaning so far over the balustrade to get a closer look that Bridget pulled her back for fear she'd fall. Although no longer young and far from beautiful, Marie Lloyd possessed an earthy exuberance combined with a mischievous cockney humor that was utterly riveting. The audience shouted the house down when she tottered about on stage miming tipsiness for "I'm a Bit of a Ruin That Cromwell Knocked About a Bit," and by the time she came to her final number, "My Old Man Said Follow the Van," she had them eating out of her hand. No one was more entranced than Millie.

After five encores Marie Lloyd left the stage, holding the armfuls of flowers thrown to her and blowing kisses, as the audience thronged out chattering excitedly.

"I want to be her," breathed Millie. "I want to be just like Marie Lloyd. She's the *best*. Oh, how I would love to hear people applaud me like that."

"Fat chance," scoffed Bridget, holding on to her hat as the cold wind hit them again outside. "Stick to cleaning grates, my love — that's where your talent lies. There isn't a hope in hell *you're* ever going to get on the boards. You're a parlor maid, my gal, be content with that."

But on the tram that took them back to Victoria, and walking across the sodden streets to Eaton Square, Millie's mind was filled with visions of "Our Marie" and how maybe one day she could be just like her.

"Our Millie," she whispered as she lay in her tiny bed. "If I practiced singing and dancing, that's what I could be one day. That's just the sort of life I'd like to have."

Chapter Three

Millie bought copies of the sheet music of the songs used by Marie Lloyd in her act and learned the songs by heart. She took to practicing them during her morning chores. Since the Swannell family was in residence at their Gloucestershire estate for the winter, she was able to rehearse enthusiastically in the kitchen, with only the stern Mr. Kingsley to admonish her.

Patsy caught her one day and watched her, hands on hips, her lip curled. "If I were an audience, I'd pay *not* to see you perform. You've no voice at all, and you dance like an elephant."

Millie blushed. "We've all got to start somewhere."

"You're mad," laughed Patsy, tossing her head. "You'll never make it to the halls, my girl."

"Wait and see," muttered Millie, through gritted teeth. "Just you wait."

Early one morning, after a more than usually spirited rendition of "When Father Painted the Parlor," Millie heard slow applause and a languid voice saying, "Bravo, Bravo! Encore!" Toby Swannell, home from his club where he'd been playing cards, leaned on the doorway of the drawing room. More than a little inebriated, his black tie hung loosely from his starched shirt, but his usually bored expression had been replaced by one of interest.

Millie jumped up from where she had been polishing the intricately carved legs of a Chippendale credenza. "Oh, sir! I'm sorry, I'm so terribly sorry, sir."

"Don't be sorry, my dear, that was very well done. I'd like to hear you sing some more." He sauntered over to the sofa, leaned back against the embroidered cushions and, lighting a cigarette from a gold case, he commanded, "Sing, my dear. Please sing for me."

Millie stared wide-eyed at Toby: a vision of sophistication as he blew an elegant smoke ring and smiled at her. "What is your name again?" he said.

"Millie, sir." She gave a little curtsy, conscious of the furniture wax on her hands and her curls escaping from her mobcap. "Millie McClancey."

"Well, Millie. Sing for me, will you? You have such a charming voice, and figure too," he observed, noticing the curve of her hips, the swell of her breasts in the tightly buttoned pale blue serge uniform, and her tiny waist circled by a navy canvas belt as she stood awkwardly in front of him.

Tobias Swannell, marquis of Leybourne, who in time would become the tenth Duke of Burghley, was a tall, elegant young man in his early twenties. His aristocratic features were already imprinted with an expression of boredom and lethargy, and there was a deadness behind his eyes that belied his years, but he had a dazzlingly innocent smile that caused Millie to grin back at him unashamedly for a second. As their eyes connected, he noticed her embarrassment and gave a comforting chuckle.

"Don't worry, Millie, Kingsley's running errands for me. No one can hear you; these doors are as thick as the walls of a moated castle."

Millie leaned against the marble mantelpiece for support. She thought she might faint. She had never seen any man or boy so dazzling. As if reading her thoughts, he drew deeply on his cigarette and cajoled her softly: "Sing, Millie, please. Sing to me."

"Oh, sir, I daren't." She glanced fearfully at the closed door. "If Mr. Kingsley hears I've been singing for you, sir, I'll get the sack for sure." She tried to tuck a recalcitrant auburn curl under her cap.

Toby smiled and strolled across to her. Placing a finger against her lips he whispered,

"Don't worry, the staff can't hear a thing, and I promise I won't say a word, if you sing for me, and me alone." His pale blue eyes bored into hers. His eyelashes were fair, his fine golden hair cascaded over his forehead, and his lips were pink and full. He was so appealing that Millie wanted to kiss his moist lips, then blushed at the thought.

"I order you to sing, Millie," Toby demanded, his voice hardening. "If you won't sing for me, then I *will* tell Kingsley."

Millie dropped the dust cloth from her shaking fingers and looked around at the intimidating room. She looked at the carved Chippendale cabinet where a priceless collection of gold snuffboxes jostled for space; at the glittering chandeliers wired with the new electric lightbulbs; and at the huge concert grand piano, covered with framed photographs of royalty, like some grand but frozen audience.

"Here?" she said, incredulously. "You really want me to sing for you here, sir?"

He nodded, his eyes fixed on her. She was a gorgeous little thing, like a delicate porcelain doll. He returned to the sofa and said, "Yes, Millie, I certainly do. Sing, Millie, now . . ."

Millie swallowed, trying to dismiss her fear. She'd read enough about performers in the weekly periodicals to realize that shyness and nervousness were not part of their makeup.

47

Summoning up all her confidence, she began to sing hesitantly in a high sweet voice, while Toby watched her intently. When she had finished, he clapped slowly.

"You're very good — you've a fine, strong voice — it's almost professional."

"Oh, thank you, sir. It's what I want to do one day, sir. To sing on the stage like Marie Lloyd."

Toby glanced at his watch. "Six-thirty. I'll be here again tomorrow morning at the same time, and I'll want you to sing for me again."

Millie let out a squeak. "Oh no, sir, I can't."

"Oh yes, Millie, you can." Toby flicked his cigarette ash onto the carpet nonchalantly. "And you will. I'm giving a dinner here tonight, and when I return from my club afterward I shall come here and expect to see you. All right, Millie?"

"Yes sir." She bobbed a curtsy as Toby stood up, stretched, yawned, then walked toward her, and cupped her face in his long slender hands.

"You're a pretty girl, Millie. A very pretty girl indeed." And without a pause he bent toward her and pressed his lips to hers. Millie's face went scarlet and she was about to protest when he walked toward the door, turned, and with a smile said, "This will be our secret, Millie, and ours alone."

Millie stared at the door, her mouth agape.

The Greek god wanted her to sing for him. "Well, I'll do my damnedest then." She giggled and ran her feather duster over the grandfather clock.

In the passage outside, someone who had heard everything crept away shaking with rage.

At Eaton Square the day passed in a frenzy of domestic activity. The young master Toby had unexpectedly decided to throw a pre-Christmas dinner party, and the staff was put out by having to organize and prepare the festivities for twenty of his friends that night.

As Bridget, Millie, and the rest of the maids and footmen bustled about in a frenzy of polishing, dusting, and cleaning, Millie's head was in a complete whirl. She could still feel the imprint of Toby's lips on hers. Still remember his pale blue eyes looking into hers as he kissed her with the arrogance that only rich men possessed. And every time she thought of him, her stomach gave a little lurch. She wanted to confide in someone about this strange feeling, but she didn't dare. Bridget was close as a sister to her, but she instinctively knew that only two can keep a secret. Little enough happened in the course of the daily work, and Bridget wouldn't be able to stop herself from confiding this juicy piece of gossip to someone else. Millie felt certain of that.

As the day progressed Millie was assigned to the dining room, where she was instructed to measure exactly the dimensions between each place setting.

"Thirteen-and-a-half inches exactly," boomed Mr. Kingsley, supervising the arrangement of a magnificent display of hothouse orchids and roses in a Georgian jardiniere in the center of the table.

"Where *did* they find those flowers?" whispered Bridget, who was placing gold and white serving plates in the middle of each array of silver knives, forks, and spoons. "Don't they know our men are dying in France?"

"I think all this extravagance is disgusting!" said Patsy. "They've greenhouses in Gloucestershire, don't y'know. That's where they grow these orchids." She looked at Millie with a disagreeable expression on her pinched little face. Millie suddenly found herself defending the family. "They pay for it all," she said, "so they're entitled to live like this." Privately she thought how wonderful it would be to be able to live in this kind of luxury.

"War or not, they'll be eating well tonight. Better than most people in England," said Bridget.

During the day the kitchen door bell had rung a dozen times as tradesmen and purveyors of fine meats, game, fish, and cheese came to the door. Mr. Kingsley would pay these men in cash while there were furtive whispers and glances down to the square in case a strolling bobby spotted them. The black market was illegal, and while it was common practice for the upper classes to have dealings with it, penalties were stiff if they were discovered red-handed.

"Must've cost a bomb," said Bridget. "It's a disgrace too, with all the shortages going on. D'you know I've heard they're even rationing bread in some places now."

"I think it's a terrible injustice with all our own poor boys starving at the front," said Tom, the young footman, who was attempting to tie his cravat with inexperienced clumsiness.

Millie went up to him. "Here, let me help you. My, you do look fine, Tom." As she tied his tie she remembered once, long ago, helping her dad to do up his tie, something he hadn't been used to wearing. It had been her grandma's funeral, and her mama had already taken to her bed with TB.

"Thanks, Millie." Tom flushed, feeling self-conscious in his old-fashioned livery of scarlet knee breeches, white coat weighed down with gold buttons, and enormous bow at his neck.

"Why aren't *you* in the army then, Tom?" asked Patsy spitefully. Millie noticed that Patsy insulted everyone at the slightest provocation.

"I've only got three toes on me left foot." Tom went even redder. "I did go to the recruitment office, but they turned me down."

"Oh really," sneered Patsy. "Pull the other one."

"Shut your mouth, girl!" snapped Kingsley. "And tighten that belt of yours too. You look slatternly."

"Yes, sir, Mr. Kingsley." Patsy smiled slyly at the butler, who averted his eyes self-consciously.

The dozen servants had congregated for inspection by Kingsley in the staff dining room, which was long, gloomy, painted a bilious shade of green and dominated by an enormous refectory table that could easily seat thirty. Male staff were now at a premium because of the war, so the servants at Eaton Square were mostly women, with the exception of Tom and the other three footmen, who were well over the age of conscription.

"You'll all be nimble and light on your feet tonight," barked Kingsley. "The young master is entertaining an important lady and he's out to impress her, so don't embarrass him."

"Important lady?" Bridget whispered to Millie. "And who might that be, pray?"

"Haven't the faintest," answered Millie, but she was certainly anxious to find out. She longed to tell her cousin about her little "audition" for Toby, but worried Bridget would only laugh at her.

★ ★ ★

At half-past eight the doorbell rang and a succession of some of the most gorgeous and refined young women Millie had ever seen entered the grand hallway, passing Kingsley as he rigidly held the door open. A red-carpeted staircase that led to the reception rooms above dominated the lofty oak-paneled entrance hall. The floor was of highly polished parquet, and on the walls hung oil paintings so old and dark that they looked almost black. The footmen took the gentlemen's top hats, cloaks, and canes, while Millie, Bridget, and Patsy were assigned to take the ladies' cloaks.

The female guests all appeared to be in their early twenties, but they possessed the poise and sophistication of the generation above them, chatting and laughing easily with one another. The ladies' youthful looks were accentuated by their exquisite heirloom jewelry, which sparkled in the candlelight, and their elaborate organdy chiffon, or taffeta gowns, some of which were daringly cut to show maximum cleavage.

Millie felt exceedingly plain and insignificant in her uniform. None of the guests looked at the maids as they carelessly tossed their cloaks to them and made their way to the drawing room.

One of the young ladies threw an ermine wrap to Patsy, who was not able to catch it before it fell on the floor. "Idiot," said the girl scornfully, ascending the stairs. "Pick it up at once."

"Stuck-up cow," hissed Patsy as she bowed apologetically. Millie almost felt sorry for Patsy, who had to kneel to gather up yards of heavy cream fur. Patsy noticed Millie looking at her sympathetically and snapped, "Those men are stuck up too — why aren't they on the front lines?"

"Perhaps you've not got eyes in your head," said Bridget, "but most of those men are old — they'll never be seeing forty again — and the two or three that are young look a bit weak to me."

"One's wearing spectacles," observed Millie.

"You can't wear specs in the army," said Bridget. "And that red-haired one — he's got a limp."

"So what about the young marquis?" asked Millie with calculated carelessness. "Why hasn't he been called up?"

"I've heard rumors that he's got a wonky eye," said Bridget. "But if you're really interested, you can find out soon enough from Kingsley. He knows where all the skeletons in this family are buried."

Dinner was to be served at half-past nine, and in the upstairs drawing room during the hour reserved for aperitifs Kingsley dispensed drinks, sherry for the ladies and whisky for the men, while below stairs the three maids gossiped about the dresses, hairstyles, and jewels the young ladies sported.

When the doorbell rang at twenty-five past nine, the maids looked at one another in surprise.

Tom went to answer the door and a vision walked imperiously into the hall. "Where's Kingsley?" the woman demanded authoritatively. Her voice had an unfamiliar accent.

"Er, ma'am, he's in the d-drawing room serving d-drinks," Tom stuttered.

The three maids stood in a row staring at this new arrival. She was exceedingly tall and exceedingly thin, wearing a fashionable silver-gray sleeveless tunic dress with shimmering paillettes embroidered on the tight bodice and panels of sheer chiffon hanging from the skirt. Her black hair was piled high in the slightly old-fashioned Gibson girl style, and her dark eyes darted impatiently around as Bridget took her white-satin-trimmed black velvet cloak. All three were riveted by this young woman who, although only a few years older than themselves, seemed the epitome of sophistication.

As the woman shrugged off the cloak, she glanced at Tom. "Tell the marquis that Miss Vanderhausen has arrived."

"Yes ma'am," said Tom, stumbling up the stairs, his face flushing almost as red as his breeches. Miss Vanderhausen looked at the maids expectantly as she coolly removed a golden cigarette case from her reticule and put a cigarette between her lips.

"She wants a match," hissed Patsy. "Quick!"

Bridget dashed over to the woman with a box she had in her apron, and Miss Vanderhausen motioned her to light the cigarette. Millie was stunned.

"Smoking? I've never seen a lady do that," she whispered admiringly to Bridget when she returned, watching as the girl drew the smoke languidly into her lungs.

"Well, she's American, isn't she? I've seen pictures of film stars smoking in the magazines. American women are all supposed to be a bit fast."

"Oh, of course." Millie stared in fascination at the first American she had ever seen, and then Toby dashed down the wide carpeted stairs toward the newcomer, out of breath and grinning widely.

"Rosemary, darling, you look ravishing as usual." He kissed the proffered white-gloved hand.

"About *time*, Toby. You might at least have waited down here to greet me," she drawled.

"Dear heart, you *were* rather late, don't you think?" Toby took her arm and led her up the stairs. He laughed and the woman turned her face to him, blew a puff of smoke, smiled seductively, and didn't answer.

Millie stood at the foot of the stairs watching the glamorous young couple go up to the drawing room arm in arm. She felt another unfamiliar sensation. Toby hadn't even glanced in her direction, and she experienced a distinct flicker of what she suddenly realized could be jealousy.

The dinner party seemed a great success, and the maids and footmen were kept on their toes, constantly refilling glasses with a variety of wines from the duke's well-stocked cellar and removing the plates from the lavish six-course dinner. They started with white soup à la reine, and then stuffed trout with tiny carrots painstakingly carved into stars and crescents. A salad of aubergines and minced beetroot followed, and the two elderly footmen staggered under the weight of the main course: a goose on a silver salver decorated with crab apples and gooseberries. A variety of ices were served for pudding; some of the younger girls were thrilled by these confections, which were still somewhat of a novelty, made possible by the advent of the icebox. After the *petites bouchées* were served, Bridget and Patsy were put to work in the kitchen helping the scullery maids carefully wash the precious Sèvres plates.

"Been in the family for years, these," said Patsy knowingly. "So you drop one, girl, and you'll be out on your arse."

When the men were left with their port and cigars, the women retired to the drawing room, where they relaxed, giggling, gossiping, and smoking cigarettes while the three maids waited to do their bidding.

Rosemary Vanderhausen stood before an Adam mirror inspecting her milk-white complexion. She took out a bright red lipstick and applied it liberally to her thin lips while Millie tried not to stare. This woman, who could not be more than twenty, seemed like a creature from another planet — so at ease with herself, so arrogant, so stylishly beautiful. Was Toby in love with her? What man wouldn't be? But, Millie wondered, if he was in love with a woman so obviously of his own class, even if she was a Yank, why did he kiss me this morning? She continued admiring Rosemary Vanderhausen's beauty and poise in spite of herself.

Rosemary glanced toward the three awe-struck maids. "I need help with the clasp of my necklace," she commanded. "It's cutting into my neck."

Millie darted forward. "I'll help you, miss," she said breathlessly.

"Damn thing, take it off . . ."

Millie obeyed, admiring Rosemary's neck, which seemed as slender and white as a swan's. She wondered if Toby had ever kissed her and felt an unpleasant stab of envy again.

Rosemary's black eyes glanced at Millie in

the mirror. "You're new?"

It was a statement more than a question. "Yes, miss," Millie removed the heavy diamond and sapphire necklace from Rosemary's scented neck. She had never seen so beautiful an object. The stones glinted and shimmered in the candlelight, and she thought bitterly that a necklace like this was probably worth enough to feed everyone in her village for a year, maybe two.

Rosemary clicked open a silver compact set with diamonds. Removing a swansdown puff, she flicked powder over her porcelain neck. "Don't gawp at me, girl," she said sharply. "Haven't they taught you not to stare?"

"Yes, miss." Millie cast her eyes down to the glittering necklace and felt hot tears gathering. The duke and duchess had never spoken to her in such an unkind fashion. Indeed, they'd never spoken to her at all really. This young woman had put Millie in her place more firmly than even Kingsley with his "hoity-toity" attitude had done.

Rosemary snapped shut her compact and patted her fine black hair as the rest of the women finished their coffee and cordials and prepared to receive the men. "Put it back on," she commanded, inclining her neck. "And don't pinch me."

"Yes, miss," said Millie, closing the complicated clasp as delicately as she could.

The men arrived, joking and talking, and

Millie noticed that Toby went straight to Rosemary to whisper something in her ear. She laughed dismissively and moved away, leaving Toby momentarily crestfallen.

He loves her, said Millie to herself, as she prepared for bed. He loves her and I think I love him. "What am I doing?" she mumbled during her fitful sleep. "Why am I thinking about him?"

But the following morning as Millie scraped cold ashes from the iron grate, Toby was there again. This time he boldly locked the door and, propping himself comfortably against the cushions on the sofa, he commanded her to sing to him. This time, without preamble, she obeyed. She wanted to please him, and she wasn't nervous anymore.

These involuntary auditions continued for over a week. Each time Millie finished a song, Toby would silently applaud, his hands never touching each other.

"Bravo," he'd mouth. "Encore!" He praised Millie's singing and her beauty to the skies, which always amazed and thrilled her, and at the end of the week he presented her with a bunch of fresh violets.

"What'll I do with them, sir? I can't afford flowers on my wages, and the other girls will wonder."

"Then I'll keep them for you, beside my bed, and tonight, Millie, you may come and see them." He bent toward her and she felt again the irresistible urge to feel his mouth on hers.

"It's too dangerous," she whispered, gazing into his eyes, which seemed soft and loving today. "Please, sir, I *can't*." She moved away from the fireplace, but his arms went around her waist and he held her tightly.

"You liked me kissing you the first time, didn't you?"

Millie couldn't answer. She tried to wriggle free from his embrace, but that strange melting feeling in her stomach prevented her. "Please, sir," she said weakly. "Please don't. It's more than my job's worth."

"Don't worry about your silly job," he whispered. "Nothing's going to happen to you, I promise."

Millie looked up into Toby's candid blue-eyed gaze. "How can you promise that, sir?" Her voice wavered. She liked the comforting feel of his arms around her, and the warm unfamiliar pressure against her thigh made her mouth feel dry. She knew she wanted him to kiss her as his arms held her closer and his hand stroked the nape of her neck and his lips drew nearer.

"Oh, dear God, we *can't*, sir."

"Oh, but we can," and his warm mouth was on hers again.

Millie was an inexperienced girl — a virgin and a devout Catholic — but the feelings that Toby evoked in her were positively wanton. She prayed to the Blessed Virgin for forgiveness as she succumbed to his kisses. His mouth was full and firm, and it fitted with her own so perfectly that she didn't even feel the need to breathe, she just drew her breath from him now and then.

The way he traced the outline of her lips delicately with his tongue made her dizzy with pleasure. As one hand stroked her back, the other pushed her mobcap away, then he buried his fingers in her luxuriant hair, caressing her head while kissing her ever more deeply.

Millie thought she was dreaming. What was he doing? Why was he doing this? According to kitchen gossip, this boy was supposed to be in love with Rosemary Vanderhausen, and what she had seen with her own eyes confirmed this.

Her mind whirled with doubts, but she was becoming so lost in Toby's embrace and the new passion he aroused in her that nothing else mattered.

But when Toby's hand moved from her hair to her neck and the fastenings of her blouse, Millie's inner voice got the better of her.

"No, sir," she pleaded. "No, please, I can't." She pushed him away and stared at him, shivering with emotions she'd never experienced. "I can't do this, sir. I'm sorry."

Toby frowned and, looking slightly annoyed, took a cigarette from a box on the mantelpiece and lit it. His blond hair fell over his forehead, and Millie stared in fascination at his beautiful mouth as he drew smoke deep into his lungs. Then he looked at her, long and hard, and held out the violets toward her.

"I think I'm taking a shine to you, Millie. So think about it. If you want to smell your violets tonight, you know where they'll be."

After he left, Millie fell onto the sofa, shaking uncontrollably. She tried to adjust her clothes and smooth her hair but kept getting distracted by the memory of his lips on hers.

"But I think I'm in love with you," she whispered. "Oh, Lord above, what do I do now?"

From behind a mirrored screen in a far corner of the room, Patsy Hooper had watched and heard everything. She glanced at her face in the mirror. She was as pretty as that McClancey girl, wasn't she? Why didn't Toby still go after *her?* She had loved him secretly during the time she had worked at Eaton Square. In her head and her heart she had romanticized the short moments she had spent with Toby until they had become a full-blown love story from a Mary Pickford film.

Her mind also often wandered to the hor-

63

rors of where she had been raised. Patsy's childhood had been one of heart-wrenching poverty and appalling degradation in the slums of Billingsgate. There foul lanes and alleys were filled with the dregs of humanity, even though they were only a few miles from the grandest houses in Mayfair. There were such extremes of riches and penury in London that only those who had experienced both aspects could truly comprehend them, and Patsy knew both sides well.

The stench of Billingsgate Market — the repugnant smell of decay, of rotting garbage, of streets sometimes ankle-deep in mud and dung — still haunted Patsy's dreams. Many men had used Patsy since her mother, Ada, had sold her, at the age of eight, to one of her best clients. "Cherry intacto," she'd leered. Little Patsy had been unprotesting, for she knew she had no choice. The act itself was no better or worse than being beaten up by the "uncles" her mother had harbored in her room, brutish men who brought other men to her mother's bed. Night after night Patsy heard the sounds they made, but they were no more disturbing to her than the cries of the costermongers, or the horses' hooves clattering on the cobblestoned street.

She'd endured it even when the men came to her bed, and as a reward she was given extra scraps of food and the occasional swig of gin. A lesser reward was when she became pregnant at age thirteen. As she became bigger and clumsier, Patsy asked her mother what was happening to her. When Ada matter-of-factly informed her daughter that a baby was growing inside her, the horror never left her and soon afterward she endured an agonizing twenty-hour labor, the pain of which almost killed her.

The birth of Patsy's baby, compounded with the near-death of her daughter, shook Ada's maternal feelings from their hibernating state. Realizing that a life of prostitution was not ideal for a fourteen-year-old girl, Ada found Patsy a job as a scullery maid at a Whitechapel gin palace. By now a raddled thirty-four, and abandoned by the pimps and "uncles," Ada Hooper decided to look after her grandchild herself. By a stroke of extreme luck she found full-time employment as a washerwoman in a brothel. Since her looks had withered, the men left her alone and Ada was able to concentrate on the little girl her daughter had borne.

Patsy was aware of her good fortune in working at the pub. Her pretty face, sturdy figure, and salty line of repartee attracted men to her, and inevitably she found herself selling her body. Though she considered them all sweaty, dirty beasts, she realized that if she could save enough money, she could get away from her sordid life and maybe move to the countryside. She could start a new life somewhere clean, away from the stench of Billingsgate and the vile men who hurt her when they invaded her body.

One night, when well into his cups, and with promises of a job as kitchen maid in a grand house in Belgravia, Alfred Kingsley had his way with Patsy for the going rate of two shillings and six-pence.

Even though she hated it, by now Patsy excelled at the art of sex because she made a man feel like a man. Kingsley didn't know what had hit him. He soon had Patsy out of Whitechapel and installed in a tiny upstairs maid's bedroom in a huge luxurious mansion unlike anything Patsy had ever known. At forty-five, he looked older but still had an eye for the ladies — and a constant urge for Patsy. She soon found that sleeping with Kingsley was a boring task indeed. In spite of plentiful food and clean lodgings, she found his fumbling attentions irritating. She insisted he give her a half-crown whenever she practiced her erotic skills on him, and soon she had nearly fifty pounds in the black tin box she kept hidden under her mattress, which was her key to a new life. In the meantime, Kingsley's lusty libido, sometimes frustrated by Patsy's increasingly regular headaches, found solace in the gentlemen's magazines he secretly read.

Millie didn't visit Toby in his bedroom that

night or any other night after that. She had persuaded Kingsley to let her take over as Cook's temporary assistant while the usual girl was sick with her monthly cramps. Kingsley, in an unusually magnanimous mood thanks to Patsy's attentions the previous night, agreed, and Millie was thus able to keep well out of Toby's way. But she couldn't keep her feelings out of the way. Thoughts of Toby, his lips, his mouth, his hooded blue-eyed gaze, intruded on her as she pounded and kneaded and mixed and stirred to Cook's instructions. She'd even stopped singing, even though Kingsley and Cook enjoyed her little "turns" now. Millie didn't want to see Toby, couldn't face him. She yearned for him, yet she tried to dismiss him from her mind.

Kingsley was a mine of information about the Burghleys. After a good evening's repast of roast pork and dumplings he sat in his chair puffing on his pipe, and in between sips of the duke's best port imparted a few salient family secrets to Bridget, May, and Millie, who sat on stools at Kingsley's feet listening intently.

"The duke doesn't have nearly the money he used to have," Kingsley said, enjoying the sound of his own voice. "The aristocracy today is being ruined — taxes, you see — they've gone up enormously to pay for this bloody war. The estate in Gloucestershire is hemorrhaging money, the landed gentry everywhere is suffering. It's all in here." He stabbed a stubby finger into his paper. "It's all in *The Times*, everything you want to know."

"I don't understand," said Millie. "They look so rich, how could they not be?"

"Oh, it's not so easy to explain to the likes of you," said Kingsley condescendingly. "But what I believe is that if they don't get some more funds in the family coffers soon — something's got to go and . . ." — he leaned forward conspiratorially — ". . . it'll be either this house or the big one in the country, or else the Scottish estate."

"What about our jobs?" Millie asked fearfully. She was settled here now, and liked it. She even liked the forbidden danger that Toby represented.

"Ah, yes — well, who knows?" Kingsley was unconcerned. As a privileged member of the servant working class, he had managed to save up a tidy little sum over the past thirty years and was not averse to the thought of future retirement, with Patsy by his side.

"You've seen the spaces on the walls of the ballroom where they've taken the good pictures down. Since the war at least a dozen have been sold — along with some of Her Ladyship's jewels too." Kingsley nodded sagely. "I know everything that goes on in this house — everything."

Not quite everything, thought Millie — stabbed by a frisson of fear. Kingsley had closed his eyes dismissively and, as Millie stepped over to the stove to make a cup of tea, Patsy sidled up to her.

"So, you didn't go up there then, did you?"

"Go — go where?"

"To see *him*, of course." Patsy bent forward and Millie felt her hot breath on her ear. "You stay away from Toby, my girl, do you hear — stay away. Otherwise I'll tell *him*." She gestured toward Kingsley, now snoring comfortably by the fire.

The two girls were alone in the kitchen, the electric light was off, and the flickering candles cast venomous shadows on Patsy's sharp face. Suddenly Millie realized that Patsy knew about her and Toby. Maybe she had even seen them together.

"So what will you do about it then?" Millie's face was flaming. "What can you do to me, Patsy?" she challenged, sounding braver than she felt.

"If I tell Kingsley, then he'll tell the master and you'll be *out*, girl. Out of this house and onto the streets, and the old duchess'll make quite sure you never get a job or work in a good house again, mark my words — you'll be finished." She stalked off, as Millie stared after her in shock.

Cook's helper would be back at her post

tomorrow, which meant that Millie would be going back to her duties as a parlor maid, back to where Toby could easily find her.

All night long, Millie anxiously tossed and turned. She tried to analyze what she felt for Toby, but whenever the image of him crossed her mind, she felt warmth coursing through her and a thrill of — love was it love? She knew she loved being at Eaton Square, in spite of the prying Patsy. She enjoyed the work, and she adored her fortnightly visits to the music halls. Her desire to be in the halls herself one day had taken permanent residence in her mind. How to achieve her goal she couldn't fathom, but a girl could dream, couldn't she?

Chapter Four
1918

The next day Kingsley assigned Millie the job of spring-cleaning the duchess's bedroom. It was now almost April, and the family was expected back at any time. Millie started as early as possible and worked swiftly. She needed to be finished before Toby found her. She was tormented by indecision. She wanted to see him, pined for him, but she knew that what she yearned for was morally wrong. She still went to church every Sunday and said her prayers religiously every night. She was a good Catholic girl and intended to remain that way.

"It's a sin," she murmured. "A sin to have these thoughts about a man." Then she wondered where Toby had been lately. Out on the town maybe? Probably at one of his clubs, Crockford's or Boodle's, or the most glamorous of all, White's. When she had dismissed these thoughts, images of his lips on hers flashed across her mind instead.

As Millie was changing the duchess's bed

linen she heard a sound and Toby appeared at the door, wearing a silk paisley dressing gown and — she noticed with a shock — evidently absolutely nothing underneath.

Toby watched her with a mocking smile as she mumbled, "Good morning, sir," and continued making the bed.

"Yes, and what a good, good morning it is." He sauntered toward her slowly, smiling all the time, one hand in his pocket, the fingertips of the other slowly brushing across his lips.

Those lips! She stared at them in fascination as he moved closer. She could smell him now. Smell the fresh scent of the shaving cream he used, smell the pomade he rubbed on his unruly curls to tame them. He was a beautiful man. There was no other word for him. The delicacy of his cheekbones, the long brown lashes surrounding those languid blue eyes, his parted pink lips, his dimples.

Before she knew it, Millie was responding to Toby's kisses. She didn't resist as he pushed her gently onto the bed, his tongue caressing her mouth.

She buried her face in his warm neck, inhaling his scent.

"Oh, my love, my love," he breathed before kissing her more deeply. Then his hand was under her skirt and she felt his fingers at the top of her cotton stockings, where they found the soft skin of her thighs.

"No, no. Oh God, sir. I can't." Millie tried to move, but she was pinned beneath him on his mother's bed like a butterfly.

"Oh, you *can*. Yes, you can, my love. I want you, Millie — I must have you — I adore you, my little angel."

Millie's mind was in a furor as thoughts she never knew existed flooded into her. She could feel Toby's hardness through the silken robe as a rush of desire overwhelmed her.

"See — see, Millie — see how much I want you?"

As Toby turned on his side, his robe slid open and revealed his nakedness.

"Oh, no, no." Millie turned away, closing her eyes — she had never seen a naked man before, only boy children, and Toby was certainly no boy.

He took her hand and placed it gently on himself. She tried to draw it away, but he clasped it over him.

"Touch me, Millie. Please touch me here."

His hand was above her thighs now. He'd pushed up the elastic in her woolen bloomers and was finding the place where she was increasingly hot and damp.

"Oh, Millie," he groaned, his left hand still pressing hers onto his erection, while his right hand continued to explore her, "I need you so." His lips were soft, so sensually loving that Millie felt all her defenses melting. All her morals — all her Catholic scruples —

evaporated in a burning of desire. This was love, wasn't it? This intense feeling that was like a hot light burning inside her — this electric current that seemed to flow between them. It was love — it must be love. As if answering her unspoken question, Toby whispered the magic words.

"I love you, Millie. You've got into my blood, under my skin. You're my angel — I love you." And for once, he believed he really meant it.

The voice that answered didn't seem to be hers. "I love you too, sir."

He looked down at her and grinned. "Sir? *Sir?* You must call me Toby, my angel — now that we're going to be lovers."

"Lovers?" Alarm bells flashed in Millie's mind. "Oh, but that's a mortal sin, sir. To love each other outside marriage — 'tis sinful."

Toby laughed. "Sinful? Really, Millie, this is the twentieth century. It's no longer a sin for people to make love to each other."

"Yes, but, sir . . ." She managed to extract herself from his embrace as she tried to make their discussion more philosophical than physical.

"Sir, loving without marriage, it *is* a sin — and if I do it I shall burn in hell for eternity."

"Well, we wouldn't want that to happen, would we?" Toby's eyes suddenly became guarded. He lay back, pulling his dressing gown over his wilting erection, lit a cigarette, and with half-closed eyes asked, "So what then would it take for a girl like you to love me *completely?*" He opened his eyes and stared at her to make sure she got the point.

"It would have to be marriage, sir," she stuttered. "My mother and my father always made me promise that I would never give myself to a man without being his wife."

"How very quaint." Toby's voice seemed distant and disdainful as he continued smoking and gazing at the ceiling. "Positively nineteenth century."

"I'm sorry," said Millie jumping off the duchess's bed. As she started pulling down her dress, the door was flung open and Patsy stood there, her face like a shrew, dustpan and brush in hand.

"Mr. Kingsley said you forgot these," she snapped, ignoring Toby, who, without moving said, "Good morning . . . Patsy, isn't it?" and continued staring at the ceiling.

Patsy glared venomously at Millie as she slammed the dustpan into her hands. "I'll talk to you later," she hissed.

"Oh, no, Patsy." Millie's voice shook. "I'll talk to you now."

She followed the maid out and across the hallway into the duke's bedroom, where the two girls faced each other.

"I'm telling Mr. Kingsley what I saw,"

75

snarled Patsy, "and you'll be out like I said."

"It's not my fault," Millie said despairingly. "I've done nothing."

"You think I'm a fool? I know that look on a man's face when he's had his way with a girl. You've done it with him, I know you have."

"I have NOT!" Millie cried.

"Don't lie to me." Patsy grabbed Millie and slammed her against the wall. "If you don't leave this house by tomorrow, girl — I'll tell Mr. Kingsley *everything* and I mean it. You'll never get a job in these parts again, he'll make *sure* of that."

Patsy lay on her bed fuming. How dare Toby want that Irish peasant slut. Why had he rejected her after he'd used her just that one night last year? For the hundredth time she relived those magic hours in her mind, the most wonderful moments of her life.

She had been plumping up the cushions on the drawing room sofa after the family had retired, when Toby's hands had grabbed her from behind, around the waist, and pressed her close to him. She could smell the alcohol on his breath as he slurred, "My, my, my, but you're a pretty little thing. Do you want some fun?"

"Oh, no, sir, I don't. Thank you, sir." Patsy had tried to wriggle away, but he only held her tighter.

"I think I can make you change your mind." He had grinned and had pushed her down onto the sofa, his pale blue eyes twinkling down at her, his soft fair hair framing his angelic face. "What's your name, pretty little thing?"

"Patsy," she had whispered.

"You look like a girl who likes a good time, Patsy. I like a good time too." Then he had pressed his lips to hers, started running his hands over her body, and she had felt not a second's compunction as she responded.

Although Patsy was only fourteen, she was hardly a naive virgin. This cherub-faced boy was a deal more attractive than Kingsley or the oafish louts she'd had to accommodate in Whitechapel. It wasn't at all hard to give in to him and his mumbled words of lust. Even though she knew he was drunk, Patsy succumbed to Toby willingly on the soft cushions of the velvet sofa. But the sweet, meaningless words he had whispered struck a chord in her and she cherished the little bit of affection he had given her.

But Toby didn't acknowledge her when he passed the young maid on the stairs the next day, and to Patsy's distress he completely ignored her from then on. She had thought that the young marquis had been interested enough in her that she might see him again, but when he continued to behave as if she didn't exist, her heart hardened and she understood that she had meant nothing. Soon after that, when she realized she was pregnant and that it couldn't possibly be Kingsley's baby, since she'd been avoiding contact with him for months, she concocted a story to him and the Burghley family about her dying mother and went back to the slums of Billingsgate. There she stayed with her cousins, the McCormicks, and, early in 1917, gave birth to her second child, a boy who was gladly adopted by Patsy's childless cousin Ella. Patsy returned to Eaton Square a little older, not much wiser, but more bitter than ever. A few months later, when Millie McClancey started work there, Patsy's resentment became all-consuming. When she discovered the flirtation between Toby and Millie, her jealousy had become so intense that she was past reason, almost becoming physically ill.

"I'm going to tell them," she mumbled to herself during a fitful sleep. "I'll tell the Burghleys, then she'll be out and then I'll get to see the young master again."

Millie spent another night in turmoil. Whatever happened, she knew she was finished at Eaton Square. Patsy wouldn't believe she hadn't slept with Toby — and Toby was by now so fired up with lust for her and she for him that she knew she would eventually give him what he wanted. In her heart of hearts Millie knew it. He was irresistible.

At four in the morning, after a sleepless night, Millie packed a small carpet bag, took her meager savings from beneath her mattress, and crept down the back staircase and out of Eaton Square forever. She left a note for the sleeping Bridget telling her she was going back to Ireland but to tell no one where she was. After waiting for six hours at Victoria Station, she took the train to Liverpool and the following day the ferry across the sea back to her Aunt Mary, back to Ireland.

Chapter Five

Aunt Mary was so delighted to see Millie again that she accepted her little white lie of losing her job "because the Burghleys are getting rid of some of their staff" and welcomed her back to her tiny cottage. It was a bit of a shock for Millie to return to the dirt floors and drafty, candlelit nights of her aunt's cottage after the relative luxury of Eaton Square, but she was a hardy soul and soon adjusted to her change of circumstances. "One day I'll have a place of my own," thought Millie, as she tried to get comfortable on the hard floor. "One day I'll be a singer good enough for people to pay money to see."

At forty Mary was as bent and shriveled as a seventy-year-old. She had been eking out a living by selling home-grown vegetables at the local market, but the crops were meager and she looked frail. Millie was so concerned about her aunt she decided she must make some money to support them both. She trekked across the fields to the nearest pub, three miles away, and so impressed the publican with her Marie Lloyd impersonation that Seamus O'Reilly hired her on the spot. "You'll entertain the regulars on Thursday, Friday, and Saturday nights, girl," he said. "They're a rowdy lot when they've been at the drink, so you'll need to put on a good show to keep 'em quiet."

"Oh, but I will, sir," Millie said eagerly. "You'll not be disappointed."

And neither were the customers. Soon The Blind Beggar became a prime site for the locals who traveled from miles around to see the singer whose exuberant youthfulness and naive, though quite unintentional, sensuality became a magnet for the rough country people.

Seamus did a roaring weekend trade. The pub was dark, noisy, and crowded, and Millie had to work hard at first to make the patrons listen to her. But listen they did and applauded her to the skies, and Millie lapped it up. The extra money she earned allowed Mary to work less in the allotment and take more rest.

Millie lived for those three nights each week when she sang at The Blind Beggar with her two accompanists: an elderly gentleman who played the accordion badly but enthusiastically and an even more ancient lady who thumped away on the piano's yellowing keys with gusto.

Millie's bashful yet bawdy delivery brought the house down every night and, on her days off, she worked tirelessly at perfecting her own style and delivery. She often rehearsed in front of her aunt in the cramped front parlor, as Mary sat in her ancient rocking chair, an encouraging and observant critic.

"I saw Marie Lloyd years ago in Dublin when she was young. She was splendid then, but she was certainly no beauty; she had a fat face and a body like an old tank. You've got her talent and spirit, Millie, but you've got a lot more because you're pretty and charming too." Pretty was an understatement for Millie these days. She was positively blooming. Thoughts of Toby lent her a subtle sensuality she had not possessed before.

One night, as Millie negotiated the dark muddy fields on her way home, a man crept up behind her and, putting his hands around her waist, pulled her toward him. She screamed and struggled, but he only laughed and, holding her tighter, whispered, "Hush, Millie, hush. It's only me, my angel."

Millie turned to see the face she loved, illuminated by the pale moon.

"Toby! Oh dear God, how in the name of heaven did you find me?"

"Elementary, my dear Millie — your cousin Bridget. It's amazing how a few sovereigns will make anyone reveal their secrets."

"But I thought she was my best friend."

"Oh, but she *is* your friend, my angel, because when I told her just why I needed to find you, that's when she revealed your whereabouts."

"And what, pray, did you tell her?"

"I told her that I loved you and I wanted to marry you." Toby's hands were caressing her hair and the back of her neck, and Millie felt herself weakening.

"I don't believe you, Toby Swannell. Your family would never allow it. Never, and you *know* it."

"Forget my family," he said huskily, covering her face in kisses. "They don't matter. It's only you that matters to me, Millie my angel, only you. You've totally bewitched me."

It was true. Since Millie had left Eaton Square, Toby found himself missing her terribly. Although he had his pick of all the eligible girls in London, he couldn't help comparing their prim and proper attitudes to the stolen moments he'd shared with the little maid. Even Rosemary Vanderhausen's glamorous sensuality was no match for Millie's virginal appeal. Rosemary kept him at arm's length, although she flirted with him outrageously. Toby had visited his usual haunts, the whorehouses and his clubs, but he found himself pining for Millie. He wanted her, and what Toby wanted, Toby usually got.

His mouth was on hers now, his kisses sweeter than they had ever been. Millie felt as if she were home, a ship returning to its harbor. Then she moved her face to breathe in his ear, "You really mean it, Toby? You really want to marry me?"

"Yes — yes, my angel. I do want to marry you, and I *will* marry you." He cupped her face in his hands and, ankle-deep in the mud of the ploughed field, they embraced again in the moonlight as he whispered, "Will you marry me, Millie?"

"Oh yes." Millie was unable to believe the turn in her fortunes. "Oh yes, Toby, my love, I will marry you. I'll marry you tomorrow if you want."

But that wasn't possible. They posted the banns at a tiny church in Balliver and, with two weeks to wait until they were able to wed, Toby persuaded Millie to move with him into the best hotel in the nearest town, although she was adamant that they sleep in separate bedrooms. However, now that they were almost as good as married, Millie's self-control and inhibitions began to crumble. The young couple spent hours together walking, talking about their future, kissing, and holding each other. Millie wanted Toby almost as badly as he wanted her, but when his ardor became too strong she tried to distract him.

"What will your parents say when you tell

them you've married their poor Irish house-maid?" she asked, gently disentangling herself from his embrace as they lay on the counter-pane of his bed, listening to the wind whis-tling outside.

"I expect they'll be furious at first, but they'll get over it. You'll be a duchess one day, my angel, what do you think of that?"

"A duchess?" Millie rose and stared at him with shining eyes. "I'd better learn me some fancy manners then."

"I love your manners as they are." Toby stood up and took her in his arms and, brushing his lips against hers, held her face in his hands and looked deep into her eyes.

"Oh, Millie, darling — why must you make me wait, my angel? We'll be married in ten days — please . . . please, I'm dying of love for you."

Then he started kissing her so passionately, yet so tenderly, that Millie's last vestiges of restraint finally evaporated. She wanted this man. Every part of her body was giving her the signals that she was ready for him, she needed him, she longed for him to take her. Only the tiniest little voice in the back of her mind whispered no, but this time she ignored it. Locking her arms around Toby's neck, she threw back her head and whispered, "Oh yes — darling, yes, yes . . . yes."

Toby picked Millie up and carried her over to the double bed. Candlelight flickered, casting dark shadows over them as he slowly undressed her, kissing and caressing her constantly. As he gently removed her bodice she started to shudder with a need so intense that her body craved only one thing — to melt into Toby's, to be possessed by him totally.

Then when they both lay naked on the white linen sheets, he made her wait until she ached with desire. Slowly, he traced the outline of her body with his soft fingers until she felt she would burst with pleasure. His lips brushed her breasts tenderly and her body arched as she touched his manhood, which was like warm steel.

When Toby finally entered her, Millie thought she would die of delight and, even though she was a virgin, his lovemaking was so considerate and skillful that apart from a tiny stab of pain she felt only joy.

During the night, he took her again and again and by morning Millie felt so in love and so loved that she wanted nothing else but to be with Toby forever, as close as a man and a woman could be.

Toby was an accomplished lover. At twenty-two he had had his share of seasoned professionals, girls who had instructed him well in the ways of what women like. All the tricks he'd picked up were thrilling beyond words to Millie, and their coupling grew ever more passionate.

But after less than a week, Toby's ardor started to diminish, and it slowly began to dawn on him that he'd made a terrible mistake. Burning with love for a servant — what could have come over him? Was it really love, or was it just lust, a physical attraction that was waning as fast as it had ignited? Toby was in a stew of guilt and remorse, and his imagined consequences of what he'd promised Millie gave him sleepless nights. He went for long walks, smoking heavily, talking and arguing with himself, attempting to put his complicated life into perspective.

How could he possibly marry Millie McClancey, an uneducated girl from nowhere, with no breeding, no class, and no family? How could he do this to his family? Bring in an outsider, a servant girl, and try to turn her into a duchess? It was sheer insanity. He could hear his parents' shocked voices in his head, and it filled him with dread.

Toby realized with a heavy heart that his passion for Millie was based on little more than lust and conquest. He was certainly attracted to her, to her bubbly personality, her gorgeous body, her divine little face — but to marry her? It was madness. How could he? Yet how could he tell Millie the truth?

Burning with guilt, Toby returned to the hotel late one afternoon to tell Millie a monstrous lie.

"I must return to London, my angel," he

couldn't look at her as he started throwing shirts into his case. "I telephoned Kingsley from the post office in the village. He told me Mother was seriously ill and that I had to come home immediately."

"But, Toby, we're to be married the day after tomorrow. Can't you wait until then?"

"I'm afraid not, my angel." Toby started to waver as he looked at Millie's beautiful body lying on the bed in her white bloomers, black stockings, and the satin corset that he had bought her. She was arousing him yet again. She had that magic. He sat on the bed beside her, his hand stroking her hair.

"I'm catching the six-fifteen boat train from Liverpool tomorrow night, so I must leave in the morning. I've got to, my sweet."

"Oh no, Toby — no. When will you be back?"

"In a few days, my angel, just a few days, that's all." He couldn't look into Millie's eyes as he started untying the blue satin ribbons on the shoulders of her lacy bodice. His hands moved to her breasts, and he heard her breath come in gasps. She was certainly sexy, this woman he had almost married. She excited him more than any other girl ever had.

"What about the banns?" wailed Millie as Toby turned her to face him and began kissing her breasts.

"We'll post them again when I get back from London," he whispered. "I promise."

Chapter Six

Toby had been gone for over a month when a frantic Millie realized that she was pregnant. Although she wrote agonized letters to Toby at Eaton Square, telling him what had happened, she only received one brief note from him informing her that his mother was still desperately ill and that Millie must be patient, he would return as soon as he could. Toby never acknowledged her condition, nor said anything more about marrying her, and her questions remained unanswered. There was nothing Millie could do but wait and pray. To make some money, she started performing again at The Blind Beggar and prayed Toby would return to marry her before her pregnancy became too obvious.

Toby faced his father in his study in Eaton Square. A severely masculine room, lined with leather-bound volumes of books, the strong smell of cigars and brandy permeated everything. The thick curtains were pulled against the sun and, even though it was a beautiful midsummer day, the atmosphere was dark and heavy. Although the war still ground on, the Season in London continued its merry way, with balls, parties, and dinners being thrown constantly. It was eight in the morning, and Toby had just returned from reveling at White's with a group of his cronies. Still in his evening clothes, hair and tie askew, he was more than a little tipsy. But he soon sobered up when he heard what the duke had to say.

"We have no money?" he repeated dully. "But that's impossible, Father." Toby sat down weak-kneed and took a swig of brandy. "What happened to it?"

The duke looked grim. "Our holdings in the colonies have been badly hit by this damn war. My investments in the stock market have also tumbled because of the war, and that bloody stupid accountant didn't sell my stocks when he should have. And the taxes, my boy. Good God, you've no *idea* how high our taxes are now."

"So what can we do about it?" Toby lit a cigarette with a shaking hand.

"I'm afraid it's not so much what *we* can do, as what *you* can do. It's all up to you now, son. There is no way the Swannells can keep up appearances, let alone our properties, without a huge influx of money."

"And where's that supposed to come from, Father?"

The duke sighed. "From you, my boy, or more accurately from your marriage to the Vanderhausen girl."

"What?" Toby sat up, shaken. "Rosemary Vanderhausen? But I don't love her, Father. This is a rotten deal."

"Love? What the hell difference does *that* make? She loves you, Toby, that's the important thing," said the duke flatly. "In fact, she loves you rather a lot."

Toby stared at his father. "And how do you know that?"

"Mr. Vanderhausen and I have had extensive discussions on this matter already, Toby. His daughter seems quite infatuated with you. Why, I simply can't imagine."

Toby cast his eyes to the ceiling. It was so typical of his father to constantly criticize him.

"Rosemary's dowry is considerable, to say the least. Vanderhausen is a generous man. After this marriage, the Swannells won't have to worry anymore, particularly if you can present us with an heir as soon as possible."

"But, Father, I . . ."

"Listen, Toby, the facts of life are often harsh. Most members of the aristocracy these days are self-destructing. There is only one thing for us, if we wish to keep things the way they are. The aristocracy must align themselves to families with money — the nouveaux riches — and the only ones who seem to have any money now are the Americans."

"Oh my God, Father, I *can't*. I can't marry Rosemary — I'm . . ." He stopped himself from blurting out that he was infatuated with Millie but he didn't know if he really was anymore. There was a pretty and willing young debutante he'd been seeing on the social circuit. She was quite enticing, and promises of further delights with her lay in store for him. Besides, he hadn't heard from Millie at all. She hadn't answered any of his letters, and with each passing day the memory of Millie grew a little dimmer.

"Toby, you are my heir, the future duke of Burghley. This Vanderhausen girl is highly suitable. Comes from a good solid Philadelphia family. Well-educated for a girl, even if the family money does come from something frightful like meat packing."

"Father, I simply *cannot* marry Rosemary," said Toby as firmly as he could. "I don't love her, and I don't think I even *like* her very much."

"Toby, you can, and you bloody well *will*." Edward Burghley fixed his son with a basilisk stare. "For the sake of our family's future you will marry Rosemary Vanderhausen, and let's pray you produce an heir as soon as possible."

Toby Swannell and Rosemary Vanderhausen were married a month later, quickly and quietly in a tiny church on South Audley Street. Because of the war, celebrations were kept to a minimum, and there was only a small reception at the Connaught Hotel afterward.

The bride wore white, and a superior expression; the groom was in a vague state of shock. He had been unable to bring himself to write to Millie about the wedding. Suffering from a large amount of guilt and self-loathing, he spent his prewedding days with his cronies in gambling clubs and his evenings in nightclubs, carousing until dawn and drinking himself into a stupor. He pushed away all thoughts of Millie and went on a mindlessly hedonistic bachelor spree.

Theirs had been a joyless wedding night. Rosemary, although icily beautiful, was an uninspired, cold, and unemotional lover. She allowed Toby to make love to her, but not a moan or a sigh of reciprocation issued from her unresponsive lips and her body barely moved.

Toby, understandably, found her frigidity a turnoff and despised himself for what he had done to Millie. As he dutifully ploughed into his bride, thoughts of his passionate young lover in Ireland were the only inspiration that got him through it.

When the telegram from the War Office arrived a week later, calling him up immediately, Toby was almost relieved.

"But I thought you said you weren't eligible because of your short-sightedness." Rosemary lay on her bed, petulantly examining her nails. "This is all *very* inconvenient, Toby. Just as we were planning the redecoration of our new home."

"Everyone's being called up now," said Toby, almost jovially. "Seventeen-year-olds and forty-five-year-olds, deaf men, short-sighted men — even queers, I've heard." He grinned at his bride, knowing how it offended her to talk of such things.

"Queers? Oh my God." She shuddered. "Well, don't be long about it. I married you to have you around, not to go off and fight with those useless French in some muddy field in Flanders."

"I'll tell the kaiser to finish the war soon, so I can return to your loving arms, dearest," he said sarcastically. "I hear all the Jerries are starving in Germany, so it shouldn't be too long now before you Yanks decide finally to come into the war."

"Don't call us Yanks," Rosemary said coldly. "We're Americans."

"Yes, dear." Toby gave a mock salute.

Why had Rosemary turned into such a pain in the neck? She had always been slightly reserved and petulant, but what had happened to her flirtatious humor and vivacity? He had only been able to make love to her two or three times during the ten days of their marriage, and each time she lay still as a stone. But, so what? He'd done his conjugal duty. He was off to the war now, and he was actually rather looking forward to it. Everyone said it couldn't last much longer. And maybe after he came back he could go back to Ireland and persuade Millie to return to London. Then he'd set her up in a little flat nearby. That would be perfect.

When Millie was four months pregnant, her aunt became seriously ill with influenza. Since all communications from Toby had ceased, an increasingly desperate Millie traipsed to the only telephone in the village, at the post office three miles away, and telephoned Eaton Square.

When Kingsley answered she was too frightened to ask for Toby, so trying to disguise her voice, she said she was a friend of Bridget's mother and could she please speak to Bridget.

"It is highly out of order for a housemaid to receive personal telephone calls." Kingsley's voice was pompous.

"Her mother's very ill," Millie replied, and Kingsley relented.

"Bridget, oh God, Bridget, I'm so glad to hear your voice." Millie started to weep when her cousin came on the phone. It was hard to hear properly, as the line was muffled and crackling. A few curious villagers queuing nearby pretended to buy stamps, but were taking sideways glances at this pretty girl who was such a success in the local pub, but who seemed so distressed.

"Is everything all right?" asked Bridget anxiously.

"No, it's not." Millie was desperate to pour out her tale of woe, but the nosy villagers made her wary.

"I'm so sorry to tell you this, Bridget, but your mam's not well. In fact, she's very bad."

"Should I come over then, Millie?"

"Oh, yes, you should, Bridget. I don't know how long your poor mother is going to last."

Millie glanced over to the postmistress's counter, and six pairs of eyes immediately swiveled self-consciously away from her. Dropping her voice to a whisper, she asked, "Where's Toby? Is he there?"

There was a brief silence.

"Didn't you know?" Bridget's voice sounded hesitant. "After the wedding he was sent off to the front — that's nearly a month ago."

"After the *what?*"

"The wedding — surely you must have known about it?"

Millie leaned on the cold wall for support. She couldn't believe what Bridget was telling her. Her legs were shaking so badly they could barely hold her up.

"W-w-what wedding?"

"Toby married that stuck-up cow Rosemary Vanderhausen. You remember her — the tall skinny American? They were married nearly two months ago. Millie? Millie? Can you hear me?"

There was silence on the line.

"Are you there, Millie?" Bridget yelled down the mouthpiece, clamping the receiver hard to her ear.

"Hello?" she heard a gruff voice say. "The little lady's here, but I'm sorry to say she's fainted, so she'll not be able to be talkin' to you just now," said the voice, and there was a click as the line went dead.

Chapter Seven

Millie opened her eyes and saw one of the village women looking down at her anxiously. Several others were clustered behind her, whispering to one another. Millie felt a stabbing pain in her gut and wetness between her legs which, she realized, was blood. She tried to sit up, but one of the women stopped her.

"The doctor's on his way," she soothed. "I think you may be losing the baby, so be still now."

Losing it. Thank God for that.

Millie realized that she was alone and in her own bed, although she had no recollection of how she had gotten there. She could remember nothing except the shock of learning about Toby's marriage. To be having a baby and her, an unmarried mother, was a heinous sin for which she would burn in hell for eternity. The seed inside her had been planted because of her wickedness and human frailty. She was an ungodly woman, and so she must suffer the consequences. She groaned as another cramp convulsed her and, in spite of the protestations of the women, she hauled herself out of bed and staggered outside to the privy.

"Please God, oh dear God, please help me out of this mess," she cried. "I can't raise a child alone." Another pain engulfed her, and she bent over in agony. "If you help me, God, I'll never give in to temptation again, I swear it. I can't have this child, I can't."

But Millie's prayers went unanswered. In spite of her vigorous exertions, marching up and down the allotment, running and jumping, soaking in boiling hot water in the old tin tub in front of the fire while drinking half a bottle of gin, the baby refused to budge.

Millie couldn't stop thinking about how Toby had abandoned her. How could he have been so cruel as to not reply to her letters about the pregnancy? How could he have lied to her so blatantly by pretending to love her and then dashing off to London to marry that American?

Aunt Mary lay in her cot, coughing and wheezing and unable to eat, and, as the days passed, she grew weaker but Millie grew stronger. Her heart began to harden against the man whom she had loved so passionately, for whom she had lost all reason, abandoned her lifelong faith in God, and become a mortal sinner.

"For that's what I am," she said to herself

bitterly. "A sinner. And I'll be paying for that sin for the rest of my life."

Aunt Mary was in extremis when Bridget arrived. The two girls stood at the foot of the old lady's bed, watching helplessly as her life slowly ebbed away.

After the funeral, when the few mourners had left, they sat in the tiny kitchen as Millie confided in her cousin that Toby was the father of her baby.

Bridget wiped her eyes, then said, "I've got something to tell you, Millie, and I don't know how to do it. There's no other way but to blurt it out." She sighed and took a sip of strong sweet tea. "You might be needing something stronger than this after you hear what I have to say to you."

Bridget opened the kitchen cabinet and poured Millie a generous glass of the cheap sherry kept for special occasions.

"A telegram arrived from the War Office just before I left Eaton Square."

"What did it say?"

"Toby was fighting in the Battle of the Marne. He was killed, Millie, killed in action. I'm so sorry." Bridget put her arms around her cousin as she sank into the hard wooden chair. Millie felt a great pang of sorrow at her lover's death, but she didn't cry or become hysterical, as Bridget had feared she might. The passionate love she'd felt for

Toby had turned to numbness. She had not allowed herself to feel anything for him since she'd heard of his marriage.

"So now my baby will be born not only a bastard but with a dead man for a father," she muttered, staring out at the sleet-covered hills. Through the loose fabric of her chemise dress she felt the baby kicking, and Bridget saw it too. Millie was too big now to tighten her corset, so she defiantly revealed her new shape.

"I've told a couple of people that after the banns were posted Toby and I went and got married somewhere else," she confided in Bridget a few days later, when her cousin was preparing to return to Eaton Square. She shrugged. "If they don't believe it — I don't much care anymore. All I know now is I've got to work. I've got to earn some money and support my baby, and the only things I know how to do are cleaning houses and singing."

Bridget stared at her cousin, who appeared to have become much tougher and more re-silient than the timid girl who had come to London only a year ago. Indeed, in the full bloom of her pregnancy, Millie seemed sud-denly no longer a girl but a woman, yet with a hardness behind her eyes that belied her youth.

"Sing then, Millie. It's what you do best, and you never were much of a cleaner,"

Bridget replied sympathetically.

Millie smiled wanly. "Around these parts you tell one person something and it's gossip in every village from here to Killarney. They'll all know soon enough about my husband's death."

The news of Millie's widowhood was greeted with enormous sympathy, and Seamus O'Reilly was only too happy to take her back to The Blind Beggar where, in spite of her size, her performances became more sparkling than ever.

On November 11, 1918, Armistice Day was declared; the Allies had won the war, and a daughter was born to Millie McClancey.

She called her Victoria, and on her birth certificate she wrote — to hell with it — the name of the baby's father: Tobias Edward Swannell.

But although there was great rejoicing all over the British Isles, Ireland was in the grip of not only food shortages but a terrible influenza epidemic as well.

Within months, three-quarters of the population of Balliver were wiped out by flu. Those who managed to survive stayed indoors to protect themselves. To exacerbate Millie's perilous situation, the bailiffs came to repossess Aunt Mary's cottage and all her paltry possessions for nonpayment of rent.

"You have two weeks to leave here and get

yourself another place," the burly bailiff announced with barely a glance of sympathy for the young girl clutching her three-month-old baby.

"But where shall I go?" she whispered.

"That's your problem, m'girl."

There was no one to take care of Victoria now. While Millie had been singing at the pub any one of a number of village women were delighted to look after the infant, cooing at how beautiful she was and how good. They had enjoyed passing her around and clucking over her. But the pub was closed and village women stayed at home now, terrified of catching the deadly flu.

Millie had only the most basic of maternal instincts for her child. She breastfed her whenever her milk started to flow and changed her when necessary, but never felt the urge to hold her baby in her arms, cuddle and kiss her, and feel the close bond that other mothers seemed to have for their offspring. Millie let Victoria cry unless it was time for a feed, so by the time the infant was a few months old she realized that crying for attention would get her nowhere. Consequently, Victoria was a well-behaved baby and no trouble at all.

There was a stone in Millie's heart where once love had blossomed, and she was single-mindedly determined that no one and nothing would ever hurt her again.

Two weeks after Aunt Mary's cottage was repossessed, Millie and her baby set sail for Liverpool, then took the train to London, which used up almost the last of her money.

Millie had obtained a copy of the marriage banns from the church and also Victoria's birth certificate because she knew she had little option now but to throw herself on the mercy of the Duke and Duchess of Burghley.

"Surely when they see their grandchild they'll help me out a bit?" she had reasoned to Bridget on the post office telephone shortly before she left.

"Ah, you know the Burghleys — hard as nails and tighter than a tick. I wouldn't put too much stock by 'em, Millie. But come here anyway, we'll work something out for you in London — I know we will."

Bridget's voice sounded weak, and she started coughing so hard that Millie thought she would explode.

"Are you all right, Bridget?"

"Sure, I'm fine," coughed Bridget. "It's just a touch of this cursed flu; I never thought I'd get it. Come back, Millie — I'll be waiting for you."

The door of the Eaton Square servants' quarters was opened by Patsy, who stared beadily at the baby in Millie's arms.

"So what's this, then?"

"What do you think it is?" snapped Millie. "She's called Victoria, as if you care."

"Got yourself in trouble, eh?" Patsy strolled inside without any attempt to help Millie with her meager luggage. Millie stumbled down the familiar steps and into the kitchen, where what remained of the staff sat around the refectory table drinking tea and looking glum. Kingsley didn't seem surprised by the appearance of an exhausted-looking Millie and her infant, and he gestured for her to sit down. Cook glanced at her sympathetically, then poured her a cup of tea, while Patsy stared resentfully as Millie slumped into a chair and sipped the hot tea gratefully.

"Where's Bridget?" she asked.

Cook and Kingsley exchanged uneasy glances, and there was a long pause while no one wanted to meet Millie's eyes.

"She's dead," said Patsy, relishing the moment and the look of shock that came over Millie's face. "She passed away last night — the flu, of course; it's killing people like flies. She's upstairs laid out on her bed, if you want to have a last look at her corpse." Patsy grinned. Millie felt hatred bubble inside her and turned her head away so Patsy couldn't see the tears welling up in her eyes.

"Here, I'll take your babba." Cook held out her arms for the angelic infant, who was happily sucking her thumb.

"She's a little beauty, ain't she?" Cook

smiled, and while the other maids clustered around Victoria, Millie slipped quietly up the back stairs.

Standing at the bedside of her only friend in the world, Millie fell to her knees, buried her face in the shabby counterpane, and sobbed her heart out. As tears coursed down Millie's face, she sobbed for Bridget's lost young life, sobbed for Toby and his infidelity and betrayal, but most of all she sobbed for her baby, whom she'd brought into this harsh world without a father and without the unconditional love she knew she should feel for her.

Chapter Eight
1919

When Millie confronted the old duke in his gloomy study with the evidence of Toby's baby, his face turned crimson.

"How *dare* you suggest that my son would *ever* have anything to do with a servant girl?"

"But, sir, look at the banns." Millie held out the precious papers. "They're signed by us both. Look at Victoria's birth certificate. It says that Toby's her father."

"Forgeries!" The duke moved menacingly toward her. "It is completely outrageous that you suggest such disgraceful circumstances occurred."

"But Toby wanted to marry me, he loved me."

"Love — *love?* If you really knew my son, you'd know he wasn't capable of such an emotion. He was a weakling," said the duke angrily. "He dallied with women, that was true, but never with a — a thing like you."

Millie's face flamed. "A thing? You call me

107

a thing? I might be that to you, Your Grace, but I'm telling you that this 'thing' is going to make something of herself and your grandchild and it'll be *without* the help of your family!"

With a shaking hand the duke pointed to the door. "Get out of this house, you little slut, and don't you dare to ever come back here again."

"Don't worry, I'm going. And I'm taking your grandchild with me." Millie turned and left before giving the old man the satisfaction of seeing her weep.

In the kitchen, baby Victoria was being cooed over by all the maids except for Patsy, who sat glowering in a corner, thinking about her own babies. She looked at everyone paying attention to Victoria and wondered how they would have treated her had she turned up with Toby's baby. He would be a year old now and still living in Billingsgate with his adoptive parents. Kingsley, with uncharacteristic kindness, told Millie that she could stay just for the night, but that she must be gone first thing in the morning.

Next day after a hearty breakfast, Cook slipped Millie a few shillings and a sandwich in greaseproof paper. With a lump in her throat, Millie hugged her, then said good-bye to the rest of the staff. Carrying Victoria in one arm and her small case in the other she walked slowly up the dank stone steps and across the road into Eaton Square's communal gardens.

It was a blustery February day, and the wind was icy. Millie sat on a bench, automatically wrapping her shawl tighter around Victoria, who had started crying. She rocked her in her arms, feeling the warmth of the tiny body against hers. She sang a plaintive ballad in her hauntingly sweet voice. As she sang, Victoria seemed to become soothed and closed her eyes, but Millie continued singing, finding comfort in holding her child.

A man watched from a nearby bench; a distinguished-looking gentleman, wearing sharply pressed gray-striped trousers, an immaculate charcoal frock coat, and a fresh white carnation in his lapel. He listened intently to the pretty young girl, and when she had finished her third song he walked over to her.

"My name is Ambrose Osborne." He handed her a card and, raising his hat, revealed a fine head of thick dark hair flecked with silver, which matched his well-clipped mustache.

"Oh sir, I'm so sorry," Millie always piped up automatically before her betters, "I didn't mean to disturb you — I'll move along."

"Nonsense, you weren't disturbing me at all." He laughed. "*Au contraire,* you have one of the most delightful and unusual voices I have heard in a long time. What is your

109

name and what do you do, my dear? Are you a nursemaid?" He glanced at the sleeping baby. "An actress? Or just a young wife?"

Millie cast her eyes downward and whispered, "I'm a widow, sir — my husband died in the trenches."

"I'm very sorry." He placed a gray-gloved hand on the baby and patted her sympathetically. "Do tell me about him, if it would make you feel better." The man sat down beside her and Millie let out a sniffle, which soon turned into a sob. Before she knew it, she'd confided everything to this sympathetic stranger, everything that is except the fact that she didn't marry Victoria's father, who of course wasn't the marquis of Leybourne, merely plain Toby Swannell.

"Well, Millie Swannell. As you may or may not know, I am a producer — quite well known in theatrical circles," he said modestly, for Sir Ambrose Osborne was, at that moment, the most successful impresario in the West End, with three sold-out musical revues running simultaneously.

"I find that you have an extremely unusual and appealing voice and, if I may say so, an exceedingly attractive face and figure too."

Millie blushed as he continued. "Please understand that I have no designs on you myself."

Millie didn't quite understand what he

meant, but what he said next made her tingle with excitement.

"I shall soon be casting for the chorus of *Hearts Are Trumps*, my new show, which we're bringing to the West End this autumn. If you would be interested in auditioning for the chorus, I would be more than happy to offer room and board for you and your baby. At my house, in Grosvenor Square, I have many young performers about your age who stay with me until such time as they either make it into my chorus line or find other employment. They earn their board by sharing the household duties and acting, for all intents and purposes, as my staff. I'd be delighted for you to join us."

"Oh, sir!" Millie's eyes shone. "Oh, sir, it's always been my wildest dream to be on the stage — I'll practice, sir — I'll practice until I'm perfect enough to get into your show."

"The word is 'rehearse,' my dear." He smiled. "You'll be able to rehearse every day with one of my stage managers, and I believe that you will succeed, for you seem to have admirable ambition and courage, as well as talent and beauty."

He rose and offered Millie his arm as they walked toward the East Gate in the direction of Grosvenor Square.

"The dormitories are in the basement and upper rooms of my house. It's a big house and, as I'm a bachelor, I like to have vigorous youngsters around me . . . keeps me young. We're all one merry bunch at number twenty-seven, and I'm sure you'll be happy with us too."

In the following weeks Millie had never felt so fortunate. There were a dozen talented, ambitious singers, dancers, musicians, comedians, actors, and actresses in residence. They cooked and cleaned in shifts, thus allowing ample time to rehearse, supervised by the cook, Sofie, Sir Ambrose's sole proper household employee. There was an atmosphere of conviviality in the warm kitchen as everyone ate together, exchanging cheeky banter. There was no standing on ceremony, no stiff formality; it was the antithesis of life at Eaton Square.

In one corner of the kitchen a baby-faced juggler would be tossing oranges in the air, in another a pretty ballerina would pirouette as a boy played the harmonica. Everywhere youthful performers were working on their craft, and Millie adored the whole environment. She barely saw her baby, for all the girls and female staff took it in turns to look after her. Especially fond of Victoria was Susie, Sofie's young daughter, who spent most of her daytime hours doting on the baby.

Sir Ambrose's mansion was like an academy for theatrical performers. The downstairs rooms contained pianos and had polished parquet floors for dancing on. One room was empty except for an entire mirrored wall along which a barre was erected for the students to practice their ballet skills.

Shortly after Millie arrived, Sir Ambrose summoned her to his study. Two of her new friends, Lizzie and Annie, joked that Millie would be "set upon" by the old man.

"He's after you, I can tell," teased Lizzie, who had a pale oval face and a sleek black bob. "Saw you in the park, and you were in this house in no time flat."

"*We* all had to audition," chirped Annie, her blonde curls bobbing. "But don't worry, just joking, I happen to know he's . . ." — she dropped her voice and looked around carefully — "one of *those* . . ."

"One of what?" asked Millie innocently.

"She means a fairy," laughed Lizzie. "Everyone knows *that,* Millie. He had that boy Noël Coward over for tea last week. Bit of a flirtation going on with those two, *I* can tell you. He was trying to get him into his new revue, but Noël didn't want to know. Said he was going to succeed by himself, even though that *Scandal* play he was in was a flop."

Millie laughed, but she wondered what Sir Ambrose wanted to see her about. Her newfound friends also had lost no time regaling her with stories of life in the "fast" lane of show business and the wolves that preyed on innocent young girls.

"Men only want one thing, and if you give it to 'em, they'll never want you again," Annie said knowingly. "And you'll *certainly* never get a wedding ring."

Millie could certainly attest to that. "I'm not interested in men," she said firmly.

"But Sir Ambrose is." Lizzie and Annie started to roar with laughter. "That poor little Johnny, the pianist. He's got to run like the wind whenever the old man comes into sight."

When Millie knocked on the door of his study, Sir Ambrose greeted her warmly, gesturing for her to sit. Millie looked around the sunlit room. Two of the walls were covered with playbills of his past shows, most of which had been very successful, while another wall was thick with framed photographs of famous performers. With a thrill Millie saw a picture of Marie Lloyd, affectionately inscribed.

"You like Our Marie." Sir Ambrose noticed her staring at the photograph.

"Ooh, I *love* her. I saw her at the Finsbury Park Empire. She was magnificent."

"Yes, she is. So tell me, Millie, my dear, what are *your* ambitions?"

"Why, to become a star of course," she breathed, "like Marie Lloyd."

"Good, that's very good. I think you could be as good as Marie. If you really worked at it. You realize of course that if you really want stardom, you have to dedicate yourself to it one hundred and one percent."

"Oh yes, sir, I do."

"Training, discipline — backbreaking work — and hard, grueling rehearsals. You shouldn't think about anything else, Millie. Nothing else should matter until you attain your goal."

"Yes, sir, I do know that, sir."

"When and *if* you make it, my dear, you'll realize that there is *nothing* more exciting in the world than the theater. When you're standing in the wings and that overture ends, the lights dim, and the curtain rises, that's the closest to heaven you'll ever get in your lifetime, Millie."

"Oh, sir, that's what I long for." Her eyes shone and Sir Ambrose thought again what an exceptionally pretty girl she was.

"This baby of yours — do you love her very much?"

Millie considered the question carefully. If she said no, would he think her hard-hearted? If she said yes, would he think she wasn't worthy of the special efforts she knew he was expending on her behalf?

"She's my baby and of course I love her." Millie swallowed — was it the correct answer? "But I can see that Susie has a good relationship with her, and I'm very happy to trust Victoria to her while I work."

"I quite agree," Sir Ambrose said approvingly. "You're a smart young lady, Millie — I think you'll go far in this crazy profession. So let Susie look after your baby and you must work, work, work."

"Oh, I'll work my socks off, sir — I promise," she smiled. "I want you to be proud of me."

"I know I will be, Millie. I'm quite sure of it."

For three months Millie rehearsed relentlessly with Johnny, the handsome pianist and voice coach. She had chosen two Marie Lloyd numbers for her audition — "My Old Man Said Follow the Van" and the plaintive ballad "I Can't Forget the Days of My Youth." She'd bought all of Marie Lloyd's recordings, which were on wax cylinders and had to be manually cranked out on the gramophone. The quality was poor, but Millie was able to study Marie's inflections and timing, adding her own feisty interpretation to the delivery.

Millie sang with cheeky charm yet innate vulnerability, and Johnny, who was rapidly becoming infatuated with her, praised her talent effusively. But charming and good-looking as he was, Millie would have none of him. "I want no more of men," she said to her reflection in the mirror every night. "They just use you up and throw you out."

Victoria was taken care of, practically full-time, by the cook's daughter. Fifteen-year-old Susie adored Victoria and insisted on becoming the baby's unofficial guardian, leaving Millie plenty of time to work on her audition and visit the music halls as often as possible.

In 1919 London was chockablock with variety and music hall theaters. The war was over, the boys in uniform had come home, and it was time for people to enjoy themselves again. Although there was still some rationing, everyone was looking forward to the next decade and, to this end, women of fashion led the way. The more daring of them bobbed their hair, started smoking cigarettes in public, and shortened their skirts to just above the ankle. A fashion revolution was happening. A young Parisienne called Coco Chanel was encouraging women to get rid of their constricting corsets, old-fashioned bloomers, and long skirts. She put women into tubular unlined frocks made of new man-made fabrics of jersey and wool, which skimmed the body. Some of her skirts fell to just below midcalf, but it was only the most avant garde of young women who would dare wear them and risk the disgust of people in the street. The majority of women still dressed modestly; they wore their corsets even though they had started to loosen them, and shortened their skirts slightly.

But in the basement of Sir Ambrose

Osborne's house, the Singer sewing machine worked full-time as the young female performers studied the fashion plates and made themselves inexpensive copies of Mademoiselle Chanel's sleeveless round-necked shifts, in simple bright colors and fabrics, which they wore with cloche hats or bandeaux.

London's dozens of nightclubs showed few signs of the ravages of war, even though there weren't nearly as many young men around to dance with the girls in their flimsy frocks. The flower of British manhood had died in the senseless war, and the young men who had returned safely from it found themselves in huge demand.

Social barriers were starting to break down as society and theatrical people began to mix together for the first time, and Sir Ambrose Osborne was one of the first members of the theatrical community to be accepted by the fast young aristocrats that called themselves the "bright young thing."

Millie was eating breakfast in the kitchen one morning when Johnny showed her a picture of Sir Ambrose on the social pages of the *Tatler*.

"He's out with the nobs again," laughed Johnny, "and he looks like he really enjoys it."

Millie idly flipped through the magazine, sipping her tea, when a photograph caught her eye. She shivered as she read: *"The Mar-*

chioness of Leybourne and her baby son Sebastian photographed at a charity tea for crippled children at Great Ormond Street Hospital."

A beautiful but hard-faced Rosemary Vanderhausen smiled into the camera, holding in her arms a little boy who looked so like Toby with his blond hair and sweet expression that Millie felt physically sick.

So Toby had had a son with that American, a boy who looked about three months younger than Victoria. It was so upsetting to Millie that she ran to her room and for the first time in months sobbed her heart out.

"How could you have done it?" Her tears drenched her pillow. "How *could* you, Toby? You told me that you loved me. Why did you leave me? Why? Why?"

"Shut up, girl," her inner voice spoke harshly. "Shut up and pull yourself together. It's done. It's finished. Toby's dead. Get on with your life, girl, and your career, because that's all you've got. That and your baby." So Millie dried her eyes, combed her hair, and went downstairs to rehearse.

"Only two more days to the audition. Aren't you scared?" asked Johnny.

Millie shook her auburn curls. "Why should I be scared when Sir Ambrose has as good as told the three of us here that we are going to pass."

Lizzie and Annie nodded.

"After all, he is one of the four people on

the committee, isn't he?" said Lizzie.

"Yes, it's just him, the director, and two of the investors."

"Piece of cake," said Lizzie cockily. "We'll walk it, girls, won't we?"

Promptly at ten in the morning Millie, Lizzie, and Annie arrived at the Alhambra Theater and were amazed to see a queue of about one hundred and fifty women of all shapes, sizes, and ages waiting for the open audition for the chorus of *Hearts Are Trumps.*

There was such keen competition for this job that the line stretched up the backstage stairs all the way to the wings and a block down Shaftesbury Avenue.

So many husbands and fathers had been killed in the war that thousands of women, young and old, were left with no means of support. Certainly the government wasn't doing much to help these wretched women and, as the three girls joined the queue, they could see poverty and hunger etched on many of the applicants' eager faces.

Slowly the three girls inched their way closer to the front of the queue and stood in the wings, where they could see some of the pathetic sights on the bare stage. When they peeked into the cavernous auditorium it was pitch dark, except for a table with a dim light on it and four or five shadowy figures sitting there. Occasionally a disembodied voice would issue instructions from the blackness.

"It's all a bit scary, isn't it?" Lizzie shuddered.

"It's exciting," said Millie. "This'll be my very first time on the stage."

"Let's hope it's not your last," said Annie.

An elderly, shabbily dressed woman croaked out the first line of a popular song and was curtly interrupted when a voice in the stalls bellowed, "Thank you. Next."

"Oh *please*, sir," the woman begged, her bloodshot eyes shining with tears. "*Please* give me a job. I'll do anything. I'll wash, I'll iron . . . I'll even clean the lavatories. My husband's killed in the war. I've got to find work. I've three children and an old mother to sup—"

"Sorry. We're not an employment agency," snapped the sharp voice from the darkened auditorium as the stage manager took the weeping woman's arm and hustled her offstage.

"Blimey," Lizzie whispered. "They're not very compassionate here, are they?"

"There's no such thing as compassion in the theater," Millie echoed Sir Ambrose's sentiments. "You've got to have guts to survive."

"Balls of brass too," giggled Annie. "Look at her."

A bare-legged, skinny fourteen-year-old

wearing a thin ragged frock teetered onstage, but didn't even manage a few bars of her song before she was dismissed, scuttling off as yet another pitiable creature took her place.

Finally it was Millie's turn. Suddenly she began to feel nervous. She took a deep breath, handed her sheet music to the bored accompanist, then launched into a spirited rendition of "All the Nice Girls Love a Sailor," doing an exuberant hornpipe at the same time. When she finished there was silence, then a bored voice from the stalls called: "Leave your name and address with the stage manager and wait backstage."

Millie scurried off with a shiver of anticipation and hope to join seven other young hopefuls in the wings. Lizzie and Annie were also chosen, and after several more sad women had made fools of themselves, the audition was over.

The house lights went up and Sir Ambrose, the director, and three other men walked onstage to inspect the twenty girls, who were standing nervously in a line. "Thank you, ladies," said Sir Ambrose. "You're all talented, pretty, and charming. Some of you can dance well enough, some of you can sing well enough, but all of you will need a lot more training. As you have potential, you're all hired, for the time being. We will start rehearsals here tomorrow at half-past nine sharp."

"And don't be late," barked the company manager, who looked like a bit of a tyrant. "Your wages will be three pounds and sixpence a week, two pounds during rehearsals, and you will supply your own makeup, towels, and rehearsal clothes."

"Rehearsal clothes? What are they?" asked Annie.

"Oh, just bloomers or shorts and a blouse," replied Lizzie.

"What are shorts?" asked Annie anxiously.

"Like trousers but cut off above the knee," said Millie, a recently converted aficionado of fashion magazines. "We'll go to Debenham's this afternoon and buy some." She let out a whoop of glee thinking about what a windfall three pounds and sixpence was, and how much it could buy. "That must be over a hundred and fifty quid a year! That's more than three times what I earned as a maid." The girls clattered down the stairs and into the pale August sunshine. "It's definitely going to be an actor's life for me from now on," laughed Millie.

Hearts Are Trumps opened at the Alhambra Theater, Shaftesbury Avenue, in October 1919. Even in the chorus line the power of Millie's sex appeal was undeniable; she was not only outstandingly talented, but her fiery mop of red curls, pert, curvaceous figure, and gorgeous face caught the audience's attention. The producers were so impressed that on the provincial tour she was given the added position of understudying the ingenue, Hannah James.

"To become an understudy after only a couple of months in the chorus is almost unheard of," said Johnny, who was playing piano in the orchestra now. "Sir Ambrose must think a good deal of you." He grinned suggestively.

"Maybe it's my talent he likes, cheeky, and don't you go getting any ideas about me and the old gent. I'm not interested in him or anyone else and he certainly isn't interested in me, if you follow my meaning."

But even if Millie wasn't interested in men, men were certainly interested in Millie. A week after the London opening Hannah James broke her arm falling down the notoriously rickety backstage stairs and Millie took full advantage of the slightly insipid "naughty girl next door" role, infusing it with all the verve and spice that Marie Lloyd would have done. She was a feast for all eyes in her fashionable flimsy dresses, and soon after her first appearance her tiny dressing room started to fill with flowers. Every night "stage-door Johnnies" clustered outside, pressing love notes and flowers into her hands, imploring her to dine or go dancing with them. But Millie was even more determined to have nothing to do with the opposite sex, for now she had neither the time nor the need for the pursuit of love.

Patsy sat in the gallery watching with fury as the audience rose to its feet to give Millie Swannell a tumultuous standing ovation.

"I don't understand what they see in her," she hissed to her companion.

Kingsley shrugged. "I think she's quite good — for an amateur, that is."

"Good?" Patsy stared at him in disgust. "I don't know why I married you, you stupid old dolt. You have no taste, no taste at all."

"Sorry, dear," said Kingsley. "It was the other girl I meant."

As Millie left the stage to a flurry of appreciative applause and whistles, Patsy wondered for the umpteenth time what she could possibly do to hurt her. *Why* did Millie have all this incredible success? Why had she been allowed to keep *her* baby? No one seemed bothered that it was a bastard child. Patsy thought about the little girl that her mother had taken care of before she passed away last year. God knows what had happened to her. Patsy hadn't heard about her mother's death until months later, and didn't much care. That little girl would be lucky if she was in an orphanage now — luckier still if she'd died. Patsy couldn't be thinking about that baby. It was her son she thought about constantly, her baby boy Edward, son of Toby

Swannell. He'd be in New York now with his adoptive parents, the McCormicks. He'd be two years old, and if circumstances had been different, he would have been the future Duke of Burghley. Patsy ground her teeth together as the curtain rose again and Millie was revealed, lolling in a giant martini glass, half-naked except for a few wisps of chiffon. The audience went wild again. Jealousy pierced through Patsy, an atavistic hatred that tasted as bitter as the bile in her throat.

Much as Millie loved the conviviality of Sir Ambrose's mansion, now that she was becoming a celebrity, she felt she should move on. So after carefully checking with Sir Ambrose as to whether she could afford it, she rented a tiny house on Fulham Road and, just after Christmas, moved in with Susie and Victoria.

"A new decade, a new life, it's about time for a new me," said Millie into the mirror, and picking up a large pair of scissors began to chop off her long red hair into a daringly fashionable bob.

Chapter Nine
1920–1922

Millie celebrated New Year's Eve at the Chelsea Arts Club Ball, dressed as a nymph. Wearing a clinging green body stocking strategically embroidered with slivers of sparkling sequins and a skullcap of green feathers, she was a sensation as she danced feverishly with many of her ardent swains who were among the five thousand revelers at the Royal Albert Hall.

That party heralded one of the wildest decades in history, and "Madcap Millie," as she was becoming known, was in the forefront of the "Roaring Twenties"; a daring young flapper determined to live her life to the full.

As the Jazz Age dawned and skirts became even shorter, the Charleston, the black bottom, and other wildly outrageous dances imported from America swept through England, and the bright young things took to partying with a vengeance. And no one partied more enthusiastically and energetically than the popular young musical comedy soubrette Millie Swannell. Even though Sir Ambrose disapproved of her late nights, Millie felt that she had paid her dues by working hard on her craft, during which time she'd stopped having fun. Now it was time to celebrate. She was young, she was becoming a star, and she wanted to bite voraciously into life.

But the one thing that couldn't tempt Millie was the attention of men. She flirted outrageously because friendly flirting was fun, but anything more intimate than that wasn't allowed. She had recently decided to accept some of the intriguing invitations with which she was inundated, so every night she went on the town. She danced with titled gentlemen in white tie and tails at the swanky 400 nightclub, chattered gaily with her theatrical peers at the 50-50, a convivial and amusing club catering mostly to performers, and dined on scrumptious suppers of sausages, bacon, and eggs at the down-market Gargoyle where, on the tiny dance floor, the clientele did the shimmy, the fox-trot, or sometimes the cockney favorite, the hokey-cokey.

Millie often danced throughout the night, returning home at dawn as Vickie's first cries were heard. She then slept until late afternoon, unless she had a matinee, secure in the knowledge that Vickie was well taken care of by Susie, a strict but loving nanny whom the baby adored.

Two years after *Hearts Are Trumps* had broken all box-office records, Sir Ambrose mounted a new revue called *Sauce Piquante*. Millie was given second-star billing below the dashing leading man, Ivor Bessant, and she performed several risqué numbers in a variety of extremely revealing costumes. She displayed her female sexuality triumphantly, even posing seminude for a series of popular picture postcards swathed in veils and wearing silk stockings and high-heeled boots. She was featured daily in the gossip columns and was definitely every young man's fancy. She danced, flirted, partied, and joked but, however much the scions of aristocratic families or handsome young actors begged for more than just a chaste good-night kiss on the cheek, Millie simply would not oblige.

She became friends with Adele Astaire, sister and dancing partner of the legendary Fred, and often went to watch them perform at the Savoy. She studied their technique in an attempt to emulate their effortless style and grace, and Adele's chic elegance made her Millie's role model.

In spite of her wild life, Millie was still deeply religious and went regularly to confession. She said her prayers each night and morning and encouraged Susie to teach Vickie to do the same.

The only time she allowed herself the indulgence of tears was when she heard of the death of Marie Lloyd.

"She was only fifty-two," she said sadly to Susie. "That's no age, really."

"Oh, I think that's really old," replied seventeen-year-old Susie, rocking Victoria on her knee. "I don't want to *ever* be that age."

Millie knew she was well on the way to the top when she was featured on the cover of the *Tatler* and everyone who was anyone realized that Millie Swannell was becoming the toast of bohemian London. Word of her sexy singing and dancing spread like wildfire, and *Sauce Piquante* became another smash hit for Sir Ambrose.

"I *can't* believe it. I can't believe that *thing* has made so much of herself." Patsy threw the magazine viciously to the floor and glared across the kitchen table at her husband quietly sipping his tea and trying to read *The Times*.

"How did she do it? How did she become a star?" demanded Patsy.

"I don't know, my dear, I simply don't know." Kingsley retrieved the periodical and looked at the familiar face on the cover. "She certainly looks attractive in this photograph, I must admit."

"She's a stupid, skinny cow. And *stop* looking at her like that." Patsy grabbed the magazine and threw it onto the fire. "She fornicated her way there, that's how she did it. Just like she fornicated with Toby." She nodded furiously, gulping her tea until it burned her throat.

Kingsley's eyes gleamed at the word "fornicated." Since he'd married Patsy Hooper two years previously, he'd enjoyed very little of what he had received the first night he met her, and what had been promised him since the time he brought her to Eaton Square. The fumbles in the parlor and the secretive kisses in the kitchen while the rest of the staff were out were now a thing of the past, after the first dry night of marital love. Patsy had held out for the gold ring with promises of passion, but had failed to fulfill those promises. "Passion!" Kingsley snorted to himself. A lifelong bachelor, he'd expected a little more from marriage than this cold, ill-tempered virago. He cursed himself for being idiotic enough to be seduced by Patsy's dainty charms, but he had been too wound up by the sexual expectation she promised. Kingsley had been badly let down, but Cook, his confidante, had told him with her usual simple logic that he had only himself to blame.

"At your age you should have known better," she'd scolded.

He hadn't. The die had been cast and, as Mrs. Kingsley the butler's wife, Patsy had become head housekeeper at Eaton Square and soon became feared and loathed by the staff. But their loathing was nothing compared to Patsy's toward Millie McClancey. She was obsessed by an irrational certainty that, if it weren't for Millie, Toby would have returned to her. Her dreams were constantly haunted by images of her son becoming the heir to the dukedom, and herself strutting around as the duchess.

"One day I'll have my revenge," mused Patsy, staring into the fire as it curled around the last of Millie's features that were still smiling at her from the cover of the magazine. "One day she'll rue giving birth to that bastard child."

Millie hurried out of the stage door. It was a freezing winter's day, and she wanted to have an afternoon nap before that night's show. Her cloche hat was pulled low over her forehead, the collar of her brown beaver coat turned up to cover her chin, and brown leather ankle boots prevented the icy puddles from freezing her feet. There were few pedestrians around because of the cold, and Millie's stage-door admirers only usually showed up at night, so she was virtually alone on the rain-sodden street.

An imposing Daimler was parked next to the pavement. As Millie passed it, a man got out and confronted her, grasping her arm so tightly she was unable to get away.

"What are you doing here?" Millie gasped.

The Duke of Burghley, who was clutching a copy of the *Tatler*, seemed extremely agitated.

"I will *not* have my family's name dragged through the mud by you," hissed the duke through thin white lips. "Who do you think you are."

Millie wrenched her arm away and looked around for a policeman. "Who do you think *you* are, Your Grace? How *dare* you attack a woman on the street?"

"I am the Duke of Burghley, and how dare *you* sully our family name by using it to perform your coarse theatrics?"

"How dare *I*?" Millie stared at him in amused contempt. "Excuse me, sir, but I almost married your son and I bore his child, don't forget. You saw her birth certificate — you saw the banns we posted in Ireland. He intended to marry me until you forced him to marry that Yankee girl." She leaned closer to the old man. "And if you bother to read Victoria's birth certificate you'll see that she was born *exactly* nine months *after* those banns, so your precious son was almost a bigamist."

"You're a liar," said the duke coldly.

"Oh, a liar, am I?" said Millie. "I was a pure Catholic virgin until your son seduced me and took that away from me. But I'll tell you something, Your Grace," she continued, her voice heavy with sarcasm, "there's *nothing* you can do to me that could ever hurt me more than your son did." She lowered her voice, conscious of the chauffeur pretending disinterest while busily wiping raindrops off the hood of the Daimler. "However, *I* can do your family and that snooty daughter-in-law of yours a great deal of harm."

"And how do you expect to accomplish that?"

"I'm a bit of a star now, you may have noticed. Newspapers are phoning me all the time for interviews and things. I've told them I'm a widow — but . . ." — her eyes glittered and she felt the anger she usually kept under control flood her — "I *won't* have a moment's hesitation about telling one friendly reporter I know my true story. If I show him those banns *and* Victoria's birth certificate, that'll be a front-page story in the *News of the World* the following Sunday, and when *that* scandal breaks, your precious family will be the laughingstock of the whole damn aristocracy."

"You wouldn't dare."

"Try me, Your Grace. I've got absolutely nothing to lose — it may even do me some good. Now, since you've raised this nasty subject, I'm going to tell you what I want to keep this little scandal hushed up. I want fifty thousand pounds put into a trust fund at a responsible bank for my daughter —

Your Grace's granddaughter, may I remind you." Millie smiled as the duke's face went even redder.

"That's blackmail. Besides which, we don't have that sort of money."

"Then *get it*, Your Grace," said Millie. "Get it from that rich bitch Toby married. She's got plenty of money. Get it, or I'll tell the papers everything." Millie was shaking inside but continued coolly, "Oh, by the way, I'm off to Broadway with this show in a few months' time and I've been thinking — I hate the name Swannell and I want nothing more to do with your family, so you'll be glad to know I've decided to change it for America. I'm shortening it to Swann — Millie Swann — nice ring to it, don't you think? Looks good on a marquee. So when you deposit the money in the bank, make sure it's in the name of Victoria Swann, of 318 Fulham Road, London, won't you?"

Millie gave a tight little smile, then hailed a passing cab and jumped in. As the duke stared after her in impotent fury, Millie gave him a regal wave.

Chapter Ten
1923–1926

Millie Swann, Ivor Bessant, Sir Ambrose Osborne, Annie, Lizzie, and the entire company of *Sauce Piquante* were waving at the hundreds of well-wishers on the docks as they set sail from Southampton to New York on the *Aquitania* early in 1923. The *Aquitania* was built like a floating hotel, with paneled staterooms and suites grandly bearing such names as "The Gainsborough," "The Reynolds," and "The Holbein," as well as a variety of restaurants and lounges. The seven hundred and fifty first-class passengers dressed to the nines all day, and every night they wore full evening dress. The trip took four days and three nights, and Millie and her friends were in heaven.

"I've never *seen* such luxury." Millie looked around the elaborate Louis XIV dining room where stewards were rolling in on trolleys small haunches of grilled antelope surrounded by mounds of Strasbourg foie gras, the edifice surmounted by peacock-feather fans.

"Wait 'til we get to New York. They say the streets are paved with gold and everyone's a millionaire." Lizzie giggled, stuffing herself with foie gras.

Millie had left the nearly five-year-old Victoria in Susie's care at their Fulham house, promising to send for them as soon as she was settled. When she had said good-bye Victoria had clung to her, tears running down her round baby face, her little body rigid with sadness. "Don't go, Mummy, please don't go — stay with us." Victoria was extremely attached to her mother, even though she saw little of her and spent most of her time with Susie.

"Now, now, dear." Susie attempted to separate the toddler's chubby hands from Millie's white gabardine suit. "Don't mess up Mummy's nice clothes." Vickie, who never sulked, tried to stop sniffling while Susie ran her hands over her unruly red hair.

"You'll visit me soon, darling, and I'll come back and see you, baby." Millie hugged her child, feeling a faint, unusual tug of maternal love. But there was no time for that. She was off to New York, off to become a Broadway star.

Millie fell in love with Broadway on her first night in New York, when she walked down 42nd Street and saw a street that was as bright as day, lit by neon lights and oversized luminous advertisements flashing on and off as though by magic. There was a smell of frying onions and hot dogs, and steam rose in great gusts from the subway. The tall buildings seemed vertical, shimmering in the brilliant light as dozens of theater marquees flashed their offerings, with the stars' names spelled out in hot white neon.

"The Great White Way," Millie breathed as she, Lizzie, and Annie strolled the streets. "It's just how I imagined it would be."

"Only better," said Annie.

Not only was the USA leading the world industrially; the American people were better fed, better paid, and generally less exploited than anywhere else. It was the land of opportunity — the sky was the limit, and there were infinite possibilities for self-advancement where the poorest of men could aspire to the highest of positions.

America was now also the most inventive nation in the world, and some people were comparing the 1920s to the Italian Renaissance or to Elizabethan England. Shiny new automobiles choked the streets of Manhattan, where everyone seemed to be in a rush, happy and eager to be part of the great American Dream. There was material abundance, freedom, and work for everyone, and the belief was that if you worked hard you won money, success, and the good life.

Recalling Sir Ambrose's advice of three years ago, Millie was determined to work extra hard, polishing and honing her performance to perfection. Broadway was not the West End. It was more sophisticated and extremely competitive. America was on top of the world in every way, and its musical theater was in a class of its own. A young lyricist and composer called Irving Berlin had recently had a smash hit with his *Music Box Revue*, which Millie loved. She and her friends also went to see everything they could. The brilliant Fred Astaire, the sophisticated Gertrude Lawrence, the easy, nonchalant Jack Buchanan, and the hilarious Beatrice Lillie were all starring on Broadway, as were the gorgeous Dolly Sisters, whose lavish costumes of feathers and beads outshone every other star and who were packing them in at the Lyceum.

At the Schubert Theater, the eponymous brothers had opened an exceedingly daring show called *Artists & Models*, the first Broadway revue to feature naked showgirls. These girls, who were not allowed to move a muscle or even sing, were draped in luscious fabrics attached to strings which, when they were pulled, revealed the titillating sight of full nudity. Millie, Annie, and Lizzie stuffed their fists in their mouths to stop giggling when they first saw the naked girls.

"You won't catch me doing that," vowed Lizzie.

"Nor me, neither," said Annie. "What about you, Mil?"

"Oh, I don't know," mused Millie. "It's very artistic, isn't it? If Sir Ambrose wanted me to show a bit more flesh, I wouldn't mind."

"If I didn't know you better, girl, I'd say you were fast," said Lizzie. "But we all know you're next door to a virgin in that department."

During the months before the Broadway opening in New York, Millie worked even more vigorously in the relentless pursuit of perfection. Even though she was not the lead, she lived for her career, and during this time she allowed nothing else to interfere with her dedication. She often stood in the wings watching the other performers and studying them, particularly Ivor Bessant for his effortless charm and insouciant delivery. Her diligence soon paid off, for on her first night on Broadway Millie Swann captured the heart of the blasé audience. For her opening number she appeared in a glass bathtub that looked to be filled with milk and topped with bubbles. She seemed to be completely nude, only her creamy shoulders showing above the bubbles, and she brought the house down with a daring song called "Won't You Come Play with My Bubbles?"

The audience went wild and gave her a standing ovation, something that was to be repeated again and again at each of Millie's appearances. Later in the show she tap-danced down steep mirrored stairs in a top hat and a skimpy costume completely covered in tiny electric lightbulbs that twinkled on and off as she twirled up and down the steps, with a dozen chorus boys in white tie and tails following her. Behind them loomed a magnificent flat of the Manhattan skyline, with windows alight, towering into a night sky that twinkled with a thousand tiny stars.

The leading critic of the *New York Times* called Millie's performance "the greatest aphrodisiac since oysters." A rival paper trumpeted the fact that "her hips moved like flowing honey," and went on to praise Millie's beauty, sex appeal, and sly, teasing delivery. From these reviews her first press nickname was coined: "First we had 'The Gibson Girl,' then 'The Ziegfield Girl,' and now, thanks to Millie Swann, we have 'The Aphrodisiac Girl,'" one starstruck critic had gushed.

Millie's rave reviews caused Sir Ambrose to raise her salary to an astonishing weekly level. Suddenly Millie Swann had become Broadway's newest star, and *Sauce Piquante* ran for nearly three years.

Thanks to the suffragette movement, women had a new improved status. They had a vote now, and they had a voice, and Millie was typical of the modern, young, emancipated woman. Female theatergoers loved her as much for that as the males did for her sex appeal.

Millie wrote regular letters to Vickie and Susie, and several times suggested that they come and visit her during summer school holidays and Christmas, but something always came up to prevent it. In truth, Susie didn't really fancy a five-day trip on a big boat to America. She was happy as a lark living in the little house in Fulham, devoting herself full-time to the care and upbringing of Victoria, and reading about movie stars in the fan magazines.

Vickie and Susie were just as close as any mother and daughter. Vickie was Susie's raison d'être, and her days and nights revolved around the little girl. She helped her with her homework and encouraged her to make school friends, even though Vickie was quite shy. Vickie was never happier than in the warm homely atmosphere of the tiny Fulham house. Susie cooked and baked, and the radio or phonograph was always playing, so the house was full of music and song. Susie bought Vickie a kitten, which quickly grew into a cat and eventually had kittens of its own.

The lives of the two were joyful, active, and full of strong familial bonds. Several times they planned to visit New York on one of the great ocean liners, but one time Vickie's favorite kitten got sick, and the following year Vickie came down with whooping cough and had to be hospitalized. Millie almost came over to visit then, but Susie assured her there was no danger and that Vickie would make a full recovery. Millie burned up the transatlantic phone lines, and from then on they spoke to each other at least twice a month.

Although Susie encouraged Vickie to write to her mother in America, as the years passed the memories of her mother's face receded more and more.

By the time she was eight, Victoria had almost forgotten what her mother looked like. Even though she dutifully wrote once a month and had a photograph of Millie on her bedside table, she had become only a faded memory to the little girl.

"A star has truly been born," thought Sir Ambrose, sitting in the orchestra stalls a few weeks after the opening night of his latest show, which starred Millie. Her name was spelled out in huge neon letters twinkling over 42nd Street:

> Millie Swann
> in
> *Debutante's Delight*

Sir Ambrose joined the vociferous applause and wild standing ovations that now always greeted Millie. The audience rose to its feet as Millie took her final bow, and none was more enthusiastic in his applause than a stocky, handsome young man sitting in front of Sir Ambrose. Square-jawed, with an olive complexion, thick curly black hair only slightly tamed with pomade, and brown bedroom eyes that seemed to hold tragedy behind them, he was impeccably dressed in white tie and tails, accessorized with glittering studs and cuff links. Two bespangled blondes who looked — to Sir Ambrose's experienced eyes — like ladies of easy virtue flanked him at either side. There was something familiar about the man's face, and Ambrose was trying to recall if they'd met when he heard a lady behind him whisper to her companion, "Isn't that Marco Novello, the racketeer?"

Sir Ambrose stared harder as the man stood up. He caught a whiff of expensive cologne and noticed that three or four satanic-looking, dark-haired men in Novello's party stayed near him, staring suspiciously at anyone who got too close.

Several other members of the audience had noticed Novello too, and there were more whispers as he moved toward the red velvet curtains that led backstage.

Sir Ambrose saw where Novello was heading and he followed, wondering if the man had made arrangements to see any of the cast. If he were interested in visiting anyone, it was bound to be Millie, thought Sir Ambrose. She was, by now, one of Broadway's biggest stars and a goddess to most men.

Chuck, the stage manager, certainly knew of Marco Novello and how powerful he was, for he greeted Novello with much bowing and scraping, clearly nervous.

Novello, having left most of his entourage behind, was only accompanied by a lanky man in his forties who had a heavily pock-marked face and hard dark eyes.

"I told Miss Swann you were coming to see her," Chuck stammered. "She said she's very sorry but she's tired and she already has another engagement for tonight."

Marco stared at Chuck coldly for a second and then said, very slowly, "Tell Miss Swann *I* want to see her, that I *insist* on seeing her. Tell her I'm a very big fan of hers. Tell her . . ." — he pressed a one-hundred-dollar bill into the protesting stage manager's hand — ". . . tell her it could be worth her while."

"Sure, Mr. Novello, I'll tell her." Chuck bounded off into the rabbit warren of dressing rooms, clutching his tip. He didn't think much of Novello's chances, but he had no choice but to ask, and a hundred bucks was a fortune.

Ambrose watched in some amusement. He knew his Millie and knew how stubborn she was. Would she be interested in meeting this good-looking mobster who, rumor had it, was one of the notorious Chicago mob, the main operators behind the bootleg liquor business? Well, he would soon find out; he'd go to see Millie himself, and he left Novello standing in the wings.

Sir Ambrose knocked on her door and Bertha, Millie's friendly dresser, opened it. Chuck scurried out. Big and jolly, Bertha was from Mississippi, and she protected Millie from her hordes of admirers and would-be Lotharios very vigorously indeed.

Sir Ambrose waited in the anteroom, which had been decorated in various shades of lavender — Millie's favorite color — idly examining the cards on the numerous bouquets squeezed onto tables and on the floor. *"Can't wait until Tuesday,"* signed *"Jack,"* jostled with *"It's been far too long. Supper at the Stork Club tomorrow? Eternal love, Irving."* Various other household names vied for her favors with exotic blooms and stacks of yellow telegrams on the tables.

"Come in, Ambrose," called Millie. "What did you think of the show tonight?"

"My darling, you were divine as usual," he said, admiring her voluptuousness as she lay on her velvet sofa sipping a glass of champagne.

"Thank you, darling." Millie sparkled, giving him a saucy grin, and Sir Ambrose saw once again what made her so attractive to men. If his desires hadn't run in other directions, he could almost fancy her himself. Her bright red bob framed her flawless face, enhancing light blue eyes that were heavily outlined in kohl, accentuating their extraordinary color. Her curved lips were painted into a scarlet cupid's bow, and her cheeks were gently brushed with rouge. Her full breasts were trying to escape over the top of a soft bandeau intended to keep them flat, as was the fashion, but only succeeded in accentuating their creamy lushness. On her feet were satin mules, and she wore a peach lace slip and matching chiffon peignoir that barely covered her splendid silk-stockinged legs.

Ambrose thought she was looking uncannily like Clara Bow, the famous movie star known as the "It" girl. Millie had realized the resemblance too and admired Clara's daring brand of sex appeal. She epitomized "the flapper," as did Millie.

"Look at this." Millie laughed merrily, dangling a gorgeous diamond bracelet. Ambrose examined it. The modern art deco design was a perfect example of the exquisite work of the master craftsmen at Cartier.

"Where did you get it, you lucky girl?"

"In these." She giggled and gestured to a basket containing one hundred lavender roses. "It was clipped to the note. Look."

Ambrose picked it up and read, *"I won't take 'no' for an answer. Dine with me tonight at 21. You are an angel. MN."*

"An angel — only one person's ever called me that before," said Millie.

"Your . . . er . . . husband?" asked Ambrose, who had always suspected the truth.

"Right," answered Millie. As she admired the bracelet, a sudden image of Toby's blond head, his blue eyes crinkling up as he smiled into hers after making love, jolted her. She shook her head to dismiss the thought and looked up at Sir Ambrose with a grin. "Generous punter, isn't he? MN? Who do you think he is?"

"He's a well-known racketeer, my dear, and he's waiting backstage."

Millie's eyes sparkled with interest. "A gangster!" she breathed. "A real live gangster. I've never met one before — now that sounds like *fun.*"

"Millie, dear, he's one of the notorious Chicago mob — he's a dangerous character. A bootlegger. His reputation is appalling. Since Prohibition he's done dreadful —"

"I don't give a damn about his reputation," Millie cut Ambrose off. "Mine isn't so hot, for that matter. Since he's so generous with the diamonds, maybe he can send me some decent champagne. This stuff stinks."

★ ★ ★

They dined at Club 21 by candlelight. Marco had sent away his entourage with the exception of Franco, his pockmarked right-hand man, who sat smoking on a chair in the foyer in a too-tight black suit, glowering at the other customers.

Millie found Marco fascinating, far more fascinating than any of the men who had unsuccessfully tried to woo her for the past five years. She was twenty-six, a bright, knowing woman of the world, totally at ease in her skin and in her daring red satin shift, and no one could ever talk her into doing anything she didn't want to.

What Marco wanted to do, and he made no bones about it, was to take her to bed. In spite of his dubious reputation, women seldom turned him down, for his silken gaze, humor, charm, and undeniable Italian good looks usually guaranteed him success.

But not so with Millie Swann. She made it clear from the outset of their dinner that she was a girl who loved to have fun and that the fun would only last to the door of her apartment.

As Prohibition was still in force, they sipped vintage claret disguised in Limoges coffee cups and regaled each other with their respective life stories, leaving out all the bits they didn't want the other to know.

Chapter Eleven
1926–1927

He came from a tiny town in Calabria on the coast of southern Italy where there was immense poverty, deprivation, and suffering, unless you were a fisherman.

In 1910, millions of people arrived on the shores of the USA, and Marcello Novello and his parents, clutching their few possessions, were among the immigrant hordes. Their optimistic crossing of the rough Atlantic Ocean on a battered old ship took several weeks. Clutching the hands of young children and old people, the immigrants arrived at Ellis Island to be processed. Women in headscarves and shawls held screaming babies, and the men all wore their best, and only, suits and caps.

Fourteen-year-old Marcello, seeing the shores of the USA for the first time, was determined to make something of himself. This was the land of opportunity, and he wanted some of the success that he had heard America represented.

The Novello family soon settled in a drafty one-room flat in the Little Italy section off Second Avenue. Marcello's father, Nico, helped his Uncle Federico in his tiny grocery store while his mother worked thirteen hours a day in a sweatbox of a factory, where the fire door was kept locked to prevent the employees from taking a break. But a year later, when fire did break out in the factory, one hundred and forty workers died, including Marcello's mother.

Nico was inconsolable and took to the Chianti bottle so completely that he was soon unable to cope with his job, and Marcello was left to make out of life what he could.

At fifteen, tall for his age, stocky, strong, and eager to work, he was soon hired as one of the numerous young numbers runners who distributed illegal lottery tickets to the ghetto souls who struggled to make a living.

After several months of observing him, Big Tony, the "godfather" for the local mob, took Marcello — now known as Marco — under his wing. Marco started by driving Big Tony in his black Cadillac and graduated to blowing safes. Big Tony taught Marco everything he needed to know about gangland life, running vice and gambling outfits, and Marco was an eager pupil.

Marco shot his first victim when he was twenty. The man was a member of a rival mob trying to infringe on Big Tony's territory in the rackets. From then on it was all too easy, and Marco had little compunction about using his shiny new .45 to protect his gang's domain. As his reputation as a ruthless killer grew, so did his reputation with women. Marco Novello was handsome, sexy, and dangerous, and women threw themselves at him, and if they were pretty he seldom turned any of them down. With old Nico dead, Marco had no parents to implore him to marry a nice Italian girl as all of his friends were doing, so he played the sexual field and enjoyed every second.

When Big Tony was gunned down by a rival Chicago gang in 1923, Marco became his natural successor and he ruthlessly took the gang's bootlegging activities to greater heights, making it more profitable than it had ever been since Prohibition was introduced. With a capacity for savage revenge, Marco destroyed the boss of the rival gang and became one of America's kings of crime — his empire grossing hundreds of millions every year.

By the time he met Millie, Marco Novello was thirty, unmarried, handsome, and very rich. He was extremely interested in the stunning redhead, who had told him as much of her own life story as she thought pertinent.

"I guess we're both self-made men," Marco joked, as Franco drove his black Hispano Suiza through the silent streets to Millie's

152

apartment, where Marco escorted her upstairs to her door. But when he bent to kiss her, Millie put a finger to his lips. "Sorry, dearie — no can do."

Marco raised his black eyebrows. "I thought we liked each other, baby."

"Oh, we do, indeed we do, I like you a lot — but if that's all that you want from me, you'll have to find yourself another girl."

"What does that mean?" Marco was so unused to being rejected that he couldn't quite believe what he was hearing.

"It means, my dear — and don't play dumb with me, Marco, 'cause I know you're not — it means I don't put out, or go all the way, or let a bloke get to first base with me or any of those things. Don't tell me you *don't* know what I mean?"

Marco held her at arm's length, meeting her candid gaze with his brooding one.

"I know what you mean, baby, but a girl who looks like you — such a criminal waste. You were made for love, Millie."

"Maybe, maybe not." She laughed. "Look, Marco, I told you — I've been married once and he was the love of my life. When and if I go all the way, it'll be with a white satin dress on my back and a gold ring on my finger. I'm being honest with you now, Marco, I hope you appreciate that."

"Sure, sure. I do. It's . . . er . . . unusual." Marco found Millie's frankness unnerving but totally disarming. "OK, OK, I can wait, Millie."

"It might be a long wait," said Millie softly. "I like to have fun, Marco, lots of fun, but I never do what I don't want to — so don't push me, please."

"I won't," he said huskily and taking her pale hand, pressed it softly to his lips, whispering, "I'll never push you, baby, but I want to see you again. Can we meet tomorrow?"

Millie thought about the many invitations waiting for her — of all the men who desired her, but for whom she felt absolutely nothing. Looking into Marco Novello's deep brown eyes, she saw a sadness there that struck a chord inside her. In doing so, it opened a chink in her heart, a heart that had been closed for a long time.

Millie and Marco were soon seen together everywhere. They went to the races at Belmont Park. They danced to the beat of the wildest jazz in honky-tonks 'til the small hours. They went to the Cotton Club in Harlem, where a new, hot young trumpeter called Louis Armstrong thrilled them with his magic sounds. They entered wild Charleston contests, which they often won. They dined at ultra-exclusive Manhattan restaurants like the Colony and 21, but equally enjoyed a shabby spaghetti house in Little Italy that served the most delicious pasta Millie had ever tasted.

Marco wore five-hundred-dollar suits and a fedora tipped rakishly over one eye. He oozed power and was immediately fawned over when he entered any room. He took Millie shopping at Lord & Taylor and Bergdorf Goodman for clothes, and to Cartier and Tiffany, where he showered her with the most beautiful baubles in the shop. They went to fashion shows at Hattie Carnegie and Lily Daché, to matinees of Eddie Cantor and Beatrice Lillie, and to tea dances at the Plaza. As the 1920s roared, so did the movies, and Marco and Millie stood in line outside the Warner Theater with hundreds of others to see the first ever movie with sound, Al Jolson's *The Jazz Singer*, which was a revelation.

When Millie wangled a long weekend off from the show, they took a night train to Miami, then crossed by boat to Havana, where Marco gambled recklessly and instructed Millie in the intricacies of baccarat, blackjack, and craps, all of which she simply adored.

Millie's lifestyle grew ever more exciting, and she epitomized the ultimate flapper. With her skirts grazing her knees, diamond bracelets halfway up her arms, pearl and jeweled necklaces swinging from her swanlike neck, Millie flaunted her sexuality. It was even more alluring because of her "good girl" reputation, which still didn't stop her nightclubbing, partying, and drinking cocktails all

155

night while reveling in being a major player in one of the gaudiest sprees in history. The Jazz Age was living up to its name. Its credo was "Live fast, die young, and leave a good-looking corpse," so the bright young things partied from dusk to dawn with no thought of tomorrow. Their bible was a new magazine called *The Smart Set*, which chronicled all their doings and in which Millie was often featured. But despite her frenetic nightlife, Millie was still an absolute professional when it came to her career. As she constantly honed her talent, her performances grew more technically accomplished and Millie became the consummate showgirl, using artifice, talent, and discreet nudity to beguile her besotted audiences.

One of Marco's many gifts was a silver flask studded with rubies. This Millie kept full of the best British gin for, in spite of her liking for champagne and wine, Millie still preferred it.

Marco was by now madly in love and completely crazed with desire for Millie, but he had no choice other than to let her do what she wanted, for she made it clear her career was all-important. However, he was fiercely jealous and he employed a spy backstage who reported to him if Millie seemed to become too friendly with anyone in the company of the opposite sex.

Unbeknown to Millie, Marco even had his mob contacts check out the Toby Swannell story and discovered the truth — that Millie had never been married. It was an ace he kept up his sleeve. But it was OK. He had skeletons too, skeletons that Millie would never know about. And as these were to do with his business dealings, he knew they wouldn't be easily traceable.

In the autumn of 1927 Ambrose Osborne mounted another new Broadway revue, called *Dream Girl*. The show was such a sensation that it ran to sold-out houses for two years, and Millie's fantastic costumes became the talk of New York. They were extravagant, daring, and diaphanous, often baring more flesh than was acceptable, but she wore them with a "devil-may-care" insouciance that was captivating.

For her first entrance she walked down a Lucite staircase wearing a skin-tight silver bugle-beaded dress slit to the thigh, with a fifteen-foot train made of white ostrich feathers. This matched her headdress, which towered above her on a steel frame and was held to her head by a diamond-studded "headache band." The audience rose to their feet to applaud her beauty.

At the finale, she appeared in a translucent silver lace dress, a diamanté bow in her hair, and crescent earrings with diamond drops that fell from her ears like tears. She stood stock still because the censor wouldn't allow movement when seminude, one high-heeled foot placed in front of the other, her arms upheld and fingers splayed out in a pseudo-ballet pose. It was the ultimate gesture of stardom, a woman at the peak of her artistry giving herself to her audience, and her sexual allure was palpable.

The critics raved again. "The most beautiful body in New York," wrote the *New York Post*, while a famous radio commentator said, "Run, do not walk to the Schubert Theater to see the cutest gal ever to hit Broadway — she can sing and dance too, but only when she's wearing clothes!"

Marco had been intoxicated with Millie for over a year, even though she'd kept him swinging on a seductive string. Her defenses were clearly weakening, but she was not about to give in to his persuasions. Although she wasn't in love with Marco, she liked him immensely, and found him excellent company. But the bewitching sexual magic that she remembered between her and Toby was missing in her relationship with the dapper gangster, however much she tried to ignite it.

Millie was reclining on a lavender chaise longue in her dressing room, fingering her armful of diamond bracelets, holding the new forty-carat emerald and diamond ring Marco had recently given her up to the light.

"He's such a lovely man. *I* wouldn't mind being Mrs. Novello one little bit," sighed Lizzie, who had become Millie's main confidante and one of the few people she trusted.

"He asks me to marry him at least once a week," said Millie.

"Because he knows it's the only way he can have you — the oldest trick in the book, clever girl. But think what you're missing, Millie. Lovemaking is fantastic — don't let it pass you by, darling. He's gorgeous, your Marco, even if he is a mobster. I wouldn't let him get away, no siree." Like Millie, Lizzie had ironed out the worst of her "below stairs" accent, and picked up some American slang along the way.

"Mmm, I bet you wouldn't. Maybe you're right, Lizzie. It's just that I don't *feel* the way about Marco that I did about Toby."

"You were a baby then, darling — seventeen years old. Romance all seemed a lot rosier when we were kids. You'll be twenty-eight next birthday, Millie, it's time you thought of your future," said Lizzie pragmatically. "You can't go on being the 'Aphrodisiac Girl' forever, y'know."

"That's for sure," sighed Millie. "Maybe it's time for me to take the plunge, Lizzie. I do like Marco a lot — just not the same way I felt toward Toby."

"What can you lose? Get him while you've

still got your looks, girl," counseled Lizzie. "Stop living in the past."

Although still ravishingly pretty, Millie was starting to become aware of middle age, which was then considered to be around thirty. She was a huge star and *Dream Girl* was still box-office dynamite, but Millie was beginning to think that there might be more to life than the thrill of applause and the constant round of "makin' whoopee." Marco's ardor seemed undiminished, but Millie was no fool. She knew that if she didn't commit soon she risked losing him, and also realized that as Marco was a handsome, virile man he must be gratifying himself elsewhere. Which was true. Marco had strong sexual appetites, and he discreetly satisfied his needs with many other willing bed partners. What else could a guy do?

Marco Novello was utterly amazed that the next time he proposed to Millie, she accepted. They were married on St. Valentine's Day 1927, in St. Patrick's Cathedral on Fifth Avenue. Afterward they gave a huge, flashy reception at the Plaza Hotel, which was a most eclectic event. Everyone who was anyone in the theater attended, mingling with mobsters and their molls. Flappers flirted with gangsters, and the nouveaux riches swapped stock market tips with notorious racketeers. Even Clara Bow — Millie's idol — had been persuaded by one of Marco's

L.A. connections to make the long train journey from the West Coast.

Susie and Victoria sailed over from London, but there was an awkwardness between the chubby nine-year-old in her stiff organdy party dress and her glamorous mother swathed in white satin and diamonds. Vickie, ever the polite little girl, curtsied, even though this was the first time in four years she'd seen her mother.

Millie took her daughter for an ice-cream sundae at Rumpelmeyers, then to Bergdorf Goodman, where she spent a fortune outfitting her in the most expensive of children's clothing, but she was unable to relate to the nine-year-old's conversation and interests. Talk of the kittens bored her, and a discussion of the best way to feed a goldfish left her cold. Conversely, talking about clothes and show business didn't interest Vickie one bit, so mother and daughter spent the day with long awkward pauses in their conversation until they went to the cinema, where they both became engrossed in the macho charms of a young actor called Cooper Hudson.

Marco soon easily won over both Vickie and Susie with his charm, but the affection that Millie professed in her letters was missing in her attitude toward her daughter. Millie didn't seem to know what to talk about, and it seemed that she really had little interest in her child.

Mother and daughter did not bond, and Vickie returned to London bewildered that her mother still seemed a stranger to her.

"If I have a baby, I'm going to love it to bits," she confided to Susie as they sat on the deck of the *Aquitania*, wrapped in blankets and watching the cold Atlantic waves. "Then it will love me too, won't it?"

"Of course, dear." Susie hugged her charge, feeling sorry about the motherly love Vickie had missed out on, but determined that she would fill that void with as much affection as possible.

Marco was aware that he should proceed carefully on their wedding night, but at the sight of Millie smiling shyly up at him, the white satin sheets of their honeymoon bed pulled up to her chin, he threw caution to the wind. She looked so delectable that Marco simply couldn't help himself. He knew he should arouse her and take his time before he satisfied himself, but he had waited too long and the anticipation of finally making love to her completely was too potent.

"You really are the Aphrodisiac Girl, baby," he breathed, sliding in beside her. "You sure do it for me."

Millie was trembling as she waited for him in her white lace nightgown. This was it. For the first time in ten years she was about to allow a man to share her bed and her body, but her body was so tight it felt as if it was twisted into a knot. When Marco grabbed her he was already raring to go, and failed to ignite Millie's fire. His kisses, which tasted of cigars and brandy, left her cold and his lovemaking, consisting of fast penetration and crude sex talk, repelled her. This was not at all how lovemaking had been with Toby, who had touched and stroked her tenderly, his gentle, slow caresses building a fire inside her.

When Marco finished he rolled off her, turned on his back, and began to snore. Millie stared into the darkness, the awful realization dawning that she was not in love with Marco at all and that maybe she had just made the second biggest mistake of her life.

Although Marco apologized in the morning for the speed and greed of his lovemaking, he was also aware that Millie had been a less than responsive bed partner.

"I should have known that she wouldn't be that hot." Marco voiced his thoughts to Franco as they drove downtown to one of his "offices" — Joe's Little Italy — a seedy trattoria on the Lower East Side. "I guess there are dames who like it and dames who don't." He tipped his fedora at an angle and adjusted the buttonhole carnation he always wore.

"You shoulda known, Boss, that when that dame didn't put out for you for all that time she wouldn't be no good in the sack — she ain't interested." Franco knew his employer's proclivities well. Marco liked sex, a lot of it, and Marco liked his ladies to like sex too. If they didn't get turned on — or at least pretend to — he wasn't the macho man he liked the world to believe he was.

"Hey." Marco scowled at Franco. "I didn't say she *wasn't* good, did I?"

"No, Boss."

"What *did* I say?" Marco leaned forward menacingly until his face was next to Franco's. Franco started to breathe heavily. In the old days before Marco had taken over control of the district, they had both been hit men, and Franco knew what Marco was capable of.

"You didn't say nothin', Boss — nothin'." Franco swallowed hard.

"Yes, I *did*, Franco — I know what I said. Maybe I shouldn't've said it to you, 'cause you're a stupid putz. So what *did* I say?"

Marco's strong hands were flexing, and Franco knew that with an expert squeeze around his neck, Franco would be history. He knew it for sure — he'd observed that bit of action many times in the past.

Sweating profusely, he managed to muster up a few brain cells to stutter, "You said, Boss, she was a lady and she fucks like a

164

lady too. Right, boss?"

"Right, that's what I said. And I guess I shouldn't've said it to you, so I don't want to hear you repeat that — ever. *Capisce?*"

"Yeah, yeah, *capisce,* Boss, *capisce.*"

"Right — glad to hear it. My wife's a lady, Franco." Marco leaned back and lit a cigar. "So she don't like sex that much. Means she won't go around lookin' to get laid with any other guys."

"She better not, Boss." Franco laughed obediently.

"Yeah, she better not, and she won't. She belongs to me now; she's my wife. Maybe I can plant a kid in her and she'll kiss all this showbiz shit good-bye."

"Yeah, Boss, yeah, good idea. You play hide the salami a lot, Boss, give her a lotta kids. That'll keep her home."

"Meanwhile," Marco checked his watch, "there's an apartment I want to visit on East Eightieth, I've just got time. You know the one."

"Sure, Boss." Franco leered. He knew the one. Who didn't? Several of the most beautiful whores in Manhattan worked there for exclusive clients only. Marco was a regular. "Guess a leopard don't change its spots," thought Franco, watching his employer stride through the entrance of the plush building.

Chapter Twelve
1929

Marco loved kids and yearned for some of his own, but although he diligently made love to his wife several times a week, she did not become pregnant. After a while, he became tired of her passivity. He realized she was acting when she sometimes tried to come across all sexy and pretend to want him; he wasn't stupid. But nevertheless he loved Millie and with the exception of their sex life, his marriage to her was reasonably happy and their lifestyle was certainly exciting.

He'd tried to persuade Millie to bring Victoria over to live with them. All of his "compadres" had broods of kids now, ensuring that their dynasties would continue. All Marco had was a famous, fun-loving flapper of a wife and a few glamorous whores on the side. He wanted a family — he needed a family. He was thirty-three years old, and what was the point of life without kids? But Victoria only came to New York at Christmas time for short visits in spite of him sending her lavish gifts.

"She's so busy with her schooling, and she's top of her form in most subjects," Susie wrote to Millie proudly.

On her rare New York trips, Marco indulged Victoria as if she were his own daughter. He wanted to spoil her, and took pleasure in her delight when he took her to Rumpelmeyers for ice-cream sodas or to Lord & Taylor for pretty dresses to disguise her plump preteen figure. He took her skating at the new outdoor rinks that were springing up all over New York, and to the theater and the movies, especially the movies. Victoria and Susie loved the movies so much that sometimes Marco took them two or three times a day.

They saw the first great musical revue film, *Broadway Melody*, and a chilling thriller, directed by the young British director Alfred Hitchcock, called *Blackmail*, which was the longest talkie ever made. But the most entertaining film of all starred a character called Mickey Mouse, with whom Victoria fell totally in love.

Marco felt proudly paternal on these outings. He liked being a regular family man, loved spoiling Vickie, and was only slightly disappointed that Millie didn't share their trips. Millie slept until four every afternoon, waking more often than not with a hangover from her heavy drinking and ceaseless partying, which was beginning to take its toll on her looks.

Millie drank and partied because, try as she might, she knew she wasn't in love with Marco. All she could muster for him was affection and friendship, and Vickie was just a sweet little stranger toward whom she tried to feel lovingly maternal but couldn't.

Marco's career as a bootlegger and major player in the rackets was going from strength to strength. The strict Prohibition laws introduced in 1920 allowed organized crime syndicates to prosper. With modern telephone and radio communications, the Mafia was able to put a stranglehold on the laws attempting to stop the public's consumption of liquor. They were making a fortune, and so was Marco.

On a freezing February day in 1929, Marco was supposed to attend an important meeting in Chicago with one of his associates, "Bugs" Moran, a notorious mobster and sworn enemy of Al Capone, the most powerful and corrupt thug in gangland. Killing one another was a common event among the rival gangs, not to mention an occupational hazard. There had been several assassination attempts on both Capone and Moran, and only the previous week Marco had narrowly escaped a car-bomb attempt on his own life.

As Marco was preparing to leave for Chicago the night before the meeting, Millie suddenly had a strange premonition. "I don't want you to go to Chicago," she cajoled. "It's our wedding anniversary, and I've planned a big surprise." Millie playfully ran a finger down Marco's bare chest.

"Hon, I've *gotta go,*" said Marco, "it's important. Bugs needs me at the meeting. We got problems with Capone's guys."

"Please don't go," she whispered, biting his ear. "I want you to stay with me tonight, and we'll celebrate tomorrow morning. It's Valentine's Day, after all."

Conjugal delights with his wife were so few and far between that Marco was tempted.

"OK. Let me make a call to Bugs. I'll tell him I'll take the afternoon train. We can still do business. The truck's not due in 'til Monday."

"Good." Millie wondered what had gotten into her. She didn't particularly want her husband to make love to her, but the intense feeling of dread she felt made her go through the motions.

At noon the next day while Marco was shaving and Millie was still asleep, he heard the shrill ring of the telephone in the hall. Picking up the receiver, he heard Franco's voice, husky with fear.

"Didja hear what happened this morning, Boss?"

"No, what?"

"A bunch of Capone's guys dressed as cops machine-gunned Bugs's guys to death in a garage in Chicago."

"No! Oh, Jesus Christ Almighty . . ." Marco sat down trembling. "How? What happened?"

"We're sure lucky we didn't go, Boss. They got them all — all except Bugs. If we'd've been there, we'd've had it for sure."

"Well, I can thank Millie for that," said Marco. "Jeez, what a lucky escape."

Before the end of the day, the "St. Valentine's Day Massacre" had gained national and international attention, and the public's outrage at the carnage triggered the downfall of many of the notorious gangs that had flourished throughout Prohibition.

Afterward Marco fell into a deep depression. He'd lost several of his friends and, after that morning of love, Millie had gone back to her normal coolness. Business was starting to go bad, and the money to keep his empire flourishing had to be found somewhere. Perhaps it was time to go legit.

A few months later, the stock market crashed, causing waves of panic and fear. All across the most prosperous nation in the world people were losing their life savings and their lives, as millionaires jumped from the tall buildings of Manhattan and millions of hardworking men became paupers overnight.

Because of Black Tuesday, practically every show had to close, and in late 1929 Broadway went dark. America was no longer in a party mood. The Depression was looming and seminude fantasy girls weren't in vogue anymore, particularly if they were pushing thirty. For the first time in years Millie was out of work and depressed, and suddenly there were no more wild parties to make her feel better about herself.

Chapter Thirteen
1933

By 1933, Millie was no longer a ravishing soubrette. She was a graying, out-of-work actress running to fat, who drank too much and too often. Marco was so sick of nagging her about it that he kept out of her way much of the time. Millie spent hours in front of the mirror convinced she was losing her looks and used the henna bottle so frequently that her curls were now bright vermilion. The emptiness of her life could only be filled with the gin bottle and, more often than not, she fell into bed at night dead drunk. They still lived in a luxurious apartment with a dazzling view of the New York skyline and sleek white art-deco furniture, but after the crash in the stock market and the repeal of Prohibition, Marco was finding it hard to make ends meet. Nor did he even bother to make love to Millie anymore — which was just fine by her, as even the touch of his hands left her cold.

"I guess I just don't like sex," she confided

to Lizzie one afternoon as they sat in a bar drinking manhattans.

"Did you *ever* like it?" asked Lizzie, an avid bed-hopper.

"Once. A long, long time ago, but maybe I imagined it. I was a virgin, just a kid." Millie shrugged. "I'd be happy if I never had to make love again."

"Oh, honey, you just haven't found the right guy," sighed Lizzie. "You don't know what you're missing."

"I don't know and I don't want to know," said Millie. "I'll leave that all to you, Liz."

When Millie returned home there was a message asking her to call Sir Ambrose. She called him back and he said without preamble, "Broadway's getting back on its feet again, darling. I want you to star in my new musical, *Bubbles*. Are you interested, Millie darling?"

"Oh, yes!" she replied enthusiastically. "Yes, yes, *yes!*"

"But you have to lose all that weight," he admonished. "Those extra pounds don't flatter you, darling — neither does that hair color."

"Oh, I will, Ambrose. I'll go on a diet, I'll stop drinking, I'll do *anything* you want me to do to be able to work again."

But when she told Marco, he was far from enthusiastic. "What the *hell* d'ya wanna do another show for? That's for kids — you're

173

no kid anymore, Millie, you're pushing thirty-four."

"So what?" she snapped. "I'm bored with doing nothing sitting around this apartment all day, watching you play poker with your buddies all night. I *need* to do something, Marco."

"So go shopping, go to lunch, do what the other gals do. Why must you go back to the fuckin' theater again?" He paused, and continued with a lie — "We've got enough dough."

"Because I love it," said Millie simply, and then thought sadly to herself, "I love it more than I do you. More than I do anything, in fact."

On the first day of rehearsals Millie was as excited and nervous as when she had first started. She had been dieting and exercising fiendishly, but she knew she was still out of shape.

"I haven't danced on stage in three years and I'm really rusty," she told the handsome director-choreographer, Luke Robbins.

"It's just like riding a bicycle — it'll all come back to you," grinned Luke.

"Well, I'm a very rusty bicycle."

"And I'm going to work you relentlessly, so it'll all come back soon enough, watch out," he replied. "Wait until I put this flabby chorus line through their paces. These kids need to work."

174

Millie sat in the stalls watching Luke, who seemed completely dedicated to his craft. Tall and slender, with a dancer's body that could be lithe and athletic one minute or provocatively languorous the next, Luke's blond hair tumbled over his forehead when he moved, and his pale blue eyes and sensitive mouth were a poem. He was a dazzling young man who stunned Millie by his resemblance to Toby. But that resemblance was only physical. Luke's temperament was the total opposite of Toby's. He was an easygoing, friendly, all-American boy; unlike Toby, whose clipped vowels and reticent, haughty manner had always given the impression of an archetypal snob, one of England's leisured class.

Luke Robbins was no snob. He was down-to-earth, intensely energetic, and so irresistibly charming and popular that half the chorus — boys and girls — had a crush on him. The instant Millie started watching Luke work, she felt a surge of feelings she hadn't experienced since she was seventeen. But there was no time to indulge these strange new thoughts, for Luke was a hard taskmaster to her too, rehearsing endlessly, making everyone go through their paces repeatedly.

"He's indefatigable," moaned Lizzie, who had been delighted to make it into the show with Millie. "Even when you think you've got it right, he makes you do it over and over again. My legs are killing me."

"He's a perfectionist" — Millie smiled — "and he's got inexhaustible energy. I admire that about him." She stood in the wings watching Luke. The score was complicated, and Luke's choreography extremely modern and audacious. He was determined to make his mark with this revue. Busby Berkeley, the film director, had recently had an immense cinematic hit with *Broadway Melody of 1933*, and Luke was attempting to simulate his intricate and demanding routines on stage. He wanted the chorus to move in total unison, and for this they had to train with military precision.

"It's impossible to get the same effect as in the movies," the producer Sam Rogers had argued. "They get to do take after take to get it right." But Luke was insistent that it could be done, and every day he made the weary cast rehearse at least sixteen hours. Neither Millie nor Ivor Bessant escaped Luke's authoritarian approach as he bullied, cajoled, and blitzed the cast into endless grueling rehearsals.

After six weeks of New York rehearsals, the show went on a short pre-Broadway tour.

In Boston, one cold winter's afternoon, Millie sat in the auditorium, yet again looking at Luke, who was rehearsing and joking with the adoring chorus girls, who were flashing their plump legs in shorts and white socks at him.

"Move it, girls," he yelled. "You all look like you're paralyzed. Buck up and lift those pig's trotters higher, ladies. C'mon, lift 'em higher! And do it at the *same* time, for Pete's sake. Oh, my God, haven't you learned *anything* in four months? Let's do it again, ladies." The girls sighed collectively and Lizzie, finishing her bit, limped off stage and flopped onto the seat beside Millie's.

"I'm a bit too long in the tooth for this, toots." She lit a cigarette and shivered. "And this theater's freezing. We're all going to get pneumonia."

"Let's go have a cup of coffee in my room," said Millie, and they walked backstage to her pokey dressing room.

"That damned Luke is breaking all our balls, y'know. He's a tartar, a regular slave-driver," said Lizzie.

"He needs to be. We're all still out of shape. He wants us to be the best we can." Millie handed Lizzie a mug of coffee and said, "He's very cute though, don't you think?"

"Join the queue, honey, they *all* fancy him — boys *and* girls. Don't tell me you do too?"

"I didn't say I fancied him." Millie coolly adjusted a curl. "But he's a looker, no doubt about that, and a talented one too."

The call boy rat-tat-tatted on Millie's door. "On stage, please. Luke needs you."

"But it's nearly midnight," wailed Lizzie. "We open tomorrow night. What's he need us for *now?*"

"He doesn't need *you*." The boy poked his head round the door disdainfully. "He wants the *star.*"

"OK, OK, I'm coming." Millie quickly slapped on a dab of lipstick and rubbed some rouge into her pale cheeks, but she still looked wan.

"You sure look a lot better than four months ago. Work agrees with you," observed Lizzie.

"I know," grinned Millie, "I still love it, I love everything about it."

"Be careful." Lizzie sensed Millie's attraction to Luke. "Don't forget you're *both* married."

"I know, I know." Millie smiled at her friend. "Hey — I'm just going to *rehearse,* that's all."

Luke was waiting on stage, practicing a difficult step with only the pianist for accompaniment.

"Hi there." He performed a complicated triple twirl effortlessly. "I want you to try this pirouette at the end of your first number. I think it'll work better for you than what we've already worked on." He was looking boyish in gray flannel trousers and a yellow sweater that almost matched his hair. He executed the step turn again. "Try it," he or-

178

dered. "And a-one . . . and step — turn — step — step, turn, turn, *turn*." He did it with effortless ease, and then turned to Millie. She attempted to follow him but lost her balance, slipped on the raked stage, and fell on her ankle, which bent under her at an awkward angle.

"Oh, God! Are you hurt?" Luke helped her up gently, but when Millie stood up, she winced as she felt a slight twinge in her ankle. Then she felt an altogether different twinge as Luke held her close.

"Are you all right?" he asked solicitously, his face close to hers. "Jesus, Millie, I'm sorry. I shouldn't be working you this late."

"It's OK, I'm OK — I think." Millie tried to walk. Luke's arm was around her waist, and she realized she wasn't hurt as badly as she thought, but she was enjoying this feeling of closeness, so she allowed Luke to lead her to her dressing room, calling to the stage manager to fetch some ice.

Millie lay on the worn sofa watching Luke as he expertly applied an ice pack to her ankle. She liked the way he was so concentrated on just that part of her body and, for the first time in years, thoughts assailed her of what she'd like a man to do to other parts of her body. Was it his uncanny resemblance to Toby that made her feel like this? It was hard to ignore these incredibly strong feelings. She was falling for him and she knew it.

Luke looked up, smiling. "You have good strong ankles, Millie — dancer's ankles."

"Thank you," she whispered, relishing the simple compliment.

For years men had heaped upon Millie the most flowery of flatteries. They had eulogized her hair, her figure, and her complexion. No praise had been too fanciful, as they had attempted to seduce her. This boy — for Luke was extremely boyish even though they were about the same age — seemed not to be interested in her as a woman at all, and his professional examination of her leg was totally dispassionate.

"I think you may have strained a tendon, but I don't think it's anything serious — does it hurt here?"

He felt her calf and Millie squeaked, "Er, no, that seems fine." By now she was barelegged, as Luke had taken off her socks to check for sprains in her other leg. She wore rehearsal clothes; tight navy-blue shorts and a white blouse fastened with tiny pearl buttons. "I think I feel a slight pain higher up here." She almost blushed as she touched her thigh. It felt perfectly fine, but she didn't want Luke's powerful yet sensitive fingers to stop their explorations.

He pressed the muscle on her thigh, then his hands moved higher and she felt all the tiny hairs on her body tingle as he probed it gently, asking, "Does it hurt here?"

"No." Millie propped herself on her elbows so that her face was inches from Luke's. "It's feeling much better now. You've got healing hands, Luke."

"So I've been told." Then he looked into her eyes, and for a second Millie thought she saw desire in them. Something compelled her to incline her head and touch her mouth lightly to his. He responded to her kiss momentarily, then drew back, a bemused look on his face. He pulled back and stared at her for several moments, then said softly, "I don't think this is a good idea, Millie."

Millie pulled away and removed his hand from her leg.

"I guess you're right," she murmured. "It's not."

Luke stared deeper into her eyes, then ran his hands over his hair, trying to tame the blond curls.

"I'll call Bert to run you home," he said quietly.

"Thanks, Luke, and don't worry. I'll be fine tomorrow for the opening."

"Of course you will." He stood up, and she felt a pang of disappointment as he moved away.

Hundreds of men had thrown themselves at Millie's feet, and now she was almost throwing herself at the one guy who wasn't interested. Was this rejection divine retribution?

"I deserve it. What the hell am I doing?"

she thought. Millie's face was flushed, and she suddenly felt embarrassed.

She went behind a screen to change into her street clothes and heard him say softly, "You know I'm married?"

"So am I." For a fleeting second Millie imagined what Marco would make of this little scenario.

"And we have a baby," he announced as she came out, adjusting her hat.

"Good for you." She was surprised to hear a tinge of sarcasm in her voice. "I had a baby — she's nearly fifteen now."

"But we don't get along." He frowned and lit a cigarette. "Haven't for a while, in spite of the kid."

"Neither do we," said Millie softly, then reason prevailed and she sat down opposite him. Taking his hand she said, "Look, Luke, I'm sorry about what just happened. I've never done anything like that before. I'm really embarrassed, and I hope we can put the whole thing behind us — forget it ever happened."

He looked steadily into her face, his yellow hair burnished by the bright makeup lights. "I don't think I want to forget it," he said huskily, and raising her up from the chair, took her in his arms. Holding her face close to his he whispered, "Do you think we should forget it?"

"No," whispered Millie, her heart beating very fast. "No, I don't."

Chapter Fourteen

They became lovers, two weeks before the Broadway opening. It was relatively easy for them to be together, as the whole company was staying at the same hotel. Although Millie and Luke had little time together because of rehearsals and performances, the few hours of lovemaking that they stole from sleep were the most joyous times of Millie's life.

She felt Luke was her true soul mate — that they had lived before and loved before. The primal passions that they aroused in each other seemed infinite, and they could not get enough of each other's bodies. Luke awoke urges in Millie that she never knew existed, and the sight of his strong muscular body excited her beyond reason. Her skin responded to his every touch, her body felt soft and new and open, and the lovers spent their time together as though in an erotic dream.

The day before the opening Millie returned to her New York apartment and was shocked when she saw Marco. In the six weeks she'd been gone, he seemed to have aged. His face seemed coarser; there was stubble on his chin and a gray weariness around his eyes. He was playing poker with his usual gang, and greeted Millie with a kiss that tasted of stale cigars.

"I'll see you later, little lady." Patting her on the rump, he returned to his game and his cronies grinned knowingly at one another.

Marco came to bed several hours later, wanting sex. Millie pretended to be asleep, but that didn't deter him. She wanted to scream as he entered her, but she lay still and prayed he wouldn't last long. Afterward he squeezed her breasts hard, turned on his side, and with a "good night, baby" was asleep with a snore.

Millie lay awake all through the night. Although her love affair was only two weeks old, there was no question in her mind that her heart belonged to Luke. This was a *coup de foudre*, and even though it was a potentially dangerous situation, she couldn't give him up. Even though they hadn't made plans to meet in New York, Millie had to see him. She yearned for him, body and soul. No man had ever made her feel as Luke did, no man except Toby, and that had been sixteen years ago, when she'd been little more than a child.

The Broadway opening of *Bubbles* was another triumph for Ambrose and Millie. In the grip of the Depression and with half of America out of work, the public was at last hungry for entertainment again, and *Bubbles* was as frothy and amusing as its name.

The company was ecstatic as the curtain came down and up again to several encores. Great baskets of blooms arrived for Millie and the other cast members, and well-wishers thronged the dressing rooms backstage, spilling into narrow corridors.

Noël Coward paid his respects to Millie, "My dear, you were *simply* divine." Jerome Kern, Ernest Hemingway, Marlene Dietrich — escorted by Gary Cooper — and even Johnny Weissmuller, fresh from his recent Tarzan movie, all kissed and congratulated her. The men shone in white ties and tails, and the women were stunningly glamorous in furs and clinging chiffon or satin gowns of ice blue, cream, or shimmering silver.

Marco presented Millie with yet another diamond bracelet to add to her collection, clasping it around her wrist himself.

"Congratulations, honey, you sure looked like a star again. The audience loved you, baby, and so do I." He bent to kiss her, but she moved her face and his lips met her cheek. Marco got the message. "OK. Listen, I've got some business to attend to, so I'll meet you later at the party, OK, kid?"

"Fine, Marco, I'll see you there."

Now that Millie had stopped numbing her

mind with liquor, she often thought about what her husband actually did for a living. She had always known he was involved with the Mob — a big player in the Prohibition game — but since that law had been repealed, she had never asked what he did and where his money came from. Thinking back, she recalled an evening a few years previously when she and Annie had discussed this. Marco had not come home the previous night, the same night that another notorious gangster, Alfredo Marinelli, had been assassinated in his Fifth Avenue duplex apartment by a masked intruder. The police had come to their apartment to question Marco about his whereabouts at the time, and Marco had said he'd been home all evening with his wife. Millie had been primed to agree. In fact, she'd been so lost in a blur of gin on the night in question that she only vaguely remembered falling into a fuzzy sleep. Had Marco been at home or not? She couldn't really recall, but it was easier to tell the detective that her husband had been with her — particularly since Marco had shot her one of his dark warning looks.

If her husband was a criminal, what did it matter? His lifestyle hadn't impinged on hers, and what her mind didn't know her heart didn't grieve for. Marco had devoured the newspapers even more eagerly over the weeks following the death, but eventually the story dropped out of the news. Marco had really prospered again after Marinelli's death. He'd bought a new fleet of trucks, and Millie received even more lavish gifts on her birthdays. When she brought up the subject of Marinelli, Marco became threatening toward her for the first time in their marriage. He was ruthless in business — it was best not to mess with him. What would he do if he discovered her affair with Luke? She dreaded to think.

Visitors came and went for another hour until finally Millie was alone. Bertha had taken her costumes downstairs to the wardrobe department, and she could hear the last of the company chattering excitedly as they left for the Waldorf. Suddenly, there was a knock on the door and Luke came in, resplendent in white tie and tails.

"You were wonderful," he said, kissing her softly on the mouth. "Pure magic."

Millie stood up, wrapping her arms around Luke until their kiss became more passionate. They stood together for a long lingering minute, intertwined, completely engrossed in each other.

"I love you," whispered Millie.

"And I love you too," said Luke.

Outside Millie's dressing room, someone who had been listening moved away from the door. Stealthily walking back along the corridor, the dark figure slid a nickel into the

187

public phone and swiftly dialed a number.

"So whose apartment is this?" Luke asked after they had finished making love. It was a cold morning, but the little bedroom was cozy with a roaring fire and the warmth of their love.

"It's Lizzie's," said Millie.

"Lizzie!" His eyebrows rose.

"I had to confide in someone . . ."

"She's the biggest gossip on Broadway. How do you know you can trust her?"

"She's been my best friend for years," said Millie, "and I've *got* to trust *someone*. Don't worry, darling, she loves the movies and she's promised to go twice a week to Radio City Music Hall so that we can meet here. She just can't get enough of Gary Cooper."

"And I can't get enough of you," said Luke, pulling her close to him again.

Although they talked about everything under the sun and laughed and made love until Millie could barely walk, they never discussed either their marital situations or their future.

Millie knew that Marco would never forgive her if he found out about Luke, and that he would never forgive Luke either. She knew what kind of a man she was married to, and what he was capable of, but she never let Luke know that.

A week later, on her way to Lizzie's brownstone to meet her lover, Millie passed a small sign announcing, *"Clairvoyant. Your fortune told here."* With fifteen minutes to spare, she entered the dimly lit room, gave the gypsy crone five dollars, and listened as the woman recited the usual clichés.

"You have success but not true happiness. Beware of a dark man in your life."

Millie shivered. A dark man? Half the men in the world were dark. Of course this woman could tell she was successful by her elegant Vionnet red wool tailored coat with the black Persian lamb collar and fox beret perched on her auburn curls.

"What about my future?" she asked, checking her watch and realizing that she would be late for Luke.

The gypsy stared at her intently for a few seconds, then looked into her crystal ball. "I'll write it down for you," she said huskily. "But, you must promise not to read it until tomorrow."

Millie stuffed the scrap of paper into her bag and walked excitedly down Sixty-second Street. Spring was in the air, even though it was only February, and she almost flew down the street in her haste to see her lover. He was waiting for her, and they tore each other's clothes off in a frenzy of passion so sublime that they soon lost all sense of time.

At six o'clock, Millie awoke from a deep sleep in Luke's arms and checked her watch.

"Oh my God! Look at the time," she gasped. "I've got to get to the theater."

"Would you like a cup of coffee, my love?" he asked, kissing the tip of her nose. "I'll make it for you while you're dressing."

He wrapped a towel around his waist and walked into the kitchen. As Millie heard the scrape of a match, she saw the piece of paper in her bag the clairvoyant had given her. Curious, she pulled it out and read the chilling words, "You have no future."

Millie heard a horrific explosion from the kitchen as Luke's match lit the gas stove, which exploded into a wall of flame. She heard Luke's cries and ran screaming toward him as, within seconds, the whole apartment turned into a flaming holocaust.

Two figures in raincoats, one small and the other tall, watched from across the street. When the blast erupted and flames were shooting out of the windows of the whole building, one turned to the other smiling and said, "Now I can sleep again."

PART TWO

Vickie

Chapter Fifteen
1933

"British Star Dies in New York Fire" trumpeted the headlines on the *Evening Standard* billboard. Vickie bought a paper as she left Fulham Broadway underground, glanced idly at the story, and broke out in a cold sweat as she read of her mother's death.

Millie Swann, glamorous British-born Broadway musical comedy star, perished yesterday in a fire at a New York apartment. Seven fire engines attempted to quell the flames. All of the other residents of the brownstone apartment on East 81st Street died in the inferno, which completely gutted the building. Foul play has not been ruled out, although preliminary examination seems to indicate a faulty gas stove caused the tragedy.

The rest of the article told of Millie's tumultuous life, but Vickie didn't bother to read it. Leaning against the cold red brick of the station, she took deep breaths to steady her nerves and then wondered why she was unable to shed even one tear for the mother she barely knew. She was upset, of course she was upset, but she realized that she should be devastated. She was an orphan now, parentless except for Susie. Devoted, caring Susie, who was more than a mother to Vickie — she was father, brother, and sister too, and she was waiting for her at their flat, tears streaming down her plump cheeks as she went to hug Vickie.

"She's gone; oh dear God, what a terrible way to go. May the good Lord have pity on her poor soul." Vickie took some comfort from Susie's arms but still couldn't muster any deep grief.

"I've spoken to Marco." Susie wiped her eyes. "He managed to get through on the telephone an hour ago. He'd been trying all night — he wants us to come to New York for the funeral."

"New York? What about school? I've got exams next week. If I want to go on to college I must get my School Certificate."

"You're just going to have to take the time off." Susie spoke unusually firmly. "I'll speak to your headmistress. We'll only be gone two weeks. We've done it before. It's your mother, dear. You have to be at her funeral."

"You're right, Susie, I'm just being selfish. Of course we must go. I just don't know why

I'm not more upset. I wish I could feel more sad."

"It's understandable, dear." Susie patted Vickie's hand. "After all, you hardly knew her. Why don't you go upstairs and take a nap before supper."

Vickie nodded, then went up to her room. She lay on her bed with its familiar pink eiderdown and stared at the framed picture of her mother on her cluttered bedside table. She wanted to be able to weep and give vent to tragic emotions like Susie had, but she felt nothing. She took out her mother's last letter, written a few weeks ago, from the pile in her bedroom drawer and reread it.

My dear Vickie,
   I do miss you, my darling child, I really do, but I realize how important your school and your friends are. I'm on tour with this new show now called *BUBBLES* and I'm having such a wonderful time. I do hope you'll come out to New York soon, and we'll celebrate after the show. I know Marco would love to see you.
                    With all my love,
                    Mama

Vickie stared at the letter. It seemed so cold and uncaring really. Millie's career had always come first. "If I ever have a child," Vickie thought again grimly, "I'm going to be with it all the time, and I'll give it so much love it'll be the most adored baby in the world."

Millie Swann's funeral was a crazed circus of sobbing fans, jostling photographers, and a bizarre mixture of theater folk, society hotshots, and mobsters. There was a huge reception afterward at the Plaza Hotel, which was supposed to be a wake, but no one, except Marco and Susie, seemed to be too saddened by Millie's death. They were all so busy eating, drinking, and gossiping that Millie was hardly mentioned.

The women were all dressed in the height of style in ankle-length floating satin or chiffon tea gowns, lightly cinched at the waist. Most of them were elegantly slender, wearing big hats bedecked with flowers and ribbons, and some carried long cigarette holders of onyx and ivory through which they puffed delicately on their cigarettes.

Vickie felt fat and frumpy in her flowered, short-sleeved rayon dress from Debenham and Freebody's in Oxford Street. The puffed sleeves accentuated her plump arms, and her untamed ginger hair looked like a messy mass of frizz beside the soigné Manhattan fashion plates with their sleek marcelled coiffures.

"They're all having such a good time," Vickie whispered to Susie. "This isn't like a funeral. It could be any old cocktail party."

"Ah, the dead are soon forgotten, dear," said Susie slightly bitterly. "Life is for the living, my pet. Don't you ever forget that. Yesterday is history. Tomorrow's a mystery. Today is a gift, that's why they call it the present."

Vickie smiled warily. "I love your home-spun homilies, Susie."

As soon as they could, Susie and Vickie returned to Marco's apartment exhausted from traveling, desiring nothing more than to sleep. But Marco wanted to talk, and talk he did, pacing around the flashy art deco, white-carpeted living room, cigar in one hand, brandy snifter in the other. His eyes were full of tears.

"You know, Vickie, your mom was a wonderful, wonderful woman and she only wanted the best for you."

"She was always writing and telling me how much she loved me," said Vickie, "but I didn't really believe her, Marco. I mean, I didn't know her at all. I didn't know what sort of person she was."

"Your mom was a star, baby," he said proudly, "and stars are selfish sometimes. They're prima donnas, divas. They aren't like ordinary people, are they, Susie?"

Susie nodded. She couldn't take her eyes off Marco, who fascinated her. Still handsome, although running slightly to fat, his masculine charisma and Italian "take charge" quality, quite touched her virgin heart.

"Well, I'm your parent now." Marco placed a well-manicured hand on Vickie's knee and squeezed it.

She could smell the strong cologne he used too liberally, which reeked of cheap carnations. She wrinkled her nose.

"I'm gonna be your daddy," Marco continued with emotion. "I'm gonna take care of you and Susie."

"I'm going to be sixteen in a few months; I don't *need* a daddy." Vickie removed his hand from her knee. The cheek of him. Even the boys that hung around the candy store never went that far. In any case, the male sex held no interest for Vickie, and from what she'd heard from Susie, who after a couple of gins could become quite garrulous, they'd brought her mother no real happiness either.

Vickie had asked Millie several times about her father, but she had consistently refused to tell her anything about him. She was fobbed off with, "Your father was a fine, handsome young man and a good soldier who died serving his country before you were born." The girl would listen wide-eyed as Millie whispered with a faraway look, "He was the absolute love of my life." But when pressed for more details, Millie was vague. "I can't talk about him, I get too upset," she'd say, at which point she'd burst into tears,

198

whether real or fake Vickie never knew, and run from the room in a flurry of emotional distress.

Vickie was brought back to the present as Marco continued, ". . . so I'd like you to stay here with me in New York. If you like, we'll get a house in Connecticut or the Hamptons. You'll like it there, it's just like England, green, countrified, and plenty of horses for you to ride."

Vickie gave a despairing glance toward Susie, who seemed hypnotized by Marco.

"But what about my exams? I take my School Certificate in three months, and then I'm down for Cheltenham Ladies' College and I'm hoping to get in."

"You'll go to college here," Marco crowed. "We've got the best colleges in the world in upstate New York — Sarah Lawrence, Vassar, Radcliffe — just take your pick of 'em. A gal can't get a better education than that. What d'ya say, honey? Your daddy wants to be a good poppa to you."

"I think it's a wonderful idea, Vickie, I really do." Susie was becoming hooked: The idea of Marco as Vickie's daddy and Susie as her mother figure was appealing, and Susie absolutely adored New York. It had really grown on her the few times she'd visited. The huge department stores, the hustle and bustle and the glamour of it — so different from plebeian Fulham. The West End was nothing compared to the Broadway theater, and as for the movie houses, that Radio City Music Hall was a regular palace of delights with its dancing Rockettes and fabulous entertainers. Nothing even came close to it in England.

While Vickie was at college upstate, Susie could go to the cinema every afternoon and take care of Marco in the evenings. He was such a handsome gentleman, he'd quite turned her head. Marco looked just like her favorite star, George Raft, who when flipping a coin in *Scarface* turned her quite weak at the knees. Just to be in the orbit of Marco, to live in his house and see him every day thrilled Susie no end.

At thirty, Susie, with her plain, stocky body and chubby peasant features, was a dyed-in-the-wool virgin and chances were that she was going to stay that way. She knew that, but she didn't mind.

The three of them discussed the pros and cons throughout the night and eventually Vickie was so exhausted that she gave in.

"OK, OK," she said wearily. "We'll go back to Fulham, I'll take my School Certificate, then we'll come back here and live with you, if that's what you want, Marco."

"Daddy," he corrected.

"Marco," she said obstinately. "My daddy's dead."

They moved into a mansion in Connecticut on Vickie's sixteenth birthday, and the following year she was accepted into Radcliffe College.

Vickie's Radcliffe days were carefree and fun. Although still gawky, slightly overweight, and shy with boys, there was more than a hint of her mother's dazzling looks in those slanting aquamarine eyes, even though Vickie insisted on wearing her thick auburn hair pulled severely and unflatteringly off her face. In certain lights she could look extremely attractive, but she was uncomfortable around most people and only really at ease when she was reading or going to the movies, particularly if they starred her favorite actor, Cooper Hudson.

Boys of her own age left her cold. Not that she'd been around the opposite sex much, as Radcliffe was a girl's college. They had their yearly proms, where Vickie dutifully pranced about with gawky teenage boys doing the fox-trot and the bunny-hop, but the young men did nothing for her.

They saw little of Marco. Involved in all sorts of deals and with several businesses to run, he stayed in Manhattan most of the time. A string of showgirls and burly sycophants still surrounded him, but every birthday and Christmas he showered Vickie and Susie with expensive gifts, and he constantly telephoned checking on their welfare.

Occasionally he would bring some of his business cronies whom Vickie didn't like at all to Connecticut for the weekend. They were all swarthy, shifty Italians who treated Vickie and Susie in a dismissive, misogynistic manner, and Vickie kept out of the way when they visited.

Every so often the newspapers would try to reopen the mystery of Millie Swann's death. Was it really an accident or had someone rigged the stove to explode? The investigators had spoken to everyone involved in Luke's and Millie's lives, but they all had alibis for that day. Millie's friend Lizzie had been shopping at Lord & Taylor with Annie, and Marco had been in Atlantic City playing in a high-rollers poker game. The only person without a watertight alibi was Luke's wife, who had been at home alone with her baby daughter all day. But the police ruled her out. She was a mousy little creature, gone to fat since the baby's birth — the sort of woman who wouldn't say boo to a goose. She wouldn't have the intelligence to plan such a monstrous act. The foul-play theories persisted, but as the years passed the mysterious circumstances of Millie's death were almost forgotten.

Vickie's summer vacations were idyllic. She spent hours riding her chestnut mare Feather, a present from Marco; swimming, lazing by the pool in the sun, and turning her pale skin the color of honey. Susie bought one of the new Kodak cameras and liked to take pictures of Vickie, particularly when she wasn't aware of the camera. Susie was stunned by how absolutely lovely she could look, far more appealing in photographs than she did in life.

Leafing through *Photoplay* magazine one afternoon, Susie read an article announcing that the David O. Selznick Studios were looking to test unknown actresses for the leading role in *Gone With the Wind*. Susie had read and loved that book, thrilling to the adventures of Scarlett O'Hara.

"The girl should be no less than eighteen and no more than twenty-five, attractive and with some acting experience."

"Vickie would be perfect," thought Susie. "She could be a wonderful Scarlett."

Vickie was nineteen and had performed quite well in some of her college plays. To her own surprise, she had actually enjoyed the experience, and Susie had been the loudest to applaud.

On an impulse, Susie put a few pictures of Vickie in an envelope, wrote her name and address on the back of the photos, and sent them off to the casting director at the Selznick Studios.

Chapter Sixteen
1938–1939

The search for Scarlett O'Hara had become a national obsession. The public had devoured Margaret Mitchell's sensational novel about betrayal and survival in the Deep South and had hounded David O. Selznick with their choices for the gutsy, gorgeous heroine. The casting director's desk was awash with photographs of young girls. Fat girls, thin girls, pretty girls, pretty ugly girls — it seemed as though every girl in America wanted to play Scarlett, but few possessed the fire, beauty and talent to bring her truly to life. Tallulah Bankhead, Susan Hayward, Lana Turner, and Paulette Goddard were just a few of the thirty-two star actresses who had been tested, but none of them had quite the right qualities, so the quest was on for an unknown.

America was movie-crazy, and *Gone With the Wind* was going to be the movie to end all movies. Hollywood was bringing gaiety and escapism to a world still recovering from the Depression, as Hitler and Mussolini rose to power. Europe was teetering on the brink of another terrible war, but America didn't want to know about wars in Europe and, ostrich-like, buried its head in the sand and went to the movies.

So the frenzied, frantic search for Scarlett swept through America as talent scouts combed high schools, towns, and villages and even held open auditions in huge city stadiums. Every girl hankered to play Scarlett. Every girl, that is, except Victoria Swann, who was amazed when a letter arrived for Susie from the Selznick Studios, summoning her for a test the day they were traveling to New York to spend a weekend Christmas shopping.

Dear Miss Miller,

The photographs you sent to us of Victoria Swann show promise. She has some of the qualities we are looking for, and we would like to screen test her for the role of Scarlett. Please call this number when you receive this letter.

Yours truly,
John Kippen
Casting Director

"Isn't this exciting," said Susie. "This could be a big break for you."

"But I don't want to be an actress," Vickie wailed. "I'm too fat, too gawky, my hair's too red and too frizzy, my hairline's too low and most actresses are idiots anyway."

"Nonsense," said Marco, who thoroughly approved of Susie's idea. "You're a gorgeous kid. Better lookin' than Loretta Young, Joan Crawford — any of those dames. They can't touch you in the looks department, baby."

"I agree," chimed in Susie quickly. "It's a wonderful opportunity, Vickie. Just think — Hollywood! You could be starring in some of those movies you love, perhaps even doing scenes with Cooper Hudson. Love scenes maybe, and they say he might play Rhett Butler."

Vickie turned on her witheringly. "That's completely disgusting, Susie, and stupid. I've got better things to do with my life than be in the movies."

"Like what? What *do* you want to do with your life, honey?" Marco's attempt at a fatherly tone sounded hollow.

"Oh, I don't know." Vickie slumped into the squashy sofa and stared out at the Manhattan skyline, which was becoming softly obliterated by the first feathery snowflakes of winter. "I don't know what I want to do yet. I'm not fearless enough to be a show-jumper, and I'm not clever enough to be a journalist. I just don't know."

Susie shivered. "Snow, I hate snow — it chills my old bones."

"Yeah, you're real decrepit now, Susie, you

must be all of thirty-five," smiled Marco.

"Thirty-four," said Susie primly, "and a lady's age should never be mentioned in polite company."

"OK, gals, listen to me." The idea of Hollywood was becoming more appealing to Marco by the minute; beautiful starlets, palm trees, golden beaches — "Hollywood's an El Dorado, it's fabulous, you'll love it," he said. "I was thinking of making a new start too. My friend Bugsy's been talkin' about moving his base of operations to a tiny little place nearby in Nevada called Las Vegas. He thinks legalized gambling could become quite lucrative out there; he's opening a casino in his new hotel. I'd be very interested in getting in on the ground floor."

"I expect your businesses aren't doing so well anymore, since Prohibition ended," probed Susie. Marco was always tight-lipped about what he did for a living.

He smiled at her and, ignoring the question, replied, "Yeah, you're right. Why not try life in sunny California for a while? What could we lose?"

Turning on all his persuasive Italian charm, Marco tried to sweet-talk Vickie into going to Hollywood. "It could be the most exciting thing that's ever happened to you, Vickie." Marco's excitement was contagious, and suddenly California seemed like a real possibility.

"Well, let me sleep on it," said Vickie. "It's

a lot to take in right now." She went upstairs yawning but feeling a little twinge of excitement. Maybe Hollywood could be fun. Even if she didn't get the part of Scarlett, going out to the West Coast could be a new adventure and perhaps she could get to meet Cooper Hudson, the handsome and married movie star.

On a warm, sunny day in December 1938, twenty-year-old Victoria Swann entered the white clapboard Selznick Studios to test for the part of Scarlett O'Hara. Shooting was scheduled to start the following January, but without a suitable Scarlett they had no movie. The studio was getting desperate. Clark Gable had eventually been signed by popular demand to play Rhett Butler, but the studio production team had yet to find the perfect girl. Today George Cukor himself was auditioning a bunch of raw recruits and was less than happy with them.

"Talentless nonentities," he'd whispered resignedly to his assistant. "OK, let's see what this one's like."

Vickie walked on to the set and stood nervously in front of the camera, next to a tall, skinny actor called Jake Marsden, who seemed equally scared. Every time he swallowed, his Adam's apple bobbed up and down like a cone and Vickie wanted to giggle. Cukor came over and gave them some hushed directions, then went back to his director's chair and barked, "ACTION!"

"Oh, Ashley, can you honestly say you don't love me? I could make you so happy — I can give you babies. You know Melanie can't give you any more babies." Vickie was trying her best, but her face was so caked with makeup that she felt tense and her voice sounded fake and tinny.

"Cut," yelled Cukor. "Cut, cut! Honey, the expression on your face is too hard. You've got to gaze at Ashley with love and passion. Look into his eyes — feel how much you need him. You want this man. You've wanted him all your life, you desire him. I want to see the yearning in your face. OK, honey, let's try again."

Makeup and Hair bustled around Vickie, adjusting her painful pink-corseted gown, rearranging her stiffly lacquered ringlets, and powdering her face. It was boiling hot on the stuffy sound stage, and Vickie was embarrassed by all the attention. As for the actor playing Ashley, Jake was so wooden he could have been carved out of a giant redwood. He was pallid, weedy looking, and not the slightest bit attractive to Vickie: Only one actor had ever interested her, and he was the unattainable Cooper Hudson, a very different proposition from the timid Jake.

"OK, kids. Ready to go?"

"Yes, Mr. Cukor," she mumbled obediently.

"Yes, sir." The lump swallowed and Vickie tried to suppress a giggle.

"Places please," called the assistant director.

The focus puller pulled the tape measure out from the camera and almost hit Vickie on the nose with it; the wardrobe woman stuck her hand down the front of her dress to hoist up Vickie's cleavage, scratching her breasts with her silver rings as she did so, and the hairdresser pulled at her ringlets so hard that Vickie felt as though she were being scalped. From behind a maze of bright lights she heard Cukor's voice.

"Are you ready? Now don't forget, honey. You love this guy. OK, let's do it. I want to *see* it in your face." Cukor came over again and whispered in her ear, "Forget it's Jake, honey, he's a lox, I know. Pretend he's one of your boyfriends. Imagine he's the one you're crazy in love with. OK?" He walked back to his chair. "And, *action*," he called.

Vickie started the scene again. Staring soulfully into the eyes of the blank-faced actor, she willed herself to imagine he was Cooper Hudson.

"Oh, Ashley," she breathed, her face starting to glow. "Oh, Ashley, I love you — I've never loved anyone else — and you love me too, don't you? Say it, Ashley, say it. Say you love me, please." As she continued with the dialogue, Jake's face disappeared and in its place she saw Cooper's. She was with him, he loved her, and all she wanted was to be with him.

"Cut. Beautiful." George Cukor beamed from his director's chair. "That was very nice, very nice indeed, honey, I think we've got it. It's a wrap."

Vickie shook her head as if to dispel Cooper's image and glanced at Jake. Yes, it was Jake, but with some sort of alchemy she'd managed to believe he was someone she loved. A few of the crew smiled at her encouragingly as Susie hurried after Vickie, who was on her way back to the tiny dressing room she shared with the next three girls who were also testing.

"That was absolutely *wonderful*, dear. You looked like you really were in love with him. I was very impressed, and so were the crew."

"Maybe I can act after all." Vickie was exhilarated by the flood of strange new emotions that welled up inside her. "But I bet you anything I don't get the part of Scarlett."

And she was right. Vivien Leigh did. But a few weeks later, Harry Feltheimer, the head of production at a rival studio, happened to see Vickie's test and, impressed by her budding beauty and extravagant and voluptuous sensuality, told his team about her.

"This one's got potential. Sign her to a six-month option."

It was 1939, and Hollywood was at the pinnacle of its Golden Age. All the studios were churning out hundreds of movies to feed the insatiable appetite of their audiences — more movies were being made than at any time before or since. It was the heyday of the silver screen, and they needed faces to fill those screens. Faces to enchant an audience always hungry for new ones. So young men and girls were plucked from all over America and Europe to be tested, put under contract, and for maybe a tiny percentage to become stars.

Vickie was signed up by Paradigm Pictures as one of the seventy-two young contractees the studio was grooming for stardom that year. Vickie was happy being under contract. It wasn't unlike college. She enjoyed the daily routine of dancing classes, fencing, deportment, elocution, and acting lessons, and the camaraderie between the young hopefuls was contagious. With Susie's encouragement, Vickie studied hard.

And then one sunny spring afternoon she met Cooper Hudson.

She was walking alone on the back lot, learning lines for a scene her class was working on. In a simple white cotton sundress and sandals, her long red hair floating in the breeze, she looked vulnerable and breathtaking. Immersed in her script, Vickie wasn't looking where she was going and she literally bumped into him. Cooper was strolling around the corner of the New York street set, talking earnestly to a man who looked exactly like an agent should look.

"I'm so sorry," Cooper apologized, bending down to pick up Vickie's pages, which had scattered all over the ground. "Do forgive me, I'm a clumsy oaf."

"That's OK — I wasn't looking where I was going, I'm sorry." Vickie became flustered. She felt her face go scarlet as her eyes met Cooper Hudson's deep brown ones and stayed there for a long minute.

"Has anyone ever told you you're an extremely pretty girl?" Cooper asked with a smile.

"All the time." Vickie tried to match his humorous tone. "I'm getting really bored of hearing it so much."

"What's your name, pretty girl?" Cooper raised one black, sardonic eyebrow while slowly looking her up and down.

"Vickie," she stammered, "Vickie Swann."

"Well, hello there, Vickie Swann," he drawled. "I'm Cooper Hudson."

"Of course you are. You look just like him — only shorter." She blushed at her audacity, but both men laughed appreciatively.

Then Cooper said, "Get lost, Bernie. I'll see you later on the set," and changing direction he took Vickie's arm. "I'm going to escort this pretty little lady to her destination, then maybe I'll cut her down to size."

Vickie giggled, but she was in a daze as they walked slowly across the back lot, Hudson gently holding her arm. Cooper Hudson, in the prime of his manhood, was utterly captivating. He knew it, and she knew it too and felt almost enveloped in his charm. How many times had she met this man in her dreams? How many times had she thought about him? Now here he was. He was giving her his full attention, and he was devastating.

Dressed in his swashbuckling costume of flowing white shirt, doublet and hose, and high black boots, Cooper Hudson was testosterone incarnate. Six foot two, with his resonant voice and engagingly dimpled grin he oozed masculinity. Known as an unabashed womanizer, he was about to reach the pinnacle of his fame with *The New Adventures of Don Juan*, a role for which he was aptly cast. The word was already out on the street that he was great in it; that it was the part he seemed born to play, for he was a magnificent animal and a dreamboat to boot, whose masculine allure had guaranteed him a place among the top ten box-office stars for a decade. Now thirty-five, his chiseled cheekbones and alluring charm made women adore him and men want to be him.

"So, you're a new contract girl?" he asked. His arm pressing on hers made her heart beat faster.

"I'm just one of dozens. You know the six-month option thing, then they drop you. I'm waiting for the ax to fall."

"They'd be nuts if they let the ax fall on you, pretty girl." He looked at her lush curves and luminous youthful sexiness. "It looks like you've got it all in spades. Can you act?"

Vickie blushed. "I don't think Katy Hepburn's going to lose any sleep, but I'm studying like crazy and they say they're going to build me up."

"So they should. You're gorgeous. You look like you've got what it takes, kid. Hey, it's not that difficult, you know, if you can hit your marks and remember your lines, with a face like yours you could make it." He grinned and his dimples deepened. "Want to come to my dressing room later and run your scene with me? I'm known to be an excellent talent spotter."

"I'd love to." Vickie didn't even blink.

"See you about six then, in my dressing room. You know where it is?"

She nodded. Of course she knew where it was. She'd strolled past it often enough, hoping for a glimpse of him.

When Cooper said good-bye to Vickie at the rehearsal hall fifteen minutes later she was already totally smitten. Cooper's sexy, knowing eyes searched her face, his full lips curving into the famous grin that entranced females everywhere.

215

"Well, kid, I'll see you later then."

"I'll be there," smiled Vickie, "on the dot."

And she was.

In her tiny dressing room Vickie feverishly tried on and discarded several outfits.

"Too girlie," she said of the organdy ruffles. "Too severe," as she surveyed herself in a stiff blue flannel tailleur and took that off too. "Oh God, I've nothing to wear," she wailed to herself. Then she had an idea and rushed over to the wardrobe department. "I need something sophisticated and glamorous for a reading tomorrow," she confided to Paul de la Maine, the head costume designer.

"My dear, I have the very thing," he purred smoothly. "We made it for Susan Hayward's last movie. It should fit you perfectly, you're about her size."

Wearing the gorgeous pale-green georgette dress with a sweetheart neckline that draped over her undulating curves, with a gardenia in her hair and liberally sprayed with Chanel No. 5, Vickie rapped on Cooper's dressing room door, promptly at six o'clock.

"It's open," he called. "Help yourself to a drink, I'm in the shower."

Vickie closed the door and looked around tentatively. The mahogany-walled room was a real man's dream den. There was a bearskin on the floor, deer antlers on the walls, and a glass cabinet containing an eclectic selection of firearms in the corner. One wall held framed movie stills of him with all his famous leading ladies, each one affectionately inscribed. Vickie was riveted reading tender messages from Greta Garbo, Joan Crawford, Bette Davis, Claudette Colbert, and dozens more.

In his ten years as a movie star Cooper had starred in over fifty films, had been nominated for two Oscars, and rumor and some fact testified that he'd bedded most of his leading ladies. Although he was married, he was irresistible to women young or old. Certainly, Vickie was no exception. She was already half in love with him now.

Cooper came out of the bathroom wrapped in a white terry-cloth robe, towel-drying his black curly hair. His dazzling teeth flashed in his deeply tanned face. Without his heavy film makeup he was even more appealing. His skin was young and firm, and she could see his chest was finely muscled with a light dusting of dark hair.

"Whisky?" He poured a generous amount into a heavy shot glass, then added a dash of bottled water. Handing her the glass he said, "Just a teardrop of water brings out the flavor."

"No ice?"

"Never ice in single malt, my dear. It's sacrilegious."

Vickie took a sip. Other than the Chianti

that Marco favored, she'd never been much of a drinker, and this whisky tasted strong and bitter. She sank into the squashy tan leather sofa, watching as Cooper threw down the towel and poured himself a generous shot.

"Salud." He raised his glass. "Here's to you and your career, Victoria Swann." He drained his glass, bending closer to her as he refilled hers too.

She could smell soap and the faint aroma of cigars. She usually hated cigar smoke, but on Cooper it seemed just right.

"So you're Millie Swann's daughter." He sat down, twirling the amber liquid. "I saw her at the Schubert when I was studying in New York. She was some dame. Who's your father?"

"He died before I was born." Vickie looked away. "But you've probably heard of my stepfather, Marco Novello."

Cooper raised his eyebrows. "Novello, huh? He's big time with the Mob. I wouldn't like to mess with him."

"Oh no, he's on the level. He's kind and funny, not at all like you'd imagine."

"Kind and funny?" Cooper laughed. "That's what those hoods like you to think." He was sitting easily on the sofa, so close to Vickie that she felt an unfamiliar feeling of excitement growing inside her. "I seem to re-member some rumor that Novello was in-

218

volved in your mother's death." He looked at her questioningly.

"Oh no, no. Not Marco, he adored my mother. Everyone says so. He was a wreck after she died, didn't get over her for years. I was fifteen and . . ." Her voice trailed off and she looked away.

"And what?" he asked gently.

"Oh, nothing." Vickie changed the subject and asked him about the bearskin rug, of which he was extremely proud.

"Shot it myself when I did that picture in Alaska. About the only good thing that came out of that movie."

They talked much more, and they laughed a lot. Talking seemed so easy with Cooper that Vickie felt she could tell him almost anything. The lights were dim, and a log fire crackled on the hearth. The phonograph was playing something dreamy by Glenn Miller, and the atmosphere was heavy with anticipation. When Cooper's arm slid along the back of the sofa it seemed totally inevitable. He looked at her with a long, slow smile spreading over his handsome face.

"Yes, you are a very pretty girl indeed, Miss Swann." He stroked an auburn curl with his finger. "And with just a little bit of talent and the right lighting and makeup, you could be divine on screen." His strong tanned hand was lightly caressing Vickie's shoulder, and then he pulled her closer and looked deep into her eyes.

Vickie felt as if no one had ever looked at her before. It was as though he could see into her soul. She felt helpless, like a rabbit caught in the headlights of an oncoming truck. When Cooper bent forward to kiss her, she felt unfamiliar desire flood through her and could only melt willingly into his arms.

Almost overnight Cooper awakened Vickie's dormant sensuality. The ultimate he-man on screen, in bed he was the most considerate and generous of lovers. After their first tryst, they met around the same time every evening. Whenever Vickie thought about Cooper, she felt herself shudder with longing for the feel of his body next to hers. Each evening as she approached his dressing room, her body started prickling with excitement, her heart pounding so hard she could hear it in her ears. She couldn't wait to be in his bed and in his arms again. And Cooper taught her well. He taught her the art of lovemaking, instructing her as if he were giving a painting lesson, showing her the strokes and the shading and the subtleties of sexual love.

Cooper adored making love, and he particularly liked making love to women who were responsive. Vickie was more than responsive. Cooper's passion stirred chords in her that released all her girlish repressions. Cooper showed her how to give and receive so much pleasure that sometimes Vickie thought she'd died and gone to heaven. She became totally open to him and fell head over heels in love.

But each night at eight or nine, after their passion was done, he'd kiss her gently on the forehead and go home to his wife.

When *Gone With the Wind* opened to rave reviews and record-breaking crowds, Paradigm decided to make their own rival to the Selznick blockbuster and Vickie was summoned, along with seven other of the prettiest contractees, to a summit meeting in Harry Feltheimer's office. He sat behind his desk flanked by two casting directors and various studio aides, surveying the girls as if they were cattle as they sashayed self-consciously into his office.

"What a bunch of dogs," complained casting director number one to casting director number two. "I wouldn't give you two bits for the lot of 'em."

"The redhead's not too bad." Casting director number two scrutinized Vickie, who was staring into space, wondering when Cooper was returning from his latest location.

"Nice tits, but her waist's too thick; pretty eyes, and the hair's good, but it's too red. She might look OK if she was lit properly."

They didn't bother to whisper and the girls could hear themselves being discussed, which made them even more embarrassed. They were asked to walk, sit, and turn; then, after a huddled chin-wag, four were told they could go, leaving Vickie, her friend Mary Lou, a virginal blonde, and Peggy, a pretty brunette.

Harry rose from his black leather swivel chair to stand in front of his magnificent Regency partner's desk, his eyes flickering over them derisively.

"Right, girlies. You gals are the best we've got, but unfortunately none of you is great, so you're all going to need to work your pants off 'cause we're going to test you extensively for our new picture."

"What's it called?" asked Peggy boldly.

Harry Feltheimer looked at her as if she'd crawled from beneath a stone and the girl cringed. He was by no means a lovable man, and he did little or nothing to pretend to be. Brusque, domineering, and arrogant, he had made Paradigm Pictures into one of the top studios in Hollywood by brilliant business sense, pitiless manipulation, and instinctive gut knowledge of what the movie public wanted. His thinning black hair was scraped over a skulllike head, greasy with pomade; his small gray eyes were coldly calculating; his nose was as sharp as his tongue could be; and a small mustache didn't quite disguise the fact that he had no upper lip. Feltheimer used people ruthlessly, whether they were actors, directors, or studio personnel. He had been at the top of his game for over a decade, and he took no hostages.

"We've bought *The Devil's Daughter.*" He almost smiled as he saw the girls' excitement. "It's as good a book as *Gone With the Wind*, and the gal who plays Regina is going to be a star. That *could* be one of you." He stared at each girl in turn. "*Gone With the Wind* made that unknown Vivien Leigh dame into a star — we're gonna do it for one of you, although, looking at you, it's not going to be easy. None of you has got Vivien's class. But that's OK because 'Regina' has got to be one part bitch and two parts whore." He smiled thinly. "You girls could fit that bill, I bet."

The girls all started to jabber excitedly, but Harry held up his hand for silence. "We start testing next week, and meanwhile you *all* go on a diet. You're all enormous. You need to lose ten pounds at least, and get some sleep, for Christ's sake. You may all be under twenty, but you look exhausted, so lay off the booze and the boyfriends, OK? All-night fucking ages a dame more than anything." His glance rested on Vickie, and she felt herself turn scarlet. Did he suspect her liaison with Cooper? They'd been extremely discreet, but there was no such thing as total secrecy, particularly at Paradigm Studios, where many who worked there made it their business to know everybody else's and flew to whisper it

223

to the gossip columnists.

"OK, that's it," said Feltheimer dismissively. "I want you all to make an appointment with the studio quack. Doctor Sandler will start you on those diet pills, pronto."

Two weeks later Vickie sat in the makeup chair while Dave Blake, one of the top makeup men in Hollywood, studied her face from every angle through a magnifying glass. He hummed and hawed, then got to work.

"We've got to emphasize the good, and camouflage the bad," he murmured, then proceeded to study every freckle, every blemish, and every pore, measuring with infinitesimal care the space between her eyes, the length of her nose, and her upper lip.

At the end of a grueling three-hour session Vickie was transformed. Her hairline was plucked back two inches, her thick red hair had been given a golden rinse and set to fall around her face in luxuriant waves and curls, and the expert use of cosmetics on her face, neck, and shoulders enhanced what was always there. False eyelashes magnified her slanting aquamarine eyes, and subtle shading gave her exquisite cut-glass cheekbones. No longer slightly plump since the stringent diet, the tight sixteenth-century costume flattered her newly slimmed curves, and her hourglass figure and amazing cleavage were unbelievably sexy. She stared at herself in the mirror.

"Wow, I don't recognize myself. You're a genius, Dave."

"I know," he said laconically, cleaning his brushes. "Now go get that role, honey."

When Harry Feltheimer saw all the actress's tests in his private screening room, there was no contest.

"A pretty girl has been made ravishing by the magic of makeup and the camera. We've found our Regina," he crowed. "That Vickie gal looks gorgeous, and she can *almost* act. We'll sign her to a seven-year deal."

"I think she could be a star, Boss," said casting director number one. "She's got that star quality."

"Yeah, but you know what they say," sighed Harry. "When you create a star, you create a monster. Keep cutting her down to size, Barry. Make her lose a few more pounds too. But *not* off her tits. Those we like."

Chapter Seventeen
1940–1943

The Devil's Daughter started principal photography in June of 1940. A roistering seventeenth-century period romp, it was an overnight box-office hit and instantly turned Vickie into a major pinup girl. But before the film was released the studio publicity genius, Russell Bane, decided to change her name. "Vickie Gordon," he said. "It's perfect for you."

"But I like my name," said Vickie. "What's wrong with 'Victoria Swann'?"

"Too prim and proper; positively Victorian," said Bane brusquely. " 'Vickie Gordon' will look better on a marquee." He promptly set to work filling the pages of magazines and newspapers with glamorous and titillating photos of Vickie Gordon, for it was essential the public knew her name before the film was released.

When Vickie wasn't filming or fitting the endless costumes needed for her follow-up movie, *Manhattan Magic*, she was constantly in the stills gallery. Paradigm made sure they had hundreds of sexy images to flood the media, and Vickie's fan mail soon swamped the studio. Within a few months she was receiving more than anyone else there.

"Beauty is youth, and youth beauty, and the only way to happiness is through illusion," mused Dan Peters, Paradigm's ace photographer, as he inspected Vickie's image through his viewfinder. "The boss is right — she's got it all, this kid."

"When you're on the screen, honey, no matter who you're with or what you're doing, the audience could only look at you — that's star quality," elaborated Dan.

Vickie smiled softly. "It's not something I can take credit for, Dan. I guess it's in my genes."

But success came with a price. Vickie was the classic slender but curvy 1940s siren, completely the opposite of her mother, who had striven for the androgynous small-bosomed look of the 1920s and 1930s. Both women symbolized the ideal female type of their era, and both women found stardom because of their looks.

For Vickie, who was fond of food, being beautiful and photogenic entailed a strict diet. With the help of the green Dexedrine pills that Dr. Sandler insisted she take every morning, and a diet that consisted mainly of cottage cheese, carrots, and lean chicken,

Vickie was able to stay at the ideal weight the studio wanted her to be. Often at night she was so hungry she found it hard to sleep, but Dr. Sandler solved that problem too with the little orange Seconal sleeping tablets he prescribed.

Soon every woman wanted to look like Vickie Gordon, while to every man she was the quintessential love goddess.

Unfortunately, there was one man to whom she wasn't.

Vickie knelt on the sand, her tight white satin two-piece bathing suit accentuating her lush body, her gorgeous red-gold hair flowing around honey-colored shoulders.

She gazed up at Cooper pleadingly. "But why, Cooper, why? Why can't you leave your wife?"

"That's something I told you I'll never discuss." He looked out to sea, a cigar clamped in his mouth, his eyes cold. "We're not going to discuss it, Vickie, so don't go on about it."

He unscrewed a small silver cup from a leather hip flask, poured whisky into it, and swallowed it in one gulp, still staring at the Malibu ocean, which was looking as cold and gray as he felt. Vickie willed Cooper to look at her. His look was like a touch, how could he resist her? She was gorgeous — even she knew it now, desired by every man she met and worshiped by the fans. In two years she had gone from being a plump, shy nonentity to a ravishingly sexy golden girl of the screen, heralded as the "Goddess of Desire." Vickie shivered as a cloud covered the sun and a tear trickled down one perfect cheekbone.

It didn't matter to Vickie that to millions of men she was their ultimate fantasy. Her ultimate fantasy was Cooper Hudson. How could he not commit himself to her?

"Don't you love me anymore?" As she spoke she knew she sounded trite and stupid, but since meeting Cooper she had not been able to think of any other man. Although much of the time he'd been on location in Africa or the South Pacific making the macho adventure movies cinema-goers adored, their trysts in his dressing room had continued regularly. Now he was back, and they'd spent a passionate weekend together at a friend's beach house.

"It's been two years now, Cooper. I don't think I can go on like this. It's not fair." Her beautiful eyes were pleading, but her actor's inner voice told her she sounded whiny and much too needy. But she *was* needy. She needed him. She lived for him.

"You're right, Vickie, it's not. It's not fair to any of us — least of all Irene."

"Irene." Vickie almost spat the name. "Irene will be fine, just fine. You don't love her, you know you don't. You love *me*. You told me you love me. You'll give her the house and money, she'll be OK."

"Vickie, Vickie, Vickie — just shut the fuck up, will you, you sound like a spoiled child."

He turned to look at her, and she saw rage and pain in his eyes.

"Don't try and run my life for me, babe — just don't."

"I'm not trying to run your life. I've been patient — but, Coop, how long am I expected to wait?"

"What are you waiting for?" His tone was cold. "What, Vickie?"

"I — I'm waiting for you, Coop."

"You've *got* me, babe. You know how much I love you — how I love making love to you."

Vickie felt another chill.

"I mean marriage — babies," she said softly.

"The whole ball of wax?" He sounded sarcastic. "That's not going to happen, Vickie — I told you when we started this thing — I'm *not* leaving my wife."

"But you don't sleep with her." Vickie felt as though she was sinking through quicksand. The man she worshiped was slipping away from her, and all of her beauty and fame couldn't prevent it.

"So?" he looked at her with a puzzled frown. "Sex is just sex, Vickie. Marriage is for life."

230

"I know, Coop." She knew the reasons, and she knew there was nothing she could do to change his mind. Having been brought up in the Catholic faith herself, Vickie knew all about the potential for guilt that came with that territory. Cooper was a staunch believer, a devout Catholic who tried in his own way to be true to his church. Vickie wasn't. She said her prayers, but she was not at all devout. Nevertheless she realized Cooper's dilemma and empathized with it.

"Life," she whispered. "How can you think that, Coop? You know you're not happy."

"Who says so?" he barked. "Who are you to tell me if I'm happy or not?" He threw back his head and tipped more whisky down.

"You're just a kid, Vic — you're twenty-two, you've got your life ahead of you. I'm thirty-seven. I made my marital bed fifteen years ago and now I'm lying in it, and no one, *no one,* not you or the studio is gonna tell me what to do. I'm *not leaving* Irene and that's it, otherwise we'll forget the whole thing. Can you live with that?"

Tears streamed down Vickie's face. "I don't know. I'll try, but I just don't know if I can."

That night they made love as if it were their last time, giving each other more sexual pleasure than they ever had before.

"You're mine, Vickie," he whispered to her, as they lay entwined together. "Aren't you, babe?"

"Yes," she whispered as she kissed her way down his chest and stomach, and further until she could taste herself on him. How could she possibly give him up? How could she? But self-preservation is a force almost stronger than love, and Vickie knew she had to. There had been too many sleepless nights, too much sobbing into her pillow. So much so that sometimes Susie would come knocking on the door to see if she was all right. It was all too clear she must end their affair. Besides, he was going on location again to Ireland next week for at least three months. She had to get over Cooper Hudson by whatever means possible. The dark stone wall of their future loomed before her; an image that wasn't inviting.

In 1941 London was ravaged by the Blitz, the Japanese bombed Pearl Harbor, America went to war, and Vickie Gordon became the troops' number-one pinup girl. No one was more thrilled with her success than Susie and her stepfather.

"She is the most beautiful girl in the world," Marco said to Susie, admiring Vickie in a slinky emerald gown, smoldering on the cover of *Look* magazine.

"And she gets more covers than any of the other glamour girls," said Susie proudly. "Betty, Rita, and Veronica are all quite jealous, they say."

All the studios had their reigning sex symbols, and photos of them adorned the lockers and walls of servicemen everywhere. Fox had Betty Grable — the cute blonde girl next door; Columbia had Rita Hayworth — the love goddess who oozed sophisticated allure; Warner's had Ann Sheridan — the Oomph Girl; and Paramount had Veronica Lake — she of the peekaboo blonde hairstyle. But none of them came close to Vickie Gordon's sizzling sexuality, on or off the screen.

The boys on active duty, and the public too, were in need of diversion and titillation, and they ate up the sanitized, overly glamorized, and heavily retouched photographs of Betty, Rita, and especially Vickie that were released by their studios. Hollywood kept the thousands of young GIs — away from home for the first time — well supplied with posters and glossy signed 8x10s of their favorite pinups.

The studios vied with one another to parade their "cheesecake" stars, dressed in the most provocative and revealing outfits possible, in the media. The most popular costumes with the boys were tight bathing suits, which showed plenty of leg, bared the midriff, and accentuated the actresses' more intimate parts. The swimming pool was considered the symbol of the utmost luxury, as much a part of the Hollywood glamour image as fast cars and gorgeous clothes, so all of the stars were constantly photographed in or around their swimming pools, and none more so than Vickie. The studio put her into the sexiest and smallest of swimsuits, some of which became almost completely transparent when wet, leaving little to the imagination of the GIs who clamored for more of her. The fewer clothes she wore, the more they wanted to see her, so she was often pictured in and around a variety of swimming pools in a variety of ever-scantier swimsuits. The golden open spaces and climate of California gave a fascinating glimpse of wealth, luxury, and hedonism to a watching world going through the horrors of war.

Although there was tremendous rivalry between the studio publicity honchos to get the maximum exposure for their stars, by 1942 there was no contest as Vickie Gordon was voted "The Girl We'd Most Like to Bring Home to Mom," "Miss Cheesecake of 1942," and "The Most Beautiful Creature in the World." Russell Bane and his cohorts at Paradigm burned the midnight oil dreaming up more and more fanciful epithets and accolades to heap upon their shiniest star.

Vickie made nine movies between 1941 and 1943, each one of which had a more outrageously frothy plot than the last. In all her movies she wore exquisite costumes, as daring as the censors would allow, yet she had a wholesomeness about her that allowed the audience to see the vulnerability that lurked behind the pancake and mascara.

But the public never knew about Vickie's illicit and often adulterous affairs. To ease her pain after she broke up with Cooper, Vickie embarked on a series of torrid romances with many of her leading men, most of whom were married. These affairs were guarded closely by the studio's publicity people, who made her publicly date several of the young contract boys. The studios spent thousands of dollars in "hush" money each year to make sure their stars' private-life skeletons stayed firmly in the closet. It was a given that most married actors playing opposite a woman as appealing as Vickie would fall for her. As long as the liaisons didn't hit the print, the studios turned their collective backs.

"You're more gorgeous than your mother ever was." Marco watched Vickie swinging idly in a hammock, deep in thought.

"Thanks, Marco." Through Vickie's half-closed eyes she could see him touching himself through the pocket of his trousers. He was so aroused by the sight of this young Aphrodite, whom he'd known since she was a child, that he went to relieve himself with his current mistress, who was in the bedroom reading movie magazines.

Vickie smiled when Marco left. She knew

the effect she had on him — had on all men — without even trying. And when she did try — watch out. Vickie had the gift of making every man she was out to catch feel like the most wonderful, important man in the world. She knew now that giving love unreservedly meant that she would be loved in return, and when she wanted a man, any man, she conquered him. In Vickie's mind, sex equaled love, so she constantly searched for real love in all her romantic liaisons.

Vickie had bought a sprawling Italian-style mansion in the flats of Beverly Hills. It was conveniently located for Paradigm Studios on Pico Boulevard, and accessible enough for Vickie to entertain her lovers discreetly. If Susie or Marco knew about Vickie's many gentlemen callers, they were smart enough to keep their mouths shut. Susie worshiped the beautiful star, and Marco had a blind spot where his stepdaughter was concerned. Since she had become such a huge star, Vickie had decided that she was going to behave like one. To forget Cooper she was on the town every night, dancing, and drinking at Ciro's and Mocombo; dining at Romanoff's, Chasen's, and The Brown Derby; partying every weekend at the beach or in movie moguls' houses with Tyrone Power, Judy Garland, Cary Grant, Humphrey Bogart, and Frank Sinatra.

"I'll be every inch a movie star and *ev-*

eryone, from the cop at the gate to Harry Feltheimer, is going to know it," she'd told Susie.

Susie just smiled and went along with Vickie's whims. She realized that all her lovers were just an unsatisfactory substitute for Cooper. She knew that Vickie's excesses and indulgences were only a cover-up for the deep need she had to be loved. And she knew too that however many men wooed her, however much fan mail Vickie received or however many magazine covers she was on, she would have traded it all to be Mrs. Cooper Hudson.

Excess became Vickie's rule of conduct as she indulged herself recklessly and relentlessly. Paradigm was paying her a fair, but not excessive, $15,000 a week and she spent every cent. Her house was decorated at enormous expense by the fashionable interior designer Elsie de Wolfe, who flew in from New York to design the glamorously mirrored white and silver living room. Vickie's closet took up the space of three rooms, overflowing with enough clothes to stock Saks Fifth Avenue. She had five hundred pairs of shoes; fifteen fur coats — everything from squirrel to ermine — and hundreds of suits and dresses. She worked, she shopped, she dated and partied. She was the life and soul of every party, but however many men made love to her she never could quite get Cooper Hudson out of her mind.

One evening, at the height of the war, Vickie, along with Betty Grable, Paulette Goddard, and John Garfield, was helping out at the Hollywood canteen. The Hollywood canteen had been founded by Bette Davis and Garfield, among others, and took its inspiration from Broadway's Stage Door canteen. It was open only to servicemen, the food was free and plentiful, and many of Hollywood's biggest names provided the entertainment and helped out with the catering. Sometimes Vickie danced with the men, sometimes she served them hamburgers and hot dogs, and sometimes she sold her kisses, which were much in demand.

Vickie was serving coffee behind the snack bar when a young marine came up to her.

"I don't believe it," he said, disbelief written all over his face.

"What don't you believe?" Vickie asked.

"That I'm seeing you! Maybe this sounds silly, but I only got in a couple of days ago, and I was pretty thrilled, especially as I was coming from overseas. Hollywood is something wonderful to us fellows, and I've been looking for something wonderful to happen, but nothing has — until now. The guys told me about this place. One guy said I'd see movie stars, and another guy said, 'Nah, nobody shows up,' and I walk in and there you are. And now, well, now here I am talking to you, Vickie Gordon. Wow! Your picture's getting me through the war." He flushed, conscious of having been carried away. "I hope you don't mind. What I'm trying to say is — on account of seeing you, Hollywood hasn't let me down."

Vickie smiled. The boy symbolized the feelings of many young servicemen. "Why should I mind?" she said gently. "You've said some really nice things, and that makes me feel good. You and your buddies are why I come to the canteen every Tuesday night."

She gave him a hug, then went over to the Kiss Booth and started selling her kisses for twenty-five cents each. Suddenly she was tapped on the shoulder and turned to meet the quizzical black eyes of Cooper Hudson.

"Hey there, beauty. How much for a kiss?" He grinned.

"A quarter each, but for you free," she said huskily. All thoughts of the pain, rejection, and yearning she'd harbored for so long were swept away as Vickie allowed herself to be pulled into Cooper's embrace and engaged in a deep erotic kiss. It was Vickie who broke away first, standing back to examine the gold leaves on Cooper's collar.

"You joined up," she said breathlessly, her heartbeat accelerating as it always had when she was close to him.

"Yup. Lieutenant-Colonel Cooper Hudson of the United States Air Force at your service, ma'am."

"Hey, Colonel, it's my turn now." A cheeky young army sergeant stood behind Cooper, throwing his quarter for Vickie's kiss up and down in his hand and eyeing her cleavage eagerly.

"I won't pull rank on you, Sergeant, but I paid for two kisses," Cooper said, and pulling Vickie toward him kissed her again. Then he drew back and whispered, "Will you join me for a drink after your kissathon?"

"Sure." Vickie could barely speak. Cooper looked devastatingly handsome in his blue-gray air force uniform, which accentuated his broad shoulders and narrow hips. How was it possible to become even more attracted to a person four years after they'd met? She smiled, watching as he sauntered away, then endured the clumsy embraces of the young sergeant and dozens more soldiers, sailors, and marines until her stint was up, and she conceded her spot to vivacious Paulette Goddard.

Cooper sat in a corner booth in the crowded bar, his usual glass of single malt in front of him, a cigar clamped between his teeth. He stood up, smiling appreciatively, as Vickie approached the table, his eyes crinkling in that old familiar way.

"You look good enough to eat," he twinkled. Vickie was glad she'd made a particular effort that evening. Her emerald satin cocktail dress was deliciously décolleté and cinched tightly to show off her tiny waist. Her auburn-red curls were swept up at each side of her head with fresh gardenias and tumbled provocatively on to her forehead and shoulders. She had applied Jungle Gardenia scent liberally to her neck and shoulders, and a fresh coating of lipstick accentuated her lush lips.

"What'll it be?" Cooper signaled to the geriatric waiter, who came stumbling over. Cooper was the kind of man whom other men loved to serve, and in uniform he was even more of a hero.

"Martini, please."

"And another Glenlivet." He sat back and surveyed her. "So my dear, you have become the toast of the armed forces. Everywhere I've been all I hear is Vickie, Vickie, Vickie. How does it feel to be the Forces' Favorite?"

"You should know, Coop; you've been at the top of the heap for a lot longer than I have."

He laughed. "I know, babe, I know, but I'd give it all up now, just to be able to serve in this goddamned war."

"Why can't you serve, and how come you're wearing a uniform then?" inquired Vickie.

"Baby, I'm pushing forty, that's ancient for

241

the military — and for the movies too, I'm afraid. But I'm doing my bit for the war effort. Propaganda, baby — I've been visiting bases all over Europe, giving pep talks, building up morale for those kids, and entertaining them with tales of Hollywood. Jesus!" He shook his head sadly. "I've seen some bad things, Vickie, real bad."

"Tell me." She saw intense sadness in his eyes and couldn't stop her hand from covering his. "Tell me everything, Coop."

They sat in the bar drinking and holding hands while he told her what he'd seen behind the enemy lines.

"Don't ever let anyone tell you war is glamorous, baby." Cooper downed his Glenlivet and signaled for another. "That's just in an Errol Flynn picture. War's the fucking pits." Coop was pretty loaded, Vickie could see that, but even drunk and slurring his words he was still the most charismatic man she'd ever known. They were almost the last people there. The lights were low, and Glenn Miller's "Moonlight Serenade" was playing. He took her in his arms; they danced so closely and he held her so tenderly that she knew she was starting to melt.

"Vickie, oh Vickie." His face was buried in her neck, and he could smell her freshly washed hair and the scent of gardenia. "You know I've always loved you, don't you, babe?"

242

Vickie caught her breath. "Then why?" she whispered. "Why have we wasted all this time? Why can't we be together — for good?"

"Ssh, baby, ssh — you know why, Vickie. You've always known."

"Yes," she said sadly, "I know, Coop." His body was so close to hers, so warm and comforting. Why did she always feel she was in a safe harbor when she was with him, when all he ever did was leave her, over and over again? But tonight it didn't matter anymore. Tonight he would be hers once again.

He was leaving for England the next morning, where he would be stationed until the end of the war.

"When do you think it's going to end?" she asked tentatively, as she lay in his arms in the moonlight, luxuriating in the heat of his body next to hers.

"Who knows? Get on with your life, Vickie, please. Don't wait for me. I'm no good for you, baby."

"Whatever you say, Coop." Vickie, stroking his hair and knowing she could never love anyone as much as she loved him, murmured again, "Whatever you say."

Vickie knew exactly when Cooper Hudson returned from leave; the hour, the date, even who picked him up at the airport. Although

243

desperate to see him again, a smart part of her brain said she shouldn't that night. She accepted an invitation to a party at Jack Warner's house instead. Jack was one of the brothers who ran the eponymous studio and his lavish parties were legendary, so Vickie had dressed to impress. A one-shouldered sea-green chiffon gown draped across her bosom and hips accentuated her luscious curves. Her hair was a luxurious mass of curls. Her emerald and diamond earrings were from Harry Winston, and she looked exactly what she was, a glamorous movie star at the peak of her form.

The Warner house was sumptuously decorated, and the magnificent marquee erected over the giant swimming pool was covered in white raw silk and sprinkled with thousands of tiny stars. The party was to celebrate the Warners' wedding anniversary, and no expense had been spared. Of course it would be paid for by his studio in any case — the cost added to the budgets of the three movies currently shooting.

Everyone hot in Hollywood was there, milling about sipping cocktails or vintage Krug and nibbling on quails' eggs, smoked salmon delicacies, and tiny potatoes stuffed with beluga.

They were all talking shop. Despite the war still raging in Europe and the South Pacific, austerity wasn't allowed to affect Hollywood's elite. As Ginger Rogers chatted to Fred Astaire about their latest pairing, Barbara Stanwyck tried to persuade Jack Warner to give her the lead in *Casablanca* opposite Humphrey Bogart. Greer Garson and Ronald Colman were congratulating each other on the success of *Random Harvest.* Every man and woman present was elegant and groomed to perfection — none more so than Cooper Hudson.

Vickie was at the opposite side of the hallway chatting to Darryl Zanuck, the tiny cigar-chewing boss of Fox, when she spotted Cooper. She hadn't seen him for almost four months, and her stomach lurched with a mixture of pleasure and amazement he was back from England, but what amazed her most was the sight of his wife.

Irene Hudson was ten years older than her husband, and she had done little to erase the ravages of time or pain, either sartorially or cosmetically. Not only was she crippled — she was holding herself up by a crutch — but her fingers were wizened from arthritis. One tortured hand held on to Cooper's immaculate arm like a bird clinging to its nest. As for Cooper, he was solicitous, taking Irene's crutch as he helped her into a chair, bending to whisper something in her ear that made her smile, and feeding her a canapé. He almost danced attendance on her, and Vickie felt faint with jealousy. *This* was her rival? Why did Cooper stay with this poor old woman?

As if answering her question Zanuck, who had been exploring Vickie's cleavage with his eyes, looked over at the Hudsons and said in his high Nebraska twang, "I don't get it either, Toots. No one does."

"What do people say?" Vickie asked idly, not wanting to arouse Zanuck's suspicions. Cooper was one of the few men she hadn't been linked to in the press, and she preferred to keep it that way.

"Irene's a Catholic too, of course — 'til death us do part, all that crap. I guess it happened because of the kid."

"What kid?"

"They had a baby — oh, must be almost fourteen years ago now. Irene was in labor for a couple of days. The doc was a quack — what the fuck they were doing using him I don't know. Anyway, eventually they had to use forceps. The result was . . ." Zanuck shrugged and glanced over again at Irene. "The doc hit a nerve or something and crippled her, and the kid was born so badly deformed that they had to put him in a home right away."

"Is he still there?"

"So they say. Apparently Irene visits him every week with the rosaries and the prayers — all that stuff that keeps you going, I guess."

246

"So that's it," Vickie whispered.

"They say that's the reason Coop stays," said Zanuck. "She's got him by the short and curlies. He ain't ever gonna leave that woman."

Vickie stared at the man she loved and felt a wave of sympathy.

"I've never seen them out together before. He usually leaves her at home," said Zanuck. "The studio won't let him bring her to public functions. Russell's done everything he can to hush it up. I guess Coop's kinda ashamed of her." Zanuck grinned, revealing the gap in his teeth, and turned his interest back to Vickie. "Now, honey, we've got a movie that Fox is *dying* for you to do, but that bastard Harry Feltheimer won't loan you out. It's called *Laura*. It's a great book, it's gonna be a blockbuster."

"I'd love to do it, Darryl. I adored the book," said Vickie vaguely. "I'll talk to Harry about it." She moved away from him, and Cooper. She didn't want to bump into Cooper, and she hoped they weren't seated at the same table.

Her date, Mike McKay, a super-cool macho actor, caught up with her. "Hey sweetie, thought I'd lost you. Everything OK?"

"Sure, Mike, sure." She clung to his well-muscled arm and thought maybe it was time to accept his proposal. Mike had left and

247

subsequently divorced his wife for her, hadn't he? Their sex life was terrific, he told her he loved her, and she told him she loved him back. So why not marry him? That should kill Cooper's ghost for good, and then she could have a baby. A child she would love and nurture like she herself never had been by her own mother.

Just as these thoughts were crystallizing in her mind she caught Cooper's eye at the next table. He gave a sad little smile, as one would give to an acquaintance, then went to help his wife into her chair. Vickie felt as though she'd been stabbed in the stomach and turned to look at Mike, who bestowed upon her a rare smile. On screen and off Mike was so cool that a smile was a rare event. It lit up his face and made him look completely adorable, like a naughty little boy. It was time to expunge Cooper for good. She had to.

Vickie Gordon and Mike McKay eloped to Las Vegas and spent their honeymoon weekend in a lavish suite at Beldon Katleman's brand-new hotel, El Rancho. Only Marco and Susie came to the wedding, as Mike's family had disowned him during his rebel years. His best friend and stunt man, Burt Johnstone, couldn't make it either, as he was in Cedars Sinai recovering from a broken leg and five smashed ribs that he had sustained while doubling for Mike.

Mike always played by his own rules and often did his own stunts unless the studio put its foot down. He was his own man, and his crystal blue eyes, overt sexuality, and he-man looks had made him one of Hollywood's most bankable and popular young stars.

Mike McKay answered to no one, which Vickie had found appealing, but not on their honeymoon night. After a fleeting but fabulous fuck, Mike threw on jeans and a T-shirt and sauntered out of their bedroom with a casual, "See you later, babe, I'm gonna hit the tables."

Vickie was outraged. "You can't leave me now, Mike." His lovemaking had been fast and proficient, but Vickie wanted cuddles, closeness, and pillow talk. Wasn't that what a honeymoon was supposed to be? "It's our wedding night."

"Sorry, babe, feel a lucky streak comin' on. Gotta follow it. Won't be long." He gave her a perfunctory kiss, and then he was out of the door, leaving Vickie seething until dawn crept through the chinks in the curtains and she finally fell asleep. When Mike ambled back in at noon he was much the worse for wear, but more than ready for some action. "C'mon, babe," he mumbled, grabbing her. "Let's have some more honeymoon fun."

"Oh no you won't," said Vickie, sliding out of bed.

"Oh yes I will." Mike grabbed her silk

nightgown and pulled her back. A simple man at heart, he was accustomed to getting what he wanted when he wanted it, and right now he wanted Vickie.

"Get *off* me, you drunk!" yelled Vickie, wriggling away from him, as he ripped her nightgown off her and threw it on the floor.

"Oh, drunk am I? Hey, *hey* baby, jus' look here what I've got for you." He pulled out wads of $100 bills from his jeans pockets. "Not bad going for a drunk, baby, and it's all for you, so c'mere and give me a kiss." He grasped her shoulders and, breathing heavily, started kissing her with fetid breath. "You can pretend to be my little whore, baby. C'mon, babe, let's fuck."

Vickie tried to pull him off her, grabbing a handful of his hair, but it was cut so short that she couldn't get a hold of it. Then Mike pinned her to the bed, his bloodshot eyes crinkling in his deeply tanned face. The smell of sweat and beer, and his fantasy that she was his whore, repelled her. She tried to fight him off, but what Vickie wanted was unimportant to Mike. As Hollywood's number-one action hero he was immensely strong and spent so much time exercising in the gym, riding his motorcycle, or doing one-armed push-ups with his stuntmen cronies that he was a mass of muscle. Vickie's attempts to stop him amused him and only aroused him more.

"Stay *real* still, babe, 'cos I'm gonna fuck you like you've never been fucked before."

"Like hell you are." Vickie was incandescent with rage. "This is *rape*," she yelled.

"Can't be rape, babe. You're my wife now — my property. I can have you whenever I want, whether you like it or not, and you'd better get used to it. So, shut the fuck up, sweetie, or I may have to slap that pretty little face around."

"You're disgusting," Vickie subsided furiously, but Mike didn't. After another brief sexual joust, in which his only aim was self-fulfillment, he went to sleep immediately. As soon as he started snoring Vickie got up and packed, took the next plane to L.A., and went straight to her lawyer's office. The marriage was annulled the following week. And that was the end of husband number one.

Chapter Eighteen
1943–1947

During the war, a photograph of Vickie in a tight red bathing suit, standing on a beach with her hands on her hips, a tantalizing come-hither look in her eyes, and her wind-swept hair blowing in the wind, was such a blockbuster that Paradigm couldn't send out enough copies to the clamoring troops. But the pressure to look perfect all the time was huge. Contractually Vickie was not allowed to even go out of her front door unless she was fully made up and coiffed, albeit by her own hand, and wearing dungarees or slacks in public was absolutely forbidden.

"You're a star and you'd better look like a star all the time," said Russell Bane. "That's what the fans want and just remember, honey, there's always some little gal coming up behind you, so you'd better keep your eye on the ball."

After her annulment from Mike McKay, Vickie was free but she still wasn't happy. She went from one picture to another, the merry-go-round only slowing down for her to indulge in another complicated romance. It wasn't enough for Vickie that the young actors and businessmen she dated often fell in love with her — her quest was for the elusive love of married men. In some way, each time a married actor fell for her and wanted to leave his wife for her, it was as if she was paying Cooper back for the pain he'd caused her and the fact he wasn't going to leave Irene.

In the twenty-two movies Vickie starred in between 1941 and 1947, three of her costars left their wives for her and one, after begging her to marry him, hanged himself when she refused. But none of them touched her like Cooper had, even though her lovers tried hard to please her and the act of love itself was often pleasurable. Cooper had been an amatory teacher par excellence, and Vickie's reputation as a *grande horizontale* had Hollywood insiders buzzing.

When the studio sent Vickie to New York on a promotional tour for *What Price Beauty?* she was delighted to be back in Manhattan again and threw herself into the publicity grind with gusto. She gossiped with Walter Winchell on his top-rated radio show, which had several million listeners; was interviewed by a sympathetic Dorothy Killgallen for the *Journal-American*; photographed for *Life* magazine by Robert Capa and *Look* by Helmut Newton; and partied with Manhattan café society.

Marco took her to lunch at the Colony. When they entered the luxurious dining room of New York's most exclusive and glossiest restaurant, Marco couldn't help noticing how every pair of eyes swiveled toward them.

"Honey, you sure are the sexiest woman in the world."

"But I don't feel it. I feel about as desirable as a plate of porridge."

Her green diet pills worked so well that she only picked at her Waldorf salad while Marco was impressed to be seated at one of the choicest tables. The instant Sirio the good-looking captain spotted the cinema's reigning sex siren with Marco Novello, he had quickly changed them from Marco's usual back booth to a red plush banquette against the wall in the front dining room. There Vickie Gordon could be admired by the other patrons against a backdrop of stained glass and exotic flowers.

Vickie glanced around the elegant interior. The restaurant was without doubt the most fashionable place in Manhattan — a Mecca for every socialite, business mogul, movie star, and upwardly mobile arriviste and a clubhouse for the older "names"; the Astors, the Vanderbilts, and the Duke and Duchess of Windsor. Crystal chandeliers cast subdued light on the famous faces who sat in recessed alcoves occasionally acknowledging each other's presence with a cool smile or wave.

"This is where the elite meet." Marco grinned knowledgeably. "It's like a club here. They're much more particular here who they let in, than at 21."

"And there seem to be more stars here than at Chasen's and Romanoff's combined," observed Vickie, who was looking particularly ravishing in a fawn Mainbocher suit trimmed with sable collar and cuffs and a tiny veiled hat tilted saucily over one eye. "Look, there's Dietrich and Paulette, and that looks like Stanwyck over there."

"But you're by far the prettiest dame here."

"Oh no, I don't think I can hold a candle to her." Vickie nodded toward a coolly beautiful blonde soigné in a black Hattie Carnegie dress of utter simplicity and a single strand of pearls. "She's ravishing."

"Who, her?" said Marco dismissively. He wasn't partial to cool, laid-back women. "I like a bit of flesh on my women. She's skin and bone."

"That's Babe Paley." Vickie, like many other women, was in awe of this icon. "She's considered to be the best-looking and best-dressed woman in the world."

"So? What's so hot about her? That black dress is nothing to write home about, and I think those three over there are a lot better looking." He gestured to the banquette opposite, where Barbara Hutton, Doris Duke, and Betsy Whitney, drop-dead chic in exquisitely stylish suits, were huddled in a delicious gossip fest.

"Those dames are *real* class."

"I agree, we could all take a lesson in culture and breeding from them."

Vickie sipped her tasty Senegalese soup, then asked, "So, Marco, how's your love life?"

Marco speared a soft-shell crab. "Busy, busy, busy, baby. I'm a busy boy in business and your papa's still got it in the other direction, honey. I've gotta fight those dames off," he boasted.

It amused Vickie that Marco still insisted on calling himself her father. Even though his business life was on the shady side, he had always been good to her and tried to be a father figure. In fact his self-delusion was rather endearing since, having gained quite a bit of weight in his early fifties, Marco was not exactly an Adonis anymore. Vickie knew that the showgirls and models who lived in his penthouse and occasionally shared his bed were mostly good-time girls only in it for the luxurious lifestyle Marco was able to give them.

But Vickie noticed Marco wasn't looking too well. There was a pallor to his normally ruddy cheeks and unhealthy-looking gray circles around his eyes.

"What are those pills you're taking, Marco?"

"For my heart. Had a little heart murmur a couple of months ago, nothin' serious. Doc gave me these pills — told me to take it easy. Ha! Can you imagine Marco Novello taking it easy!"

"No I can't, but maybe you should." Vickie looked concerned as Marco swallowed his pills with a gulp of red wine, and he winked at her. Then his eyes lit up as a swarthy figure, followed by a couple of thuggish-looking goons, swaggered past their table. Marco immediately jumped up and stuck out his hand.

"Frank, hey Frank, it's Marco, long time no see, pal. How're you doin'?"

Frank Costello, the notorious gangster, swept cold eyes over Marco. "Doing great, Marco — who's this lovely lady?"

"My daughter, Vickie Gordon. Vickie, meet Frank Costello."

"Of course, delighted, Miss Gordon." Costello's deep voice held the faintest hint of menace. "I like your movies."

Vickie shook the hoodlum's proffered hand. He had overdone the expensive cologne, but he was beautifully dressed and impeccably groomed. This man was one of the most feared mobsters in America, but his aura of respectability seemed to negate his villainy. Certainly the waiters and maître d' couldn't stop fawning all over him, and every conversation in the room had ceased when he entered.

Costello smiled faintly at Vickie, then moved on to his booth. Marco sat down with a pleased smirk.

"Great guy, Frank, great guy. We go back a long way — we had some real good times."

"I bet," smiled Vickie. "I heard Prohibition was a riot."

As the waiters cleared away the soup course and served them the Colony's world-renowned chicken hash, Vickie confided in her stepfather, who more than anyone seemed to understand her constant search for elusive love.

When she'd finished telling him about her latest abortive affair with a famous leading man, Marco leaned back, lit up a Havana, and said, "The trouble with you, honey, is that you confuse fucking with being in love."

Vickie blushed. "Well, that's certainly calling a spade a spade."

"Listen, I've seen how you behave with guys. I read between the lines in the gossip columns, and you know Susie tells me everything, don't you?"

"I'm a fool as far as men are concerned," Vickie confessed. "I try to be everything to them."

"You just want them to love you, baby. I know, I know. I'm still looking for Mrs. Right myself. I've got a string of broads and I

don't really give a damn about any of them."
He patted her hand, raising himself slightly
out of his chair as Merle Oberon, the quin-
tessence of style in charcoal gray flannel and
fox furs, nodded to them as she was escorted
to her booth. "Beautiful dame, beautiful," he
whispered, gazing after the fabled movie star
admiringly. "Now *there's* a dame who knows
how to get any guy, and she knows just how
to treat 'em too."

"How so?"

"She's a ball breaker, honey. She treats 'em
mean and she keeps 'em keen — know what
I mean? While *you*, my little beauty, lay it on
with a trowel." He paused. "Now, honey, I
don't know how to say this without sounding
crude . . ."

"Be crude, Marco." Vickie toyed with her
food and smiled. "Why change the habits of
a lifetime?"

"Well, you're not at all like your mama."

"In what way?"

"Well to be frank, honey, your mama
wasn't interested in making love."

"Really? I guess some women are like that."

"But — hey." Marco clapped his hand on
Vickie's shoulder. "That was her generation,
honey. Women weren't *supposed* to like it, but
they had to put up with it. Only whores liked
sex, that's the way it was then."

"But this must have affected your marriage,
Marco?"

"Baby, without putting too fine a point on it, I did what lots of guys did, I got it elsewhere — get it?"

"Got it." Vickie was intrigued by Marco's confessions; he usually played his cards close to his chest and rarely spoke of her mother to her.

Marco drained his claret, called for a brandy, then continued. "That didn't stop me lovin' her one bit. In fact, I loved her *more*. Y'see, baby, to men sex is one thing and love is a completely different department. Men love sex, but they don't have to love the gal they're havin' sex with. That's the problem that most women have with men, they think when they're gettin' laid they're gettin' loved. I guess you feel that way too, huh?"

Vickie sighed. "It's always the same, Marco. I actively go out to seduce *them*. I seduce them with total attentiveness. I make them feel like they're the greatest, most special guy in the world — so naturally they fall in love with me."

"And then?" Marco surveyed her through a haze of cigar smoke, his eyes narrowed. "Y'know, even if you think you're getting what you want, you're not, Vickie."

Vickie shrugged. "Please don't be shocked, Marco. You see, unlike my mother I like making love, but to enjoy it I have to feel I'm *in* love, and then I get hooked."

"So what's wrong with hooked?"

"Hooked on the sex, which I *think* is love. It's kind of stupid, don't you think? But of course sex usually wears off." She sighed and lit a Camel. "Three times a day becomes twice a day, then once, and then after several months it's down to once or twice a week — just like an old married couple — and the romance starts to fade."

She smiled ruefully, unable to meet Marco's frank stare.

"But that's typical, honey. That's the way guys are."

"Is it me or is it men, Marco? Because when I get into bed at night and I want to be loved, if they decide that they want to read or listen to Jack Benny, I feel rejected."

"Well you shouldn't, baby. That's the nature of the beast. It doesn't mean they don't love you, hon, but it, er, it takes a lot of energy to, er, you know, er . . ." He looked embarrassed and Vickie patted his hand and smiled.

"I understand what you're getting at."

"If the guy feels secure with a gal and comfortable, he doesn't need to prove it all the time like he did in the early days."

"You are a wise old owl, Marco. But I definitely think I have a big problem. It's Cooper. I still love him and that's *crazy*. It's insane. Maybe I should see a shrink." She sipped her martini.

"Don't say that, baby."

"Psychoanalysts are all the rage in Hollywood these days, lots of my friends are going and they say it helps. Not that I've seen any difference. They're all still crazy," she laughed.

"Well, you don't need a shrink, honey. What you need is to forget Cooper, for Chrissake. Find a really good man next time round, and realize that he can love you plenty, even if he doesn't jump you all the time." A spasm of pain crossed Marco's face as he signaled to the waiter for the check. "C'mon let's go, kiddo," he said. "End of lecture. Let's go shopping."

"Thanks, Marco." She kissed his cheek. "You give good advice."

As they stood on the corner of Madison and Sixty-first Street, Marco started rubbing his left arm, then, his face suddenly turned ashen. He leaned against the railings for support. "Hey, honey," he slurred. "I don't feel so good — let's catch a cab and get the hell outta here."

Suddenly he slumped to the pavement, with a sickening crash, his mouth fell open, and his eyes rolled back in his head. As Vickie bent over him she knew immediately that Marco Novello was dead, and her screams echoed down the cold canyons of Madison Avenue.

Chapter Nineteen
1948–1950

As her films deteriorated into frivolous crowd pleasers, Vickie's love life became more frenetic. Her public epithets "The Sexiest Woman in the World," "The Goddess of Desire," "The Woman No Man Can Resist" had certainly held true throughout the war. Vickie's beauty had seemed indestructible as she went from man to man, from party to party, and from picture to picture.

When she began to gain weight the studio put her on a stricter diet and gave her even stronger pills to quell her appetite, and when the pills kept her awake at night, Dr. Sandler prescribed even more powerful doses of sleeping tablets. Soon Vickie was drinking too much, popping too many pills, and still looking for love in all the wrong places.

Then, when she was simultaneously involved with three different men, Vickie discovered she was pregnant. At first she was thrilled, but when the reality of having a fatherless child hit her she became totally distraught. As much as she had fantasized about having a baby, it was too terrifying to contemplate.

"So who's the father?" asked Susie as they sat in the breakfast nook while Vickie ate her minuscule portion of cottage cheese and grapefruit.

"Would it horrify you if I told you I didn't know?" Vickie spooned some cottage cheese into her mouth and made a face. "This is the most revolting food ever made." She pushed it aside. "It tastes like mush. Can I have some Ritz crackers and cream cheese and strawberry jam, please?" She looked pleadingly at Susie.

"Getting cravings already, are you?" Susie could never refuse her anything, so she brought the goodies to the table and Vickie fell upon them with gusto.

"I feel like I haven't eaten in a year," she said as she spread cream cheese thickly onto the crackers and dolloped large spoonfuls of jam on top.

"I guess the diet pills aren't working then?" asked Susie.

"I stopped taking them yesterday."

"I see." Susie sipped her strong English tea and regarded Vickie with her stern nanny look.

"Well, you know what'll happen, Vickie. You'll gain ten pounds in a month and the studio will have a fit."

"Oh hell, I was only thinking of the baby. Screw the studio," said Vickie bravely. Then she subsided again, looking scared.

"Oh God, what am I going to *do*, Susie? I was always so careful. My damn diaphragm must have had a hole in it."

"Are you going to tell any of these men what's happened?"

"Are you kidding? Gary and Gene are married, and besides I don't love them." Vickie sighed. "As for that young assistant director, I hardly think he's in the position to support a kid."

"Well, let's face it, you can't have a baby without a father," said Susie pragmatically. "It'll be the biggest scandal to hit this town since Fatty Arbuckle killed that starlet with the wine bottle."

"Loretta Young managed it," mused Vickie, locking her fingers under her chin and staring out at her lush green lawn. "She and Gable had an affair on location, and she went missing for a few months and then adopted a little girl."

"Sure, but at least she *knew* who the daddy was and Loretta's a devout Catholic. We know you're not a devout Catholic, Vickie."

"True. I'm not a devout anything — the only thing I seem to be devout about is sleeping with unsuitable guys. Oh hell, Susie, I'd love to have a baby, I want a baby. I'd love it to death, you know I would."

"But you *can't* have this one, sweetheart. Not if you want to continue having a career. This is Hollywood, Vickie, and you're a big movie star. If you do go ahead, then you'd better find a husband real quick."

"No," Vickie shuddered. "I tried marriage with someone I didn't really love — that was a fiasco and a half. There's only one person I could marry." As she turned away, her eyes started to fill with tears.

"Now, now, don't start on *him* again, please dear." Susie passed Vickie the Kleenex. "Lord knows you've been carrying this torch for Cooper for over seven years now. It's about time you let it go out."

"I know." Vickie blew her nose. "But even if Cooper is the only man I'll ever love, I guess I ought to get a hold of myself and find someone suitable anyway. After all, I'm nearly twenty-nine."

"But not yet," said Susie. "You've got a lot of years left to make movies still. Don't waste them. Give it five more years, then start looking for Mr. Right, OK?"

"I guess you're right. I want my child to have her own father, not just a stepfather like I did." Vickie blew her nose again, then brightened. "Do you know I'm the only actress under contract at Paradigm that hasn't had an abortion?"

"Good Lord, how do you know?"

"Oh, the girls talk about it all the time.

The makeup department's a hive of gossip, and you can find out lots of information there about all sorts of things."

"Such as?"

"Such as they say that scientists are working on some sort of pill that women can take every day that will stop them getting pregnant when they don't want to. Wouldn't that be great?"

"I don't believe it," said Susie. "That's impossible, how could it work?"

Vickie shrugged. "No idea, but if it does happen it'll certainly beat that disgusting diaphragm. And another bit of information I discovered is that the man to get rid of unwanted *bambini* is a Dr. Javier Tranusco, and he plies his trade down Mexico way — Tijuana, to be exact."

"Is that where you're thinking of going?" Susie asked quietly.

"Susie, you yourself told me I can't have this baby and, to be perfectly honest, I think the responsibility would overwhelm me. Now I know you'd take care of it, of course you would. But this career's been hard won, and I know a child would destroy it. Plus what do I say when he or she asks me who their real father is?"

Susie crossed herself. "I know it's a sin, my dear, but I'm sure that God will forgive you. It's best, if you don't mind, if you make the arrangements yourself. When I go to confession I don't want to have that on my conscience."

"Of course, I understand." Vickie squeezed Susie's plump arm. "Please don't think I'm being callous, Susie. You don't, do you?"

Susie shook her head. "No, my dear, I don't. You must listen to your heart."

But in the end, Vickie didn't need to go through with the difficult decision. It was taken out of her hands when, a few weeks later, she was devastated by a miscarriage.

By 1950 Vickie Gordon's movies weren't pulling in the punters at the box office as they once had done. She had tried to get more interesting and dignified parts, but to the studio she was just a gorgeous commodity with cleavage and sexy costumes. They didn't want to know about finding serious roles for her. Frothy extravaganzas were becoming démodé. The public wanted to see harsher, reality-based movies and more down-to-earth stars, like Marlon Brando, Robert Mitchum, and Jan Sterling. Movies of the caliber of *Sunset Boulevard* and *The Asphalt Jungle* were what the public flocked to see. Now, with the advent of television, escapist fantasies and musicals could be viewed in the comfort of the home, and movies had to become grittier to offer something different to the cinema-goer. Although Esther Williams still swam in underwater sequences and Gene Kelly and Fred Astaire tap-danced insouciantly together, Hollywood's Golden Age was almost coming to an end. Like every other Hollywood star, Vickie's clout was weighed on the scales of box-office success, where only the grosses of their latest picture proved their worth.

A new young starlet was on the rise, and she was fast overtaking Vickie in the popularity and pinup girl department. At twenty-four, Marilyn Monroe was eight years younger than Vickie and her sexy baby face was irresistible to fans. Several years earlier, Vickie had seen the writing on the wall. The scales were not tipping in her favor.

Vickie met the intellectual screenwriter Charles Anderson at a beach lunch at Elia Kazan's house. Kazan, who would later achieve mass popularity and critical acclaim with the gritty *On the Waterfront*, was considered to be the most talented and brilliant director of the day. Vickie was now desperate to break away from the frothy capers that she was typecast in. Her agent had taken her to the lunch in the hopes that Kazan might be interested in casting her in his next movie. To this end, Vickie had thought long and hard about the right way to look. She didn't want to appear like a Hollywood glamour puss, so she scrubbed her face, pulled her hair back in a chignon, and wore a simple white shirt and trousers. Although Kazan did not seem terribly impressed with her, Charles certainly was.

Charles Anderson had been linked with the notorious Hollywood Ten, a group of actors, directors, and producers blacklisted by the film studios for supposedly being sympathetic to Communism.

In 1947, Anderson, along with novelist Dalton Trumbo, director Edward Dmytryk, screenwriter Ring Lardner, Jr., and six others, were subpoenaed by the House Un-American Activities Committee to answer questions about the Communist influence on the motion picture industry. When Charles and the others refused to answer the questions, citing the First Amendment, Charles was convicted of contempt of Congress, fined $1,000, and jailed for one year in a federal prison. After that he was blacklisted, his passport taken away from him, and he was considered officially unemployable in the States. Unable to get a play produced under his real name, Charles had resorted to the pseudonym Elton Bernshaw.

He was by no means a dreamboat. Shorter than Vickie, he had a chiseled ascetic face, thinning brown hair, and was fifty years old. But his plays were world-renowned and his charm and wit legendary. He was immediately smitten by Vickie as they stood in line at the buffet — relatively simple fare by Hollywood standards. Hot dogs and hamburgers were the order of the day, and the handsome young actor Paul Newman was doing the honors with the salad, mixing it with his own special homemade dressing.

Vickie hugged Paul. A good friend of Kazan's from New York, he was making his first movie, *The Silver Chalice*, at Warner Brothers.

As Charles Anderson greeted him, Newman said, "Vickie, you know Charles Anderson," and Vickie shook the hand of the famous playwright.

"I've always thought you were a much better actress than your material," said Charles.

"You certainly know your way to this actress's heart." She smiled.

"I saw you a couple of years ago in that comedy film you made with Mitchum. It was a complete piece of crap, but you were excellent and charming. You reminded me of a young Lynn Fontanne. Have you ever thought of doing a play in New York?"

"Broadway? Why no. Actually, I think the studio would kill me if I even suggested it. They think of me as their personal and private property — I can't do anything without checking with them."

Vickie considered helping herself to some potato salad but decided against it, as she'd gained a pound last week. In front of the camera, every pound she put on added a year to her face. Charles took her plate and gestured to a small sofa close to the window where they could look out onto the ocean. They sat down and she sipped her wine while he proceeded to analyze her last four movies.

"You have a vulnerable quality that I believe has been obscured by too much cosmetic enhancement and complicated hairstyling." His eyes twinkled behind black-rimmed glasses. "You are a natural beauty and you can act too, so why haven't you tried to get stronger roles — meatier parts? Is it because you're too good-looking? Or are you just lazy?"

"No, it's because I'm a bond slave to my studio. When I started they signed me to a contract with options, and since they kept picking up the options I just went along with it. I guess I am lazy really, but it beats working in a factory."

"Pity," he said. "The play I just wrote that Kim Stanley is starring in now would have been perfect for you."

"I don't think I would know how to move or act on a stage. It's a whole different technique."

"Your mother was on the stage, I seem to remember. It's usually hereditary; I'm sure you'd be wonderful. I'd like to write a play for you."

"You would?" Vickie's eyes sparkled.

"Yes. You'd be magical on stage. You have a voluptuous sensitivity that is intriguing. How long does your contract have to run?"

"Well, I'm starting a new role in a film called *Manhattan Princess* in a few months after I finish the one I'm shooting now." She made a face. "Actually, we're doing some of the locations in New York — I'm amazed, actually. All my films have been made on the studio lot on the cheap, with just a backdrop indicating either Chicago, Acapulco, or Rome."

"Why haven't you gone on location? Other movies do."

"Paradigm doesn't like spending too much money on my kind of film," she said ruefully. "But, however second rate they are, they still seem to make money."

"Yes, the public loves you, but they won't continue to if your films don't improve."

"I've asked for better scripts, better quality material, but they just don't want to know."

"Even though you're such a big star?" He smiled the kind of smile that Vickie had seen a thousand times from men. The smile that told her he was attracted to her, extremely attracted to her. Usually she only liked tall, handsome men, usually actors, but this man seemed to have a lot of integrity. He was so interesting and knowledgeable that he quite fascinated her as he launched into a dissertation on the state of Broadway theater in depth.

"I want to write a play for you," he announced at the end of lunch. "And I know exactly what it's going to be about."

It was a whirlwind courtship. Vickie and Charles met every day at his office on the Paramount lot. He was writing his first screenplay for the studio but, being a multifaceted Gemini man, he seemed able to accomplish two things at once. Vickie was excited about the play and, encouraged by Charles, she started reading voraciously: Henry James, Faulkner, Goethe, and James Joyce. Charles took her to Los Angeles's little theaters to study and learn about stagecraft. She worked with an acting coach on serious pieces like *Medea* and *The Rose Tattoo*, and Charles boosted her ego as he helped and stimulated her.

"He's my first mentor, can you believe it?" Vickie told Susie. "The first man who seems to genuinely care for *me*, the real woman, and not some fantasy goddess."

Because Charles's friends were more bohemian than the Hollywood mob, Vickie took to going around without makeup and in casual clothes — but the studio was far from pleased.

"You look *hideous*," Harry Feltheimer had barked when he'd caught her having lunch with Charles in the commissary, wearing a plaid shirt and dungarees, her face devoid of makeup and her hair scraped back from her face.

"What the *hell* are you thinking about?" Harry had made such a scene that half of the diners stopped eating to listen to him. "Put some paint on and get your hair done. You can't be seen like that. You're a star, for Christ's sake. Try to look like one."

"*This* is the real me," said Vickie boldly.

"The real you doesn't *exist*," replied Harry, lowering his voice. "You're just a bunch of Technicolor images that guys like to drool over. Don't ever forget that, little lady. You let the fans see you looking like this and they'll start turning away from your pictures in droves."

"They have been anyway. My last two pictures have been terrible. That's why the box office has been so bad."

"Or maybe it's because you're getting a little age on you, cupcake. You're not nineteen anymore — thirty-two is getting up there, sugar. The fans like young, fresh meat, like Marilyn."

"Thanks a lot, Harry. You're a real pal."

"Just a little warning," said Harry, walking off. "Lay off the booze too, you're looking bloated."

Charles patted her hand complacently. "Take no notice. His ethics and ideals are as shallow as a puddle of cat piss."

"It's hurtful, but I'm used to it. I'm just a

commodity to them."

"Well, let *me* try and change all that," said Charles.

The next day Vickie was summoned to Feltheimer's office. "You know that guy you're seeing is a Commie, don't you?" Harry snarled.

"What do you mean?" Vickie hedged. She'd heard the rumors, but she and Charles had never discussed it.

"I mean that he was one of those Red bastards our industry tried to get rid of. After the war, your Mr. Anderson refused to testify in the McCarthy hearings. He was working in the theater with the rest of those goddamn Reds and he wriggled out of it in some way, but it didn't ruin his career like it did Larry Parks and Dalton Trumbo. He's bad news, Vickie, we don't want one of our stars involved with a Commie prick like that."

"Oh, for heaven's sake, Harry." Vickie stood up, exasperated. "I'm not a child. I've been under contract to you for nearly twelve years. When are you going to allow me to be myself? To do what I think is right for *me* for a change. I've always been at everyone's beck and call and done what you wanted — acted in cheap froth, and I've never complained. Why don't you give me a decent part — a strong role for a change?"

"Paradigm makes entertainment pictures.

Not bolshie crap like Kazan and Eddie Dmytryk. So you want out of your contract, Vickie? OK. You've had a good run. After *Manhattan Princess* wraps we'll talk."

"Fine with me."

"Hey, you're not thinking of marrying this guy, are you?" Harry's tiny eyes became even narrower.

"As a matter of fact, I am," said Vickie quietly, although until that moment she hadn't really taken Charles's proposals of marriage seriously. He said he was in love with her, but apart from some chaste kisses he hadn't made any kind of pass. Although she didn't find him physically appealing, it was obvious he was falling in love with her.

Anyway, what did sex mean? Relationships built on sex never lasted. As Cooper had said long ago, "Sex is just sex, that's all it is — so enjoy it just for that, baby, and don't expect much more from a guy if you're having great sex with him."

Maybe she should accept. Maybe she could be happy with Charles, even without good sex. He was intelligent and witty, he'd taught her a lot, and he loved children. It was definitely time for her to have a child. At thirty-two her clock was ticking.

That night Vickie accepted Charles's proposal and slept with him for the first time. The earth did not move, but Vickie was beginning to realize that the passionate love-making she had indulged in with her string of lovers had not fulfilled her in the slightest. Cooper — ah, Cooper. Would she ever stop thinking about him? Probably not — Vickie answered her own question. Like the song said, she'd got him under her skin, and she'd just have to live with it.

After Charles and Vickie married, he became totally immersed in his new screenplay, and the play he was writing for her was forgotten. His work became all-consuming, and now that Vickie was his wife she came very much second in his life. Buried in writing and research all day, Charles seemed only perfunctorily interested in Vickie's discussion of her own days at work when she came home at night after shooting *Manhattan Princess.*

Over a period of six months they drifted apart so much that Vickie, still craving permanent love, realized she wasn't going to get it in this relationship. She had hoped to conceive, but that hadn't happened either. She wondered if the miscarriage she'd had three years earlier had ruined her chances of having a child. It was a sobering thought that kept her lying awake at night, along with doubts about her marriage, which seemed barren and empty. Now the sharing side was gone, and the physical side had never been there in the first place. After less than a year, Vickie reluctantly decided to divorce Charles Anderson. And that was the end of husband number two.

Chapter Twenty
1952

In 1952 the studio sent Vickie to London to attend the Royal premiere of *Manhattan Princess*. She stood in the lineup chatting with Dirk Bogarde on her left and John Mills on her right, both leading lights of the British silver screen, waiting to meet the royals.

"I knew your mother, you know," said John. "I was in the chorus of *Hearts Are Trumps* in 1921."

"You must have been thirteen," exclaimed Vickie.

"Around about that age," grinned John. "Your mother was enchanting and so talented. I can see the resemblance."

"I didn't think anyone remembered my mother anymore."

"Oh yes, we old-timers do. Did they ever discover the real reason behind her death?" Vickie shook her head as John said, "Oops, look out, here she comes."

Vickie craned her head to see Princess Margaret Rose, followed by various equerries, walking slowly down the line, shaking hands and chatting with each celebrity. She was a pretty young woman in her early twenties, and when they came face to face Vickie performed a deep and elaborate curtsy as the studio had instructed her to. Was it Vickie's imagination or did a flicker of disapproval cross Margaret Rose's face as she was faced with Vickie's lush *embonpoint*, which was pushed up and displayed like two luscious cupcakes in a shop window?

The princess had little to say to Vickie but a lot to John Mills and Dirk Bogarde. Vickie then greeted a succession of elderly aristocrats and was pleased and surprised to find herself suddenly face to face with a tall, attractive young man who raised her white-gloved hand to his lips, saying, "I'm enchanted to meet you at last, Miss Gordon, I've been a *huge* fan."

Vickie was glad that he didn't mouth the usual empty platitudes that she'd heard too much of in her few days in London. He seemed engagingly down to earth, and his light green eyes and thick black hair were a stunning combination.

"I'm so sorry, I missed the introduction," said Vickie. "Please tell me your name?"

"Sebastian." His smile was enchanting. "Sebastian Swannell, at your service, Miss Gordon."

"Call me Vickie." She smiled into his eyes,

which were almost like a mirror image of her own, for seconds their eyes were locked.

After the premiere Lady Sarah Cranleigh was throwing one of her exclusive parties for the cast. Her magnificent Georgian house in Belgravia was packed with an eclectic mixture of aristocracy, society, and *nouveaux riches*. Artists, film stars, fashion gurus, and fashion victims mixed with politicians and pseudo-intellectuals as two hundred of the most beautiful, notorious, and favored people in London drank, gossiped, and danced the night away. In the enormous oak-paneled reception rooms oil portraits of Lady Sarah's ancestors looked down from the damask-draped walls in silent disapproval.

The two most beautiful people there were, without doubt, Victoria Gordon and Sebastian Swannell. Vickie was wearing a simple white silk dress split to the thigh, which showed off her long tanned legs perfectly. Her thick red-gold hair flowed around her shoulders, and without the studio's usual application of heavy cosmetics her true beauty shone through. Admiring whispers followed her as she drifted around the crowded salon like a gorgeous butterfly.

Sebastian was accompanied to the party by his widowed mother, Rosemary, the Duchess of Burghley, a tall imposing-looking American in her mid-fifties. Vickie had found the duchess's slate-eyed stare and her insistence on the formality of addressing Vickie by her surname, when introduced, slightly disconcerting.

The duchess was intrigued yet puzzled by the younger American woman. There was something strangely familiar about her, but perhaps it was because she was a world-famous movie star. What the duchess was not aware of was the instant attraction that had sprung up between her darkly handsome son and the lovely actress.

At thirty-three Sebastian Swannell, Marquis of Leybourne, the eleventh Duke of Burghley, was one of the most eligible bachelors in England. He had dated a series of eligible girls, from Princess Margaret to the American ambassador's daughter, Sharman Douglas, to the young English actress Jean Simmons, but none of the relationships had been serious.

Watching this vision of desirability, Sebastian was instantly captivated by Vickie, and lost no time in engaging her in conversation. His wide-set eyes sparkled appreciatively into hers and Vickie, equally attracted, flirted with him openly, the rest of the party forgotten. At one o'clock Sebastian drove Vickie to the Dorchester in his Bentley Continental.

"When can I see you again?" he asked with diffident schoolboy charm.

"Tomorrow night is all I have left in London. I've got to leave the next day for L.A."

"Perhaps we could dine together then?"

"I'd love to." Vickie hoped she didn't sound too eager.

"I'll pick you up at eight. I can hardly wait." Vickie turned to Sebastian, expecting him to kiss her, but he brushed her hand with his lips after he escorted her to the revolving door. "Until tomorrow then; the hours will pass too slowly for me."

"I told you to call me Vickie."

It was past midnight, the lights were dim, and the music mellow at the 400, one of London's most exclusive nightclubs.

"Very well, Vickie." The disc jockey was playing "People Will Say We're in Love" from the hit musical *Oklahoma* and on the tiny darkened dance floor Sebastian held her very close to him with the utmost gentleness.

"Don't smile and gaze at me — your eyes are so like mine," Vickie sang softly, then looked up into his eyes and said, "They are, you know."

"What are?" He was lost in the feel of her body next to his as they swayed to the music.

"Your eyes. They're the same color as mine and almost a similar shape."

"Amazing." He smiled down at her. "Maybe that's a sign from the gods that we're meant for each other."

Vickie knew this was all happening far too fast and far too soon, but there was something hypnotic about the way he looked at her. She felt she could almost drown in Sebastian's eyes.

"I know that you are not only beautiful but a good person," he murmured in her ear as they danced, the other patrons pretending not to notice the celebrated couple. "Beautiful and good, the perfect qualities in a woman."

"I don't know about that." Vickie was surprised by his rather old-fashioned way of speaking, then realized that he was English, after all, and a blue-blooded aristocrat too. Weren't English gentlemen supposed to be quite stuffy and reserved? Well, this one was certainly starting to break out of the mold, for she could feel his hardness as their bodies moved to the romantic rhythm.

"I don't think I am a terribly good person, Sebastian. But beautiful? Maybe in this light, but you should see me in the morning." She laughed.

"I don't believe you." He held her even tighter as the disc jockey put on Sinatra's "You and the Night and the Music."

"I think I know what you are really like, Victoria. You are an angel, a perfect angel, and the perfect woman for me."

"Now you're going too far." She tried to draw away, but Sebastian was insistent. His arms were strong, and there was no mistaking his obvious attraction to her, nor hers to him. When Sebastian suggested that she come back to his Grosvenor Square flat for a nightcap, Vickie hesitated for barely an instant. She wanted Sebastian to make love to her, and she felt no false inhibitions about it. The affairs she had indulged in over the past few years, her catastrophic marriage to macho Mike McKay, and her dull marriage to Charles Anderson had never expunged the ghost of Cooper Hudson from Vickie's subconscious. He still haunted her dreams and, try as she might, she had never succeeded in banishing him from her thoughts. Perhaps this young duke could be the man to make her finally forget Cooper.

At Sebastian's elegant flat they drank more champagne, then he started kissing her so passionately she felt a pulse of lust. When he knew she was ready, he carried her into the bedroom still kissing her and undressed her gently.

Lying naked on Sebastian's intricately carved four-poster bed canopied in dark crimson velvet, Vickie watched as he took off his clothes, then walked toward her smiling. Then to her shock, he started tying one of her ankles to the bedpost with his tie.

"What are you doing?" Vickie sat up, but he pushed her back softly, murmuring, "I won't hurt you, my darling. I want you to be my prize, a beautiful, ravishing prize that I have caught. I wouldn't dream of hurting you, my love, I promise. Relax, please relax, I know you will enjoy this."

Vickie lay back and watched Sebastian with wary fascination as he tied her ankle. Certainly there was something strangely exciting and forbidding in what he was doing; none of her American lovers had ever attempted to do anything that even approached this almost religious and powerfully erotic experience. She watched Sebastian's purposeful movements as he opened a drawer of the cabinet at the bottom of the bed and removed several more silk neckties with deliberate slowness. The room was suffused with the heavy fragrance of scented candles, and the walls, hung with red velvet tapestries, cast a glow of carnality that excited Vickie more than she could ever have imagined. Sebastian was like a priest going about his duties, and she was the sacrificial lamb laid on his altar. As an actress Vickie had always enjoyed experiencing new sensations. This one was promising to be a major trip.

As if reading her thoughts, Sebastian whispered, "I am going to make love to you, Vickie. But first, you must be a blessed maiden whom I shall sacrifice to the barbarian. That is why I am tying you up. I want to worship your body as it should be worshiped. You are an idol, and I idolize you, my darling." He tied her other leg, then each of her wrists, whispering, "You're so beautiful, the most beautiful creature I've ever seen." Then he lay on the bed beside her, stroking her and murmuring, "You are exquisite, like a piece of Sèvres porcelain."

Vickie almost wanted to laugh, but when he leaned over to kiss her, she responded eagerly. He kissed her mouth and breasts for a long time. She couldn't touch him, but she could see that he wasn't responding; then, as his lips began their journey down her body, Sebastian suddenly fell back onto the pillow and closed his eyes.

"Sebastian?" whispered Vickie. There was no answer, except a tiny grunt, as he turned away from her. "Sebastian, are you all right?" She started to shout his name, but Sebastian snuggled deeper into his pillow, then began snoring deeply. Vickie felt like a butterfly pinned to a board.

"Bastard." She tried to claw the silken cords off her wrists. "For God's sake, let me *go*. How dare you do this to me? What kind of a sick monster are you?"

Sebastian's answer was another tiny snore.

After an hour of struggling, an exhausted Vickie finally managed to loosen her bonds and free herself. She returned to the Dorchester so angry that she was unable to sleep. "He must be insane," she mumbled as she tossed and turned. "I definitely shan't be having anything more to do with him."

Chapter Twenty-One

The following morning, while Vickie and Susie were finishing their packing for L.A., one hundred white roses arrived for Vickie with a note from Sebastian, full of profuse apologies.

Can you ever forgive me for being so drunk, my dearest darling angel? I am utterly ashamed of my appalling behavior. Please, please, please forgive me. I know I have been disgusting, a fool, and a drunken lout, and if you never want to see me again I shall understand. But please, I beg of you, give me another chance. Let me see you again before you leave. Please. Your devoted slave, Sebastian

Vickie tore the note into pieces. She was going to forget about Sebastian, but after a couple of glasses of wine on the plane she confided in Susie.

"The instant I saw him I felt as though we

289

were meant for each other. There was this surge of, God, I don't know — adrenaline. It was as though we'd met before, it was so intense."

"It was just lust," Susie observed laconically, looking out of the window at the clouds. "But at least he pushed Cooper out of your mind for a little while."

"Maybe. When I first saw Sebastian, he was so attractive my stomach went into a knot."

"Maybe it was that time of the month."

"Susie. Stop. Don't you believe in love at first sight?"

"It's happened to you too many times. That kind of attraction only happens in the movies. Listen, my pet, that duke sounds like a world-class psychopath. Forget about him. You've got many other fish to fry."

"I know." Vickie sighed. "But other than Cooper, none of them have ever made me feel like Sebastian did, for those first few hours together. It was like yin and yang — as though we were one."

"Forget about him, Vickie. If a man did that to me, I'd never go near him again."

"Well, there's going to be several thousand miles between us now, so I'm sure I won't."

Two days later Susie brought an exotic orchid plant to Vickie's dressing room. Nestled at the base, among the leaves, was an exquisite 1920s Cartier diamond bracelet and a note from Sebastian, again begging for forgiveness.

"Send it back," Vickie instructed Susie. "I'm with you, I don't want to have anything more to do with that weirdo."

During the week several more cartloads of flowers arrived, all of which Susie sent back, and after a few weeks Sebastian obviously got the message and the floral tributes ceased.

It was the last film under her Hollywood contract. *The Girl from Indiana* was another trivial no-brainer with a ridiculously convoluted plot, but Vickie threw herself into the movie with a vengeance. Vickie was once again a regular at dinners in the grand houses of stars and producers, and occasionally thoughts of Sebastian Swannell and what he'd done to her, and had not been able to do to her, crossed her mind. In spite of herself, she was still intrigued by the young duke.

Three months later Hollywood royalty put on their best bibs and tuckers to entertain British royalty. Princess Margaret was coming to town, and every host and hostess worth their Sèvres was vying for her presence at their beautiful homes.

Vickie was uncharacteristically without a man in her life, so she asked Dino, her handsome hairdresser and a well-known Lothario, to be her escort to producer Irwin Kline's party.

"Smile, sweetheart, we're on candid camera," Dino quipped, as they drove up to a mountainous creation of white marble and Corinthian columns. "This whole thing looks like a huge wedding cake."

"It's like an old plantation mansion transported from a Civil War movie," laughed Vickie.

"Yeah, it was built by Clara Bow in the twenties, and it's said that the reason the bedrooms are so enormous is because she entertained several lovers at a time in them."

"Really? How many?"

"Dozens," said Dino.

"When Irwin first brought his wife, Jane, to look at the house, she announced, 'I won't marry you unless you make it bigger,' so he added a ballroom, an ice-skating rink, and a mahogany-paneled screening room that seats fifty." Dino was an expert at Hollywood trivia.

"Nothing like excess," remarked Vickie, as they entered the great reception hall. Italian baroque carved wood sculptures were interspersed with trompe l'oeil statuary in wall niches, and the enormous room was lit by a central chandelier of yellow and gold crystal. The crème de la crème of Hollywood were drifting in and out of the half dozen reception rooms, their artificial laughter mingling with a string quartet playing Mozart. All the women were elegantly dressed.

Most of the producers' and directors' wives were in long gowns, and expensive diamonds, emeralds, and sapphires glittered on their tanned wrists and necks. They were mostly older women in their late forties and fifties, though few in Hollywood ever dared admit to being a day over thirty-nine.

The younger women were the current crop of stars or the wives and girlfriends of actors. They stood on the Aubusson carpet, gossiping, flirting, and drinking pink champagne, and, although some of their jewelry was fake, their beauty was not.

The host and hostess stood imperiously just inside the door of their galleried reception-cum-ballroom door, greeting their guests. Irwin Kline was still one of the most influential and important men in Hollywood. The CEO and largest single shareholder of Scalini Studios, he was also one of the biggest private shareholders of the Ford Motor Company and Coca-Cola. Although he looked like two hundred and fifty pounds of condemned veal, money was his middle name, and he made it and spent it with equal ease. His wife, formerly Jane Harrison, was from a socially prominent, mega-rich Pasadena family that moved into California when the Indians moved out. Jane Kline, tonight dressed in Mainbocher's appliquéd black velvet, was a veritable pillar of Los Angeles society. Tall, skinny, and blonde, she had a horsy attractiveness that appealed to certain men. Women liked her because they thought she was no threat to them. She supported important charities, gave memorable parties, and men liked her because she could tell a bawdy joke with the best of them, sit a horse better than most and, it was rumored, gave one of the best nonprofessional blow jobs in town.

Beside them stood Princess Margaret, to whom Vickie curtsied when she was introduced. Princess Margaret looked Vickie over dismissively, obviously not remembering her, then became diverted by Dino, who gallantly kissed the royal glove and zeroed his black eyes into hers with his familiar sexual come-on. It had seldom failed to entrance any woman he wished to impress, and the Queen's sister seemed no exception, for within seconds they were chatting animatedly. When Vickie was introduced to the man who stood beside the princess for a second, she was dumbstruck as Sebastian Swannell formally extended his hand.

"How are you, Miss Gordon?" he asked. "Sebastian Swannell at your service."

"Hello again." Vickie regained her composure and smiled coolly as he inclined his head in a small bow. "I'm extremely well, thank you, Your Grace."

"Do I take that enchanting smile to mean that you have forgiven me?" His glowing eyes looked even more seductive in his tanned face.

"Maybe." Vickie looked up at him in the way that most men found irresistible. "I've had some time to think about it, so yes, perhaps I could forgive you. But you had better be plenty persuasive, Your Grace."

"Oh please. We've surely left formalities behind us by now. Shall we?" Before she could protest Sebastian took her arm and steered her on to the quiet terrace. "So again, I must apologize a thousand times for my revolting behavior. Cognac doesn't agree with me." His sincerity and boyish charm seemed genuine. "That situation has never happened before. You see I've only gone out with a few girls, but I've not been really involved with any of them."

"Really? Why not?" The thought crossed Vickie's mind that he might be homosexual.

"Because of the war. I joined the navy when I was twenty-one, then after it was over I was too busy running my houses and the estate to get serious with anyone." He put his hand on hers. "But since I met you, I want to be with you, Vickie. I haven't stopped thinking about you and kicking myself for what an ass I've been. I believe I have found in you the perfect woman for whom I've been searching for years. Will you let me see you again . . . please?"

"I don't know, Sebastian." Vickie sipped her champagne, trying to sort through her confused thoughts. "I can't just pop over to

295

see you in London. My life is here, I work here."

He laced his fingers smoothly into hers, and her heart started racing. "I understand your reluctance to become involved with me, but please at least let me see you again. I *must*. I'm staying at the Beverly Hills Hotel all week. Let's meet, even if it's just for lunch. Please, Vickie?"

Vickie couldn't deny her attraction to Sebastian. Was the incident at his flat indeed a stupid misjudgment brought on by too much alcohol? She needed to believe that it was. She would ask him when they met. Her feelings for him were too strong not to see him again. She would give him another chance.

The following night Sebastian took Vickie for a romantic dinner at Chasen's. She wore a décolleté cream chiffon dress, with spaghetti straps and pearl drops in her ears. With her long hair loose on her shoulders she looked like a princess in a fairy tale. And in his midnight-blue suit, a white shirt complementing his tan, and pale green eyes, Sebastian made the perfect consort. The two made such a striking couple that some of the diners couldn't keep their eyes off them, and the way Sebastian looked at Vickie made all the women feel a tinge of envy.

Sebastian made no reference to the night

in London except to refuse cognac at the end of dinner. "It does bad things to me." He smiled enigmatically and looked appealingly into her eyes. "Would you like to go dancing?"

"I'd love to go dancing. And I don't have an early call tomorrow."

"What time do you usually have to go to work?" he asked as they drove down Sunset Boulevard in his rented Cadillac.

"I get up at about five to be in makeup by six or six-thirty. It's hell — but beauty is everything in Hollywood, so a girl's got to suffer."

"Good grief! Five *a.m.?*" Sebastian nearly drove off the road. "In London that's usually when many of my friends go to bed."

"I know, life is totally twisted around in this part of the world. We shoot at least twelve hours a day, and that doesn't include makeup and hairdressing. In any other job everyone would go on strike."

"Aren't you getting bored by it all?"

Vickie didn't answer, her perfect profile so still it was like a newly minted coin against the blackness of the window.

"I guess I am," she finally said slowly. "I've been making movies for nearly thirteen years now, and I think I'm reaching the end of my shelf life."

Sebastian snorted. "You? Don't be absurd, you look like a child."

"I'll be thirty-five in eight months, and in Hollywood that ain't young anymore."

"Ridiculous. I'm nearly thirty-five too. We're both still young, Vickie."

Vickie grinned. "Thank you, kind sir, but this is Hollywood and for an actress thirty-five is almost crone time."

He laughed. "You're the prettiest crone I've ever seen."

The parking attendant jumped to open the door as they drew up to Mocombo, and as they entered the nightclub he whispered, "And I think I'm falling in love with you."

The maître d' seated them with a flourish as all eyes swiveled toward them.

"This is all too fast," Vickie said faintly. "Much too fast."

"I'll give you time — all the time you need, my angel," then, taking her hand, he led her onto the crowded dance floor.

For the next few days, they saw each other as much as possible until Sebastian had to return to London. He wooed Vickie with extravagant presents and gentle kisses, but when he became too ardent, she resisted. She wanted this relationship to be special, different from the others. Vickie couldn't stop thinking about the handsome Englishman. It soon became apparent that neither could he stop thinking about her. They talked constantly long distance on the telephone, and he bombarded her daily with forests of flowers.

"This guy's got it *real* bad," said Susie as she ushered in yet another colossal basket of Vickie's favorite white roses. "I counted one thousand roses. One thousand! I've never seen anything like it, and, although I think this guy must be crazy, he certainly is crazy for you."

"I guess he likes me." Vickie smiled wryly. "What do you think I should do about him, Susie?"

"Do you want him?"

"I think I've wanted him since I first saw him. We've talked about children. He really wants them too. It's time I tried to have a baby, Susie. I'm getting on, you know."

"What about that night?" asked Susie darkly.

"Oh, it was just a game, a silly game, and he was drunk. I don't think he would have hurt me. He's gentle and sweet and kind."

"They're all gentle and sweet and kind when they want to get into your panties. If he started off the relationship like that, what does he do for an encore, whips and chains?"

"It was just *once,* Susie. I handled it then and I know I'll be able to handle him. He really does love me, Susie, and I think I love him. That's all that matters."

"Well, I think he's a nut case. I've never

trusted those cold Brits."

"May I remind you that *you* are an Englishwoman," smiled Vickie.

"Not for years, dear — I pledged my allegiance to the flag in 1942, and there's no going back for this U.S. citizen."

"Look, Susie, let me trust my own instincts, will you? I know I've been unlucky with my past marriages, but I believe Sebastian's a wonderful man and a good person. I think I could be very happy with him."

"If you say so." Susie shrugged. "So be it. I'll keep my fingers crossed."

That night as Vickie was preparing for bed, the telephone rang and the voice that turned Vickie's heart into a fist asked softly, "My angel, how are you?"

"Oh I'm fine, darling. A little tired, but the picture only has a month of shooting left. Then I'll be free."

"Free to marry me?" asked Sebastian.

"But, darling, we still don't really know each other."

"It doesn't matter." His voice was calm but insistent. "I knew when I saw you at Sarah's party that I could fall in love with you. Vickie, could you love me enough to marry me? Please say you could. Say that you will be my wife?"

There was a pause, then Vickie burst out joyfully, "Oh yes, yes, of course I'll marry you, darling — whenever and wherever you want me to."

"Then let's do it as soon as possible. Let's get married. I love you, my darling. Do you mind giving up your film career to come and be my wife and the Duchess of Burghley?"

Vickie laughed. "Would I *mind?* To be frank, I'm sick and tired of being a movie star. I've lived in a fishbowl all my adult life and I'm beginning to hate it. My career's almost over in any case. I don't want to act anymore; I want to be with you. Yes, Sebastian, I'll marry you. Yes, yes, I will."

"I can't believe it, my angel." He sounded close to tears. "You'll never regret it, my love — I shall make you so happy, so terribly happy, my darling."

Vickie paused and, plucking up the courage said, "One thing, Sebastian — we've never really discussed it, except in a roundabout way, but what happened that first night in London . . ."

He interrupted her. "My angel, that night was just one of those awful stupid things that men do when they're overtired and drunk," he said sincerely. "It will never happen again, my sweet, please believe me. I promise you, I shall never humiliate you like that. I couldn't my love, I just couldn't."

"Don't worry about it anymore, darling," said Vickie soothingly. "I believe you, I really do."

Chapter Twenty-Two
1953

When Sebastian told his mother that he intended to marry the movie star Vickie Gordon, Rosemary Swannell was outraged. They sat in the anteroom off her bedroom — a room as stiffly formal as the duchess herself.

"As the only male left in both our families, it certainly is time you married and gave us an heir, but to do so with some divorced film actress? How can you even *think* of bringing a flighty creature like that into our family and into our lives?"

"Victoria is not a typical actress at all. She's a wonderful woman, kind, sweet, and sincere, and I love her — in fact, she's the only woman I have *ever* loved. So whatever you say, Mother, I intend to marry her."

"Well," the duchess said grudgingly, "you've gone out with every eligible female in England, so I suppose it is time you married — for everyone's sake and the family line."

In the duchess's bedroom next door her personal maid crept closer to the door to listen more carefully. Patsy Kingsley had been Her Grace's maid for over thirty years and there was little that she didn't know, either about the duchess or the entire Burghley dynasty. And there was nothing that she couldn't find out about either.

The wedding was held at St. Margaret's, Westminster, in August 1953. It had not been an easy feat to arrange a church wedding because of Vickie's two divorces, but the Burghleys knew the right people who could pull the right strings.

Vickie had engaged one of the Queen's favorite couturiers, Norman Hartnell, to design her wedding gown. He had made a spectacular but elegantly simple dress of cream Duchesse satin. The tight bodice and long fitted sleeves accentuated her perfect arms and tiny waist, and her ten-foot train was to be held aloft by half a dozen tiny aristocratic toddlers. Sebastian would have liked five-year-old Prince Charles, the Queen's firstborn son, to be one of them, as Sebastian had been an usher at Queen Elizabeth's coronation at Westminster Abbey the previous year and the Burghleys were longstanding friends of the Windsor family. All the senior royals — the Queen, Prince Philip, the Queen Mother, and Princess Margaret — were invited to the wedding, but because Vickie was a divorcée, they all turned down the invitation, much to the old duchess's fury.

"You see what you've done, Sebastian, bringing this outsider, this commoner, this *actress,* into our family. We are now ostracized by the entire Windsor clan."

"I'm sorry, Mother, I don't care. I love Vickie and I'm marrying her, and if you're not happy with having the nuptials at St. Margaret's, we'll elope."

"Heaven forbid." The duchess sat down, dabbing her forehead with a lace handkerchief, as Patsy brought her a cup of camomile tea, glancing at Sebastian with a look of barely hidden hostility. But mother and son ignored her — *"Pas devant le domestiques"* wasn't necessary in front of Patsy. She had complete access to all of the duchess's private papers, bureau drawers, and trunks and she more than anyone knew where any family skeletons were buried. But Patsy was a trusted servant and loyal supporter of the Burghley family and would never betray any confidences or knowledge to any outside party.

"Well, I hope the Grosvenors, the Devonshires, and the Marlboroughs accept," fumed Rosemary, "otherwise we'll be finished in society, and I won't be able to show my face."

One of Vickie's ex-lovers, John Fitzgerald Kennedy, a handsome young Democratic senator from Massachusetts, had married a beautiful society girl called Jacqueline Bouvier a few months earlier, and they had accepted, but Sebastian had deterred Vickie from inviting too many of her Hollywood friends. "Lana Turner and Ava Gardner? Really, my dear, they're not quite one of us. I don't think they'll fit in, don't you agree?"

Vickie agreed, loving Sebastian enough to bow to his judgment. "I really don't care that much about my Hollywood pals anymore; true friendships are capricious in L.A. Out of sight, out of mind, that's the order of the day."

Since Vickie's last two pictures had done badly at the box office, the studio had been relieved not to have to honor the final two years of her contract, but she didn't care anymore. She was optimistic that 1953 was a good year for marriage and that her third one would be her last.

Although many aristocratic families in England had accepted wedding invitations, the dowager duchess had put her Ferragamo foot down firmly when Vickie requested that Dino give her away. "I will *not* have a hairdresser involved in the ceremony." Her lips curled dismissively. "And I assure you that the Royals would not have been happy about someone like that either." So Vickie was escorted down the aisle by Sebastian's distant cousin, Basil, a man she had only met the previous week.

As the bride and groom stood at the beautiful altar, the sun streamed in great colorful shafts through the stained glass windows of St. Margaret's, and the organ music of the "Wedding March" filled the rafters. Tears ran down Susie's cheeks as she clutched Dino's arm, her eyes fixed on the gorgeous creature.

"Our little girl's done well, hasn't she?"

Dino nodded. "Her hair looks great too," he said proudly. As she floated down the aisle, Vickie was ecstatic she was marrying a man she loved. Sebastian had finally made her forget about Cooper, and she hoped that a new and wonderful life was beginning for both of them.

The honeymoon took place on a yacht in the Mediterranean; a lazy month of cruising, sightseeing, and shopping in Portofino, Monaco, Cap Ferrat, and St. Tropez. Vickie was expecting some tender lovemaking on deck beneath the stars, but Sebastian was not an ardent lover. He tried to please, and even though his amatory expertise couldn't touch Cooper Hudson's, Vickie loved him, so she concentrated all her efforts on becoming a good wife and hopefully soon a mother.

They returned to their Gloucestershire country house in September, when the hunting season was in full swing. Sebastian was immediately fully occupied in organizing the hunt meets, so it was up to Vickie to plan the elaborate house parties that accompanied the hunts. For this she leaned heavily on the dowager duchess for advice and expertise.

Many of the manners and rituals of the English aristocracy seemed quaintly strange to Vickie's American way of life, but she was eager and determined to learn.

"I want to be the best duchess I possibly can," she told Susie, who had become Vickie's personal secretary and assistant.

"Oh you will, I don't doubt it," said Susie. "Just like you became the biggest and the best star."

"This is even more of a challenge." Vickie frowned, consulting the list of guests for her first dinner party. "Now I don't remember, is a marquis more important than an earl? Should I seat the earl of Dunthorpe on my right or on my left?"

"Darned if I know," answered Susie.

When Patsy Kingsley had first seen the new Duchess of Burghley, she had stared at her long and hard. All the staff were lined up in the great hall of the Gloucestershire estate to greet the newlyweds. The butler, the under-butler, eight footmen, three cooks, and a dozen assorted maids made their obeisances to the young couple as they passed graciously down the line of servants.

Vickie was nervous. This was her first official day as the duchess, and she was concerned she might be overdressed in her cream wool suit with its cinched waist, full flowing skirt, and a tiny veiled hat. She glanced up at the heavy dark walls, from which dozens of Burghley ancestors seemed to glare down at her. The light from the stained glass windows cast somber shades of blues and purples into the corners of the cavernous hall, yet despite the sunshine it was extremely cold.

Vickie was surprised when she met the piercing stare of the dowager duchess's personal maid. It was obvious that Patsy Kingsley was not going to be in her camp, for an odd, unwelcoming expression crossed her chilly features. Vickie moved quickly over to greet the cook, thinking she would keep out of the way of that particular person, who seemed to emanate hostility.

As for Patsy, she could hardly believe her eyes when she first saw the duchess, or Vickie Gordon, as everyone knew her. Suddenly she recognized those candid blue-green eyes and trademark red hair, which was starting to frizz from the long journey. Vickie could only be Millie McClancey's daughter, she had to be. She was the right age, and Patsy remembered that Millie had called the child Victoria after the late Queen.

As soon as she could escape from the lineup, Patsy rushed to her attic room and placed a long-distance phone call to Los Angeles where her son Eddie was now based.

On the manicured lawn at the Gloucestershire estate, Susie also met Patsy Kingsley for the first time and an instant mutual loathing began.

The women were a study in contrasts. Robust and good-natured, Susie was ever ready with a quip and a joke. Patsy, two years Susie's senior, was skinny and dour, with a permanently sour sneer etched on her sharp features. To Susie's annoyance, she immediately started criticizing Vickie.

"Calls herself a duchess," she sniffed disparagingly, watching as Vickie set off on a morning shoot. "Those clothes are more suitable for a weekend in Las Vegas than a pheasant shoot. My poor dear departed husband, Mr. Kingsley, would turn in his grave if he'd seen Her Grace dressed that way."

"And what pray *is* wrong with the duchess's outfit?" Susie looked across the expanse of green lawn to where the party of eight was walking toward the woods. "I think she looks lovely."

Vickie was wearing plum-colored plus fours, new brown shiny boots, and a tailored brown corduroy jacket, which was perhaps a touch too "haute couture" for country life. On her head perched a jaunty orange cap, and Susie had to admit to herself that Vickie did look more like a Hollywood movie star than an English country lady. The two other women in the group were dressed down but far more suitably in thick tweeds, brogues, and dowdy headscarves.

"So common," sneered Patsy, "she has no idea either how to dress or how to behave as a duchess should."

"She's still a star," snapped Susie. "She's much more Vickie Gordon superstar than the Duchess of Burghley."

"All actresses are trash. And from what I've heard about your precious employer, she's always been known as a whore and a slut."

"What did you say?" Susie wheeled on the older woman, her eyes full of fire. "Just who are you calling a slut?"

"I do *know* people," said Patsy smugly. "People who live in Los Angeles. And I've also read a great deal about your Miss Vickie. In fact, there's not much I don't know about her."

"Such as?"

"Such as, her mother was a second-rate musical performer who married a gangster. Such as, your precious Vickie slept with half the actors and directors in Hollywood before she managed to hook the duke. Gary Cooper, Cary Grant, and Frank Sinatra are just some of the dozens of men she went to bed with. Then there was that married one who left his wife for her, but when she got shot of him he turned to drink, and then the queer one who killed himself."

"And just where do you get all of your *mis*information?" Susie asked with heavy sarcasm.

"It's common knowledge among certain people, and everyone in Hollywood knows that she was on her way out. Her studio was fed up with having to pay through the nose to keep all her adulterous affairs hushed up."

"Who told you all this?" Susie's face flamed.

"Never you mind." Patsy started to leave, but Susie grabbed her by her scrawny arm and, mustering as much menace in her voice as possible, hissed, "I wouldn't start telling any of the staff those lies."

"Oh really, why?"

"Because since I've been here, *I've* heard a few juicy stories concerning your young duke."

"What stories?"

"I've heard things from sources a little closer to home than your rubbishy newspapers." Susie was beginning to enjoy herself. "The duke was in the war, wasn't he? At sea for years and years?"

"Of course he was in the war! He's a patriot and an Englishman. He fought for his country." Patsy was beginning to look rattled.

"Ha! He fought, my foot. Sebastian never saw any action. He was stationed on a ship outside Portugal. There was no enemy action there, just a lot of *other* action," she said meaningfully.

"What are you insinuating?"

"I'm saying that Naval Officer Sebastian Swannell on overseas active service from 1940 to 1945 was *very* active in ways that nice people don't talk about."

"I don't want to hear any more." Patsy turned away again.

"Well, you won't. Not another word. Not from me anyway. But you'd better keep your trap shut about Vickie. OK? It's not her fault that she's so beautiful that every man she met wanted to sleep with her."

The two women stared at each other with rampant hostility, then Susie stuck out a plump hand.

"Deal?" she asked sweetly.

Patsy stared at her intently, and Susie saw hatred in her snakelike eyes. Then Patsy proffered a bony hand to shake and stalked off. Susie watched her go.

Why *did* Patsy know so much about Vickie's life? Only the insiders, studio personnel and those who worked on her films, were really aware of all her love affairs. The studio had done plenty of backpedaling with the press to hush up rumors, especially when Troy Townsend, one of her leading men, had been found hanging by his dressing gown cord in a bungalow at the Beverly Hills

Hotel. Ace Paradigm publicist Russell Bane had managed by some alchemy to reach the suicide scene before the police did and pocketed the incriminating note that implicated Vickie.

Troy had written that it was because of his unrequited love for Vickie that he'd killed himself. If the media had found that out, they would have castigated her forever. But they didn't because Bane had destroyed the note. So how did Patsy know — or did she? Susie shrugged; she had better things to do than worry about that bitter old biddy.

Vickie seemed terribly happy and fulfilled these days. She'd adjusted to being the Duchess of Burghley effortlessly, and Susie had no intention of bursting her beautiful bubble by revealing what she had discovered about Sebastian.

Chapter Twenty-Three
1955

Occasionally, when the brandy flowed too freely after dinner, Sebastian would light scented candles in their bedroom and try to persuade Vickie to indulge in a little bondage.

"You know it's really quite fun, angel," he cajoled, coiling a Charvet tie around his wrist and flicking the end of it lightly against his bare thigh. "You'll grow to like it."

Vickie could see the obvious tumescence that had parted the gap in Sebastian's silk dressing gown and his rather small cock endeavoring to make a personal appearance.

"Darling, I'd love to make love with you." She was reclining on pillows, looking delicious in a pale pink pajama top, her long legs unfurled provocatively. "But why can't we make proper love? We don't need all those silly tie-ups."

"But I *want* to tie you up. If you love me, you'll let me do it." Suddenly Sebastian looked like a sulky little boy deprived of his toy car.

Vickie sighed. It was the time of the month when she knew she was at her most fertile, and she was more determined than ever to have a baby, but after trying for nearly two years Vickie was finding it increasingly difficult to arouse Sebastian's libido.

"If I let you tie me up, will you make love to me properly then?" she whispered.

"Of course, my darling, of *course* I want to make love to you. You're my angel, my priceless beauty, I adore you."

Oh, but actions speak louder than words, thought Vickie. If he really loves me, why does he hardly ever manage to make it? Reluctantly Vickie allowed her husband to kneel and to slip silken bonds over her wrists and attach them to the bedposts. As he crouched before her she favored him with her mouth, hoping for the desired effect that would ensure conventional consummation. Her expert ministrations soon made Sebastian rigid and he slid slowly down her body, uttering appreciative groans. Vickie expected him to pleasure her for a minute or two, but no, Sebastian had other ideas.

Swiftly he tied her ankles together, then pushed her legs high above her head. With one hand he jammed her feet against the headboard and with the other he started to shove his small but rigid penis inside her, but not where Vickie expected it. As Sebastian thrust himself brutally inside her, she felt a searing pain.

"That's the wrong way, you idiot."

"No," he gasped, "I like it."

"Please, Sebastian, don't do this, you're hurting me."

Sebastian ignored her; his face contorted as he pounded into her a few more agonizing times, and then climaxed with a little shriek of satisfaction. Vickie wriggled herself from under him.

"How dare you," she sobbed. "How *dare* you humiliate me by doing something so horrible."

"I'm sorry, angel; I couldn't help it. Your little bottom is so firm and taut. It's just like a boy's."

Sebastian had rolled off her and was lying limply on his back, eyes closed, a beatific smile on his face.

Vickie shuddered with revulsion. "Get these goddamned ties *off* me, you pervert. We've been attempting to make a baby for almost two years. I told you today was the right time for it, and you don't even want to try."

Vickie was pulling her wrists against the ties so violently that she could feel them cutting into her.

"It's obvious you don't *want* a baby anymore," she sobbed.

"Oh no, my angel, I do."

"Then undo these ridiculous ties, for God's sake."

Sebastian undid the bonds, then turned to her, his face pleading. "I want a child, you know I do."

"Then *why* can't you make love to me properly, at least once or twice a month?" Vickie sat up, rubbing her bruised wrists and ankles, trembling with anger. "Because if you don't start doing that, Sebastian, I want no more of this marriage."

"No, no, my angel, don't say that."

"I mean it. Your mother never stops telling me how we've got to have a child to carry on the line. Well, I don't care about your goddammed line anymore. I'm sick of all the pomp and ceremony that I have to put up with and all the bullshit that goes with it. I'm thirty-seven years old this year and I want a baby, Sebastian, for me, for *us*, not just for the future of the Burghleys."

Vickie's beautiful face was flushed, her red hair tumbling around her shoulders, and she was shaking with sorrow and rage.

"I'll give you a child. I promise I will."

"How, Sebastian? How? I'm not going to get pregnant *that* way, and you know it."

"I couldn't help it, I couldn't." He turned over toward her and Vickie saw that his penis was erect again. Vickie knew it was now or never for this month, and even though she felt humiliated and used, she lay down and resignedly guided her husband into her.

Chapter Twenty-Four
1955–1960

Six weeks later, when Vickie knew for certain that she was pregnant, joy filled the Burghley household. No one was more thrilled than Vickie and no two people more solicitous than Sebastian and Susie. Vickie was pampered, spoiled, and indulged like some indolent pet poodle, and the nine months positively flew by.

Vickie spent a great deal of time in bed daydreaming, yet too often her thoughts strayed to Cooper Hudson. She kept up with his exploits and the careers of her other contemporaries via the fan and news magazines, *Photoplay*, *Picture Post*, and *Life*. After the war, Cooper had returned to film-making and still featured in movies regularly. At fifty his rugged macho-man looks were weathering well. He was never photographed with his wife, indeed she was rarely even mentioned in any article, but he was never pictured with any other female either, other than on set with one of his costars. Even after all this time those pictures hurt Vickie, as she knew that he was almost certainly involved in a romance with one of them. Cooper was a sexual animal, and in spite of herself Vickie still felt a pang of desire whenever she thought of him.

The intrusive tabloid press didn't exist in 1956, so stars and celebrities went about their lives with impunity, secure in the fact that no scandal would ever touch them. However, a new magazine called *Confidential* had started up and many closeted homosexual movie stars had become fearful of discovery.

Rock Hudson was so intimidated by threat of exposure by *Confidential* that he had been forced to enter into a phony marriage of convenience and, as Vickie read "Rock's Story" in *Confidential*, she couldn't help thinking about her own husband.

It seemed clear that Sebastian too was probably a closet homosexual, but with a child growing inside her, Vickie refused to confront that disturbing thought. Besides, Sebastian was so unbelievably solicitous, bringing her constant gifts and flowers, sending her notes, and professing eternal love, she didn't want to think about it.

Vickie's baby was born on a cold February morning in 1956. A pretty little boy, he had Sebastian's black hair, Vickie's delicate features, and the amazing pale eyes of both his parents. All the love that could be lavished on a child, Vickie lavished on her son, and for the first time in years she was utterly content.

"Isn't William the most gorgeous little boy you've ever seen?" Vickie watched proudly as the child ran around on the emerald green lawn of the grounds of Burghley, laughing and chasing one of the dogs.

"And look at his eyes," said Sebastian, smiling, "blue-green and wide apart — just like yours and mine."

"Sometimes I think we could be brother and sister," teased Vickie.

"And our birthdays *are* only twelve weeks apart. Speaking of which, what do you want for yours, my darling?" asked Sebastian, linking his fingers with hers.

"Oh God, don't remind me. I'm going to be *so* old." Vickie gave a mock groan. "Forty — I'm *really* ancient now."

"Never. Not you, my darling. You are eternally young and beautiful, one of nature's miracles."

He bent to kiss her, but Vickie moved her head away. Since Wills's birth, there had been even less sex between them than before, and she was happy to keep it that way. After all, she was a mother now, and it wasn't seemly to have sex. Not until it was time for William to have a little sister. Then maybe she'd start watching her calendar again.

On Wills's fourth birthday, he wanted to go to the London Zoo. A giant panda had recently been imported from China, and the newspapers had been full of news about Chi-Chi for months. Sebastian was going to drive them there in his new Ferrari, which William absolutely loved, but Vickie wasn't sure the car was safe.

"Take the Bentley, darling. It's safer than that racing car."

"But Wills insists." Sebastian was dressing. "He absolutely insists on going in the Ferrari. You know how stubborn the little blighter can be."

"Oh I know, I know." Vickie smiled fondly and then attempted to get out of bed when a stabbing pain assailed her.

"What is it, darling, what's wrong?" Sebastian rushed to his wife, who lay on the bed white-faced, her hand on her head.

"It's nothing. I've just got another of those horrible headaches." She lay back weakly, wincing from another twinge.

"Then you shouldn't go to the zoo," Sebastian said firmly. "You know the doctor said that when you get these migraines you must rest."

"I know I'm supposed to, but it's Wills's birthday, I want to be with him."

"It will be his birthday all day, angel. Susie

and I will take him to the zoo, then we'll be back in time for tea and birthday cake. And don't forget the big party with all his little friends tomorrow. You'll want to be well for that, won't you?"

"All right then." Thankfully, Vickie swallowed a couple of strong painkillers, then sank back onto the pillows.

Little William, a bundle of mischief with black curls, dimples in his chin, and a cheeky disposition, came running into the room.

"Come on, Mama and Papa," he yelled excitedly. "Get up. Chi-Chi's waiting. Let's go."

"Mama's not feeling too well, Wills," said Sebastian. "She has to stay in bed."

"Oh — sorry, Mama." Wills's desire to see the panda outweighed his toddler's compassion. "Hope you feel better, Mama." He waved gaily to her. "Can we please go *now*, Papa?"

"Yes, yes, *yes*. My, we're impatient today." Sebastian kissed Vickie briefly on the forehead and picked up his son.

"Bye, Mama, bye-bye." The little boy started chatting excitedly to his father, and Vickie smiled as they left the room and she sank into a fitful sleep.

It was dark. Too dark. Vickie awoke with a start and glanced at the bedside clock. It was a quarter to five in the afternoon.

"Good God, I've been asleep for hours."

322

She rang the bell for her maid. But where were Sebastian and little Wills? They'd been gone since ten that morning. The zoo was only an hour and a half's drive from the estate, so why weren't they back yet? What had they been doing?

Teatime was four-thirty every afternoon. It was a ritual. As Vickie attempted to get out of bed, the door opened and Sebastian stood there, his face a mask of shock.

"Hello, darling — where's Wills?"

Behind Sebastian, she saw Susie, tears running down her face as she rushed to Vickie's bedside and held her tightly, sobbing, "I'm sorry, I'm sorry, I'm so sorry."

"What *is* it?" Vickie almost screamed. "Tell me what's happened, for God's sake."

"There's been an accident," Sebastian said heavily, sinking into a chair. "On the way back from the zoo. I couldn't help it. I couldn't . . ." He buried his face in his hands, his shoulders heaving with grief. "It wasn't my fault. It wasn't."

There was ice in Vickie's stomach and a feeling of deep dread.

Susie attempted to speak through a torrent of tears.

"It's the baby — it's little William — oh, Lord Jesus, Vickie, I'm so sorry, so, so sorry." She started lamenting, rocking herself to and fro, holding on to Vickie at the edge of the bed.

"Tell me what's happened, *please*," whispered Vickie. "I can't bear it."

The old duchess had entered the room, standing like a statue in the doorway, her normally cold expression grief-stricken. In a composed voice she explained.

"William was sitting in the passenger seat," she spoke matter-of-factly. "A truck came down the lane — it was going too fast — much too fast."

"It was coming straight toward us." Sebastian looked up, wide-eyed and tear-stained. "I had to brake, I *had* to . . ." He paused and started sobbing again.

"For God's sake, is he badly hurt?" said Vickie. "Tell me, tell me please."

"He's gone," Susie said through sobs. "He was thrown through the windshield and . . ."

"No." Vickie felt as if she wanted to die as well. "No, no, no, not my baby, not William."

All of her love had been plowed into that little boy — all of her hopes and dreams for the future. She was going to cherish him and love him as she herself had never been loved and cherished. Now he was gone, on his fourth birthday. It wasn't possible. It couldn't be.

"How can I go on living?" Vickie fell back on the bed, sobbing and shaking with grief. Susie sat in the chair next to her holding her hand. She put cold compresses on Vickie's brow and mumbled words of condolence, but there was no consoling her until the family doctor gave Vickie sedatives that sent her into drugged oblivion. The pain of the loss of her little boy was too great. Vickie's heart and soul felt dead, and she knew she would never be happy again.

Chapter Twenty-Five
1962

The next few years passed in a haze for Vickie. Unable to get over the death of her son, she went through life on autopilot, addicted to tranquilizers and alcohol. Since it was still imperative for the Burghley family to produce an heir, she dutifully, but reluctantly, allowed Sebastian into her bedroom once or twice a month, but she failed to become pregnant again.

"You're in your mid-forties now, m'dear," said the genial doctor. "The chances of falling pregnant at your age are extremely slim, I'm afraid."

Vickie took long, solitary walks on the estate, trying to work out what to do with her life. As the Duchess of Burghley, she had had to return to her duties. The house parties, pheasant shoots, and the Season of balls and parties in London still continued. The show was expected to go on. In fact, only a few short months after William's death it was clear to Vickie that she was expected to put on the full British stiff upper lip and carry on as usual. But without her vodka and pills she would have found it impossible.

Vickie's life with Sebastian became extremely shallow. They slept in separate bedrooms, made love only in an attempt to conceive, and he was far more interested in being with his aristocratic companions hunting, shooting, and fishing than he was in being with his wife.

Vickie was lonely — and a desperate sadness and longing for a child consumed her until she was obsessed with the idea. As she tramped the fields and lanes of Gloucestershire, Vickie started to think about what she wanted to do now. A Hollywood agent had approached her to take the starring role in *Imitation of Life*. It had been a juicy script and a great role for a forty-something woman. Vickie had felt the familiar rush of actor's adrenaline as she read it, but when she broached the subject with her husband, he flew off the handle.

"No Duchess of Burghley can *ever* demean herself by acting. You promised you'd give it all up when we married. Why start on this silly quest again?"

"Because I need something to do with myself."

"You're a *duchess*, Vickie. Join another charity and get this house more organized. It's a mess. We've got Princess Margaret and

327

Snowdon staying next weekend. You know how persnickety she can be. I hope you've planned some entertainment," he said coldly.

"I've got Sinatra flying in," she said sarcastically, "and Sammy and Dean too." She then went to call the agent to turn down the part that her contemporary, Lana Turner, played to considerable acclaim. But Vickie didn't mind. She didn't need anything anymore, she just felt totally dead inside.

Early in 1963, Vickie went to Rome. Valentino, a new, young designer, had invited her to attend his couture collection, so with nothing better to do she decided to stay at the Hassler for a few days and take in some of the other fashion shows and a touch of culture too.

The party at a grand palazzo on the Appian Way after Valentino's show was a huge success. The young Italian was being lionized, and Vickie went up to congratulate him.

"My dear, you look beautiful." Valentino looked her up and down appreciatively. "I love what you're wearing."

It was a cold January night, and Vickie was dressed appropriately in a long midnight-blue velvet gown of utter simplicity. She wore some of the Burghley family jewels: a magnificent sapphire and diamond parure of necklace, earrings, and bracelet, and her hair was swept up in an elegant chignon.

Vickie accepted Valentino's compliment graciously and after congratulating him, searched for her placement at one of the twenty round tables, each of which was set for twelve people.

"Long time no see." The laconic familiar voice shocked her so much that Vickie could hardly answer.

Cooper Hudson was holding out a gilt and red velvet chair for her, smiling down with that look in his eyes that always made her stomach twist with longing.

"Yes, it's been ages. How are you, Cooper?"

The actress in Vickie took over as she smiled graciously and sat down beside the man she'd been in love with for over two decades. Her heart started hammering as strongly as it had when she'd been twenty-two, and she could feel her thighs starting to tremble.

She looked at Cooper. He was nearly fifty-nine, his black hair was turning silvery-gray around his temples, but it was still thick and curled attractively over his collar and he wore his dinner jacket with the same casual insouciance that he wore jeans and a denim shirt. Although the sun had etched deep lines in his tanned face, his lips were still firm and sensual, and his dark brown eyes had not lost their twinkle. In fact, he had lost very little in the way of looks or sex appeal as the woman on his left obviously realized, immediately engaging him in animated conversation, leaving Vickie to contend with the Arab arms dealer on her right.

After the first course — scrambled eggs topped with beluga caviar served in a brown eggshell in a Georgian silver cup — Vickie, having downed two stiff vodkas, glanced toward Cooper and the woman whom she knew. Lady Graydon, the wife of a recently knighted industrialist, had nouveau riche written all over her. Her deep orange tan exaggerated the wrinkles on her sun-ruined skin, the blonde bob was just a touch too golden to be natural, and in spite of the January cold, she wore a sleeveless, backless dress, which couldn't disguise the sagging skin on her arms.

Vickie and Sebastian had recently spent the weekend with them at their flashy Wiltshire estate in which most of the antique furniture was fake and the pictures second rate. In spite of vast amounts of money, the Graydons still looked like what they had been, a poor boy from Lancashire and a shop assistant from Essex.

Sally Graydon was giving Cooper the full brunt of her charm. She'd already issued an invitation for him to join them on their boat this summer, and Vickie watched as a horsey laugh issued from her mouth — in which there appeared to be far too many teeth.

"Gives a new meaning to the phrase 'social climber,'" grinned the Arab, who then proceeded to grill Vickie about all the famous stars she knew in Hollywood.

Although Vickie turned toward Cooper after the first course, Sally Graydon was not about to let go of her prey and her arm rested on Cooper's shoulder, making it difficult for him to change direction and talk to Vickie.

Vickie shrugged inwardly. So what. Cooper was out of her life — he might as well be dead and buried. "You wish," said her inner voice. "His flame still burns inside you and you know it, girl."

When Valentino rose to make a short speech, Cooper finally extracted himself from the woman's clutches and turned to Vickie, his eyes burning into hers. He didn't need to say anything; his look was enough, and Vickie knew that whatever he wanted she was willing to give him, and wherever he was going tonight she was going with him.

Chapter Twenty-Six
1963

They had never needed to talk. He held her hand tightly as they walked into her hotel suite. The lights were low, and from the window the golden floodlit dome of St. Peter's shimmered in the moonlight. Wordlessly his arms folded around her, his lips found hers, and for an endless moment they kissed until Vickie thought she had never been kissed before. Then, effortlessly, he picked her up and carried her into the bedroom.

Cooper's lovemaking was as tender and passionate as it had been the first time. When he was inside her, his fingers laced with hers and he kept looking deep into her eyes. With every erotic motion Vickie's senses told her she was home. No matter that it had been eighteen years since their last encounter — it was as if it were yesterday. The familiar feel of Cooper's body moving rhythmically with hers, the intimacy of his touch on her flesh and the feel of his mouth and tongue on hers drove Vickie to an intensity of desire she had never believed she would experience again. Their hunger for each other was so intense that they couldn't stop making love, couldn't stop craving each other's bodies. When he came, he looked deeply into Vickie's eyes, smiling with such sweet passion that she felt she could die of love for him. She bit her lips to prevent herself from blurting out, "I love you, Coop, and I always have and I always will." Too many times she'd said it, too many times he'd hurt and rejected her. For this magical night Vickie knew she must live only for the moment. And so she did.

They made love for hours, stopping only to smoke, to sip champagne, or to whisper softly as they lay in each other's arms. He was so lovingly affectionate that Vickie wanted to scream, "Why can't you be with me? Why can't you leave your wife? We belong together, you know we do." But she didn't.

As dawn broke, their appetites were temporarily gratified. They slept for an hour or two until he awoke her, once again aroused, and brought her to her peak again and again. When Vickie awoke at noon he was gone; the indentation of his head on the pillow and the rumpled sheets the only evidence that they had been together.

Vickie lay in bed all day thinking, reliving over and over again her gorgeous night of passion. She wondered if he would telephone, but she suspected he wouldn't. He was leaving Rome that morning for New York and then California, where she had overheard him telling Lady Graydon that his wife was in a nursing home. Her heart heavy with sorrow, Vickie feared she would never see Cooper Hudson again.

Later that day, he called her from the airport. The line was crackling, and she could hardly hear him, but his intention was clear. He would be coming to England in three months, and he wanted to see her. Would she see him? Of course she would. Vickie hung up, glowing with euphoria. Cooper had told her he would be staying at the Dorchester in April; he was shooting an action movie at Pinewood Studios. She would call him there. She would see him again; she could hardly wait.

Vickie spent the next two days strolling the winding streets and piazzas of Rome in a golden daze of happiness. She wandered down the Spanish Steps to the Piazza d'España, buying armloads of bright winter flowers from the old women who crouched on the cold stones patiently waiting for customers. She sipped cappuccino at Doney's café on the Via Veneto, watching the colorful parade of pimps and prostitutes; predatory young studs in black sweaters and tight white pants and miniskirted starlets seeking their fortune in the Eternal City. There was a sensation deep inside Vickie of life, and two weeks later, by the time she was only one day late, Vickie knew unequivocally that she was carrying Cooper's baby.

Vickie's second pregnancy was greeted with huge rejoicing by the Burghley family again. Susie in particular was thrilled to see how blissfully happy Vickie had become again.

As the weeks passed, Vickie was back to her old self and at every house party and social event she sparkled as she never had before.

As the life within her grew so did Vickie's joy, but she was still counting the days until April, when Cooper would arrive in London.

In March Vickie started hemorrhaging so badly that the doctor confined her to bed.

"If you do not stay off your feet entirely for the next six months, there is no guarantee that at your age that you will carry this baby full term," he warned.

Vickie took to her bed obediently but spent most of the time daydreaming about her new baby and about Cooper.

"Cooper, hi, it's Vickie."

"Hey, babe, good to hear from you. How're you doin'?"

"I'm doing fine, Cooper, just fine. I heard

335

you were in town. I'm in Gloucestershire, but I'd love to see you." There was a silence in which she sensed his hesitation.

"Yeah, well I'd love to see you too, babe, but I'm kind of busy on this picture right now. I'm really sorry I didn't call before but publicity's been on my tail all the time, they're running me ragged."

"I hoped you might be able to visit me because it would be rather difficult for me to come to London." She paused. "You see, I'm expecting a baby." This time there was definitely a pause — a long one.

"Well, that's great, honey, I'm real happy for you — isn't that what Sebastian's family wanted?"

"Yes, Cooper, it is, but . . ." Vickie dropped her voice. Was it her imagination or was there a click on one of the other house lines? Had someone picked up?

"Cooper — I *have* to see you," Vickie whispered. "I must. Please, it's terribly important. I need to see you, just to talk, to tell you . . ." She trailed off. If someone was listening, this could be dangerous.

"Well I'd love to talk to you but, Vickie, why do you need to see me to talk? Can't we talk on the phone? I don't have much free time, babe. This picture's a bitch — nothing but underwater stunts and jumping in and out of helicopters. I've only been here a week but I'm exhausted already. I'm too old for all this. Why don't you come to Pinewood, honey? We can have lunch. Or meet me at the Dorchester for dinner. I'd love to see you, honey, I really would."

He dropped his voice in the familiar sexual way that still thrilled her.

"I'll have to check with my doctor. Maybe. I'll let you know." There was another awkward silence, and then Vickie took the plunge. "How's your wife?"

"The same. She's in a home now. Having care," Cooper answered flatly.

He'd never wanted to talk about his wife, and Vickie was too tired to pursue the conversation. Too many years, too much water under the bridge. What witchcraft in Cooper made her feel this way, so helplessly lovelorn, even though all her instincts screamed "No"? Here we go, thought Vickie, the old runaround again. He'd done it to her many times throughout the years. Why had she put up with it? Love, of course. She had been a slave to this man's love, believing in her heart of hearts that he loved her too.

Vickie had wanted to tell Cooper about their baby, to share with him the joy it was bringing her. But not on the telephone. If he couldn't spare the time to come and see her, she wasn't going to bother anymore.

"OK, Cooper. Fine. I'll call you when the doctor gives me the all clear. Maybe we can have lunch then. Good luck with the movie."

She hung up, not waiting for his answer. She wasn't twenty-one years old anymore; she was a mature woman who was finally getting what she had always craved. Given that it was not Sebastian's child, which he and his family must never know, it would perhaps be better that she not tell Cooper the truth about her pregnancy. If Sebastian ever discovered that the baby wasn't his — what then? They had been drifting apart for a long time now, in spite of their monthly sexual congress. Having another man's baby would surely drive them further apart and ultimately the child would suffer.

No, Vickie would keep this secret all to herself. Whoever it was who said "Two can keep a secret only if one is dead" was wise indeed.

Chapter Twenty-Seven
1963–1965

The Honorable Lucinda Rosemary Swannell entered the world in October 1963. Weighing six pounds seven ounces, she had a perfect baby's face, her father's black hair (thank God both Sebastian and Cooper were dark-haired, thought Vickie), and the wide-apart aquamarine eyes of both her parents.

Vickie was totally thrilled with her baby girl, but she soon realized that the family was not.

"A girl," the dowager duchess said scornfully to her son. "We don't need a *girl* — you *must* have an heir, Sebastian. You simply must. You'll be forty-five soon. You're the last of the line, and you've *got* to produce a son."

"Well I can't start trying yet, mother, can I? The baby's only two months old." Sebastian petulantly stuffed a cigarette into an onyx holder. His mother was starting to irritate the hell out of him. But she was right, of course. The Burghley line was all that mattered and he knew it.

"In one month's time you'd better start trying again," the duchess said ominously. "If you don't produce a boy within the next two years, it will be far too late for Victoria. I'm sure I don't need to point out that she's your age, Sebastian, she's almost too old to have another child."

He noticed that the maid, who was arranging the dowager duchess's post on her desk, seemed to be taking her time about it. Patsy was the old duchess's confidante, and she seemed to trust her totally. Sebastian had never liked or trusted her, but he rarely dared disagree with his mother about anything. "All right, Mother, all right," Sebastian sighed. "We'll try again."

But a month later, when Sebastian entered Vickie's bedroom to make his intentions known, she sent him packing.

"Can't you see I'm feeding Lulu," she said.

"But I want to make love with you. We've got to try for a boy." Sebastian glanced away disdainfully from the infant at her mother's breast. "For God's sake, Vickie, *must* you suckle that child yourself? You're like a fucking peasant, for God's sake. No one does that anymore, no one."

"Well, I do," said Vickie firmly. "And I'm going to look after her myself as much as possible. I don't want my baby brought up by servants and nannies."

"Right. Then may I make an appointment

with you, my dear?" he asked sarcastically. "I would like to have sex with my wife some time this century."

"I feel like a brood mare," said Vickie darkly. Then, realizing that she did indeed still have a duty to the family, she sighed and said, "All right, Sebastian, let me rest until the New Year, then we'll try again."

Once every month during 1964 and 1965 Sebastian came to Vickie's room and they made clinical, dispassionate love. Sebastian performed like an automaton, and Vickie was finding the act more and more distasteful. She was never turned on by him and dreaded these monthly assignations.

One day Vickie arrived at the Eaton Square house unexpectedly. Sebastian thought she was in Gloucestershire with Lulu, but Vickie had forgotten an important appointment at the dentist's.

Exhausted from extensive root canal work, she let herself into the house, as the servants were away. Entering her bedroom, she was confronted by the sight of Sebastian in bed with a muscular young man.

"It's not what you think!" cried Sebastian as Vickie fled the room in shock.

"You could have fooled me," Vickie yelled, banging the front door behind her.

Vickie was calm as they sat in the morning

room of their Gloucestershire mansion, two days later.

"I want a divorce, Sebastian — this marriage has become a farce."

"Oh, for God's sake, Vickie, stop being so old-fashioned. Don't forget I was at sea for five years, this kind of thing was quite common — it's no big deal."

"Not to this kind of woman. Our marriage is a sham and you know it. Let's cut our losses, Sebastian. I'll leave with Lulu and the coast will be clear for your mother to find a nice young English rose to produce an heir — one who won't mind you dallying with the occasional pretty boy."

Sebastian gazed into the fire, misty-eyed.

"It isn't that I don't love you, Vickie, you know that I do."

"But you're not *in* love with me. I understand. It's the oldest line in the book, Sebastian. I've even said it in my movies. It's OK darling, I'm not in love with you either."

"What is it anyway, Vickie, 'love'?" He sighed. "I really did love you madly once, but when two people start the day-to-day business of living together, love wears off, doesn't it?"

"I guess so." Thoughts of Cooper became a kaleidoscope in Vickie's head, and she struggled to banish them.

"Let's end it then, Sebastian. No hard feelings?"

He held out a manicured hand as from up in the nursery they heard the faint cries of eighteen-month-old Lulu. "Maybe you're right, Vickie."

"I must go to her." Vickie was reacting in an almost Pavlovian style to the sound of her hungry infant. "She wants to be fed."

"Oh, for heaven's sake, Vickie," Sebastian snapped. "Isn't it time you weaned her? Let Susie give her a bottle. What you're doing is obscene."

"No, Sebastian, it's not. Lulu is my child, and she is going to be loved utterly and completely by me. I will never leave her and I will never abandon her and I mean that with all my heart." She blew her husband a kiss at the door and he gave her a faint wave.

"Good-bye, my dear, and I wish you the best of luck."

"And the same to you, Sebastian — I really hope you get what you desire."

PART THREE

Lulu

Chapter Twenty-Eight
1966

The Dowager Duchess of Burghley stood stiffly in front of the French windows in the drawing room at Eaton Square, glaring at her son, who lounged on the sofa. Despite her seventy years, the duchess's back was firm and straight and she held herself with an even more aristocratic demeanor than when she had been a debutante. Her wiry personal maid, Patsy, busied herself putting more coals on the fire, occasionally glancing in Sebastian's direction with ill-disguised contempt.

Sebastian was letting his mother do the talking, and she was in full-blown matriarchal mode. She had not been as angry as he feared when his bisexuality had been revealed, but she was now adamant about his future.

"Of course you must divorce the actress immediately. You have to give our family an heir, Sebastian, you simply *must*. I suggest you marry Emily Woodroff-Hamilton. She's in her twenties, a fine robust girl from an excellent family, highly suitable."

"But, Mother, I don't love Emily." He sighed.

The duchess gave her son a withering look. "What has *love* to do with anything?" she asked, sipping fruit tea from a delicate Wedgwood cup. "Don't be so naive, Sebastian. Do you really think I loved your father?"

"You — you didn't?" he stuttered.

"Of course not. Oh, I was fond enough of him, he was quite a charmer, but all of that love stuff is for novels and films. In real life you marry for the right reasons, and the right reasons in this case, my dear son, are to continue the Burghley line. Do you understand?"

He did understand and so the die was cast. Vickie and Sebastian were quietly divorced and, even though she was entitled to keep her title, Vickie decided against it. "They don't give a damn about duchesses in Hollywood and neither do I," she told Susie. "I'm going back to California and back to my maiden name." Sebastian had given her a reasonable amount of child support and, in spite of protestations from his mother, Vickie also received a handsome settlement of two million dollars.

"It will be enough to buy a house for you and the child. You should invest the rest, and we sincerely hope that we won't be hearing anything more from you," said the dowager duchess crisply.

In Los Angeles, Vickie installed Lulu, Susie, and herself in a bungalow at the Beverly Hills Hotel, known to the locals as the Pink Palace because of its rose-colored rococo exterior. Lulu was enrolled in a kindergarten at nearby El Rodeo School, and Vickie spent her days searching for the right house, which was difficult because nothing seemed to be suitable or the right price. Vickie had never been smart with money and, although Sebastian had advised her to find an honest financial adviser or business manager, she put her two million dollars into a current account at the bank and gradually started eating into the capital. Vickie adored her daughter. She indulged her whims, gave in to her occasional temper tantrums, and lavished on her all the love and affection that Vickie had never received from her own mother. Little Lulu knew how to manipulate Vickie, and from the time she was three she became an expert at getting her own way.

"Did you see this?" Susie passed the obituary column from *Daily Variety* to Vickie.

It was a beautiful California spring morning, and the Santa Ana winds had blown away all traces of smog. The two women were sunbathing on the tiny terrace outside their hotel bungalow while Vickie scanned the latest *Los Angeles Times* residential section yet again.

Irene Hudson, 75, scriptwriter of the 1940's hit Dead Men's Prayers, died in her sleep at the Kirkpatrick Nursing Home in Pasadena. She is survived by her husband, actor-turned-businessman Cooper Hudson, and a son.

"So she's finally gone," said Vickie. "I wonder what Cooper's going to do now?"

"You going to call him?" asked Susie.

Vickie shook her head. She had confided everything in Susie. "If he wants to see me, he can soon find out where I am. You know I've tried hard not to think about Coop, but every day I see more and more of him in Lulu."

It was true. The little girl had the same black curly hair, full lips, and stubborn streak as her father, but she had also inherited her mother's cerulean eyes and affectionate, fun-loving nature.

"Well, I hear Cooper's become quite a whiz in the investment business now that his acting career's on the wane. Maybe it's time you looked him up again," suggested Susie. "After all, he is the only man you ever really loved."

"Fat lot of good that's done me. He's never given me anything, except Lulu of course."

"Don't you think you should tell him about her? Now that his wife's passed on, maybe he'll be more interested."

"In me, you mean? Susie, you are the only person who knows how devastated I've been by Cooper's rejections. Yet I always took him back again because I was young and I couldn't resist him. I'm forty-eight now, Cooper's over sixty. Do you *really* think sparks of passion will ignite at our age?"

"Why not?" asked Susie. "Wasn't it Oscar Wilde who said that age isn't important unless it concerns wine?"

Vickie smiled, put down the paper, and examined her bank statement again. "This really isn't good, Susie. Do you realize I've gone through over a quarter of my settlement in a year? At this rate, if I don't organize myself into buying a house and investing the rest of the money, I'll be broke in five years."

"Well, since there're no producers on the horizon standing in line for you, dear, you must do something," urged Susie. "Find some financial person to help you."

"Oh, Susie, it's so hard to trust any of these Hollywood business managers. You remember how the studio took care of everything for me when I was under contract? They rented my houses, bought my cars, found the right advisers to handle everything. I don't *know* anyone here anymore, Susie, and there are so many shysters and crooks around."

"Well, you'd better get some help quick. I'm too old for the poorhouse, dear." Susie picked up the telephone directory and thumbed through it. "Ah, look, here it is, Hudson and Brown Investment Brokers. That's Cooper's firm, dear. Call him. What can you lose?"

Vickie raised her eyebrows. "Certainly not my virginity!"

They met in the Polo Lounge for drinks, almost thirty years since they had first met on the Paradigm back lot. Cooper was already seated in a green upholstered booth in the far corner near the pianist, a shot glass of malt whisky in front of him, a cigar in his hand. When Vickie arrived, he stood up to hug her and inspected her face at close range.

"Vickie, you still look beautiful, honey."

"Still?" Vickie smiled and sat down. "I hate that word, don't you?"

"Guess I do, but it'll have to do until they invent a new one. Martini?"

She nodded and he signaled for the waiter while Vickie studied his profile. For a man in his sixties Cooper looked amazing. His iron-gray hair was still thick, and the lines in his deeply tanned face only seemed to exaggerate his forceful masculinity. As usual, his clothes were beautifully cut but worn with the casualness of a man who didn't really care how he looked. Vickie felt like a teenager again as he turned to her, his dark eyes as piercing as ever.

"So you're no longer the duchess of Hidey-Ho, or whatever it's called, then?"

"Thank God." She took a sip of her martini, aware of Cooper's inspection. She had dressed carefully in a short pale-gray shift dress that accentuated her beautiful legs, discreet pearls, and her auburn hair was swept into a chic chignon. She was confident that she was still a beautiful woman — she knew that by the number of men who asked her out on the dates that she seldom accepted.

But she wasn't interested in men anymore; her life revolved around her daughter. However, this man, the father of her child, the man she had loved for three decades still made her heart flutter like a virgin bride.

"I'm sorry to hear about your wife."

"No, you're not. There's no need to lie to me, Vickie. We've never lied to each other, have we, babe?"

"Does holding back the truth count as a lie?" The martini had made Vickie bolder.

"What do you mean by that?" He regarded her quizzically.

"I have something to tell you that you may not want to hear, but I feel I should tell you, for both our sakes, and for Lulu's."

"Who the hell is Lulu?"

Vickie finished her martini and took a deep breath. "Lulu is our child, Cooper. Lucinda is her real name, and she's your daughter."

"My what?" For the first time ever Vickie

saw a look that was almost of fear cross Cooper's face.

"We have a child, Cooper. That's why I wanted to see you in England, to tell you. Do you remember that night in Rome almost five years ago?"

"I certainly do, Vickie, how could I forget. But a *child* . . . *our* child? How can you be so sure it's mine?"

"Because I wasn't sleeping with my husband and I wasn't sleeping with anyone else either, and she also looks and behaves exactly like you." She smiled. "In fact, she's a regular little madam."

Cooper signaled for more drinks, then stared at Vickie for a long time. "So what do you want me to do about her?" he asked slowly. "I'm not acting that much anymore. Are you asking me for child support?"

Vickie's face flushed. "Of *course* not. How could you think I'd do such a thing, Coop? Sebastian supports her. I wanted you to know because . . ."

Her voice trailed off and she sipped her fresh drink, aware of the faint strains of the pianist playing "I'm Through with Love" in the background. How apt, Vickie thought ruefully, that Cooper could only think about his daughter in monetary terms instead of as a potential relationship. Is this what I want for Lulu? Vickie surveyed the man of her endless dreams yet again and noticed that he was actually looking a touch shopworn, even in the flattering dim light of the Polo Lounge.

"You've spent all your life running from commitment as far as I was concerned, haven't you, Coop?" Vickie tried to keep her voice light, but the barb hit the mark.

"I told you that years ago, Vickie. I'm not the guy for the long haul. I can't make it, honey, never have, and it's far too late for that now," he said ruefully.

"Never mind what you are or were, Coop, that's not important. I just want you to see Lulu. She's beautiful, slightly wild. She's an amazing mixture of you and me."

He drew on his cigar and surveyed Vickie through the smoke, and then he smiled.

"OK, Vickie, I'd like to see the kid too, just to see what the old genes were capable of."

"You did well . . . we did well," Vickie whispered. "Why don't you come to tea on Sunday, you'll see what she's like then. And by the way, this *wasn't* the reason I called you. I'm interested in starting up an investment portfolio, and I need some advice."

"Now for that you've come to the right guy," said Cooper and launched into detailed descriptions of the services and benefits his company was able to offer. At the end of an hour, Vickie was impressed enough to make plans to entrust her remaining one and three-quarter million dollars to Hudson and Brown to invest for her. Although she was aware of the familiar sexual glint in Cooper's eye, she resisted the impulse to take him up on his offer to see his newly acquired apartment on Wilshire Boulevard.

"From now on, darling, it's going to be strictly business between us." She noted the flash of disappointment in his eyes. "Those days are all behind us, Coop."

Chapter Twenty-Nine
1968

Vickie's reluctance to become involved with Cooper again so completely bewitched him that he began to pursue her in earnest. He wooed her with flowers and his talent to amuse, and Vickie's good intentions began to waver when faced with the full battery of Cooper Hudson's legendary charm. He took a complete shine to his daughter, indulging her even more than Vickie and Susie did.

One afternoon, a week after Cooper and Vickie had met, they sat with Susie on the tiny lawn outside the bungalow watching the pampered child throw herself about, screaming, on the grass.

"Why's she acting up?" asked Cooper.

"Because I wouldn't buy her a pony for Christmas," laughed Vickie.

"All my friends have pets," wailed Lulu. "Why can't I have one too?"

"You can have a kitten or a puppy, a rabbit, a goldfish or a hamster, but I'm not letting you start to ride. It's far too dangerous." Vickie had been thrown off a horse in one of her early films and now had a deep-seated fear of them.

"Hey, little lady, calm down." Cooper went over to the sulky child and started whispering in her ear, and Vickie and Susie stared in amazement as a cheeky smile spread across Lulu's face. She stood up, stopped crying as Cooper wiped her eyes with his handkerchief and, without protest, allowed him to lead her by the hand to the back gate.

"We'll be right back," grinned Cooper.

"Where are you going?" called Vickie.

"I'm taking Lulu riding," he yelled in a voice that brooked no argument. "They have these little ponies on La Cienaga and Beverly Boulevard. They're safe as houses, Vickie. Don't worry, they've never lost a kid yet."

Before she could answer, Cooper and Lulu were gone. Susie started laughing and Vickie stared after them, openmouthed. "They've sure got a lot in common, those two. Peas in a pod. Both stubborn as mules, and both got to get their own way."

"You're right," Vickie said grimly, "but I'm not happy about having my authority overruled."

"Don't see you've got much of a choice, Vickie. You know that whatever Cooper wants, Cooper usually gets. And I'll say one thing for him — apart from the fact he can charm the birds off the trees — that girl adores him and he's certainly a fine father figure, which is more than we can say for the duke, right?"

"True," Vickie sighed. With Sebastian's re-marriage and the birth of his twin boys, communications had been sparse between him and Lulu. The child support checks arrived regularly enough but, apart from a Christmas card, Lulu's legal father might as well not have existed.

"Cooper's a good influence on her, mark my words," said Susie. "You should let him see more of her." And more of you too, Susie thought privately. She knew Vickie was still in love with Cooper. He had come back into her life with a vengeance and, try as she might, Vickie knew her defenses were crumbling.

Cooper invested wisely and well for Vickie. He found her a charming little house in the flats of Rodeo Drive and helped her decorate it with the quiet English country taste she had developed while married to Sebastian.

"It's across the road from Gene Kelly's, so we can play volleyball with his gang some-time," he said.

The balance of the money he invested brought Vickie a modest income and, with the $600 a month from Sebastian, all ends were quite easily met.

But it was inevitable that they would become lovers again. Cooper was too irresistible and Vickie was still too much in love with him, in spite of her denials to herself. He wooed her and he won her and, on June 1, 1968, they were quietly married in the Beverly Hills Presbyterian Church on Rodeo Drive. Even more quietly — so that only he, Vickie, and Sebastian knew — Cooper adopted Lulu. She was now his, naturally and legally. He liked it that way; so did Vickie.

Patsy Kingsley read about the wedding in the newspapers as she sat by the fire in the basement kitchen of Eaton Square, which had hardly changed at all since 1918.

"That slut," she sneered to no one in particular. Even though she was old now, the hatred Patsy had nurtured toward Millie McClancey was like a disease that still festered inside her. She was able to indulge her intense dislike of Millie's daughter in gossip sessions with the dowager duchess, who also had nothing but scorn for her former daughter-in-law.

Although Rosemary confided many secrets to her maid, Patsy had never let the duchess know her own secret. She could never let anyone know about the child she had borne more than fifty years ago. That was her and her son Eddie's secret. Eddie had moved with his surrogate parents, the McCormicks, to New York in 1919, where he still lived. It was with the teenage Eddie that she had plotted and achieved Millie's death in 1933, and it would be through Eddie, again, that she believed she could eventually get even more revenge either on Vickie or her daughter, whom Patsy believed to be the product of incest.

Up in her sparse bedroom, Patsy took out her writing paper and penned a letter to her son in New York, a man she had not seen in many years but whom she believed should really have been the rightful Duke of Burghley had circumstances been different.

When Millie McClancey had suddenly disappeared from Eaton Square early in 1918, Patsy had been delighted. Then, when Millie's letters to Toby started to arrive, Patsy's curiosity had gotten the better of her. One of her jobs was to deal with the post, which, due to the war, was erratic, but it was still supposed to be collected and delivered at least once a day. Patsy had made it her business to always greet the mailman first thing in the morning and rifle through the letters. Then one day she recognized Millie's handwriting on a letter to Toby. When Patsy had read the contents of that letter, she had had an actual physical fit. Trembling uncontrollably, she had thought her lungs would burst before she could release her pent-up, choking fury. Throwing on her bonnet and cloak, she had run out in the pouring rain to nearby St. James's Park and, to the astonishment of the flocks of pigeons, screamed in a crazed rage until she fell exhausted onto the sodden grass.

She had kept the letter. She had kept all seven of them, each one increasingly pleading and beseeching about Millie's impending motherhood. Patsy was glad that her rival was suffering so much.

"Now she'll know what it's like to have a bastard child," she'd muttered to herself. Patsy also managed to purloin some of Toby's letters to Millie; an early one in which he vowed undying devotion to Millie and the later ones in which his interest was obviously waning. She kept them, her most prized possessions, tied with blue ribbon safely in the back of her drawer. Throughout the years Patsy had read and reread Toby's early letters, imagining herself to be the recipient.

She still harbored an all-encompassing, unreasonable passion for the young duke with whom she had shared a few fumbled moments on the sofa so long ago. In Patsy's twisted mind, Millie had become the reason that Toby had abandoned her and their baby. Bizarrely, she imagined that he would have married her and joyfully embraced the paternity of her son. She spent thousands of sleepless hours staring at the ceiling in her bleak bedroom, thinking of what might have been.

Patsy's calculated marriage to Kingsley had been a means to an end and a way to get up in the world. Even though he meant nothing to her, Patsy was convincing enough to persuade the old butler that she was mad for him, cleverly withholding her favors until he made an honest woman of her.

Shortly before Ambrose Osborne's *Bubbles* revue opened on Broadway in 1933, the Duke and Duchess of Burghley had spent a season in New York. They had taken a small entourage with them while staying at the Waldorf-Astoria, among them Kingsley and his wife, who had become the duchess's personal maid. Patsy had been following Millie's career avidly through newspapers and periodicals, so when she read in *The New York Times* that Millie was starring in a new revue, one in which her son, Eddie, was part of the backstage staff, working as an apprentice electrician, she was first in line at the box office the following day.

When Millie made her first entrance on the stage, rising like Aphrodite from a giant seashell and clothed in a flesh-colored leotard with shells appliquéd in strategic locations, Patsy wanted to scream with rage. Even she could see her hated enemy's beauty and sensuality, could sense the sexual arousal many men in the audience seemed to be experiencing. "Delicious," breathed the man next to her in rapture, "the most ravishing creature on Broadway." Patsy gave him a vicious stare, then turned back to the stage. She sat in a world of her own in the upper circle, pure jealousy consuming her.

During the show she could only think of how much better her life would be if this woman didn't exist. "If she were dead I could sleep at night," she whispered to herself.

Afterward she met her son Eddie in a nearby diner. Over supper she told him the full story of his parenthood and who he really was. Eddie had been shocked and then, with his mother egging him on, his shock turned to anger, then to a desire for revenge. "If this woman had not stolen the young duke from me," Patsy snarled, "I would have been married to him and *you*, my son, would be a duke and have riches galore."

Eddie was a simple man and obedient, so when his mother said they must dispose of "that redheaded witch," as Patsy called her, he agreed to help. In the following weeks, with Eddie's help, she had watched and waited and spied on Millie. Because of Eddie's electrical expertise she was eventually able to settle her score with her rival.

As Patsy stood with her sixteen-year-old son on Sixty-second Street, shivering in the bitter February cold, she had watched the brownstone building explode and catch fire, and had clutched hold of Eddie's arm and laughed with glee. It was he who had rigged the gas stove to explode, for Eddie's mind had been filled with the poison that his surrogate parents, the McCormicks, and his real mother had instilled in him over the years toward Millie and the Burghleys. Aware that he should be a duke with a fine estate in the English countryside and a mansion in London, Eddie was bitter. He was a poor boy just lucky enough, in the days of the Depression, to even have a job. If it helped his mother to get her revenge, he would do his bit.

When she read the New York tabloid headlines that screamed, "Famous Star Dies in Holocaust," Patsy allowed herself a rare smile. She had been vindicated — for a while at least.

Chapter Thirty
1980

The Honorable Lucinda Swannell grew up surrounded by family who loved her, people whom she took totally for granted. The more her mother, "stepfather," and Susie lavished attention and devotion on her, the more selfish and willful she became.

Now seventeen, her looks were spectacular. She had inherited the best of both her parents, although unaware that Cooper was her real father. At five foot nine, her wide-apart, enormous blue-green eyes had a guileless innocence that belied the naughty little girl she could often be. Her thick, curly black hair tumbled in a profusion of curls and waves around her heart-shaped face and shoulders that no hairdresser's expertise could ever have achieved. Her eyelashes were so dark and thick that some people thought she was wearing false ones, and her pouting full lips gave her face a sensual, almost carnal, look.

To the boys at Fairfax High, Lulu was a magnet, catnip to all the males, even the teachers. She wore the tightest T-shirts and the shortest miniskirts and, when she walked down any street, her undulating bottom, round and firm as a peach, caused many heads to turn.

She lived a privileged Beverly Hills life, wanting for nothing, her every whim catered to. Her closets were bursting with clothes, shoes, and jewelry. Her dressing table was clogged with dozens of bottles of perfume and hundreds of cosmetics she had no need for, and her private telephone never stopped ringing with boys begging for dates. But Lulu had no time for boys.

As a young teenager, her passion had been dancing. Hoping to become a ballerina, she had taken daily ballet classes since she was four. But to her enormous disappointment, when she auditioned for the prestigious Vanessa Cheyney Ballet School, she was turned down because of her height. Lulu went into a sulking rage that lasted for a month. Then she started to hit discos and nightclubs every weekend with a coterie of acolytes, mostly boys, whose only use to her were as dance partners. She was bitter about not being able to fulfill her lifelong ambition and only dancing, any dancing, relieved her anger.

Her family was concerned about Lulu's partying, particularly when she started coming home later and later each night.

"You know what teenage guys want?" said Cooper angrily. It was past three in the morning, and he and Vickie had been waiting for their daughter to return home since midnight. "All they want is sex — lots of it, as often as possible, and they don't care who they have it with." He paced up and down the living room, cigar clenched in his mouth, occasionally glancing out of the window.

"Well, you should know, darling. You were like that once yourself."

"Yes, but I don't want your daughter . . ."

"Our daughter," corrected Vickie.

". . . OK, OK, I don't want Lulu to be a receptacle for some pimply-faced kid's libido."

"What quaint old-fashioned terminology, darling. Don't worry. Lulu's told me she hasn't the slightest interest in boys. In fact, she told me she found the whole idea of them repugnant."

"Good. I hope she feels the same way for a few more years yet. She's too damn beautiful for her own damn good. But even if she's not interested in them, you can be darn sure they'll always be sniffing around *her*."

The front door opened and closed with a bang — Lulu seldom had any regard for whom she might disturb — and their daughter slouched into the room and threw herself on to the sofa.

"It's three o'clock — where the hell have

you been?" Cooper's voice was meant to intimidate, but it didn't succeed.

Lulu smiled slyly. "I've been at the Daisy, Pop." Vickie noticed that her pupils were completely dilated, and there was a spaced-out, faraway look on her face. "You know, the disco where everyone goes. It's all happening there. Natalie Wood, Ryan O'Neal, they're all there. It's fun."

"The Daisy closes at two and it's only down the street, so where *were* you?" Cooper looked so angry that Lulu giggled even more.

"Oh, chill, Pop, I just had a couple of beers to cool off and then I . . ." She fell back onto the sofa, gazing trancelike at the ceiling.

"And then you what? Answer me, Lulu, otherwise I'll . . ."

"Otherwise *what*, Pop? I'm seventeen, y'know, so don't threaten me, OK?" Lulu yawned dismissively, stretching her tawny limbs like a cat.

Cooper could see her nipples through her almost transparent red silk T-shirt, and the tight hot pants she was wearing left nothing to the imagination.

"What the hell are those things you're wearing?" Cooper demanded.

"They're hot pants, Pops."

"They're . . . quite revealing," interjected Vickie, hoping to avert another fight between Lulu and her father.

"Well, Mom, everyone *knows* what I've got down there. They can look, but they can't touch, no way, no siree!" She started giggling and bent to roll down her knee-length Lurex socks.

"Have you been taking drugs?" asked Cooper.

"Have I been taking drugs?" she mimicked sarcastically. "Get real, Pop. Of *course* I've been taking drugs, as you call them — all the kids do. But it's only pot. It doesn't hurt you."

"Doesn't hurt you hell." Cooper went over to the sofa, gripped his daughter by the shoulders, and started shaking her. "Pot, dope, speed, LSD — they're all poison. They make you do things you shouldn't do."

"Oh, stop, Pop. You're an old man. You don't know anything about people my age, what we do, how we feel. Face it, Pop, you and Mom are both from the dark ages."

"That's enough, Lulu." Vickie wondered where she had gone wrong in raising this recalcitrant, ungrateful girl. She had given her every bit of love — and what had she got in return? A sulky, spoiled disobedient child who seemed to care nothing about anyone except herself.

"I won't have you taking drugs, do you hear?" Cooper was in full fury now. "They're poison, they'll destroy you, besides the fact that it's a criminal act and you could go to jail."

"Oh, cool it, Pop — you don't know *anything*. Besides, you're not my real father, so what right do you have to think you can boss me around?"

"He has adopted you and he has every right as my husband," said Vickie quietly, "and as the head of this household."

"Well, I don't give a shit." Lulu wrenched herself away from Cooper and stood up. "If you don't like what I do, then fuck you all. I'm getting stifled here. I'll leave home and go to New York."

"New York?" asked Vickie faintly. "You don't know anyone in New York."

"Oh, no?" A sly grin crossed Lulu's face. "There's this model agent guy I met. He said I was a natural to be a model. He gave me his card; said anytime I wanted he could get me work. He said I could be bigger than Brooke Shields and Cheryl Tiegs."

"Bullshit," boomed Cooper. "You've got your education to finish. You're still in high school — we've got great plans for you."

"Yeah — what?" Lulu yawned again and lit a Marlboro, not bothering to hide her antipathy toward her parents. "What plans, Mom? What do *you* want me to do with my life, huh? Be a ham actor like you guys were? No thanks, no way."

"Of course not, Lucinda. With your brain you could be anything you want. We just want you to have a full education."

"Well, that sucks, frankly." Lulu inhaled deeply. "I wanted to be a ballerina but I'm too damn tall, so that's a no-no, but I'm *not* too tall to be a model and that's what I'm thinking about."

"But New York?" said Vickie. "Where would you live? Who would look after you?"

"Mom, I can look after myself — you have no idea. Don't you think I've been looking after myself for the past four years? Every time I leave this house I have to keep all my wits about me."

"What do you mean?"

"Oh, Mom, wake up and smell the coffee. I mean that practically every guy who looks at me tries to make a pass at me. You'd be amazed how creepy most guys are." She shuddered and stubbed out her cigarette.

"I don't think I'd be that amazed." Vickie's mind flashed back to her own days of wine and roses. "But I guess in my day men were more gallant about things."

"Well, this is the eighties, Mom, and they ain't gallant anymore. Guys'll do anything to get into your pants, *anything* — spike your drink, knock you out, flatter you by saying the most ridiculous things . . ."

"So, how do you handle them — these guys who come on so strong?" Cooper sat down, trying to be calm and play the patriarch game. He ran a hand through his thick white hair and sighed. He was tired. This girl was wearing him out.

"It's easy, Pop. I tell them the truth."

"And what, pray, *is* the truth?" asked Vickie.

"I tell them I like girls! And I do, Mom, I really do, and I guess I've finally got to admit it to you. So if you really want to know where I've been tonight, I'll tell you."

"Where?" Vickie managed to croak, her heart filled with dread.

"With Liza, at her parents' house. They're out of town so she and I . . ." Lulu's voice trailed off and a dreamy look came into her eyes.

"So . . . so what?" Cooper's face was pale with shock. This revelation came totally out of left field — boys he could handle, but girls? His beautiful daughter preferred women to men? Cooper knew he wasn't modern enough to accept that, and all of his old-fashioned conservative attitudes were thrown into confusion. "Tell me, Lulu — what's going on?"

"Well, if you must know, we spent the whole evening in her parents' bed." Lulu was enjoying the shocked amazement on Vickie's and Cooper's faces. "You know that Liza's dad owns a casino in Vegas, so they've got a mirror on the ceiling right above their bed. You'd be amazed how sexy that can be, Mom." She looked at Vickie challengingly, relishing the shock on her mother's face.

"Oh my God. I don't want to hear about it." Vickie got up, trembling, and started collecting glasses and emptying ashtrays. "I can't listen to this anymore, Lulu."

"Then don't ask, Mom, because believe me I have no inhibitions in talking about it, none at all. I'll tell you everything you want to know. Ask me. Ask me what we do; I'm sure as my *parents* you're interested." She grinned and her raven curls tumbled across her forehead. Vickie thought she looked like a dark angel — or a devil.

"Enough." Cooper stood up. He seemed to have aged in the last half hour, and his tanned face was several shades lighter. "I'm going to bed. I don't want to listen to any more of your filthy stories."

"Filthy? What's filthy about sex, Pop? You liked women's bodies. So do I." He started to answer, but Lulu interrupted, "Hey, Pop, I *know*, OK? A couple of the kids in my grade are the *grand*kids of women you slept with. You were quite a stud, weren't you? Quite a stud. And you, Mom, were a nymphomaniac, weren't you? Screwed your way through Hollywood, so they say."

Vickie, too, had turned extremely pale, and Cooper seemed to be visibly shrinking with shock at this venom from his beloved daughter.

"Stop it, Lulu," Vickie said in a shaking voice. "Can't you see how much you're hurting your father?"

"My father?" Lulu shrieked, jumping up and down, her pupils so dilated her eyes looked almost transparent. Vickie thought she looked like a werewolf — a gorgeous, wild werewolf crazed by a full moon.

"You're not my fucking *father*. My father's the Duke of Burghley, and I'm the *Honorable* Lucinda Rosemary Swannell." She gave a little mock curtsy. "I'm a fucking English aristocrat, and you and Mom are just ancient old actors, old, *old* actors that nobody wants to know about, yesterday's news — relics."

"You're wrong." Vickie was in so much shock that her voice was merely a whisper. "Cooper *is* your father, Lulu — he's your natural father. I . . . didn't want to tell you, but . . ."

"Oh, bullshit, Mama. I don't buy it. Don't try and make things better."

"I'm not listening to any more of this." Cooper grabbed Lulu's arm and half-dragged her toward the stairs. He pulled her up while she held on to the banister, screaming at him. Vickie was weeping bitterly. What had turned her daughter into this monstrous creature?

"You'd better go to bed right away or I'm calling the doctor." Cooper's voice sounded muffled and hoarse. "It's not just pot you've taken, it's something else, something mind-altering, because you don't know what you're saying."

Vickie stumbled up the stairs behind Cooper and Lulu, struggling to control her tears. "We'll forgive you, Lucinda, because you're obviously drugged out of your mind."

"Not too fucking out of my mind to speak the truth, Mommy dearest," she yelled. "So now that you know the truth, what are you going to do about it, huh?" She stood at the top of the stairs, hands on hips defiantly.

"We'll discuss it tomorrow." With a super-human effort Cooper pushed his daughter into her bedroom, where she slumped onto her bed, her hair fanning out on the pillow. She lay still for a moment, then jumped up screaming even more obscenities. She started throwing ornaments, CDs, anything she could, into the fireplace, slurring her words and becoming extremely agitated.

"Take no notice, darling," Cooper whispered to Vickie as he closed Lulu's bedroom door and put his arms around Vickie as they walked to their bedroom. "I'm calling Dr. Northridge right now. It isn't Lulu speaking, it's the drugs. Get into bed, darling, try and relax."

Vickie lay down, closing her eyes wearily, and Cooper picked up the telephone and started to dial. Suddenly Vickie heard the phone clatter to the ground and a loud thump as Cooper collapsed onto the carpet clutching his chest in agony.

"Oh God, oh my God! Cooper, what's

wrong?" Vickie threw herself onto the floor calling his name, listening to his harsh, rattling breathing. She could hear her crazed daughter still shouting and throwing things in her room as she dialed 911 with shaking fingers and watched her beloved husband's face turn ashen.

But it was too late. When the ambulance arrived ten minutes later, Cooper Hudson was already dead of a massive heart attack.

Chapter Thirty-One
1981

Half of old Hollywood from the "golden era" attended Cooper's funeral service. Then they came to Rodeo Drive to pay their respects to his widow. Cooper had been immensely popular and a huge star in his prime, and many of his contemporaries — Frank Sinatra, Gene Kelly, and Cary Grant — were just some of his peers who wanted to tell his widow how much Cooper had meant to them.

"They don't make 'em like Coop anymore." Sinatra's piercing blue eyes were sorrowful. "He was a real man, one of the boys — y'know what I mean?"

"Yes, I sure do." Vickie smiled, thinking of the thirty years when Cooper had been so busy being a man's man that he hadn't had time for her. Never mind. She'd had twelve wonderful years with him and even though neither of them had been in their prime, they had been totally committed and full of love for each other. "I guess twelve years is a long time to be happily married in this town."

"You bet, honey." Sinatra winked. "I never made it past seven!"

Vickie had been told by her physician, Dr. Northridge, that even though he was in his mid-seventies, Cooper had been in peak physical shape and could have lived for many more years. It had been shock that had caused his heart attack. Vickie sat next to Susie, listening grimly, as Susie squeezed her hand supportively. Although Susie loved Lulu, she blamed her for his death, and her main loyalty had always been to Vickie.

Other men friends of Cooper milled about in the living room, drinking Scotch and reminiscing about Cooper's exploits and adventures, while the chintz-covered sofas overflowed with old friends of Vickie's. Lana Turner was chic in black silk and a matching turban. Ava Gardner, her luscious raven hair brushed severely back, chatted with Hedy Lamarr, who was still almost as dazzling as when she'd played Delilah. Katharine Hepburn, the epitome of casual style in a men's-cut gray flannel suit, imparted some advice to Vickie about coping with the death of someone who'd been worshiped.

"When Spence died, I thought I'd died too," she confided. "It's going to take a long, long time to get over him, Vickie. You have to grieve — that's part of the healing — but then you must get on with your life."

"What life?" Vickie's voice was hoarse, but

she was dry-eyed. The doctor had given her some valium, which made her feel almost surreal, surrounded as she was by so many people she hadn't seen in years. "You had your career to return to, Katy, and you were still young enough to get on with it. I'm sixty-two and there aren't many parts for the glamorous grandmother type."

"You should try," said Hepburn. "You're still a name even though you haven't worked in years. Get an agent. Get back to work, Vickie. It'll be good for you. You know what they say, 'Once an actress, always an actress.' It never gets out of your blood."

Vickie smiled. "I don't know how I could. My life revolved around Cooper and Lulu. Now he's gone and she's become . . ." She couldn't finish the sentence. She didn't want Katy Hepburn to know that her adored daughter was becoming a monster, someone whose cruel tongue and selfishness had been driving a wedge between mother and daughter since before Cooper's death.

Vickie glanced over to where Lulu was chatting with Cary Grant and felt her chest tighten. Lulu had killed Cooper as surely as if she'd stabbed him through the heart. It was going to be hard to continue living in the same house with this alien stranger.

Vickie needn't have worried. Although Lulu made an attempt to commiserate and comfort her mother, her apologies sounded hollow and fake. Vickie's heart was closed to her. Suddenly she saw clearly that all the years of care and unconditional love that she, Cooper, and Susie had lavished on this girl had been wasted. She had turned out to be a callous, heartless little shrew, and Vickie couldn't bear to be around her. Only Susie gave Vickie the sympathy and comfort she needed. Only Susie understood how she felt.

A few days later, returning from placing flowers on Cooper's grave, Vickie found a note in the front hall. It was addressed to her, in Lulu's writing. She took it upstairs and read it slowly while lying on her bed.

Dear Mom,

I'm really sorry about what I did and I know you won't be able to forgive me. It wasn't my fault, you know, that Cooper died. What I said I didn't really mean, it was the drugs talking like he said. I guess they sold me some bad stuff. I hope you can forgive me one day, because even though you may not believe me, I did love Cooper and I do care for you.

But anyway, Mom, I don't belong here anymore. I'll be eighteen soon and I want to go my own way. I'm off to New York to take that guy up on his modeling offer. I'll keep you posted.

Sorry for being me. I guess I'm just a

spoiled Beverly Hills brat after all, but I've got to do my own thing and maybe one day I'll learn to be a better person.

Love ya, Mom
Lulu

Vickie lay back on the bedspread, staring at the ceiling. "My life is over," she whispered. "There's nothing left anymore."

When Patsy read about Cooper Hudson's death in the *Daily Mirror*, she laughed and laughed until tears ran down her sunken cheeks. Then she went to see the dowager duchess, Rosemary, now bedridden and almost blind, to tell her the good news about the demise of Vickie's husband, and they both had a glass of sherry to celebrate.

Chapter Thirty-Two
1985–1986

Lulu hit New York like an Amtrak train barreling into Penn Station, and New York ate her up. True to his promise, Lew Ackerman, head of the Ackerman Agency, had no difficulty in getting jobs for the gorgeous teenager. Within a year Lulu was featured in *Cosmopolitan*, *Glamour*, *Mademoiselle*, and *Seventeen* magazines, and within two years she had made the cover of all of them, plus dozens of others.

By the time she was twenty, Lulu Swannell was the supermodel all of the great photographers were dying to shoot. She was temptation incarnate, desirable yet unattainable and every man's fantasy, and her life became a mad whirl of traveling to new cities, airports, photographic studios, and celebrity parties. Lulu loved to party and dance. Wherever the beautiful model went, people fell over themselves to meet her. She partied in Rome and in Rio de Janeiro, in London and in Lima, her dizzying pace accelerated by alcohol and drugs.

By 1985 Lulu was competing with the top models of the day — Iman, Cheryl Tiegs, Brooke Shields, and Verushka — for the plum assignments. *Vogue, Harper's Bazaar, Town & Country,* and *Vanity Fair* were at her feet, for she had the chameleon ability to look glamorously haughty and sophisticated in evening gowns, elegantly casual in sportswear, and innocently ingenuous for the youth market.

But her youthful magnetism was tempered by black bouts of depression, for Lulu's life was fueled by her craving for drugs. Since she was exceptionally well paid, buying them was no problem at all. Her drug of choice was cocaine and, after two years on the modeling merry-go-round, she was unable to get out of bed in the morning without snorting at least two lines of the magic powder.

Men flocked around Lulu like lions at feeding time, but she had no interest in the male sex whatsoever. She found most men physically repulsive, and though she was occasionally tempted by one of the gorgeously buffed and depilated young male models with whom she worked, her attraction for her own sex always eclipsed their appeal and she only had relationships with women. In that respect she wasn't alone.

By the mid-eighties many beautiful and intelligent women were turning away from sex with men. Women had striven to have it all in the twentieth century, and now that they had freedom, emancipation, and equality with men, they were beginning to find them sadly lacking in the qualities of sharing, commitment, and the ability to love that they, as women, needed and in fact possessed.

The eighties were in full swing, and the acquisition of money and all its trappings ensured instant social success for the arrivistes who were the movers and shakers of the day — and Lulu was one of the biggest movers and shakers of them all.

One summer morning, while Lulu was staying at the Byblos in St. Tropez, the photographer she was working with, Alice Turner, called her.

"Darling, we've been invited to a beach party at the Voile Rouge. It's only five minutes' drive. Let's go, we'll have fun and we don't have to work today. It's just your scene — it'll be amusing, I promise."

"It sounds a lot more amusing than what went on last night."

"Bad trip?"

"Ghastly. But I've had a couple of Bloody Marys with breakfast, so I'm feeling much better."

"Bloody Marys with breakfast?" Alice tut-tutted on the phone. "I don't know how you still manage to look so good, girl."

" 'Cos I'm only twenty-two," Lulu laughed.

"And I'm going to have fun *now*. I don't care how I look by the time I'm forty — I'll be an old hag then anyway, so it won't matter."

"That's what they all say. Wait until you hit thirty-five, Lulu; then you won't be so arrogant."

They arrived at the beach restaurant to find their lunch companions already in high spirits, consuming large quantities of deep-fried sardines and Mersault Perrieres. Fifteen people sat at the long rectangular table, all sun-tanned, all beautiful, and all casually dressed à la St. Tropez.

Lulu and Alice were greeted with delight, and chairs were moved to make room for them.

Splash, the famous rock star renowned for his flashy showmanship and clothes, was holding court, his admirers hooting with hilarity at his outrageously bitchy jokes. The hot St. Tropez sun had brought out the sun worshipers, who sprawled on the sand on the periphery of the group, their almost naked bodies glistening with oil and sweat, lapping up every bon mot from the Olympian summit of the celebrity table.

Not all the people there were beautiful, however. A London estate agent, made rich by the property boom, ran soaking from the sea to embrace everyone at the table and plant a dripping kiss on Splash, who mopped up with good grace. His huge flapping shorts were printed with raunchy candy bar motifs: *Mr. Goodbad, Knickers, Munch This.* He was undeniably pleased with himself.

Many of the sun-worshiping men of all ages, shapes, and sizes were more elaborately arrayed than the women. Some men wore diamond pinkie rings, which sparkled in the sun; a few had discreet applications of cosmetics on their bronzed faces; and a handful flaunted the tiniest of posing pouches that became totally transparent when wet.

A woman of indeterminate age, whose naked bosoms hung flaccidly almost to her waist, squatted on a bar stool like a wizened brown monkey, drinking a pink drink with a pink straw that matched her Day-Glo visor and bikini bottom. She glared disdainfully at the beautiful young mannequins who were modeling the most outrageous beachwear while trying to avoid the groping hands of drunken, sweating men as they paraded through the massed tables.

Lulu was chatting gaily, savoring her white wine, when a voice said, "Hi there. My name's Jan. Jan Phillips." She shook a firm hand and looked up into a beautiful, smiling face.

"I'm Lulu Swannell."

A pair of the greenest eyes she had ever seen stared at her. "*The* Lulu Swannell? Well, you're even more gorgeous in person." Jan's eyes roamed admiringly over Lulu's body in her cream silk sleeveless sweater and thigh-length matching pleated skirt.

"Thanks, you're rather lovely yourself." Jan had tousled brown, wavy hair and a slightly crooked mouth that looked as if it were ready to burst into laughter at some secret joke.

Their summing up of each other was distracted by a loud whistle blowing and, to the sound of a Dixieland jazz band playing the Wedding March, a wedding party trooped into the restaurant, jumped onto the bar, and proceeded to dance a wildly uninhibited samba.

"Why are they all wearing only black and white?" asked Lulu.

"It's a black and white wedding, y'see?" Jan gestured to the giggling newlyweds. The pretty Guyanan bride wore only an uplift Wonderbra and a long white tulle skirt, while the Glaswegian, ginger-haired groom — pasty-faced and freckled — was in black Lycra bicycle shorts and a checked cap. They were surrounded by boisterous friends all in black and white costumes, who were spraying magnums of Cristal over everyone.

"They do it for the publicity," explained Jan. "They party here on the beach, go crazy, dance like dervishes, and then announce that everyone's got to visit the Hysteria club, 'cos the action will be even hotter than today."

Lulu studied a waiter who was dancing

through the tables, balancing a tray full of drinks and wearing a black spandex minidress accessorized with silver crucifixes, bangles, and an ankle bracelet. On top of his punk haircut he wore a large black cardinal's miter draped with yards of white tulle that trailed on the ground, but he handled it as elegantly as if he were a catwalk model.

Claude the jovial patron, came to greet the celebrity table. A good-looking man of fifty, he wore nothing except a tiny thong of pink leather, which revealed not only that his buttocks were flaccid, but that he was in dire need of a bikini wax. A Havana cigar clenched between his teeth, he affably clinked glasses with everyone before samba-ing his way back to the wedding party.

"He's overdressed." Jan laughed as Claude wobbled his bottom among the tables of appreciative patrons. "Usually his costume is a terrycloth robe *without* the sash, which he pulls open at every opportunity to show the punters his willy. Sometimes he even ties a red ribbon around it!"

"I've heard that's the latest thing in Paris this year."

"So, you want to come to Hysteria tonight?" Jan looked at Lulu, an open invitation in her eyes. "A bunch of us are going — it'll be fun."

Lulu stared at the other girl. She found her extremely desirable, and it looked as though the feeling was mutual.

"Sure, why not? I've got a shoot in the Place des Lices with Alice in the morning, so I can just fall out of the club and straight into makeup."

"You know, I'm a model too," said Jan. "Not as successful as you though, and I never will be either."

"That's silly, you're beautiful."

"Maybe but I'm too short for catwalk and my boobs are too big for editorial. *Vogue* and *Harpers* won't go near me, but I do a bit for *Cosmopolitan* and . . ." — she leaned forward confidentially — "I do some of the men's magazines too."

"You do beaver?"

"I sure do." Jan grinned. "It can be quite a turn-on sometimes. You'll have to work with me one day."

Lulu already knew she'd like to do more than work with Jan, who was almost, if not more, as outrageous as she was, and later that night, after they had danced the night away at Hysteria, they inevitably became lovers.

But Jan didn't last long. After Jan came Suzette, then Molly, then many more, some of whose names Lulu found it hard to remember. Most of her romances were short-lived, and none of her relationships brought her any real fulfillment. Often the girls she made love to were only doing it for kicks and, sooner or later, went back to the opposite sex. Lulu's affairs were emotionally ungratifying; the only thing that really gratified her was cocaine.

But her modeling career went from strength to strength. Annie Liebowitz photographed her in the dead of winter, standing on a bleak Long Island beach, buffeted by the wind in a belted raincoat, with four greyhounds straining at their leashes. Herb Ritts shot her from a crane at the Film Festival in Cannes, lying on top of a red Cadillac surrounded by screaming fans, with a "cat-that-got-the-cream" expression on her face, wearing nothing but red roses and diamond-studded sunglasses. And Phil Stern did a superimposed double-spread montage of her for French *Vogue*, in which she wore the latest haute-couture evening gowns from Lacroix, Ungaro, and Valentino. The resulting effect made it look as if she were chatting to herself in all the photographs.

Lulu's popularity was due in large part to her androgynous, finely muscled body, on which her gorgeous, exquisitely feminine face, bosom, and buttocks negated any suggestion of masculinity.

"She can look like a goddess or a gamine," announced Helmut Newton, who adored using her because she wouldn't hesitate to do the outrageous things he asked her to do.

For a hosiery advertisement so shocking that most magazines wouldn't print it, Lulu lay inside a giant seashell, wearing only black stockings, garters, and a velvet ribbon around her neck, gazing into the camera with her famous "fuck you" expression that her devoted fans everywhere tried to emulate. When the poster hit the billboards, ninety percent of them were stolen overnight by besotted fans. She was the flavor of the month — the model everyone wanted to use, the girl every girl wanted to look like.

One hot day, during an exhausting shoot with Patrick Demarchelier, Lulu went to her dressing room and got out her white magic powder. She needed a pickup badly. She inhaled it deeply, then with trembling hands lit up a joint and, leaning back, allowed the soothing smoke to permeate through her. It made her feel wonderful, in total and peaceful harmony with herself. It was a peace that she did not receive from lovemaking anymore, or from any of the superficial relationships she had been involved in. She lay back dreamily, feeling no pain, feeling wonderful, finally feeling exactly like the famous and successful supermodel that she was. The fact that she needed to take a huge amount of coke and heroin to get that glorious feeling was something Lulu didn't allow herself to think about. Nobody knew how hooked she was. Besides, everyone took drugs these days. Why should she be any different?

The man lay on his bed staring at the seminude photographs of Lulu Swannell in the magazine. She looked like a white witch who could put a curse on any man, but she looked like a goddess too — his goddess.

Certainly he'd felt cursed by her since the first time he'd seen a picture of her in one of his wife's fashion magazines. He often waited until his wife was out, then took the magazines to bed and pleasured himself, holding Lulu's image before his eyes. It was all the more of a turn-on because what he now knew about her disgusted him — and that excited him even more. He thought about what his grandmother had told him last week when she'd come over for his father's funeral. He didn't quite understand everything the old lady had told him — she had become impatient with him and made him promise to come and see her at her hotel. She hadn't seemed that upset by her son's death, and Al McCormick hadn't been too cut up about his dad Eddie's death either. The old man had been an OK father, but he'd lived and breathed show business. Even though he was only an electrician backstage on Broadway, he liked to think he knew everything that was going on, and his years working at one of the Hollywood studios during World War II had given him the inside track on all the scandal.

Young Al had followed him into the business but had failed to find the theater as fascinating as his father. He preferred working at the television studios in Brooklyn, where as an electrician on a daily soap opera he was quite well paid.

At her son's funeral, Patsy had sat dry-eyed in the front pew of the little Irish church in Hell's Kitchen, wearing a dusty, old-fashioned cloak and bonnet and leaning on her stick. She was a tiny, shriveled old thing, but she still had a lot of mental energy. Al soon found that out when, at her invitation, he went to visit her in her hotel the next day. He guessed she must be at least eighty-five but spry as a weasel as she hobbled over to an ancient brown leather holdall and from it removed some letters tied with frayed blue ribbon.

"These are your heritage." Her smile revealed yellowing teeth, then she proceeded to tell him a long and complicated story that revealed that he had aristocratic English roots and should have been a duke. Al didn't really understand, and became irritated when the old lady rambled on and on without even offering him a cup of tea. However, when he heard her say the name Lulu Swannell he pricked up his ears.

Patsy dragged out a well-worn copy of British *Vogue* from her holdall and pointed to the cover with a shaking finger.

"*That's* her, that's the girl."

Al studied the picture. It was an image he hadn't seen before, and he started becoming slightly aroused. Lulu was sitting on the beach in a white bathing suit, her head thrown back, big white sunglasses on her nose, lush lips parted as if to receive — what? Al knew what he'd like to put into those lips, but he had to concentrate. The old lady was jabbing him with that finger again but speaking slowly enough now for him to understand.

"That girl is an abomination. She is the product of incest — do you hear? Her mother, Victoria Swannell, married Sebastian Swannell, the eleventh Duke of Burghley, but Sebastian was really her half-brother because they both had the same father. Incest is a crime, a filthy crime. She's the spawn of the devil. She shouldn't be allowed to live."

"I don't get the incest bit." Al had never been the brightest bulb on the tree.

"Sebastian and Victoria were *both* fathered by the tenth Duke of Burghley — Toby Swannell," Patsy snapped impatiently. "*Now* do you understand?"

"Yeah, yeah, I get it." Al was shocked and revolted. A kid born of a brother and a sister? He could see why his grandmother was upset — it was wicked, sinful. "How do you know all *this?*"

The old lady sighed and blew her sharp

nose. "Because I *saw* what was going on. That tart, Millie, was panting after Toby for months! Of course, he didn't claim the child Victoria as his, as it wasn't his fault." Patsy paused, and continued with a simper, "It was a different story for me, of course. Your dear departed father, my son Eddie, was *also* the son of Toby Swannell. We had a romance," she said proudly. "A wonderful love affair, but it had to be a secret, so I had to give poor little Eddie up for adoption."

"You mean *you* and that duke?" Al shook his head. He couldn't imagine this ancient hag ever having a romance with anyone, let alone a member of the aristocracy. "And out of that, you had Dad?"

"Right, right," Patsy continued excitedly. "Toby's and my baby was Eddie, your father, but I couldn't tell a soul. I was only fifteen when he was born — I would have been shunned by everyone. I would never have been allowed to work for the Burghleys again, so *that's* why your father had to be adopted by my cousin, Ella McCormick."

Al scratched his head. "So what's the point? It's nineteen eighty-six. No one gives a damn about illegitimate kids anymore — it's no big deal."

"Ah, but there's money to be made . . ." A crafty look crossed Patsy's face. "Big money." She handed him a copy of *Architectural Digest* with a picture of the magnificent Burghley estate on the cover. "This could all be yours, Al." She flipped excitedly through the pages, showing him the splendid interiors. "It *should* be yours by rights. You are Eddie's firstborn son. You deserve everything, including the money."

"Money?"

"Yes," crowed Patsy, "and I'm going to tell you how you can get it, so listen to me carefully."

On her twenty-third birthday, Lulu bought a luxurious penthouse on Central Park West and moved in with her latest girlfriend, Saskia Barret.

Saskia was as petite, curvaceous, and blonde as Lulu was tall, athletic, and dark, although not nearly as beautiful and successful as Lulu. They had formed an instant attachment the previous month while shooting the cover of Klaus Mueller's latest album. Helmut was the photographer, and the money was so good that Lulu couldn't be bothered to turn it down. Besides, the eroticism of the idea appealed to her. Three women, all naked except for elaborate gold jewelry, gold leaf headdresses, and with shimmering silver makeup dusted all over their bodies and faces, were to be entwined around the famous German pop star, who was clad only in a black leather G-string with a silver-studded leather dog collar around his neck. Klaus leaned against a phallus-shaped ivory pillar while Helmut gleefully arranged the girls in tastefully erotic poses. Helmut was in his element, fussing around the girls and making sure that even though they were nude none of their more erogenous zones would be exposed to the camera.

Saskia crouched at Klaus's feet, her arms reaching up to caress his thighs. Bettina, a flame-haired model with large breasts, posed slightly behind the pillar, standing on a small plinth. Her right breast rested on Klaus's muscular shoulder, while her left leg bent at right angles so that it was draped across his chest. Her left hand fondled his hair. Lulu, the *pièce de résistance* of the portrait, leaned disdainfully against the other side of the pillar, her head thrown back in seductive abandonment, her arms extended to the top of the pillar, and her perfect body glistening with a sheen of silvery oil while Klaus's hand lightly grazed her hip.

At least, it was supposed to lightly graze her hip. Twenty-two-year-old Klaus had only been on the charts for six months. Plucked from the obscurity of a small village in Bavaria, he had hit a nerve with every *fraulëin* over ten and under twenty and, in Germany, was riding as high as Mick Jagger in his heyday. He had his pick of women, a surfeit of them, and was by now quite jaded by the intensity and love-starved adoration of the young groupies who had stalked him constantly and unquestioningly and unconditionally gave themselves to him at the snap of a finger.

These three haughty models, their superior Aryan bodies so sensuously close to him, began to arouse the young star's libido. As his G-string began to strain under pressure from his burgeoning desire, the hand that was supposed to be grazing Lulu's hip snaked up to her breast. Without a second's thought, Lulu turned and whacked Klaus across the face, dismantling the artfully posed tableau and causing Saskia and Bettina to scramble out of their places and dissolve in peals of helpless laughter.

"Order, order, we must have *order*." Helmut ran his fingers through his hair in desperation. "It's taken an hour to get you kids into the right positions, and now you've gone and ruined the whole damn thing! Idiots, you're all idiots . . ."

"Sorry, Helmut." Klaus was painfully aware of his huge erection, which, in spite of the muffled giggles of stylists, makeup, and hair personnel bustling around the fallen tableau, refused to subside.

"I need a ciggie break." Saskia, helpless with laughter, went to join Lulu, who sat in a corner of the studio un-selfconsciously naked.

Saskia admired her splendid form, which

was splayed out with such casual abandonment that everyone could see her intimate parts. Lulu didn't seem to care who saw her naked. She knew she had an incredible body — which she was in fact using as bait to lure Saskia into a possible liaison.

"What I *really* need is a coke break," whispered Lulu. "I don't have any on me, as you can see, but I've got a stash in my bag in the dressing room . . . Helmut?" she called. "Can we have five minutes please?"

"Sure, sure." The photographer was staring in dismay at Klaus's prodigal growth, which refused to be tamed even though he was attempting to hide it with a towel around his waist. "Can't you get rid of that bloody thing?" he screamed in German at the embarrassed pop star.

"Nein, nein," the blushing boy went to whisper in Helmut's ear.

"I don't believe it." The old man shook his head incredulously. "Well, you're not going to get any action with those three hoity-toity princesses . . . what about her?" He gestured toward a moderately attractive hairdresser whom he had noticed glancing admiringly at Klaus as she gelled his hair. "I'll arrange it for you — but make it fast, you hear?"

"Ya, ya. It's always fast — that's the trouble."

The famous photographer went to procure the hairdresser for Klaus and pushed them into an empty dressing room.

"Make it quick," he barked.

"See what I mean?" Saskia giggled, observing the whole transaction. "It'll be wham, bam, then no thank you ma'am with him and the hairdresser. Their 'relationship' will last about two minutes, I reckon."

"Then we've got time for a toot," said Lulu, "a quickie . . ."

Bettina was chatting with the stylist at the coffee stand, so the girls were alone in their dressing room.

After Lulu had laid out two generous lines of coke on the dressing table and given Saskia her own rolled-up $100 dollar bill to snort it with, they stood up and examined each other's silvery bodies in the mirror.

"You're beautiful," whispered Lulu, gently running her hands through Saskia's silky hair. "Quite ravishing." She looked deep into Saskia's gray eyes, not wanting to go further. She wasn't sure if this girl would be receptive to a female lover, but it didn't take long to find out.

"So are you," whispered Saskia, pulling Lulu toward her until their breasts touched and gently exploring Lulu's mouth with her tongue.

But it was Lulu who pulled away. "We can't do this here. The makeup people will kill us if we smudge anything."

"But I can do this," Saskia breathed huskily and fell to her knees before Lulu, "if you would like me to."

They were idyllically happy for months. Although Lulu had made love to many women and girls in her short life, she had never fallen in love before. With Saskia she found a soul mate, a true partner, with whom she experienced heights of the sapphic love she had only dreamed about.

Saskia expressed the feelings of many women when she said one night as they lay in bed after making love, "The trouble with most guys is that once they've fucked you a few times, they think they're doing you a favor getting it up again. Since they're basically lazy, it's easier to get it up with someone new rather than make the effort with the old partner. Most of them are dirty and crude, and the idea of kissing a body covered in hair disgusts me." Lulu laughed and, running her hands down Saskia's slender, velvet-skinned body, bent her head to trace the outline of Saskia's breasts with her lips.

"And they don't have these little playthings either." Lulu's lips closed around Saskia's nipple as she felt her start to respond again.

"Now, if you were a guy," Saskia whispered, "all you'd want to do now is shove it in and pump away until I'm sore."

"Well, I wouldn't know," whispered Lulu,

caressing her lover's breasts with her mouth. "I just know that I can give you what I like, and you do the same for me. It's perfect."

Chapter Thirty-Three
1986

Occasionally Lulu received brief notes from her mother or Susie, telling her nothing in particular. But the latest letter from Vickie said she was thinking of returning to work again because there had been some financial problems.

"Work, at her age?" scoffed Lulu. "That's ridiculous."

"Maybe it's because her life is so empty," suggested Saskia.

"Yeah, she always led a boring life, and you've no *idea* how deadly dull Beverly Hills can be," said Lulu. The girls lay on a bearskin rug in front of a roaring fire, having just made love. It had not been as earth-shatteringly wonderful as usual and, although Lulu was perfectly content with Saskia, it appeared the converse was not true.

Turning toward her lover, Saskia murmured, "You know, Lulu, we always do the same thing when we make love."

"So? What's wrong with that? I thought you liked it."

"Sure I like it — I liked it a lot."

"*Liked* it, past tense? What do you mean by that?"

"Well, maybe we should bring a little variation into our sex lives, spice it up a bit, y'know."

"You mean, like, another girl?"

"No, I mean like with a guy."

"A guy!" Lulu sat up in shocked disbelief. "But you don't *like* men. You told me that many times!"

"Oh, I know, I know, but they have their uses. Some of them can actually be quite fun." Saskia idly twirled a strand of blonde hair around her finger and stared into the fire. "If he were the right guy, Lulu, it could be a great trip for all of us."

"There *is* no right guy," said Lulu flatly. "Jack Lemmon spoke the truth in *Some Like It Hot* — 'they're all rough hairy beasts.' I don't want to have anything to do with men sexually — ever."

"You would if you met Leon." Saskia smiled dreamily. "You wouldn't be able to resist him."

"And just who the hell is Leon?" A horrible pang of jealousy gripped Lulu, and she didn't like it one bit. It was the same kind of feeling she remembered from watching an incident between her mother and Cooper years ago.

She had been about six or seven years old,

and she'd absolutely worshiped Cooper. He was tough and funny, and he bought her ice-cream sodas and expensive toys and took her to ride the ponies. They rough-and-tumbled together and did all kinds of fun things that daddies do with their little girls. Yet what he did with her mother that horrible afternoon was revolting. But even though she had hated it, Lulu couldn't stop watching.

Her father had been standing beside the bed on which her mother lay naked. A strange red thing stood out between his legs. It looked rigid and angry, but that didn't seem to bother her mother, who put out a pale hand, stroked it lovingly, then brought it toward her mouth. Little Lulu thought she was going to be sick, but she continued watching in morbid fascination. As her mother did this, her father's face contorted in a sort of ecstasy. Then, just when Lulu thought she couldn't bear to watch anymore, her father got on top of her mother with a grunt and shoved the thing inside her body.

Lulu thought she would faint from disgust, but she continued watching through the crack of the half-closed door, her hand clapped over her mouth to stop herself from gasping. And she could see everything quite clearly — see the repellent red thing as it moved in and out of her mother, see her father's face screwed up as though in pain. Then her mother started moaning and squealing and Lulu wanted to say "Stop it, Daddy, you're hurting Mommy." But she couldn't stop watching the shocking scene. Her mother was thrashing about as if in agony, and her father was going faster and faster inside her, and he was moaning now too.

Then they both let out a long moan together and he collapsed on top of her. Lulu ran to her room, blinded by the tears streaming down her face, her throat aching from wanting to scream, and buried her head in the pillows.

Lulu had tried to push this memory from her mind, but sometimes in her dreams the image of that big frightening object her father had between his legs made her wake up screaming. She had never mentioned this incident to her parents, since they were of the generation that never discussed the "facts of life" with their children, so Lulu's knowledge of sex and procreation was picked up in the playground. And the facts she learned were dirty indeed. Schoolkids seemed to know a lot of loathsome things about men and women. They whispered innuendo and filthy stories, and they told her that what her ma and pa had done was called "fucking" and that it was the most vile act of all.

Even Lulu was impressed when she first got a look at Leon Jefferson the third. Six

foot two with sleek black curls framing a car-
amel-colored face, his chiseled cheeks and
Roman profile made him look like a dark
Greek god. His eyes were so deeply blue they
were almost black, and the sweetest of smiles
transformed his slightly brooding looks into a
cherubic countenance.

Although it was a cold February night,
Leon's white shirt was open to reveal a muscular mahogany chest, and faded blue jeans
hugged his sculpted bottom, while a black
leather jacket was casually slung over his
broad shoulders.

"Hi, I'm Leon." He smiled an angelic
smile, revealing a set of teeth Farrah Fawcett
would have envied, and looked Lulu up and
down with cool detachment.

Lulu, looking particularly ravishing in a red
Lycra cat suit that hugged every curve, was a
touch put out by the boy's cavalier attitude.
So accustomed was she to every male over
the age of twelve reacting to her beauty that
Leon's obvious disinterest piqued her.

"Yeah, hi Leon, I'm Lulu. Take a seat." He
strolled into the living room and threw himself onto the dark leather sofa with elegant
insouciance. Lulu sashayed out to the
kitchen, calling over her shoulder, "Help
yourself to a drink; there's Stoli, Scotch, and
Chardonnay on the bar."

Saskia was in the kitchen checking the
baked potatoes.

"What *are* you wearing? It looks like a French maid's outfit!" laughed Lulu.

"It *is* a French maid's outfit." Saskia was bending over the oven, her tight black satin dress so short that her white ruffled panties were revealed. Black fishnets, patent leather ankle straps with heels so high that she could hardly walk, and a little frilly apron completed her look. "I hired it at Western Costume. It was in an old MGM movie."

"Don't you think the outfit is a touch *de trop* for this evening?"

"Not for what I've got planned for us." Saskia grinned.

"And what's that?" Lulu dipped a finger into the juice of one of the succulent oysters clustered on a silver dish.

"Wait and see. Now scoot, Lu. Get out of my kitchen. I'm the boss here, so go flirt with Leon."

"I don't think he's the flirty type. Hey, what's with the baked potatoes?"

"*Pommes paysanne*." Saskia gave a pleased smile. "These potatoes are going to be stuffed with Sevruga, my dear. It's a feast fit for a king — and I'm going to serve it to you and Leon myself."

"You? Why? The servile bit's never been your scene, sweetie. Slightly out of character, don't you think?"

"Don't worry, I've got it all planned. *Girl*friend, we are going to have so much fun!

409

Go make Leon talk. In ten minutes I'll call you guys in to dinner and then . . . let the entertainment begin."

"I've made about as much of an impression on Leon as Roseanne Barr would. I must be slipping . . . or is he gay?"

Saskia gave a tinkling laugh. "Gay? Leon? No way, honey. He can fuck for the USA, that one."

"Oh, so you've done it with him, have you?"

"Of course!" Saskia seemed unconcerned as she pried open the heavy tin of Russian caviar. "Plenty of times. Now don't go getting all jealous on me, honey, please. We're doing this to spice our love lives up a bit. You know I love you, don't you?"

"Actually, I don't," said Lulu sulkily. Saskia was beginning to disconcert her. Although she professed commitment and love, Lulu felt a distance between them. And although their lovemaking was great, it was as though Saskia looked down at their couplings with detached objectivity.

"Well, I do, so scram. Go chat up the stud. You said you'd do it for me, didn't you?"

"I guess so." Lulu sighed. She strolled into the living room, poured herself a large Stoli on the rocks, and sat beside Leon, who was looking extremely relaxed on the sofa, intently watching a ball game on TV, occasionally yelling out an expletive at the screen. His feet were up on the coffee table, a shot glass of Jack Daniels next to them, and he looked completely at home.

So at home, in fact, that he didn't even bother to look up or stand up when Lulu sat down.

"Well, two can play this game," she thought and, picking up the latest *Vogue*, started reading an article intently.

After they had ignored each other for about ten minutes, the door to the kitchen was flung open with a "Ta daaaa! *Dîner est servi, mademoiselle et monsieur.*" Saskia scurried back to the kitchen, humming the theme song from *Dr. Zhivago.*

The table had been set for just two. "What the hell is Saskia up to?" thought Lulu. This was supposed to be a *ménage à trois,* not a gourmet feast *à deux.* "Eat," yelled Saskia from the kitchen. "Don't wait for me." While she was eating and looking covertly at Leon, Lulu became more intrigued in spite of herself. He certainly was gorgeous. He also had a hearty appetite, smacking his lips appreciatively as each new dish or glass appeared, served on French china by a slyly smiling Saskia.

By the time Lulu had finished the second course, she was beginning to feel mellow. Whether it was the Swedish aquavit, subtly flavored with fennel and aniseed that burned her throat with aromatic fire, and which

Saskia insisted on refilling several times; the oysters, which tasted more delectable than any she'd ever eaten before, or the exquisite taste of the caviar tempered by the earthiness of the baked potato, she didn't know, but she was definitely relaxing.

Saskia had given them a fine white Châteauneuf du Pape with the oysters and when the lobster was served, surrounded by tiny pyramids of prawns and baby asparagus, another ambrosial white wine appeared, this time an elusive Château d'Yquem.

Leon and Lulu sat opposite each other at the long table, neither speaking a word. He grinned at Saskia when she was serving and . . . was that a wink Lulu caught them exchanging? Although suddenly that didn't seem too important. But why had Saskia not put flowers in the middle of the table?

The Venetian chandelier cast a subdued glow, there were black candles in elaborate eighteenth-century silver candlesticks on the white lace tablecloth, and the cutlery had been fastidiously polished. Dreamily, Lulu noticed the chandelier lights slowly dim until the room was lit only by the flickering black candles. The door to the kitchen was opened and Saskia's voice said, "Ready when you are, Mr. De Mille."

Lulu felt as if she were floating through space. A wonderful feeling of euphoric contentment seemed to surround her. She leaned back against her suede chair and idly watched Leon's muscled body moving gracefully as he strode to the door. She felt an unexpected stirring of lust inside her as she looked at his bottom in the tight jeans, and a sudden appreciation for the male physique enveloped her.

Leon returned, pushing a large trolley on which lay an enormous silver salver enveloped by a domed silver cover. His muscles straining, he lifted the tray and placed it on the center of the table, then with great care he removed the top.

Saskia, round and pink and golden, lay elegantly sprawled on the salver, lying on what looked like a cushion of marshmallows. On her breasts and pubis was sprinkled a white substance which looked to Lulu like confectioner's sugar — or maybe cocaine. Saskia lay still, arms at her side, legs slightly apart. The strains of Handel's *Messiah* came through the room, adding an almost churchlike ambience to the scene.

Lulu watched fascinated, as with swift movements Leon ripped off his shirt and jeans and stood naked at one end of the table, his huge cock resting on Saskia's calf. Lulu felt herself flood with sexual desire. Leon was beautiful and every part of his oiled muscular body was honed to perfection. He was a carnal delight as he stood before Saskia, who looked almost like a sacrificial offering. This wasn't like watching her old mother and father at all; this was theater, a pure, exotic, erotic performance — and it was turning her on, a lot.

Slowly Leon moved up against Saskia's body until his mouth opened to her pubis, and as he started licking the white substance off her she started writhing in ecstasy. When it was gone and his mouth had explored her for a while, he moved up to her breasts and did the same thing.

Lulu was mesmerized by this sensual display of sexual love. The two protagonists seemed totally un-selfconscious and unaware of Lulu as they indulged in their sexual delights. She felt herself getting wet, but not for Saskia. The way Leon was holding Saskia, with tremendous gentleness and strength; the way he enjoyed kissing her lips and breasts made Lulu want him to do the same to her. Then Saskia started to moan huskily.

"Fuck me, baby, fuck me *now*."

And so he did. Expertly, exquisitely pleasuring Saskia until she burst into a delirium of sexual frenzy.

"Now," he smiled softly, "it's Lulu's turn." He looked at Lulu for the first time, a question in his eyes, and she nodded mutely. Her body was hot and aching for what he offered. For the first time in her life she wanted a man to make love to her, and she didn't even bother to think why.

He fucked her on the bearskin rug in front of the fire, then he fucked her on her bed. When she begged for more he took her on the cold marble bathroom tiles, then he poured bubble bath into her Jacuzzi tub and took her again under the foaming hot water.

Lulu lost count of the number of times she came. Her body felt as if it were just one sexual organism as every touch and thrust from Leon caused her paroxysms of ecstasy. It was as if she'd never been made love to before.

After a while Saskia joined them in the tub and they ended up, the three of them together, on Lulu's bed, until dawn's light crept through the curtains.

They spent the next day and night together, and the different permutations of lovemaking with which they experimented gave new meaning to the joy of sex. Lulu's libido was prodigal and quite matched that of Leon, who performed with such verve, vigor, and delight that he made Lulu's dislike of men totally evaporate. And during the two-day bacchanal, Saskia made sure that she spiked Lulu's drinks with ground-up ecstasy pills, sprinkling them in abundantly.

When Lulu finally awoke on Monday morning the apartment looked like downtown Beirut — discarded clothes, empty champagne and whisky bottles, dirty glasses, overflowing ashtrays; not to mention the various bottles and tubes of lotions and potions with which the threesome had anointed one another's bodies that were scattered on every surface and all over the floor.

But of Leon Jefferson the third there was no sign, and Lulu felt more than a pang of disappointment. She had enjoyed being made love to by a man far more than she'd ever imagined. "Maybe it could become a habit," she mumbled to herself. She lifted her head off a pillow that felt like it had been stuffed with cement. Her eyes were puffy and swollen, and her lids were stuck together. She reached for the Visine and felt like she wanted to vomit.

"This is the mother of all hangovers," she muttered, downing three aspirin.

"How do you feel, sweetie?" She turned to Saskia, who looked adorable, curled asleep in the rumpled satin sheets, a beatific smile on her cherubic face.

"Like shit. Let me lie here and die." Saskia groaned as she awoke, and the full force of the hangover hit her too. She opened a bleary eye and exclaimed, "Oh God, I feel like hell — but was that fun or what?"

"Yeah, it was fun."

"So what do you think of Leon? Isn't he Mr. Super Stud?"

"I guess he is. He's certainly got staying power."

Saskia threw off the covers, revealing pert

breasts, and yawned. "Maybe you'll start swinging both ways now. You think you could get to like guys better now, Lu?"

"Maybe not *better*." Lulu ran her hand over Saskia's exposed breast. "I still prefer the fruit of the fig to the fruit of the banana."

Saskia moved away mumbling, "I've gotta go back to sleep."

Lulu punched in the numbers for her answering service, listened for a few seconds, then hung up with a frown. She checked the illuminated clock.

"That's weird, it's twelve-thirty and not a single call from the agency. It is Monday, isn't it?"

"Mmm, guess it is." Saskia had snuggled under the covers, her secret smile still in place.

"Come to think about it, they only called me twice last week with work. Maybe I'm getting old hat." She staggered into the bathroom and stared at herself in the mirror. "God, I even *look* like an old hat." She surveyed her sunken, bloodshot eyes and her complexion, which was sallow and had blotchy red marks all over it. "Damn that Leon and his five o'clock stubble," she said crossly, and slathered cream liberally on her parched skin. "I've got more bags than Vuitton. No wonder I prefer girls."

Lulu couldn't reach her agent on the phone for two days. He didn't return her

417

calls, and she was getting panicky. On Tuesday she and Saskia went to Devils, an unsavory disco dive frequented by the more raunchy members of the gay community, male and female. By the time they arrived at midnight, Lulu had done so many lines of coke that she felt invincible, untouchable, and free as air.

She danced wildly with Saskia, then they started kissing in front of the other dancers, which wasn't unusual as many of the same-sex couples on the dance floor were doing the same. Everyone was crushed together in the tiny room, and a strong smell of sweat, dope, and booze drenched the place. Most of the boys were bare-chested, grinding their pelvises lasciviously into each other to the heavy metal beat. Some of the women were bare-chested as well, and an orgiastic atmosphere, heavy with sexual arousal, permeated the tiny club.

As Lulu and Saskia were dancing, a large crop-haired woman came up behind Saskia and started fondling her breasts.

Lulu's head was thrown back. The music was making her feel lubricious and she couldn't wait to get Saskia home, but this bull dyke was pissing her off.

"Beat it, bitch," Lulu snarled.

"Who's going to make me?" challenged the fat, ginger-haired woman, her leather cat suit unzipped to the navel and straining at the seams. "I like her." She cupped one of Saskia's breasts and licked her lips, her tongue making sucking motions. "I like her a lot."

"So do I," growled Lulu, noticing that Saskia, instead of avoiding the woman's hands, actually seemed to be enjoying her caresses. Lulu reached out, grabbed the fat lesbian by the collar, and slapped her across the face. "I told you to lay off. If you don't I'll flatten you, you bitch."

"Oh yeah, who you calling a bitch, bitch?"

With that the woman clutched Lulu's hair and the two fell to the ground, kicking, yelling, and punching each other in the face. An excited crowd, Saskia at the fore, gathered around cheering them on as they rolled over and over each other on the floor, screaming obscenities at each other. The rotating mirrorball in the ceiling cast surreal shafts of light on them, and the DJ turned the music up a decibel or two higher.

"Now, that's what I call a light show!" he laughed with excitement at the fight, clapping his hands to the music.

Then there was a crack as Lulu, who had caught hold of the woman by her thick neck and banged her head several times violently on the wooden floor, gave one shove too many. The woman's head lolled back, blood started seeping out of her mouth, and she lay very still. Everyone went silent in shock and horror, then someone screamed "She's dead! The bitch killed her!" and the crowd erupted in panic, rushing toward the exits before the police arrived.

An ambulance shrieked to a halt six minutes later. Paramedics applied first aid to the supine woman, then put an oxygen mask on her face and whisked her on a stretcher into the ambulance.

The police arrived shortly after and the cop, a redneck with fascist tendencies, started reading Lulu her rights.

"C'mon, sister, you're coming down to headquarters with us." He looked Lulu up and down contemptuously. In her black leather ripped miniskirt, white shirt hanging out, torn stockings, barefoot, and with dirt and blood caked all over her face, she looked a wreck; nothing like the world-famous model she was.

"But I haven't done anything. *She* started it. It was just a little spat."

"C'mon, you dyke," snarled the cop, snapping handcuffs around her wrists, "tell it to the judge."

Someone had tipped off the paparazzi, and a grainy photograph of Lulu, handcuffed and bloodied, being dragged out of the police car and into the precinct made the front pages of the *Times*, the *News*, and the *Post*, as well as much of the world's press. The gossip columns couldn't wait to add their ten cents' worth of venom to the story. New York buzzed with salacious details of what had really happened at Devils. Although Lulu had been popular with stylists and photographers who had to deal with her on a regular basis, the editorial staff of magazines had never warmed to her. They had thought her to be arrogant and egotistical, a girl whose high and mighty attitude toward those around her made her enemies but, because she was so smoking hot with the public, they had used her. But now, as each day more lurid innuendo about Lulu's lesbian lifestyle surfaced, her reputation was being ripped to shreds.

A week later she sat in her agent's office.

"No one will touch you." He frowned. "None of the advertisers, editors, or photographers want you in their pages. You've really done it this time, Lulu. They say you're poison."

"But Tom, I'm the top model in New York. You said that yourself last year."

"Last year you were, sweetie. This year you ain't. You're nearly twenty-four now, Lulu, and that's not young in this business anymore. I've got girls on my books, fifteen-, sixteen-year-olds that have the kind of look the mags want now — fresh, young, innocent. That's what everyone's searching for — new faces."

"I've *never* looked innocent," said Lulu.

"True, but when you started out at seventeen you had that bad little girl look and a baby face. Wake up and smell the coffee, Lulu, it's not there anymore. You're looking dissipated. Too many drugs, too many late nights, too much sex. Sure, you're beautiful, but beautiful girls are a dime a dozen in this profession. And you carry on the way you are, you won't be nearly so beautiful in five years' time."

"But surely you can get me something? Maybe in Europe?"

"The story's broken in Europe too, sweetie. My phones have been ringing off the hook all week. They want to know the gory details, but they *don't* want to know about using you. And I'm sorry to tell you this, but your contract's been canceled with the hosiery company."

"Why?" Lulu ran a despairing hand through her hair.

"Morals clause, sweetie."

"But that poster was one of the most famous in the world." Lulu was now indignant. "People stole it off billboards. They collected it. It was a classic — a goddamn collector's item!"

"I know, Lulu, but you've got to face facts, sweetie. You've had almost six years in this game, most of them at the top. Nothing lasts forever. You'd better leave New York for a while, let everything blow over. And thank your lucky stars you didn't kill that carpetmuncher, otherwise you'd be in the slammer for a long, long time. I hope you've saved some money, kid, 'cos you won't be making it in this game anymore."

Lulu didn't step out of her apartment for a month. She hardly ate, slept all day, snorted copious amounts of cocaine, and smoked equally copious amounts of pot. She felt utterly miserable and alone. Her friends avoided her, and when she called the two or three she thought were trusted confidantes she got coldly polite excuses. Saskia was in New Zealand doing a bathing suit layout for *Women's Weekly* and had several more assignments lined up in Australia afterward. Lulu was alone with her thoughts and, since she didn't want to face them, she chased them away with drugs.

When Al McCormick saw the photographs of Lulu splashed all over the tabloids, he was so disgusted by the revelation of her lesbianism that he threw out all the magazines he'd been hoarding.

"I don't ever want to think about that devil-bitch again," he muttered as he crouched in the basement of his house in Queens, feeding the now offensive journals into the incinerator. He fingered the crucifix about his neck. "She's poisonous trash. A woman who loves another woman is worse

423

than a whore, she's filth."

His grandmother's words came back to him. *"She shouldn't be allowed to live, Al. Someone like that deserves to die."*

Chapter Thirty-Four
1987

"I don't believe it." Vickie stared at the lawyer's letter in alarm. "It's not possible! This is an absolute nightmare."

"What? What's the matter?" asked Susie, who, though suffering from arthritis, was gamely watering the plants in the garden. The sprightly eighty-two-year-old limped through the open French windows into the sunlit living room that was filled with comfortable, well-worn furniture.

"Here, read it." White-faced, Vickie tossed the letter at Susie, then went to the bar to pour herself a stiff brandy. She sat on the sofa and put her head in her hands. "We're ruined, Susie, practically wiped out."

"It's not possible. How? Why?" The old lady sat down stiffly in her favorite chair in front of the TV.

"I've been dreading this letter. I've been asking Fred Brown questions about my portfolio and various other investments for months, but he's been evasive or out of town and he's never returned any of my calls." She continued plaintively, "Coop used to explain everything to me and even on those silly newfangled computers I could see and understand that my finances were solid."

"Those things are impossible to work," sighed Susie, "like all this technology stuff today. I can't even use the oven anymore, it's so complicated."

"Well, *this* is really complicated." Vickie knocked back her brandy and went to the bar to pour another one.

"Will you read it to me, Vickie, dear? I've forgotten my glasses. Is it really such bad news?"

"The worst. Listen to this." As Vickie read the lawyer's letter out loud, Susie looked perplexed.

"I don't understand, dear, I'm sorry."

"I'll cut to the chase, Susie. Fred Brown has embezzled *all* of my money. He's sold my stock, taken the profits, and mortgaged this house to the hilt."

"Where is he now?" croaked Susie, aghast.

"Disappeared. No one knows where to. Scampered off to South America or the Far East, I guess. Wherever he's gone, no one will ever be able to find him, I'm sure of that. He had complete power of attorney over me, so he could sign *anything* in my name. He must have been siphoning off money for years. He's also done the same thing to several of his other clients, if that's any consolation."

"Cooper must be turning in his grave," said Susie.

"Oh God, Susie. This would never have happened if Cooper were still alive." Tears glistened in Vickie's eyes. "What are we going to do?"

"I don't know, dear." Susie looked worriedly at Vickie. They were such good companions, more like mother and daughter now, and Vickie's problems were always Susie's.

"I have no income whatsoever now." Vickie drank half of her brandy, then sat down. "The payments on this house are five thousand a month. But that bastard Brown has remortgaged it so many times that even if I sold it I'd only get about twenty-five or thirty grand."

"It can't be true." The old lady felt quite faint. "I often heard Cooper say before he died that this house was worth over a million."

"Well, it's *not* now," said Vickie grimly. "We can sell some of my stuff, I suppose, but I don't have that much jewelry and I've never bought really good pictures or furniture. We'd be lucky if we get twenty thousand for the lot."

"There's always Lulu," suggested Susie. "She's making plenty of money. She could help you out."

"There is *no* way I'm going to ask my daughter for anything," said Vickie vehemently, *"no way."*

"Why not? You gave her everything when she was growing up. She owes you."

"No one owes *anyone* anything in this life, Susie; I learned that long ago. Remember what Katharine Hepburn told me on the day of Cooper's funeral? She said 'You must grieve, then you must get over it, and you should try and get back to work; it's a great healer.' "

Susie nodded eagerly. "That's a wonderful idea, Vickie. Get back into acting again. You did some very good films, you know."

"Susie, darling, face it — most of my movies were mindless froth. But the only work I *know* is acting. The last time I acted was in 1953! Do you think that any producers would hire an actress who's been out of the business for over thirty years? Do you think *anyone* remembers me?"

"Of course they do! Like they remember Alice Faye, Loretta Young, or Betty Hutton. Your movies are on American Movie Classics all the time, and you still get fan mail."

"You sound like Max in *Sunset Boulevard.*" Vickie smiled.

"And I suppose you're Norma Desmond?"

"I'm a great deal older than Norma was," said Vickie. "She was only fifty, but I'm sixty-eight. I certainly don't have any illusions about trying to look like an ingenue again, and I don't have any illusions about Hollywood either. This is a coldhearted town where friendship means nothing and box office means everything." She sighed. "Most producers and studio heads hate actors, but they hate actresses even more. And if those actresses happen to be over *forty*, their chance of getting work is minimal. No, Susie, the possibility at my age of being able to make any kind of a living out of acting is about as high as that of finding teeth in a chicken."

"Nevertheless," Susie shrugged, "why not give it the good old college try."

Vickie smiled at the old woman's spirit. "Maybe I'll call Lou, my old agent, if he's still alive. Ask him if there're any granny roles going for a sprightly sixty-something."

To Vickie's utter astonishment, her agent, Lou, was not only still alive, but was still in business too. And he found Vickie a job almost immediately. She sat in his tiny office in a high-rise building on Sunset Boulevard feeling strangely excited at the thought of working again. She heard the telephone ringing nonstop in the anteroom and the receptionist's voice making appointments for young hopefuls. Although Lou's agency was small, he represented quite a few hot new actors.

"It may not be the kind of gig you were looking for, honey, but the one thing you can say about daily soaps is that it's regular work and it pays pretty well too."

"A soap? What's the name of it?" asked Vickie.

"It is called *Sons and Lovers*. The new USBC network — that's the United States Broadcast Corporation — is starting shooting in the fall. They're going head to head against *Days of Our Lives*, and they want to make it look more like those prime-time evening soaps, more like *Dallas* and *Flamingo Road* — glamour, y'know what I mean? Old-time glamour and lots of sex."

"Well, I'm not very glamorous anymore," Vickie said objectively, smoothing her sensible gray pleated skirt over her still slender legs. "And as for sex, forget it." She had gained weight in the last few years, and looked nothing like the alluring sex symbol she had once been. Her face reflected the full life that she had lived; her flaming auburn hair was now salt and pepper, but she was comfortable with her body and with herself, and not at all dismayed that her previous size six was now a size fourteen. She possessed a calm serenity and poise that was appealing and which didn't depend on looks or youth.

"Honey, face it. You're not going to be playing the vamp. They're holding auditions now for *that* part. No, the producer thought

430

you'd be perfect for the matriarch of the family, y'know? Think Jane Wyman on *Falcon Crest*. Great part, lots of style and power."

"It sounds exciting, but the start of the project is almost eight months away. I need to make some money *now*, Lou. Any ideas for something in the meantime?"

"Nothing's happening right now that I know about. Everyone's cutting back, so you'd better tighten your belt and go on a budget. Do you realize that less than five percent of the Screen Actors' Guild members over the age of fifty are working in movies or TV? You're lucky the network wanted you for this job, Vickie, damn lucky. Ann Miller, June Allyson, and Joan Fontaine have all been salivating for it, but the network wanted someone with a touch of class, and that's you, honey, in spades."

"I guess my time as the Duchess of Burghley paid off after all."

"You know, one thing I don't understand, Vickie. With all the years you worked at Paradigm, don't you have any 'fuck you' money at all?"

"What's 'fuck you' money?"

"A little stash, twenty or thirty grand you keep under the floorboards or in a black box somewhere. Then if the going gets rough you can say 'fuck you' to the world."

Vickie shook her head. "Unfortunately I

431

haven't, Lou. Not a dime, I'm afraid."

"Too bad." Lou became businesslike. "OK, honey, then you'd better stay in L.A. till you get the call to leave for New York. They definitely want you, but it's a lot cheaper to live in Hollywood than in Manhattan. I'll try and get you a couple of TV guest shots, but it won't be easy, honey. Most actors are desperate for work, and over-forty actresses are a dime a dozen these days. The casting directors practically rule the roost; so unless one of them's your friend or you're sleeping with them, they're not gonna push for you. They've all got their favorites, and they're the ones who work all the time."

"OK. So, I'll pack everything up, sell my house, rent a little apartment in Westwood, and tighten the purse strings."

"Good girl," said Lou. "You're one smart woman, Vickie Gordon."

"I wish I always had been," said Vickie ruefully. "My wisdom has only come with age."

That afternoon Vickie told Susie about the offer. "So in eight months, we'll be off to the Big Apple and I'll be starting work again."

"Well done, Vickie. I *knew* you could do it." The old lady sat in her armchair, watching the television and trying to see well enough to embroider a cushion. She'd always loved needlepoint, but her eyesight was giving her a few problems and her new glasses didn't seem strong enough.

"You'll come to New York with me, won't you, Susie?"

Susie smiled and squeezed Vickie's hand fondly. "Where else would I go, dear? I think you and I are joined at the hip, together until death us do part."

"Great, we'll just hang in here until October and then, like the song says, 'We'll hit Manhattan like a farm fresh egg.'"

Chapter Thirty-Five
1987–1988

Vickie had tried contacting Lulu several times, initially as soon as the photographs of her outside the police precinct had hit the press, but her daughter's telephone line had been disconnected and Vickie's letters were returned "addressee unknown." She wanted to tell her she was coming to New York in the fall, so she also sent a letter to Lulu via her agent, who returned it saying that Lulu was out of town and that he didn't know her whereabouts. Although Vickie had forgiven her daughter for the ghastly outburst that had killed Coop, she had still not been able to forget about it. She realized that, even though she had loved Lulu unconditionally, that love had not been returned and their relationship had been very much a one-way street. Vickie no longer tortured herself with thoughts of what might have been, or what had gone wrong between her and her daughter. She accepted what had occurred and recognized that, even though she didn't have a close bond with Lulu, she was extremely fortunate to have a companion as loyal as Susie.

A week before leaving for New York, Vickie received a synopsis of the series she was to work on and a large pile of future shooting scripts.

"Thank God my part is relatively small, otherwise I just wouldn't be able to cope with learning all this stuff," she told Susie. "I'm *stunned* by the amount of dialogue some of the actors will have to learn each day."

"What's it about?" Susie, an avid soap fan, asked eagerly.

"Oh, they're this very rich but dysfunctional Manhattan family. There's the father, that's Stanley Croft, who's married to Marina, that's me, a small but telling role, I hope — I don't want too much dialogue. We have five sons, some of whom are rascals, some of whom are saints, and they, of course, all have girlfriends, wives, and ex-wives. Fortunately, my sons' and their various lovers' wranglings take up most of the scenes."

"It sounds wonderful," Susie beamed. "Better than *All My Children*."

"I wonder who they're going to get to play Tamara?" mused Vickie, flicking through the scripts. "That's a hot role."

They were sitting in their little rented apartment, overlooking Tompkins Square

Park in the East Village. The November leaves were still falling, and they could see several well-wrapped children frolicking in the park.

"Who's Tamara?"

"Tamara Barrymore is the evil little seductress who makes life hell for three of my sons. Great part. Sort of a baby bitch." Vickie consulted the synopsis. "It looks like she doesn't come in for a while. Everyone just talks about her a lot, to get the audience prepared."

When Vickie stepped onto the sound stage of USBC Studios, she felt like a total alien. It was a hive of activity, with all the usual hustle and bustle of a film set. Giant cameras roamed over the thick black cables that snaked across the floorboards like venomous reptiles. Everyone watched out for them as the cameras moved dizzyingly fast, and it was up to each actor to keep out of their way.

Most of the actors had worked in other daytime soaps and knew the drill, but for Vickie, the coddled princess of 1940s and 1950s films, it was a slightly irksome revelation to have to take care of herself all the time. At Paradigm she had always been surrounded by an entourage of hairdressers, makeup artists, dressers, and secretaries, following her around slavishly. Now she was lucky if during taping the makeup girl gave her a quick flick with the powder puff. Vickie took to carrying a purse whenever a scene called for it so that she could repowder her face in her own mirror.

Susie had offered to come with her to the tapings. "I'll be your personal assistant," she'd said eagerly. "All the big stars have personal assistants these days. The bigger they are, the more they have."

"Thank you, darling, but I'll manage fine," smiled Vickie. Since the old lady's eyesight made it difficult to even walk around the apartment, negotiating the perilous studio floor would be far too dangerous.

Vickie felt somewhat of an outsider at work. Except for Stanley Croft, whom she knew from the forties, and who played Maxwell Williamson, Marina's husband, she had little in common with the array of long-limbed, long-haired, lissom twenty-something actresses and the buffed and toned handsome actors, who spent more time primping in front of the mirror than the girls did.

But even at his best, Stanley was still a crashing old bore who liked nothing more than a good long reminisce about the "good old days." He had never been a major player in Cooper and Vickie's heyday, but he'd done enough *cinema noir* and B-movies to have a few entertaining stories. Unfortunately, these anecdotes tended to be repeated with monotonous regularity and Vickie, like the rest of the cast, soon found herself avoiding the boring old codger. Not that there was much socializing. Every weekday, cast and crew came in at eight a.m. to rehearse and block their moves. This took about an hour, during which time the director, frantic in his glassed-in control gallery above the stage, screamed instructions at the actors and the five cameramen as to where they should go. While this was all going on, the actors desperately attempted to learn their lines.

Stanley had a hell of a time memorizing his. On the first week he made a couple of unfortunate dries, prompting the producer to reluctantly give him idiot boards — his dialogue written in oversized black letters and held behind the camera, where he could see them when on set. Even though Vickie would have liked to have these, she was too proud. Watching the young cast mocking Stanley behind his back, it strengthened her resolve to spend more time studying her script. Live television was a tremendous challenge.

Around nine a.m. it was time to get into makeup and hair. These departments were lively centers of gossip and warmth. There were only two hairdressers and three makeup men, not really enough for a basic cast of fifteen, but they were jolly souls who always kept the coffee percolating and the radio and heaters on full blast. For Vickie this was almost the most enjoyable part of the day, as everyone munched doughnuts, sipped coffee, and read the newspapers while gossiping and working on their lines. The "wrecking crew," as the department was affectionately called, worked feverishly on their faces and hair, and there was much jostling for position as to who would be the last to be done. At eleven a.m. they had a technical run-through and at twelve-thirty they were on the air live, hopefully to an audience of many millions.

From across the noisy, crowded set, Al McCormick watched the middle-aged lady who seemed to hold herself slightly aloof from the rest of the young cast. So this was the famous Vickie Gordon. This was the woman whom his grandmother, Patsy Kingsley, loathed with such passion. How an old woman like his grandmother could bear such an ongoing grudge for another old woman was beyond Al's limited perception, but he realized he could use it to his own ends.

He tried to remember what Patsy had told him about Vickie at his father's funeral. He couldn't really remember any of it, but she had given him that packet of old letters. Maybe he should finally read them. And maybe he should write to his grandmother to tell her the news about working with Vickie. She could probably do with a bit of cheering up.

Patsy Kingsley sat in the dimly lit basement kitchen reading and rereading her grandson's letter.

It was unbelievable. It was preposterous that Vickie Gordon was back and working in a TV series at her age. Patsy was so enraged that she had to have a swig of gin from the bottle she kept in secret in the pantry behind the flour. The new butler, Mr. Winters, regarded her coldly. There was little love lost between the two of them but, since the ancient maid was the confidante of the even more ancient and practically senile dowager duchess, until the old aristocrat popped off the perch, Winters was saddled with Patsy and her whines, complaints, and criticisms. Betty the cook, a florid young country girl, couldn't stand Patsy either, and neither could the two maids. In 1987, the Burghley staff consisted of less than half of what it had been seventy years ago, but the workload hadn't become any lighter. Eaton Square was a huge house and, between the five of them, the servants not only looked after the dowager duchess but also took care of the duke, Sebastian Swannell, who was now in his late sixties and rather weak and crotchety. His wife, the Duchess Emily, some twenty years younger than her husband, was a tartar for cleanliness and had a nasty habit of running her fingers along the chimney pieces behind the Limoges figurines and ormolu candlesticks to check for dirt and dust. She also slept in a separate bedroom from the duke and insisted on fresh linen sheets daily. Thankfully their twin sons, Jonathan and Andrew, were rarely at Eaton Square, spending most of their year at school at Eton or at the family's Gloucestershire estate.

But nevertheless Patsy found plenty of time to sit and brood. She had become obsessive in thinking about what might have been had things gone her way. Al's father, Eddie, as Sebastian's older brother — she snorted at the comparison between the two — would be the Duke of Burghley, and she, Patsy, would be where the dowager duchess was most of the time; reclining on a gilt and canopied Louis XIV bed, in a lush room full of Oriental rugs, gilt-bronze clocks and urns, silk sofas, and eighteenth-century oil paintings. Thick green brocade curtains would prevent the daylight from disturbing her slumbers, and Winters would waken her every morning with freshly squeezed orange juice and toast, served on a silver tray. Patsy sighed with pleasure as her fantasy continued. Silver picture frames and knickknacks — which were a nightmare to dust — would still clutter every surface, and she would be sure that the priceless French clock on the chimney piece was wound every day. The clock had always fascinated Patsy, with its glazed enameled dial surmounted by a gilt monkey holding a parasol; all of which was balanced on the back of an elephant. The clock struck every hour, which was usually the signal for Patsy to get her mistress another one of her endless cups of tea.

The duchess had always lived a pampered life, but now that she was almost blind she spent her days listening to opera on the ancient wireless she refused to part with, or boring Patsy as she rattled off long lists of problems, slights, and insults she perceived herself to have suffered. An avid reader of the new *Hello* magazine, Patsy in turn was able to amuse her mistress by describing in detail the godawful outfits most of the royals and celebrities wore in its pages, and she gave vivid descriptions of the nouveaux riches' ghastly homes. The old lady quite enjoyed this and, since Patsy was always on her best behavior around her mistress, they got along reasonably well, considering the cantankerous nature of both women.

Patsy was so skinny she looked almost like a scarecrow when, in the privacy of her bedroom, she let her long grayish-white hair down. Patsy had been proud of her thick, auburn hair — "my crowning glory," she'd often boasted to her husband, Kingsley, when she had allowed him to stroke it occasionally.

Now Patsy sat brooding in her tiny dormer room under the eaves, the same sleeping quarters she had inhabited since 1916 and to which she had returned after Kingsley's death. She took a nip of gin, bit into a chocolate digestive biscuit, and ruminated for the thousandth time on what she could do to hurt Vickie Gordon. Maybe a bit of blackmail to pass the time until Al could claim his rightful heritage? To reveal that Vickie's lesbian daughter, Lulu, was the product of an incestuous marriage might be a good place to start. She'd think about it — this sort of thing couldn't be rushed, after all.

Chapter Thirty-Six
1988

Sons and Lovers was doing well. It still had a long way to go to beat *Days of Our Lives*, but after a couple of months it started getting a loyal following and the network was pleased.

"We've found a fabulous kid for Tamara. Twenty-five years old. Never acted before but, boy-oh-boy, what a face and *what* a body."

The show's producer, Jerry Goswell, was indulging his cast with one of his monthly get-togethers at Sardi's. They sat together convivially at a long table under framed caricatures of theatrical greats, past and present, chatting and telling showbiz tales. The three actresses who played the current girlfriends of the sons looked miffed at this announcement. If a new girl was being brought in, it probably meant curtains for one of them. The show was on a strict budget, and the producers could only afford a certain number of above-the-line salaries. The cast knew this, so the skinny blonde with the silicone breasts, the sultry redhead, and the chic brunette looked at one another nervously.

"What's she look like, this Tamara?" asked Wendy the blonde. "And what's her name?"

Jerry paused — he had to be careful. The girl had had some really terrible press some time ago, but he couldn't be sure that the cast wouldn't remember the scandal and refuse to work with her. "Hey, it's a surprise." He smiled winningly. "We'll call her Tamara, for now. She's tall, great boobs, gorgeous pale green eyes, and flaming red curly hair. She photographs magnificently — used to be a model."

Wendy and Tippy, the brunette, breathed a sigh of relief, while the redheaded Sandy looked concerned. "She's a redhead?"

"Like Rita Hayworth," said Jerry, "only better."

"Who's Rita Hayworth?" asked Wendy.

Jerry sighed. He'd been a producer for forty years and realized that many actors were idiots, but the ignorance of their own business that these three bimbos possessed simply amazed him.

"Rita was the greatest sex goddess of the 1940s, along with our lovely Vickie here."

The girls looked pityingly at Vickie.

"Hard to imagine, isn't it?" whispered Wendy to Sandy.

"When does this glamourpuss start work?" Sandy was concerned but curious.

"Her first day is January eighth. We'll give her a couple of scenes, see how she does. It's a pretty goddamned terrific role. We tested twenty girls, but she turned out to be *it*." He smiled triumphantly and puffed on his cigar, perversely enjoying the obvious unease of some of his cast. And they could well have reason to be uneasy. Acting was a perilous profession, with no job security at all. If any of the cast of *Sons and Lovers* were fired they could be out of work for God knows how long or, even worse, become so associated with the character they played that they could never live it down.

On the wall behind Vickie, an Al Hirschfield caricature of her mother, all saucer-eyes, tiny heart-shaped face, exaggerated cupid's bow lips, and an aureole of flaming curls, smiled out at the world. Vickie looked at the caption, *"Millie Swann,* Bubbles, *Belasco Theater, Jan. 1933."*

Nineteen thirty-three had been the year her mother had died, Vickie mused. Had it been an accident, or was she murdered? Even now, more than fifty years after her death, Vickie and the media sometimes wondered and theorized about what had happened to glorious Millie Swann, "The Aphrodisiac Girl."

On an early morning in January 1988, another aphrodisiac girl threw on faded blue jeans, furry boots, and a sheepskin coat and flew out of the front door. She didn't bother with makeup; she'd get that at the studio. Besides, she knew she was beautiful enough without cosmetic enhancement.

Outside her apartment building on Sutton Place South, she hailed a yellow cab that braked to a halt, squirting dirty slush over her boots.

"Four fifty-five West Fifty-fifth," she ordered, clambering in, "and make it snappy."

"Que? Donde está?"

Lulu looked angrily at the dopey driver, who had obviously not even bothered to learn the language of his adopted country.

"Tenth Avenue," she coldly enunciated the words. "Fifty-fifth Street. Can you find that?"

The driver didn't answer, made a screeching illegal U-turn, and sped down the icy streets well over the speed limit, but Lulu didn't let it bother her. New York cabdrivers were an occupational hazard for those who lived in Manhattan. She leaned back in her seat and went through her lines yet again. She'd memorized them thoroughly, but she remembered her mother telling her, when she was about eight and in a school play, "Listen, darling, when an actor goes onstage, or before the camera, if he's the *slightest* bit nervous, those well-learned lines can disappear like smoke, and you're left with egg all over your face." Vickie had laughed and continued, "Luckily, there're always take two and

447

take three, and sometimes even take ten, so you're well protected in the movies."

"But can't it be kind of scary?" little Lulu had asked.

"There is nothing to fear but fear itself." Vickie had ruffled her young daughter's black curls fondly.

"And I bet today's going to be real scary," thought Lulu, returning to the present with a jolt as the taxi driver shouted at a pedestrian. "I'm going to be in front of sixteen million viewers and I've only acted at school and in magazine layouts. That *is* terrifying." She imagined her mother's reaction when they'd meet and wondered whether she knew that Lulu had been cast in the same show — presumably not, as Lulu had used a different name. It was a hoot, really, appealing to Lulu's bizarre sense of humor.

There'd be all sorts of questions, of course. "Where have you been? Why didn't you write?" and all the guilt trips Vickie could lay on her — except that Lulu had such a high guilt threshold that she rarely, if ever, expressed contrition for any of her deeds.

The cab drew up with another squeal of brakes. Lulu tipped the driver generously, then, because he didn't thank her, she deliberately left the cab door open.

"*Puta,*" snarled the cabbie, "*chíngate y la puta que te parió.*"

She gave him the finger and the security

448

guards at the front desk grinned, approvingly, looking Lulu up and down appreciatively. They handed her the plastic ID card with her name on it, which enabled her to come in and out of the studio without hassle, and a runner showed her to her shoebox of a dressing room.

"We'll do the first run-through and camera blocking in ten minutes," the pretty, rather overweight girl said, envying Lulu's slim figure as she carelessly threw her coat on a chair and lit up a Camel.

"What's your name, honey?" asked Lulu.

"Jamie. I'm the second-second AD, otherwise known as the gopher."

"What's that?" Lulu idly fluffed out her luxuriant curls in the mirror, admiring the effect of herself as a redhead. She still wasn't quite used to it. She'd washed and redyed her hair that morning, but even without setting or drying it, it looked like an advertisement for Vidal Sassoon.

"Go-fer this, go-fer that." Jamie grinned, revealing little gappy teeth and too much gum. "Officially we're known as runners. Can I get you anything?"

"No, thanks — maybe later." Lulu bestowed upon Jamie her most dazzling of smiles, a smile that rarely failed to cast a spell on anyone who received it. She was the new girl now, and she realized the pitfalls. She needed allies and, since she was starting out, this girl would have to do to begin with. Throughout the day she chatted and giggled with Jamie until the young AD was completely besotted by her. Particularly when Lulu told her how pretty she'd be if she lost weight.

"I'll help you," Lulu said. "I know all the tricks."

Vickie was over at the craft services table drinking a mug of decaf and chatting to Stanley and Morgan, who played one of her sons, so she didn't see Lulu at first.

"They say the ratings are dismal," sighed Morgan.

"We're going down," said the older thespian gloomily. "I've heard rumors that if our ratings don't pick up, we'll be dropped by February."

"Shit, what a bummer. Hey, man, I *need* this gig." Morgan swallowed a couple of painkillers, hoping to get rid of his pounding headache.

"We *all* need this gig," said Vickie quietly.

"Well, maybe the new storylines with this bitchy vamp will pick things up . . . Oh-oh! Wow! Well, *helloooo there!*" Morgan stared across the bustling set to where a red-haired vision in blue jeans stood in the center of the maelstrom, casually flipping through her script.

"Now that's what I call a looker." Morgan

ran a hand through his immaculate blond coif. "That must be Tamara. I'm introducing myself before the other guys get in there." He strode off, all macho charm and sparkling teeth, but the other four "sons" were all already clustering around the new arrival, positively falling over themselves to say hello. Tippy, Wendy, and Sandy stood slightly apart, staring jealously at the group over which Lulu was already holding court.

"She's not wearing makeup, and she looks *that* good?" Tippy hissed incredulously.

"Don't be ridiculous. I can see from here she's got on a truckload of mascara, and blusher too, I'm sure of it. And she must have spent two hours on her hair," sniffed Wendy.

"Well, face it, girls," said Sandy, "we all give ourselves a little enhancement before we go on set. Don't want to frighten the crew to death, do we? C'mon, let's go say hello. Make like we're delighted for her to join our happy band of strolling players."

The three actresses sauntered over to Lulu, now completely surrounded by well-wishers, mostly male, and Jamie, who was functioning as handmaiden.

"I guess we'd better say hello to her, too," Vickie said to Stanley, advancing toward the circle. "Poor kid, she's probably scared to death."

Then Lulu turned toward Vickie, and for

the first time in eight years mother and daughter were face to face.

"Hi, Mom, it's good to see you again." Lulu didn't look at all nervous as she smiled, stepped away from the group, and held out her arms to her stunned mother.

Vickie was paralyzed. She stood completely shocked as her long-lost, once-beloved daughter hugged her, whispering, "Hope you aren't too shocked, Mom. I wanted to surprise you."

"Well, you certainly did that." Vickie's voice sounded muffled and her limbs seemed numb. "I'm totally stunned and confused. What are you doing here, Lulu?"

"Shhh, don't call me, Lulu. I've changed my name, Mom, as well as my hair color. I had to because of the scandal. I'm Rebecca Swann now. You like that name, Mom?"

"Yes, I do." Vickie responded automatically.

"I'm playing Tamara," said Lulu. "I'm the girl who, when she comes into the room, makes all the other girls want to leave it."

"Well, you're certainly able to do that," said Vickie, appraising her daughter. "But, Lulu, I want to know where you've been! What have you been doing? It's been over seven years."

Lulu sighed. She could have written this dialogue herself.

"Mom, it's my first day. I'm nervous as hell and I want to be good. Can we meet later and I'll fill you in?"

"All right," said Vickie faintly. "I'll take you to tea at the Plaza and you can tell me everything then." Moving like an automaton, she walked onto the set.

After blocking and camera rehearsal the cast was given an hour and a half for hair, makeup, and wardrobe. When Lulu appeared, exquisitely made up and coiffed, wearing a simple black pantsuit with a white shirt, the crew — a cynical bunch of TV veterans — was more than impressed.

"Wow, I've seen them all — Turner, Gardner, Lamarr," the old gaffer, Ted, said appreciatively, "but I ain't never seen any dame as beautiful as that one, and I've been in the business forty-five years."

"You're right," whispered Al McCormick, "she's gorgeous."

Much too gorgeous, he thought. He'd recognized her instantly. She might have changed her name and the color of her hair, but he'd studied her pictures for hours on end. He knew who she was and what she was. Too good-looking for her own good. It wasn't fair for a woman to tempt men like that. It wasn't right that she should be in all those magazines with her nipples sticking out and that "I want to be fucked" look on her face when he knew that she preferred to do it with women. She was a temptress — an evil fascinating witch who so inflamed men

453

with her image that they were forced to do disgusting things to themselves.

"I'd sure like her to sit on my face for about a day," sniggered another electrician.

"Those knockers — are they real?" asked another admiringly.

"Who cares? They look good enough to eat, if y'know what I mean!"

The guys guffawed and went back to work, pulling lights and cables around the set and trying not to bump into the actors, who were clutching their scripts and mumbling furiously to themselves.

Al was in a turmoil of lust and disgust as he stared unashamedly at the woman of his darkest fantasies. He could well believe she was the product of incest. That was why she was so dangerously alluring. The Bible would say she was conceived in corruption by fornicating sinners. She was the devil's decoy, and she had to be punished. But before that, there were other things he had to do to her. Things he had only imagined doing as he'd gazed at her seductive image in the magazines. He had to have her. He had to fuck the lesbian bitch and then he had to hurt her badly. His grandmother would approve of that. She'd promised him money if he did something to hurt Lulu or Vickie — either of them. What might she give him if he destroyed Lulu? Patsy was a faithful servant who was going to get a heap of money when the old duchess died. If he really pleased his grandmother, maybe she'd leave him everything.

Morgan, Tippy, and Sandy had the bulk of that day's dialogue. Morgan still had one hell of a headache from getting smashed the previous night at Chicago Blues. He usually didn't drink that much, but it had been one of those nights, and even six Excedrin hadn't exorcised his hangover. In fact, it was so bad that he couldn't seem to retain any of his dialogue, and, ten minutes before airtime, in a panic, he rushed all over the set writing certain key words from his speeches on bits of paper, which he stuffed in drawers, behind flats, and in a newspaper. Hopefully these words would spark his failing memory into spouting the right lines. He was sweating profusely, having the actor's worst nightmare — he couldn't remember a single line.

Lulu stood on the sidelines watching, amused and terrified at the same time. This was it. Live prime-time television. Even though it was only a soap opera, her big moment was coming up and she was going to play it to the hilt.

Mother and daughter sat in the Plaza Hotel Tea Room, eating cucumber sandwiches, sipping Earl Grey tea, and filling in the gaps of their separation. Little old ladies nibbled cream cakes and gossiped, a string quartet played in the corner, and the atmosphere was thick with gentility.

"Where did you go after that terrible incident when you were arrested? I tried to find you, but you'd been released from jail and no one knew where you were at your building. I left a lot of messages, Lulu."

"I know you did. I went to Arizona, then Mexico, Mama, to Acapulco actually. I had some friends there, and I was gone for several months. I had to sort myself out, get my life back on track." She sighed, then looked Vickie straight in the eyes. "Especially as I was now responsible for another life."

"What do you mean . . . ?"

"Yes, Mama, I had a baby. Can you imagine me, who only liked girls, getting pregnant?" Lulu shook her head and poured herself another cup of tea.

"But how?"

Lulu grinned. "The usual way, Mom."

"I mean was it *planned?* Did you want to have a child?" Vickie was feeling quite faint. It was too much turmoil for one day — seeing her daughter for the first time in years, then discovering she was an actress in her show, and now finding out that she had a grandchild.

"No, of course it wasn't planned." Lulu waved away the pastries from the hovering waiter. "I was at the top of my game, Mama, the number-one model in America." Lulu felt self-conscious about her mother seeing her softer side. "You think I'd want to throw all that down the tube for a kid?"

"Well, why didn't you get . . ."

"An abortion? C'mon, say it, Mom, don't be shy." Lulu leaned forward, her pale eyes flashing. "Do you remember, after you married Pop, every Sunday at church, Mom? All those preachers telling us abortion was a mortal sin, same as murder?"

"Yes, I do. Cooper was a staunch Catholic in spite of his lifestyle, and he wanted me to embrace the faith as much as he did. I tried," she bit her lip, "I did try, but in spite of my nightly prayer sessions since childhood I never bought into that dogma."

"But that saved a life, Mom. Cooper's beliefs saved my baby's life."

"So that's why you couldn't go through with it?"

"I guess so. Even with all the drugs, and my girlfriends and my crazy life, that little old Catholic doctrine that Pop made me follow proved to be real strong."

"Who's the father of your baby?" asked Vickie quietly.

Lulu shrugged. "Leon. His name's Leon. He doesn't know about the baby and I don't want him to either. We weren't exactly close." She smiled to herself, remembering how close she and Leon had been for a couple of days.

"What does he do?" Vickie felt she had to keep this conversation going. Lulu wasn't particularly forthcoming, and she kept staring into space with a faraway smile on her face. "Don't you think you should tell him? It would be nice for the child to at least know its own father."

"He's black, Mom. He's also a bisexual, and a paid stud." She looked into her mother's face for her reaction.

"Oh my God, the oldest taboo of all." Vickie fanned herself with a napkin. It suddenly seemed to be much hotter in the tea room.

"You think I want to bring a gigolo into my life? Into my baby's life? No way, Mom, no way."

"Were you in love with him? You must have at least *liked* him?"

Lulu let out a peal of laughter. "Mama, you are *so* old-fashioned. Just because you had to fall in love — or at least pretend to love every guy you slept with — doesn't mean *I* have to. It's the eighties, Mom, not the forties. All that love stuff's a myth. And it never lasts."

"It did for me," Vickie whispered, but Lulu didn't hear her as her beautiful brow furrowed in thought.

Even though her cynical words were those of a liberated modern woman, Lulu still felt bitter. She had loved and trusted Saskia because she had believed that she loved her too, but she'd realized that love left you open to hurt. She had been devastated when Saskia had dumped her, without even the courtesy of a face-to-face good-bye, an opportunity to discuss and resolve their problems. Lulu had just received a classic "Dear John" letter from Saskia on the same day she discovered she was pregnant.

That was when Lulu had gone on a two-month bender. Although she tried to forget, the sad memories of that time still intruded on her consciousness too often, like a flashing image from an MTV video. As she listened to her mother droning on, Lulu remembered her trip to hell.

She'd gone to some bar alone, got fiercely drunk and been persuaded by a person, or persons, unknown to attend a party in a seedy downtown apartment. The other party-goers weren't her usual crowd of models, actors and photographers. They were creatures of the night, with ruined bloodless faces that looked sickly and corrupt. A blue pall of marijuana smoke had hung in the air like a noxious cloud, and the acrid chemical smell of crack cocaine had permeated the atmosphere as the lifeless party-goers tapped their vials and cooked their opiates on their personal tin spoons.

Lulu had taken a big hit of the unfamiliar crack. It had seemed like just the panacea she craved, but afterward she remembered nothing. Until she came to in an unfamiliar bed in an unfamiliar room with three unfamiliar faces grinning at her.

"You enjoy that fuck we give you, honey?" grinned the pale, pimply one in the back-to-front baseball cap. "You sure looked like you did. You were squirmin' an' squealin' like a stuck pig."

"You sure are hot," the one with a broken nose had leered. "You're the best I've had for a long time."

"Want some more, bitch?" Another strapping young man, practically naked, with a lithe athlete's body and smooth skin had flexed his biceps. "There's plenty more where that came from, ain't there, guys," he'd mocked.

"Where am I?" Lulu had asked weakly.

"Where are you?" he mocked. "You're with the toughest motherfuckers in the city. And you owe us — we protected you from the others."

"What others?" Lulu had felt like throwing up all over the stained blanket that she lay on. Her entire body ached, there were ugly bruises on her arms and an agonizing pain inside her. She could feel blood trickling down her thighs — something was happening — was she losing her baby?

"Those doped-up fuckers, the ones we took you away from. They were enjoying you a lot little lady, they'd have left you dead. We rescued you, so we gave ourselves a little reward." He started preparing another shot of crack for himself, grinning widely, his eyes roaming over her half-naked body.

Lulu had thought she would pass out again as disgust, like a poisonous snake, crawled all over her. Her panic started to intensify as the most strapping and menacing of the pack strutted toward her, his intention obvious as he rubbed his rising tumescence through his baggy jeans. With an instinct born of terror and self-preservation, Lulu suddenly projectile vomited toward the guy, hitting him in the stomach with a full blast.

"Shit, bitch, look what you've done," the punk squawked furiously, rubbing at his splattered musculature. He grabbed a bandanna from his compadre's head to angrily wipe himself down, detumesceing rapidly. "After all we did for you, woman, you throw up all over *me* — on Mad Maxie? I'm the man — the main man here."

"Can I go to the bathroom, *please?*" Lulu's nausea was rising up again. "I'm going to be sick."

"Yeah, yeah, go to the fuckin' bathroom, clean yourself up. You ain't fit for no one the way you look now."

The three men turned away from Lulu contemptuously as she staggered on shaking legs to the half-open door of the bathroom.

She'd glanced around the room for her clothes but there was just the musty fetid bed, a filthy sagging sofa and a table, pocked with cigarette and crack burns. The window had been so covered with dirt that she had not been able to tell whether it was day or night.

Naked, bleeding, and terrified, Lulu fell on her knees in front of the dirty bowl and threw up again and again. Then suddenly she realized she was hemorrhaging badly. She tried to stem the flow with a dirty towel hanging from the basin, before collapsing onto the rotten floorboards, doubled over in agony. Before she'd passed out she managed to call out faintly, "Help, please help me, I think I'm losing the baby," and then the blessed relief of unconsciousness had overcome her.

The emergency services had found Lulu lying at the bottom of the exit steps of Roosevelt Hospital, where the gang had dumped her. They had then sped off in their stolen car, still high on crack, ear-shattering music echoing after them on the rain-soaked streets.

Fortunately it was a slow night at the hospital, and Lulu was taken care of before she lost too much blood. She had been feverish and hyperventilating during the long night and her temperature rose so high that they didn't think she'd make it. But Lulu wasn't aware of anything. She was out cold, mercifully dead to the world.

They had managed to save the baby, just, and when Lulu regained consciousness she had telephoned her bank manager to instruct him to transfer sufficient funds to the hospital's account so they could move her into a private room. There she had lain slowly recuperating, thinking long and hard about her screwed-up life.

When she was well enough to leave the hospital, Lulu had put her apartment on the market, packed a small bag and gone to Sedona, Arizona, where she checked herself into a rehab clinic. She remained there until her baby was born. Then, her apartment sold and her addiction hopefully beaten for good, Lulu had flown with her daughter to Acapulco, where she rented a tiny casita near the beach, staying there until her little girl was three months old.

Chapter Thirty-Seven
1988

Vickie was curious to see her first grandchild, but Lulu was tight-lipped about the baby girl's whereabouts. All she would say was that she was being taken care of "in a safe place," but she wouldn't elaborate. She was as closemouthed about details of her daughter as Millie had been in revealing any information about Vickie's father to her.

Vickie became resigned to not seeing the child, but she didn't have time to dwell on it because *Sons and Lovers* was all-consuming. With the advent of "Tamara the Temptress," as the tabloids dubbed Lulu, the show suddenly started to sizzle as it hadn't done in the first three months.

The producers decided not to give Lulu too many scenes in each episode initially. "We'll break her in gently," said Jerry Goswell.

"She's got star quality in spades, that's for damn sure." Director Roger Harris was rerunning this morning's live broadcast, considering his choice of shots and angles to see if they had been the best, and what he could do to improve the show.

"She heats up the screen and she gives great face. Look at that." He stopped the projector, freeze-framing an enormous close-up of Lulu. Her slightly parted lips and eyes slanted in anger gave her an almost she-devil look. "The camera loves her, she's a knockout, this girl. Where'd she come from? What's her background?"

"She was a model." Jerry shrugged. "We had an open audition and she turned up. It was a no-brainer. She beat the rest of the kids hands down. We're getting mail. Every day there're two or three dozen letters for her. Tamara seems to have hit a nerve with our lady viewers."

"We only *have* lady viewers," said Roger witheringly, "and only ladies of a certain age, at that."

"Well, what the network's seeing is that the younger viewers are starting to tune in — the teens and twenty-somethings. They're thrilled; those are just the magic demographics they pray for."

"Why aren't these kids at school or work?" asked Roger sarcastically.

"How the fuck should I know? All I know is Lulu's getting warm, and warm means she's gonna be hot, and the network wants us to cash in on her while she's on the burn."

"Fine with me," Roger started, rerunning a scene in which Tamara blew her fuse at Morgan. "She's certainly making mincemeat out of *him*."

"Yeah, I think it's maybe time Morgan had a little accident," mused the producer, picking his teeth with a gold Tiffany toothpick. "Maybe after he marries Tamara and she becomes a part of the family, he dies. Then we'll have confrontation after confrontation with the sons, the girlfriends, and the parents. Let's get those writers on the phone," he said gleefully.

Al McCormick slid an arc light into position where the gaffer had instructed him to and watched Lulu strut her stuff. She had certainly pulled out all the stops today as she sashayed around the set in a scarlet dress, cut so tight it was like a second skin.

"Slut," he thought as he lugged lights and cables around the set. "Filthy trash." She was just as bad as the character she played. Everyone knew now that she was Vickie Gordon's daughter and that her real name was Lulu, although professionally she was still known as Rebecca; what they didn't know was that she was conceived in almighty sin with Vickie's own brother, Sebastian. She was slime, an aberration — and it was almost time for him to strike.

The other three young actresses stood behind one of the cameras staring at Lulu jealously. "How come she gets to look like that and we have to wear these *schmattas?*" snarled Sandy, who was becoming more desperately insecure each day. During the months that Lulu had been on the soap, everyone knew that the ratings were rising and everyone knew it was because of her.

"She must be screwing the costume designer," said Wendy spitefully. "Got to be."

"Oh, fat chance; he's gayer than May Day." Tippy, being the only blonde on the show, had less reason for insecurity than the other two.

"You can see *everything*," Sandy squeaked indignantly, "the crack in her ass, her nipples. She might as well be naked."

"That's a Halston for sure." Wendy knew her fashion. "I saw it in *Vogue* last week. It must have cost at *least* a couple of grand."

"And this piece of crap I'm wearing had the price tag still on it," moaned Sandy. "Two hundred bucks at Macy's, can you imagine? And I'm supposed to be *rich*."

"So how come she gets all the best clothes?" whined Wendy.

"She's fucking someone, for sure," said Sandy bitterly. "Either Jerry or Roger. One of 'em's got to be sticking her."

"Or maybe a network suit?" asked Tippy. "They're the guys holding the purse strings around here."

"Cow," hissed Wendy under her breath. "And she's *much* too thin. She looks like an X ray, and don't you think her head's too big for her body?"

"She looks like a lollipop lady," giggled Wendy, and the three of them bit into their jelly doughnuts and roared with laughter.

Lulu finished her scene, glanced at the three girls huddled together, and grinned. She knew she was pissing them off big time. But they were stupid. They were like lazy sheep, doing everything the director told them to and stuffing their faces at craft services so that their waistbands had to constantly be let out. Wardrobe had confided that to her. She spent a lot of time in wardrobe. She herself had found this dress at a secondhand store on Third Avenue. It was a Halston, from the sixties, which she'd bought for $150, along with several other glamorous vintage pieces that suited Tamara's electric character perfectly.

Natalie, the wardrobe mistress, had been thrilled when she'd come in with the garments and the receipts. "They're *fantastic*, Lulu. I can't believe you got these so cheaply. You're really making my work easier for me."

"If you want, I can find more," Lulu had suggested.

"Oh, but don't tell anyone *you've* found these clothes, will you? The producers will think I'm slacking if you do."

"Of course not, Natalie." Lulu had bestowed upon the woman her most dazzling smile. "It'll be our little secret."

Lulu's six years as a model had given her a tremendous sense of style, and knowledge of where to find the best and most original clothes at the lowest prices, and she used that knowledge on the show to great advantage.

What Tamara would wear in each episode started to intrigue more and more female viewers, and the "Tamara Look," slinky, sexy and sassy, started to be emulated by women all over America.

Soon Lulu was a rising star. The network knew it, the public knew it, and the cast of *Sons and Lovers* knew it — although several members weren't too thrilled about this huge rise in popularity that had nothing to do with themselves. Conversely, others had no problem with reaping the rewards of being in a hit show.

"Of course it's very good for our ratings. If this continues we'll have a job for life. Daytime soaps last for years. I, for one, am extremely happy about her success," confided Stanley.

"So am I," answered Vickie fervently.

They stood at the craft service wagon while Stanley ate a massive breakfast of fried eggs, bacon, sausage, and waffles. Lulu joined them, pouring herself a black coffee while noticing that Stanley's costume needed letting out again.

"My dear, how are you? *Loved* you on Johnny Carson last night, well done, you looked lovely," smiled Stanley, his false teeth glinting in the arc lights.

"Thanks, Dad. Oh, sorry, I mean Stanley." Lulu winked at Vickie.

The two women exchanged smiles. Although not closer than close, there was an agreeable familiarity between them, and they had even started having dinner together once or twice a week.

Her daughter was some piece of work. Vickie had always known that, although she had inherited much of Cooper's *chutzpah* and charm, her beauty and hauteur too often made her enemies.

The remaining two ingenues sidled up to the cart.

"Here come Cinderella's ugly sisters," Lulu whispered to Vickie.

" 'And then there were two.' " As red-headed Sandy had foreseen, the unfortunate actress had been fired, her character trapped in a burning building never to return. Now Tippy and Wendy, becoming extremely worried about their own futures, had started a simmering vendetta against Lulu.

Cool greetings were exchanged as Tippy and Wendy bellied up to the bar to heap their plates with danishes, doughnuts, cheesecake, and pecan pie. Lulu sipped her sugarless coffee, smiling at them sweetly.

"You should eat something," snapped Wendy. "You never eat — you need the energy. Here, have one of these, they're delicious."

She shoved a jelly doughnut toward Lulu, who recoiled. "No way, that's junk food!"

"You're too skinny. You look like a ghost . . . it doesn't photograph well, you know," said Tippy. "You're beginning to look like Karen Carpenter."

"Have you got anorexia?" piped up Wendy. "You really should gain some weight, Lulu."

"And look like *you?*" Lulu pinched the fold of fat that hung over the waistband of Wendy's too-tight jeans. "No thanks, darling. Didn't your mama tell you that you can never be too thin or too rich?"

"Well, everyone certainly thinks *you're* too thin." Wendy was close to tears from pure jealousy. One of her ambitions in life had been to be a guest on Johnny Carson's *Tonight Show*. She'd begged the network and the studio publicists for a slot, but they had said that Johnny wasn't interested in a daytime soap star. Now he'd had that bitch on for two whole segments. It wasn't fair.

"On Johnny last night, you looked scrawny."

"Oh, who says so?" Lulu answered coolly.

"I have got *eyes,* you know. Several of my friends called and said you were just skin and bone."

"Well, it's better than being just blubber and fat." Lulu had had enough of this catty exchange. "You're pathetic, Wendy. You eat like a pregnant pig. Can't you see what you're doing to your body with all that food? Just remember, 'eat junk: become junk.'" She started walking away, but Wendy grabbed her by the shoulder and swung her around.

"Are you calling me junk?" she screeched. "Are you?" Wendy was a hefty girl, definitely running to fat. She pushed Lulu so hard that Lulu lost her balance and crashed into the craft service trestle table, collapsing to the floor as popcorn, tuna fish, and cookies rained down upon her. Then, as if in slow motion, the glass percolator full of coffee toppled over and smashed onto Lulu, who was trapped among the junk food wreckage.

Luckily the percolator had been almost empty, so Lulu wasn't badly hurt, but the story made all the papers. Once again Lulu was on the front page of the tabloids, this time leaving the hospital with a bandaged wrist and head and a cheery wave to her fans.

"SOAP STAR SLIPS UP," a banner headline blared. But the fan mail just kept on coming.

Chapter Thirty-Eight

Don Lowell, a hack on the *National Informer*, was looking for a scoop — any scoop. As he sifted through the latest stories on actress Rebecca Swann — known only to her family and colleagues as Lulu — his mind was definitely inching toward something, but he just couldn't get at what it was. Frustrated, he threw a rival paper's report on the hospital incident onto his desk and glared at the article in frustration. As he did so, a photo of Lulu's face, swathed in bandages that covered her gorgeous hair, jolted his memory and everything fell into place. Five minutes later, Horace Reid, the editor of the *National Informer*, was slapping him on the back in excitement. "Holy shit! It *is* Lulu the Lesbian!" he crowed as the paper's staff gathered round to see what all the fuss was about. "Remember that dyke model a couple of years ago — had a fight in a gay bar and knocked out some muff-muncher? Hold the front page, boys, we got a good one here!"

A week later Jerry Goswell stalked onto the set, his face a thundercloud, holding a copy of the *National Informer* as if it were a dog turd.

"I want to speak to you, Rebecca, and you too, Vickie, as soon as possible, please."

The assistant director looked panicked. "We're in the middle of blocking, we need them. There's only an hour and a half to air-time."

Jerry's eyes narrowed. "OK, OK, tell them as soon as shooting's finished, I want them in my office, pronto — *capisce?*"

"Yeah, boss, sure." The AD was sweating. It was a tough job being in charge of a daily live soap and ADs burnt out extremely fast. He was looking forward to taking early retirement and becoming a school bus driver — it would be less stressful.

In the week since the fight between Lulu and Wendy at craft services and the subsequent publicity, *Sons and Lovers'* ratings had soared, and the network was ecstatic.

"We want more of that gal — she's becoming a national heroine — even if she is playing a bitch," said the CEO of USBC.

"But with this lesbian scandal the public could turn off just as fast as they've turned on, so we better be quick," said the head of talent. He knew only too well that TV viewers were a fickle lot, always eager for something or someone fresh on the horizon.

Summoned to Jerry's office, Vickie and Lulu sat opposite him on uncomfortable leather chairs in front of his enormous desk. Jerry brandished the *National Informer* in front of them.

"So, what's this story all about?" he snarled. "We could start hemorrhaging viewers because of it. You better explain why you didn't tell us the truth about your past, kiddo, and it'd better be good."

"There's nothing to explain." Lulu was coolly unfazed by the producer's legendary anger. "You never asked me if Rebecca Swann was my real name, and it doesn't say anything in the contract about that. I didn't lie. Anyway, I changed it legally and that's how my social security reads now."

"There's a morals clause in your contract, y'know, which says that if you're discovered doing *anything* illegal — like drugs or dope or jail — we can fire you."

"So fire me." Lulu lit a cigarette and calmly blew a smoke ring. "I've been clean since I've been on the show and, let's be honest Jerry, you'd never have hired me in the first place if you'd known who I was and what I'd done."

"Yeah, you're right, we wouldn't. The network would have had a fit; they're not keen on lesbos."

"And you would have lost the best thing

that's happened to daytime soap since Susan Lucci," said Vickie quietly.

"Well, the shit's gonna hit the fan, and it'll be my balls on the rack. Jesus, Rebecca, how could you?"

"How could I what?"

"How could you *do* all that stuff? Look at you!" He held up the *National Informer* cover, which in lurid color showed the old photograph of Lulu being dragged into the police precinct, covered in blood, her clothes filthy and ripped to shreds. Next to that picture was another one of Lulu as Tamara glamorous and smiling, and a small picture of Vickie. The headline blared "EXCLUSIVE! THE DOUBLE LIFE OF TAMARA" and, on the undersling, *"We reveal the sordid past of the wild-child temptress of daytime soap and daughter of a famous movie star!"*

"This could ruin us," fumed Jerry. "Ruin *me.*"

"Why should it ruin *you?*" Lulu asked. "It looks like it's me that's going to be ruined."

"As the producer, the network holds me responsible for whom I hire."

"I haven't committed a crime. It's not a criminal act to be a lesbian these days."

"Don't say that word — please." Jerry's face went an even deeper beet red. "You're supposed to be the sexy slut every guy wants to hump. When the public finds out that you're a dyke, that's when the shit will really

really hit the fan."

"How? Why? How do you know?"

"Because of fucking Middle America. Bible belt rednecks who never even go down on their own wives, let alone *think* about women doing it to each other."

"That's not a crime either," said Vickie.

"Look, *bubula*." Jerry was exasperated. "We don't care about the legality here, it's *perception*. Our viewers, whom we depend on to keep this show on the air, see Tamara as a sexy, savvy, ruthless vixen. The men all want you, the women want to *be* you. Not the other way around."

"Oh, horse-plop," laughed Lulu. "We're nearly in the nineties. Half the world's gay now, didn't you know, Jerry?"

"Not in Middle America, they're not. They don't want to know about fags and dykes, and Middle America makes up most of our ratings."

"So, what do you want me to do? Hold a press conference? Saying . . ." — she put on a babyish voice — "very sorry everybody, I've been a bad, naughty little girl and I'll never do it again."

"*Will* you do it again?" asked Jerry.

"Do what?"

"Do it with another dame. The press'll be watching you like hawks. If they catch you even going to the movies with some chick, they'll nail you, and that will be the final nail in the coffin for *Sons and Lovers*."

"Why?" asked Vickie. "What will happen?"

"Let's face it, much as I hate facing it: We were on the brink of canceling the show. Rebecca saved it. If we lose her, we lose the lot. Shit, shit, shit, what a fucking situation!" Jerry sank into his chair, sweating profusely. His fat face looked so close to crying that both women actually started to feel sorry for him.

"What do you want me to do?" asked Lulu gently. "I'll do anything you ask, Jerry. I love this show and I want to continue in it."

"Me too." Vickie put her arm around Lulu affectionately.

"OK, we're gonna have to work our asses off, but I think we can save it. We'll send out a press release." Jerry started to pick up. "You'll admit what you did and you'll say you were very young, you made mistakes, blah, blah, blah. You'll never do it again. You'll do a couple of interviews, maybe with Barbara and then with Larry, and maybe, just maybe, it'll all blow over. And please, Lulu, I *beg* you, if they ask you if you still prefer girls could you just tone it down a bit, for the sake of the ratings?"

Chapter Thirty-Nine

Fueled by his grandmother's incessant letters from England telling him that he owed it to his family and his dear departed father to get their rightful dues, Al had started surveillance on Lulu right after the latest scandal broke. He couldn't believe that she had come through it again unscathed, unpunished, and almost more popular than ever.

Patsy knew all about it in London. Although few American daytime soaps were shown in England, there had been several stories about Lulu in the gossip columns and, as she was the daughter of an ex-Duchess of Burghley, also a famous fifties' movie star who'd had a colorful life of her own, the tabloids had a field day with the story.

With great difficulty Patsy had managed to figure out how to telephone her grandson long distance. Her ancient voice had crackled along the wires. "I'm sending you some more letters to go with the ones I gave you after your father's funeral." She had gone to the local library and made the harassed assistant spend hours photocopying the letters for her. She wasn't stupid — she'd keep the copies carefully. She had wanted to keep the originals of the letters near her, as it was her greatest delight to read and reread them, but now she thought it best to send them to the person who could start using them — soon. "Don't do anything with them yet, do y'hear? Just put them with the others, and wait until I tell you what to do."

A few days later the letters arrived, and Al was curious to read them. The writing was difficult to read, spidery and ill-educated, written on thin paper that was yellow with age.

August 15, 1918

My Dearest Toby,

My heart is breaking because you have not answered my letters. Surely you must realize the predicament I am in, my dearest love. We were supposed to marry, and because of that I let myself give in to you although it was against my upbringing to do so. What am I supposed to do, Toby? I have been with child for nearly six months now, and I don't know what is going to happen. Please come back to me. I know you love me, you told me so many times.

Please, Toby, I beg you, don't let our

child be born out of wedlock for that is a mortal sin too. I will wait for you my love, please come.

Your faithful and loving Millie

The last letter was the most interesting, and the most incriminating for Ms. Lulu Swannell. It was dated November 27, 1918, and it was addressed to the Duke of Burghley at the mansion at Eaton Square.

Your Grace:

I am writing to you because I am at my wits' end, and I beg that you will help me out of my terrible predicament.

Your son Tobias and I were to be married. He promised to do so, and I have the banns to prove it. I know that my dearest Toby has passed away in combat, and for that I am more sad than you could ever know. I offer my deepest sympathy to you and the duchess.

Because I was engaged to your son I allowed things to happen between us which should not have happened, but he told me so many times that he loved me and I believed him. Our baby was born two weeks ago. She is a beautiful little girl whom I have christened Victoria after our dear departed queen.

I beg you, kind sir, to send me and the child a little bit of money, for there is a famine here in Ireland and everyone is terrible hungry. Please, sir, I beg you for charity's sake and the sake of your grand-daughter, help me out in this time of terrible need.

Most sincerely yours,
Millicent McClancey

Al grinned malevolently. Stupid ignorant bitch. All of the women descended from her were stupid bitches too. The worst one of all was Lulu, and these letters were now absolute proof that she was the product of incest. He'd bide his time.

The gay community embraced Lulu whole-heartedly. They admired her for coming out so boldly, which for a female celebrity in the late eighties was unusual. The more traditional-minded viewers liked her, too, for the fact that Vickie Gordon and Lulu were real-life mother and daughter appealed to their family values.

As for the young audiences, since taking drugs was perceived as a cool thing to do, Lulu became something of an icon to them, and *Sons and Lovers* gained ever more popularity in the elusive youth market as well.

Lulu was hotter than she'd ever been as a model, and was now making the covers of the more important magazines. *Life*, *People*, and *Vanity Fair* eulogized her in major features, and her love life became the subject of endless tabloid speculation. But Lulu kept her mouth shut about that, and if she were seeing anyone, be they male or female, no one — not even the sneaky tabloid paparazzi — ever managed to catch her with them.

Wendy had become so enraged by Lulu's incredible success that she went on an uncontrollable eating binge. In spite of repeated warnings from Jerry, Roger, and the network brass, she continued stuffing herself until her weight ballooned to 150 pounds. When wardrobe could no longer disguise the size of her stomach, the writers had the idea to write in a pregnancy. Shortly after, realizing the pregnancy could bizarrely go on for seasons, they finally had her character die in childbirth.

Only Tippy was left now as Lulu's competition, but even though the writers crafted excellent conflict scenes between them, Lulu's attitude and presence ran circles around the other actress. Her aura pervaded the show, and when she wasn't on the screen or being talked about by the other actors, viewers complained.

Rebecca Swann and Susan Lucci were now the most popular drama queens on daytime TV. Everyone loved them, and everyone loved to hate them. But nobody hated Lulu more than Al McCormick. To get rid of her had become his obsession.

Chapter Forty
March 1988

Lulu let herself into her dark apartment and without turning on the lights walked across the marble foyer to the bar. She poured herself a stiff Stoli on the rocks, yawned, and stretched. She was exhausted. She'd had a shitload of dialogue that morning, and then a fashion shoot all afternoon for *Glamour* magazine. Now all she wanted to do was to watch the Oscar telecast from her bed and then go to sleep.

She lit a cigarette, then strolled out onto her balcony, surveying the glittering lights of New York City as they shimmered in the cold night air. Now that she was making a thousand dollars an episode, she could afford to rent this furnished apartment in a fashionable neighborhood of Manhattan. Maybe one day she could afford to even buy one again. She was getting commercial offers now for skin and hair products, and they were becoming more and more lucrative.

A heavy snow had started falling and, shivering in the icy air, she turned to go back inside, but stopped as she saw a figure silhouetted against the glass sliding doors. The tall, thickset man stood stock still, breathing heavily, then took a step toward her. He wore dark clothing and a black ski mask, and in his right hand he held a knife, which glinted in the dim moonlight.

"What do you want?" Fear made bile rise in Lulu's throat. The man didn't answer but took another menacing step toward her, fingering the blade of his knife in his black-gloved hand.

This was the scenario of nightmares: trapped by a knife-wielding maniac on a narrow terrace forty floors above street level.

Lulu looked around for a weapon, anything to protect herself, but all she had was a shot glass in one hand and a Marlboro in the other. Summoning up every bit of bravado, she demanded again in a shaky voice: "Who are you and what the hell are you doing here?"

The mask moved as the man's lips stretched in a sinister smile. There was something familiar about his teeth. There was a gap in the middle and one of his eyeteeth was crooked. She knew she'd seen that before somewhere.

"You got a great view here, lady, must've cost a packet. Pays to be a slut, don't it?"

He moved toward her with palpable hostility, and Lulu edged along the balustrade until her back was flat against the brick wall that separated her apartment from her neighbors. Cornered between the wall and the balustrade, she had nowhere to go. She bent her head to the side and saw the sheer walls of the building below her. She was on the fortieth floor. It was a long way to jump.

Then, with a grunt, he was on her, his burly arms pinning her to the wall, his teeth bared in that horrifying smile, his breath rasping in his throat like a death rattle. "You're never going to get away from me, you bitch — never, you hear?" His wheezing voice was like an old man's, but by the strength of his grip Lulu could tell that he was a strong, fit man in his thirties. He twisted one arm behind her and she dropped the glass, her only weapon. Then he bent his head so close toward her that she could smell his stale breath.

"I want you, lady, an' I'm gonna have you before I throw you off this balcony."

"No, please. I've got money. It's in the safe — I've got jewelry too. I'll give you anything you want, only please let me go."

Lulu started sobbing and heard herself begging, but she didn't care. She was trembling violently in his agonizing grip. His hands were like vises on her arms, and he held her as easily as if she were a two-year-old. He laughed, and she thought she recognized that coarse brutish sound.

"You think I'm gonna let you *go?* Are you crazy, lady? I've been planning this little surprise for you for months, sweetie pie. I've been dreaming about it. Now let's get you inside where we can get real cozy, OK?"

Lulu had closed her palm gently around her lighted cigarette. She felt it singeing her flesh, but she had to hold on to it — it was the only weapon she had. Maybe she thought she could burn him with it and escape during those vital seconds of surprise. She must wait for him to let his guard down. It was her only chance.

The intruder dragged Lulu by her shoulders into the living room. He'd obviously been preparing for her, as there was some rope on the armchair in front of the fire. The chair was on a fake monkey skin rug made of acrylic fiber. It wasn't Lulu's taste, but a fan had left it with the doorman and she'd put it down there temporarily.

As he forced her down into the chair, Lulu realized the man was too covered by his clothing for her to be able to burn him with her cigarette, so instead she flicked it, still smoldering, behind him as far away as she could, praying it would start a fire on the carpet. She knew the sensitive fire alarm was on the ceiling above. She sat still as a stone as the man surveyed her, panting, his pupils heavily dilated. Thank God he hadn't noticed the cigarette. She'd heard that in situations like this it was best not to struggle but to stay calm so as to be able to call upon reserves of strength and courage at the right time. But when was the right time going to be? Fear had turned her stomach into a block of ice, and her legs started trembling uncontrollably.

The man bent down to caress her thigh, then raised his head and his tongue slid out of the black ski mask and slowly licked his lips. She wanted to vomit. Then he started tying her legs to the chair. Lulu was fortunate not to be wearing her usual blue jeans and sneakers. She had on heavy black leather pants, a sheepskin coat and fur-lined boots, but she could still feel the ropes cutting into her ankles.

Al was enjoying himself — very much indeed. "Are you havin' fun, sweetie?" He grinned, tightening the ropes on her legs to the chair. Then he sat back on his heels to survey his work, holding the knife between his teeth: He had an almost satanic appearance. Then he grinned again and, reaching into his back pocket, took out some papers tied together with a rubber band.

"Before I tie you up thoroughly, sweetie, I want to show you something. Here. Read 'em. They're interesting. It's your legacy, Lulu Swannell. It's where you come from. It proves you're pond slime, a freak, and that you shouldn't have been allowed to live."

"I don't understand." Lulu took the yellowed sheets of paper and glanced at the old-fashioned handwriting on them. "What are these? Who wrote them?"

"Well, let me explain, sweetie pie." Al sat back on his heels and with a flourish removed the ski mask, staring at Lulu triumphantly. "Recognize me? You probably don't. You're too much of a stuck-up bitch to have anything to do with the likes of us."

"I think I do recognize you." Lulu realized she *had* seen this man before, on the set lugging lights or cables. She'd noticed him staring at her sometimes, but that was no big deal. All the guys stared at her. "You work on the show, don't you?"

"Right. Al McCormick at your service. So you do remember me after all. Now, you're curious about these letters, aren't you?"

"What are they?"

"They're my heritage, sweetie." His small eyes became even narrower. "*My* heritage that was taken away from me, ruined by your fucking grandmother and the rest of your goddamn family."

"I don't understand anything you're saying." Lulu realized that this person was a lot more deranged than she'd originally thought. "I never knew my grandmother. Why don't you just let me . . ."

"Read the letters," his face became purplish-red as he put his hands around her neck and started to squeeze. "Read them, and then get ready to pay for the sins of your ancestors, bitch."

The second-second AD got the call from the head writer just as she was settling down on the sofa to watch the Oscars in front of her tiny TV. This was always one of Jamie's favorite nights, and she'd made herself a special dish of spaghetti and meatballs, to be followed by Häagen-Dazs chocolate chip ice cream with caramel sauce. Tonight she wasn't following Lulu's diet.

"We've got rewrites," barked Ed Carson. "Major. You gotta get them over to Vickie, Stan, and Rebecca ASAP."

Jamie knew better than to argue. A gopher's job was a thankless task, at everyone's beck and call twenty-four-seven. She was the lowest person on the totem pole, but she was lucky, wasn't she? She was in showbiz, in a top-rated TV show, and how the folks back home in Milwaukee envied her.

"Get these copied right now, then run them over to the actors and make sure you deliver them *in person*, d'you hear? And have 'em sign. I don't want any of my cast moaning about not having their lines in time."

Privately Jamie thought that giving actors ten or twelve pages of new dialogue the night before they were due to shoot was extremely unfair, but who was she to complain? She was, after all, just the gopher, a nonperson.

"But what if they're out?" she asked. "It's eight o'clock, they could be at dinner or at an Oscar party."

"Then you wait, kid, for 'em! C'mon, you know the score. You wait until you see them, and you put these babies right into their hot little hands, got it? It's a big denouement scene tomorrow, and we need everyone to know what they're doing for a change, especially Stan. You better get to him first — he takes the longest to learn his stuff."

"But he lives in Brooklyn," Jamie wailed. "In this weather it'll take at least an hour to get there."

"That's what we pay you for," snapped Ed. "Now skedaddle, kiddo, time's a-wastin'."

Throwing on boots and an anorak, Jamie managed to finally hail a cab, which floundered through the unseasonably thick slush to Ed's apartment in the West Village.

An hour later, having delivered Stan's and Vickie's new pages and had them sign a receipt, Jamie stood in the foyer of Lulu's apartment building arguing with the desk clerk, who was ringing Lulu's apartment.

"I tell you, she must've stepped out." The bored clerk hung up and checked his watch. Only two more hours on this shift and he'd be out of here and back to his new little wife. He couldn't wait.

"In this weather? There's no one out there in this horrible night. Everyone's at home watching the Oscars . . . except me, that is."

"Well, she's not answering," said the clerk flatly, "and I can't let you go up there — that's the rules."

"Then I'll wait." Jamie sat down on the leather banquette and stared at the clerk defiantly. "I'll wait all night if I have to, because I *know* she's up there. She told me her plans," Jamie confided proudly. "She said she'd be doing a magazine shoot and she was staying in to watch the Oscars alone. Did you see her come in?"

"Sure, about an hour ago."

"And you've not seen her leave?"

"Nope, but if she did, I could've been on coffee break."

Jamie went over to the doorman standing inside but shivering in his fancy uniform.

"Did you see Miss Swann leave here tonight?" she asked him.

"No, ma'am. In fact, no one's gone out all night in this storm. It's bitter out there."

"Right, thank you."

Jamie dialed Lulu's private number on her mobile phone, but only her machine answered. She left a message saying she was downstairs waiting and had strict instructions to deliver these new pages personally. Then she sat down again and prepared to wait.

Lulu heard the telephone ringing in the study. Heard the answering machine click on and Jamie's voice saying she was in the lobby and had to see her. Lulu looked at Al. He'd told her his name now, told her that he was some sort of distant relative, a cousin from Ireland. She had tried to read the letters he put in front of her, but the words swam in front of her eyes.

Time, time, she *had* to play for time. She knew the rules of this building. They had strict instructions not to let anyone up unless they were expected and then announced. Al must have managed to slip by unnoticed while the desk clerk was occupied, she thought miserably. Then suddenly her heart leapt. The cast had each been given a gift two days ago to celebrate their ratings — these new portable phones that were supposed to revolutionize communications. Jamie, who was something of a techno-wizard, had shown her how to use it. Lulu hadn't paid much attention at the time, just thrown it in the pocket of her sheepskin. It must still be there!

The maniac was babbling again. Lulu tried to pay attention to make him think she was listening to his ravings about being the Duke of Burghley. What was he talking about? How could he be a duke, this burly oaf with the slack mouth and demented eyes? He was a psycho, the kind of stalker the studio had warned her about. How the hell had he managed to get into her apartment?

"So now you know the whole story; what do you think I should do about it?" he asked slyly. "What would you do, huh?"

Lulu's brain was racing wildly. She had to keep him talking. The man was fingering the knife, pointing it toward her, then spinning it around by the handle. He never took his eyes off her. Then suddenly, behind him she saw a tiny spiral of smoke issuing from the acrylic carpet. The cigarette she'd thrown had ignited the carpet. How long would it be before Al noticed it was burning and stamp it out? It was still only a tiny plume of smoke, not even a flame. Oh God, please let it be enough to set off the alarm, she thought. This building was tremendously fire sensitive. Several times she had set the alarm off when she was just cooking dinner.

Lulu raised her eyes to the flat white alarm in the ceiling that was almost directly above the smoke. *Please* let it go off, please, she prayed as she had never prayed before. Please, God.

Jamie was cold, bored, and sick of being stared at by the desk clerk. Where *was* Lulu? If only there was another way to get in contact with her . . . Suddenly, Jamie remembered that she'd programmed Lulu's mobile phone for her. The actress hadn't seemed too adept at using it, complaining that she was useless with technology, but as Jamie punched in Lulu's number she prayed that it was at least switched on. It was, and it started ringing.

In her pocket, the mobile phone started beeping. Lulu heard it and so did Al. With a snarl he leapt onto her and tried to find the phone in the folds of her thick sheepskin coat. Lulu's chair fell over backward as she desperately tried to press the answer button. But Al's bulk was on top of her, his hands around her neck. Through the panic haze in her brain, Lulu noticed that he'd dropped the knife, and she could smell the smoke from the carpet, which had started to ignite. With a superhuman effort she shrugged Al off her and pressed the answer button on her cell phone. She tried crying for help, but she couldn't speak. A pair of hands had come around her neck and was squeezing the life out of her.

On the other end of the line, Jamie listened in horror to a savage voice bellowing, "I'm going to kill you, bitch. You filthy whore."

Then she heard the shrill screech of a fire alarm and Lulu's hoarse voice calling, "Help, someone, please help me!"

Screaming at the doorman to call the cops and the fire department, Jamie, followed closely by the clerk, ran for the stairs.

With mounting frenzy Patsy read the story on the front page of *The Sun*. "STALKER ATTEMPTS TO KILL SEXY SOAP STAR," the headline blared. Beneath it the caption read *"Would-be murderer dies of smoke inhalation in fiery holocaust at Rebecca Swann's Manhattan apartment. Actress critical but will survive."*

"Idiot!" The vocal cords on her ancient neck stood out like yellow rope, and her hands shook so convulsively that she could barely hold the paper. "Stupid, clumsy, lunatic *fool*. You couldn't even do *that* properly." She read the article again, her ancient face contorted with malevolent impotence, her mind racing. With Al gone, she'd never be the Dowager Duchess of Burghley, but if she planned it carefully, she could get rich yet — she'd been right to keep copies of the letters. Both Vickie and her slut daughter would pay millions to keep Lulu's birth secret out of the papers. Feeling better, Patsy folded up the paper — a shame about her grandson, but at least she wouldn't have to pay him off now — and prepared to get on with her morning's duties.

Sorting the mail five minutes later, she was intrigued to find an envelope addressed in her maiden name, embossed with the name and address of a firm of lawyers in America. She slit it open with a grimy fingernail and read:

Dear Ms. Hooper,

I have been instructed by my clients, Ms. Victoria Gordon and Ms. Lucinda Swannell, to forward the enclosed copies of these documents, which they feel may be of interest to you. They have said that your knowledge of the contents of this letter should "end everything, once and for all."

They would also like to express their condolences for the death of your grandson, Mr. Albert McCormick.

The letter finished with the usual pleasantries, but Patsy was blind to them. Enclosed was a copy of a medical DNA test showing without a shadow of a doubt that Lulu's father was a man named as Cooper Hudson. Stapled to this were copies of formal adoption papers, the reason given, "Natural Father."

Patsy Hooper Kingsley dropped her head onto the wooden kitchen table and, for the first time in seventy years, sobbed her heart out.

EPILOGUE

NEW YORK
MARCH 2002

The women were escorted down the aisle with great deference; for two of them were, after all, icons. Some of the audience recognized Vickie and Lulu from their popular long-running soap opera, and they nudged one another, pointing toward them and muttering excitedly. Susie, in her wheelchair, was being pushed by Jamie, Lulu's long-term partner. At ninety-seven, the old lady was still incredibly alert and recent laser surgery had improved her eyesight so much that now she only needed spectacles for long distance.

Lulu's luxuriant black hair, now back to its natural color, had been fashionably straightened so that it fell like a sheet of ebony to her shoulders. In her sleek black satin pantsuit and white bugle-beaded T-shirt she was the epitome of the chic modern working woman. In full bloom, she oozed style and confidence in herself and her own sexuality.

Vickie held on to her daughter's arm slightly, although she had little need of support. At eighty-three, she was maturely beautiful and, although she had not held the years at bay physically, her upright posture and serenity gave her a classic elegance that many women envied. Her full-length gold-and-brocade coat, trimmed in sable, suited her comfortably upholstered figure perfectly. Her hair was cut short, and a flattering auburn rinse complemented her creamy skin.

As they were shown into their front row seats, heads craned forward for a better look at the mother and grandmother of one of tonight's stars. Radio City Music Hall was the venue for the concert to celebrate the real millennium, the proceeds of which were going to UNICEF to fight world hunger and poverty. Many major international music and recording stars were going to perform, and the buzz was electric. Master of ceremonies Billy Crystal had the audience in stitches with his opening monologue, and then, one after another, a glittering parade of entertainers came onstage. The crowd was relishing the lineup ahead. Madonna was to perform a duet with Rod Stewart; George Michael and Robbie Williams would pay homage to musical greats of the past like Frank Sinatra and Fred Astaire; Luciano Pavarotti would thrill with "Nessun Dorma," and, as the grand finale, the Rolling Stones would be reunited yet again.

The evening didn't disappoint. Each act

was more spectacular than the last and each performer more brilliant than the one before. A shimmering array of movie stars introduced them. Julia Roberts, Denzel Washington, and the two Toms — Cruise and Hanks — had all given their time and talent. The aim was to raise five million dollars for this extraordinarily worthy cause.

Toward the end of the first half, Billy Crystal stepped up to the microphone. "What can one say about a living legend? A lady whose career has spanned more than sixty years? Her glamour and talent made the G.I.s and servicemen of World War II go into battle with a smile on their faces and a pinup picture of her in their kitbags. She starred in more than thirty of the most entertaining and sparkling comedies and musicals of the nineteen forties and fifties, and for the past fifteen years she has enchanted us as the patient, long-suffering matriarch of one of America's best-loved daytime soaps. Shakespeare said it best, ladies and gentlemen, when he wrote, 'Age cannot wither her nor custom stale her infinite variety,' which, translated from the original Hebrew text, actually reads 'this lady has lots of *chutzpah.*' Please give a big welcome to the very lovely Miss Vickie Gordon."

The audience stopped laughing from Billy's cracks in time to rise to its feet as Vickie swept confidently on to the stage. She hugged Billy, then stood in front of the microphone, her heart thumping wildly. She took a deep breath and tried to stay calm as she looked down into the sea of applauding people. Then, when they finally sat down, she spoke.

"Ladies and gentlemen, many years ago I came to this theater as a child for a charity evening and sat pretty much in the same seat as I am sitting in now to watch my mother, Millie Swann, perform one of her songs from the hit revue she was starring in, called *Bubbles*."

Several of the older members of the audience remembered and started clapping and cheering again, but Vickie held her hand up for silence.

"Millie Swann was considered to be one of the great musical comedy stars of the nineteen thirties. She started in the chorus of revues in London and, by dint of tremendous hard work and showmanship, went on to Broadway, where she became a legend. Tragically, my mother died much too young, but I know if she could have been here tonight she would be more than proud to watch the mesmerizing talent of our next performer."

Vickie looked down into the first row and smiled at Lulu, who gave her mother the thumbs-up sign.

"She's the fourth generation of a show-business dynasty, and I am honored to be her grandmother. Her mother, who is also here tonight, is my own daughter, Lulu Swannell, who, as you know, has just received an Emmy for her performance in *Sons and Lovers* and a People's Choice Award for 'The Most Popular Actress on Daytime TV.' "

Another huge round of applause swelled throughout the audience, many of whom called out Lulu's name. She stood up, cheeks flushed, eyes sparkling, and turned to acknowledge the cheers that greeted her. Then she sat down as Vickie continued, smiling fondly at her daughter, whose eyes seemed to be filled with tears of emotion.

"Tonight you will meet a young lady who, although only fourteen years old, has been performing and writing her own songs since she was twelve. She made her singing debut in a shampoo commercial and, after studying at the Grace School of Theater and Fine Arts, was discovered by the talent-spotting entrepreneur Samuel Prince, who signed her to a five-year recording deal. Before she was thirteen, she was at the top of the charts in both the U.S. and Europe, and her — ah — original style of dressing has been copied by teenagers all over the world." Vickie grinned mischievously and the audience erupted in laughter, for everyone knew that the girl's outrageous and overtly sexual outfits were a fashion phenomenon that for the past year since she became famous had been scandalizing parents and schoolteachers worldwide.

"Her latest single, 'Devil's Eyes,' has been number one for six weeks, and she has just received her first Grammy for best new recording artist. The level of fame that my granddaughter has achieved at such an early age can be difficult to deal with, but she has handled it and herself with enormous intelligence and maturity far beyond her years. So, without further ado, ladies and gentlemen, it gives me great pleasure to introduce my granddaughter, who bears the same name as my own mother — please welcome the latest in the line of the Swannell girls — Miss Millie Swannell."

The lights dimmed and Vickie left the stage and hurried to join Lulu, Jamie, and Susie in the audience. The curtains swung open and the stage exploded into flashing laser beams and a cacophony of loud rock.

On a steel platform stood Millie, a caramel-skinned, sultry-eyed teenage wild child, almost a mirror image of her mother, Lulu, but with the same saucy smile and flaming red hair as her great-grandmother coupled with the smoldering sexuality of her grandmother Vickie.

A guitar was slung around her body, and the audience gasped audibly at the audacity of her costume. It was backless, almost frontless, and slashed up both sides; the shimmering silver fabric revealing the apparently unclad cheeks of her round derriere.

"How the damn thing stays on her I'll never know." Lulu shook her head. "It's like two Band-Aids and a Handy-Wipe."

"It's all attached to that strap that goes between her legs," whispered Susie knowledgeably, "and the reason her top doesn't fall off is because she has toupee tape sticking all over her chest."

"It's a miracle of gravity defiance," said Vickie, "but she's made that look all the rage with the kids."

As Millie gyrated and pranced to the lusty lyrics, thrusting her pelvis and shaking her body like some devilish young dervish, the audience burst out into wild spontaneous applause and Vickie imagined what Cooper would have thought about his granddaughter. She was free-spirited and bold, just like he had been. In fact, Millie Swannell was everything a modern pop princess should be: outrageous, exotic, scandalously sexy, with a pure throaty voice and talent and energy to spare.

"And they used to call *me* shocking." Lulu admired the lithe acrobatic contortions of her daughter. "I was like a nun compared to her."

"It's the modern way." Susie looked over at Vickie during a break for audience applause.

"Your mother scandalized society in London and New York in the twenties and thirties by having her skirts way above her knees, showing her stocking tops, and going to speakeasies with gangsters."

"Tame stuff," smiled Vickie. "I was considered a loose and shameful woman because I went to bed with a few men. Some of them married, I admit."

"And it was a few, too." Susie shook her head. "My dear, you were practically a *virgin* compared to what goes on with the girls these days."

"And they say that Millie's corrupting the youth of today." Lulu grinned as her daughter threw her guitar to one of the band members and did several backflips — revealing erotic glimpses of even more flesh — her bright red curls intertwined with fake silver braids whipping about her face.

"Nothing changes," sighed Vickie as Millie launched into her finale with a series of whirling, brilliantly executed *grand jetés* and *jetés en tournant.*

"Plus ça change, plus c'est la même chose."

"She's going to go far," observed Susie, "just like both of you did, my darlings. I predict that young Millie Swannell is destined to be a very big star for a very long time. She has what you both *and* her great-grandmother had in abundance. Star quality."